THE HEAVENLY TABLE

A NOVEL

DONALD RAY POLLOCK

Harvill Secker
LONDON

1 3 5 7 9 10 8 6 4 2

Harvill Secker, an imprint of Vintage,
20 Vauxhall Bridge Road,
London SW1V 2SA

Harvill Secker is part of the Penguin Random House
group of companies whose addresses can be found
at global.penguinrandomhouse.com.

Penguin
Random House
UK

First published by Harvill Secker in 2016
First published in the United States in 2016 by Doubleday

penguin.co.uk/vintage

A CIP catalogue record for this book is available from the British Library

ISBN 9781910701621

Printed and bound in Great Britain by Clays Ltd, St Ives PLC

Penguin Random House is committed to a sustainable future
for our business, our readers and our planet. This book is made
from Forest Stewardship Council® certified paper.

MIX
Paper from
responsible sources
FSC
www.fsc.org   FSC® C018179

For Patsy always
and
For Barney, the best dog ever, who
passed away October 1, 2015

THE HEAVENLY TABLE

I

IN 1917, JUST as another hellish August was starting to come to an end along the border that divides Georgia and Alabama, Pearl Jewett awakened his sons before dawn one morning with a guttural bark that sounded more animal than man. The three young men arose silently from their particular corners of the one-room shack and pulled on their filthy clothes, still damp with the sweat of yesterday's labors. A mangy rat covered with scabs scuttled up the rock chimney, knocking bits of mortar into the cold grate. Moonlight funneled through gaps in the chinked log walls and lay in thin milky ribbons across the red dirt floor. With their heads nearly touching the low ceiling, they gathered around the center of the room for breakfast, and Pearl handed them each a bland wad of flour and water fried last night in a dollop of leftover fat. There would be no more to eat until evening, when they would all get a share of the sick hog they had butchered in the spring, along with a mash of boiled spuds and wild greens scooped onto dented tin plates with a hand that was never clean from a pot that was never washed. Except for the occasional rain, every day was the same.

"I seen me two of them niggers again last night," Pearl said, staring out the rough-cut opening that served as the only window. "Out there a-sittin' in the tulip tree, singin' their songs. They was really goin' at it." According to the owner of the land, Major Thaddeus Tardweller, the last tenants of the shack, an extended family of mulattoes from Louisiana, had all died of the fever several years ago, and were buried out back in the weeds along the perimeter of the now-empty hog pen. Due to fears of the sickness lingering on in a place where black and white had mixed, he hadn't been able to convince anyone to live there until the old man and his boys came along last fall, half starved and looking for work. Lately, Pearl had been seeing their ghosts everywhere. The morning before, he'd counted five of them. Gaunt and grizzled, with his mouth hanging open and the front of his trousers stained yellow from a leaky bladder, he felt as if he might join them on the other side any minute. He bit into his biscuit, then asked, "Did ye hear 'em?"

"No, Pap," Cane, the oldest, said, "I don't think so." At twenty-three, Cane was as close to being handsome as any sharecropper's son could hope to get, having inherited the best of both parents: his father's tall, sinewy frame and his mother's well-defined features and thick, dark hair; but the harsh, hopeless way they lived was already starting to crinkle his face with fine lines and pepper his beard with gray. He was the only one in the family who could read, having been old enough before his mother passed for her to teach him from her Bible and an old *McGuffey* borrowed from a neighbor; and strangers usually viewed him as the only one of the bunch who had any promise, or, for that matter, any sense. He looked down at the greasy glob in his hand, saw a curly white hair pressed into the dough with a dirty thumbprint. This morning's ration was smaller than usual, but then he remembered telling Pearl yesterday that they had to cut back if they wanted the sack of flour to last until fall. Pinching the hair loose from his breakfast, he watched it float to the floor before he took his first bite.

"Only thing I heard was that ol' rat runnin' around," Cob said. He was the middle one, short and heavyset, with a head round as a chickpea and watery green eyes that always appeared a little out of focus, as if he had just been clobbered with a two-by-four. Though as stout as any two men put together, Cob had always been a bit on the slow side, and he got along mainly by following Cane's lead and not complaining too much, no matter how deep the shit, how small the biscuit. Even telling time was beyond his comprehension. He was, to put it bluntly, what people usually referred to in those days as a dummy. You might come across such a man almost anywhere, sitting on his haunches around some town pump, hoping for a friendly howdy or handout from some good citizen passing by, someone with enough compassion to realize that but for the grace of God, it could just as easily be himself sitting there in that sad, ragged loneliness. Truth be told, if it hadn't been for Cane looking out for him, that's probably how Cob would have ended up, living out his days on a street corner, begging for scraps and the occasional coin with a rusty bean can.

The old man waited a moment for the youngest to respond, then said, "What about you, Chimney? Did ye hear 'em?"

Chimney stood with a dazed look on his pimply, dirt-streaked face. He was still thinking about the splay-toothed floozy with the fat tits that the old man's raspy squawk had chased away a few minutes ago. Last night, as with most evenings whenever Pearl passed out on his blanket before it got too dark to see, Cane had read aloud to his brothers from *The Life and Times of Bloody Bill Bucket,* a crumbling, water-stained dime novel that glorified the criminal exploits of an ex-Confederate soldier turned bank robber cutting a swath of terror throughout the Old West. Consequently, Chimney had spent the last few hours dreaming of gun fights on scorched desert plains and poon-tang that tasted like honey. He glanced over at his brothers, yawning and scratching like a couple of dogs, eating what might as well have been lumps of clay and listening to that nutty bastard prattle on about his black buddies in the spirit world. Of course, he could understand Cob buying Pearl's bullshit; there weren't enough brains in his head to fill a teaspoon. But why did Cane continue to play along? It didn't make any sense. Hell, he was smarter than any of them. Being loyal to any old mother or father was fine up to a point, Chimney reckoned, no matter how crazy or senile they had become, but what about their own selves? When did they get to start living?

"I'm talkin' to you, boy," Pearl said.

Chimney looked down at the shelf of greenish-gray mold growing along the bottom of the cabin walls. A simple yes or no wasn't going to cut it, not this morning. Perhaps because he was the runt of the family, rebelliousness had always been the bigger part of his nature, and whenever he was in one of his defiant or pissed-off moods, the seventeen-year-old was liable to say or do anything, regardless of the consequences. He thought again about the juicy wench in his dream, her dimpled ass and sultry voice already fading away, soon to be extinguished completely by the backbreaking misery of swinging an ax in another hundred-degree day. "Don't sound like no bad deal to me," he finally said to Pearl. "Layin' around pickin' your teeth and playin' music. Christ, why is it they get to have all the fun?"

"What's that?"

"I said the way things is goin' around this goddamn place, I'd trade even up with a dead darkie any day."

The room went quiet as the old man pulled his slumped shoulders back and tightened his mouth into a grim leer. Clenching his fists, Pearl's first thought was to knock the boy to the floor, but by the time he turned away from the window, he'd already changed his mind. It was too early in the morning to be drawing blood, even if it was justified. Instead, he stepped closer to Chimney and studied his thin, triangular face and cold, insolent eyes. Sometimes the old man almost found it hard to believe the boy was one of his own. Of course, Cob had always been a disappointment, but at least he had a good heart and did what he was told, and Cane, well, only a fool would find fault with him. Chimney, on the other hand, was impossible to figure out. He might work like a dog one day and then refuse to hit a lick the next, no matter how much Pearl threatened him. Or he might give Cob his share of the evening meal, then turn around and shit in his shoes while he was eating it. It was as if he couldn't make up his mind between being good or evil, and so he tried his best to be both. Not only that, he was woman-crazy, too, had been ever since he first found out his pecker would get hard. And he didn't give a damn who knew it, either; you could hear him jerking it over there in his blanket two or three times every night, especially if Cane had read to him again from that goddamn book they treasured like a holy relic. Pearl thought about something he had once heard an auctioneer say at a livestock sale, about how when the stud gets older, the litters get weaker, not only in the body, but in the head, too. "Don't just go for your animals, either," the man said. "Had an old boy back home caught him a young wife and decided at fifty-nine he wanted to bring one more of his own into the world before he dried up for good. Poor thing was born one of them maniacs like they got locked up in the nuthouse over in Memphis."

"What happened to it?" Pearl had asked.

"Sold it to some banana man down in South America who collects such things," the auctioneer replied. Back then, Pearl had dismissed the notion as part of some sales pitch to run the bidding up on a pair of young bulls, but now he realized there might be some truth in it. Though he hated to admit it, from the looks of things, his seed had already lost some of its vigor when he and Lucille made Cob, and by the time he shot Chimney into the oven, it had gone from slightly tepid to downright sour.

Even so, perhaps because he was the youngest or had yet to grow the scraggly beard his brothers wore, Chimney was still the one that reminded Pearl of his dead wife the most. He leaned closer and stared into the boy's eyes even more intently, as if he were peering into a smoky portal to the past. Chimney looked over at his brothers again, took the last bite of his biscuit. The old man's breath reeked of stomach gas and rancid drippings. A solitary bird began to twitter from somewhere close by, and suddenly Pearl was recalling a long-ago night when he had walked Lucille home from a barn dance just a few weeks before they married. The autumn sky was glittering with stars, and a faint smell of honeysuckle still hung in the cool air. He could hear the gravel crunching beneath their feet. Her face appeared before him, as young and pretty as the first time he ever saw her, but just as he was getting ready to reach out and touch her cheek, Chimney shattered the spell. "Hell, yes," he said, "maybe we should ask them niggers if they'd be a-willin' to—"

Without any warning, Pearl's hand whipped out and caught the boy by the throat. "Spit it out," he growled. "Spit it out." Chimney tried to break away, but the old man's grip, seasoned by years of plowing and chopping and picking, was tight as a vise. With his windpipe squeezed shut, he soon ceased struggling and managed to spew a few wet crumbs from his mouth that stuck to the hairs on Pearl's wrist.

"Pap, he didn't mean nothing," Cane said, moving toward the two. "Let him go." Though he figured his brother probably deserved getting the shit choked out of him, if for no other reason than being a constant aggravation, Cane also knew that getting their father too upset this early in the morning meant that he would push them twice as hard in the field today, and it was tough enough working a slow pace when you had but one biscuit to run on.

"I'm sick of his mouth," Pearl said through clenched teeth. Then he snorted some air and tightened his hold even more, seemingly resolved on shutting the boy up forever.

"I said let him go, goddamn it," Cane repeated, just before he grabbed the old man's other arm and wrenched it behind his back with a violent twist that filled the room with a loud pop. Pearl let out a piercing howl as he jerked free of Cane and shoved Chimney away. The boy coughed and spat out the rest of his biscuit onto the floor, and they all watched in the gloomy half-light as the old man ground it into the dirt with his shoe while working the hurt out of his shoulder. Nothing else was said. Even Chimney was temporarily out of words.

When Pearl was done, they all followed him out of the shack single-file. Cob stopped at the well and drew a pail of water, and they carried it, together with their tools—three double-headed axes and a couple of machetes and a rusty saber with a broken tip—along the edge of a long green cotton field. As the sun crested the hills to the east, looking like the bloodshot eye of a hungover barfly, they came to a swampy piece of acreage they were clearing for Major Tardweller. He had promised them a bonus of ten laying hens if they finished the job in six weeks, and Cane figured they might just make it at the rate they were going. He peeled off his ragged shirt and draped it over the top of the canvas bucket to keep the gnats and mosquitoes out, and another day of work began. By afternoon, with nothing but warm water sloshing around in their guts, all they could think about was that sick hog hanging in the smokehouse.

2

THAT SAME MORNING, several hundred miles away in southern Ohio, a farmer by the name of Ellsworth Fiddler went to wake
his son and discovered he was already up and gone. He stood for a
moment looking at Eddie's empty bed, then walked to the barn on
the slim chance that he might be there, but there was no sign of him.
Going back to the house, he checked to make sure Eula, his wife, was
still asleep, then slipped down into the cellar beneath the kitchen. Just
as he feared, there were at least two more jars of his blackberry wine
missing. "I never should have let him have that first taste," he mumbled
to himself, thinking back to last Christmas. The holiday had been a
gloomy one, mostly because Ellsworth had lost his and Eula's life savings to a con man in a checkered suit the previous September, and he
thought that sharing a drink with Eddie might brighten things up a bit
for the boy. Ellsworth's own father had allowed him a glass every night
from the time he was twelve, and he'd turned out all right, hadn't he?
Looking back on it, though, he should have known better. Eddie was
already prone to daydreaming and telling fibs and shirking his chores,
and even a little hard cider sometimes did strange things to people
like that. And sure enough, ever since that first sip, down in the cellar
listening to Eula moving around in the kitchen above them while she
stuffed the Christmas bird, a tough, stringy Tom that he'd traded Roy
Cox some old harness for, the boy had become, on top of everything
else, a regular boozehound.

He was just emerging from the cellar when Eula came into the
kitchen. "What are you doing?" she asked.

"Lookin' for Eddie," Ellsworth said nervously. "He ain't in his bed."

"You mean he's gone?"

"Well, I can't find him."

"But even if ye can't, why would you think he'd be down there at six o'clock in the morning?"

"I don't know," Ellsworth said. "I just—"

Shaking her head, Eula walked to the boy's room to look for herself. Ellsworth waited on her to say something when she came back, but instead she lit the kindling in the cookstove, then dipped some water from a bucket into a pan for coffee. He went back out to the barn and fed the mule; and a few minutes later, she called him to the table and he sat down to a couple of eggs and a bowl of gummy, tasteless oatmeal. Jesus, he thought, this time last year there would have been sausage and gravy, maybe even pork chops. Though sick and tired of thinking about the swindle, the tiniest things reminded him of it all over again, even his breakfast. It was an ache inside him that never let up, something he figured would probably gnaw at him the rest of his days. A man riding a red sorrel mare had stopped him and Eddie along the road one bright afternoon toward the end of September last year, and casually asked if he might know someone who'd be interested in buying fifty Guernsey cows at twenty dollars a head. "Why so cheap?" Ellsworth had asked suspiciously. He knew for a fact that Henry Robbins had paid over twice that just a couple of weeks ago for some Holstein calves.

"Well, to tell ye the truth," the man said, "I'm up against it. My wife's took sick and the doctor says she won't last another six months if'n I don't get her to warmer weather."

"Oh," Ellsworth said, "I hate to hear that."

"Consumption," the man went on. "Nolie never was in any good shape, not even back when I married her damn near twenty years ago, but I didn't care. And I still don't. Wasn't her fault she was born sickly. I'd gladly make a deal with ol' Beelzebub just so she might draw one more breath. The way I see it, a man that don't do everything he can to uphold his marriage vows ain't much of a man." He pulled a soiled handkerchief from his coat and patted his eyes with it. "Anyway, that's why I'm in a hurry to sell."

Ellsworth was impressed with the man's speech; he felt much the same way about Eula, though he wasn't sure he'd go so far as to trade around with the Devil, no matter how bad things got. "How much would them cows figure up to altogether?" he had asked, unable to calculate such a high number on his own.

"A thousand dollars," Eddie spoke up.

"That's right," the man said. "Boy's got a good head on his shoulders, don't he?"

"I reckon," Ellsworth murmured, looking past the man at a yellow finch that had just landed a few yards away in a crabapple tree. He and Eula had a thousand dollars put back, but it was all the money they had in the world, and it had taken them years to save it. Still, if he could convince her to go along with this, he'd own more cattle than anybody else in the township. And if he didn't buy them, somebody else surely would before the day was out. It was just too good a deal to pass up. He took a deep breath. "I'd have to talk this over with my wife first," he said.

"I know exactly what you mean," the man said. "I don't spend a dime without talkin' it over with Nolie."

The man had followed them home, waited in the front yard while Ellsworth went inside the house. He found Eula sitting at the kitchen table having her afternoon cup of coffee. Pacing back and forth, he explained the situation twenty different ways in increasingly glowing terms, occasionally stopping to remind her that he knew as much about cattle as Henry Robbins, and then some. "We could have one of the best dairy farms around," he told her. "Or, we could just take 'em to auction and double our money. Either way, it's the chance of a lifetime." Of course, she had been resistant, as he had known she would be, but after an hour of his going on about it with no sign of a letup, she reluctantly gave in. She went into the bedroom and returned with the money jar she kept hidden under a loose board behind the dresser. "You look those cows over good before you go to handin' him this," she said.

Three hours later, he and Eddie and the man passed through a wide, sturdy gate to a large farm set between some wooded hills in Pike County. Ellsworth looked about admiringly at the rolling green pastures and acres of corn and hay and the freshly painted barn and scattered outbuildings and the brick two-story house set back among some tall oaks. "Quite a place ye got here," he said.

"Yes, it is," the man said. "The Lord's been good to me."

Ellsworth had wondered what was going to happen to the land, but he hated to ask. After all, the old boy was already taking a beating on his livestock. He remembered later that he'd been a little surprised at how soft the man's hand seemed when he shook it to finalize the transaction. And then there was the checkered suit coat and pants that he wore, another warning sign that Ellsworth, in what he later shamefully realized was his hurry to take advantage of someone else's misfortune, chose to ignore. "Well, I hope your wife gets to feelin' better," he'd said, as he watched the man stuff the money in his pocket without even bothering to count it, then scribble out a receipt on the back of an old envelope with a pencil stub.

"So do I," the man answered. "I don't know what I'd do without her." His voice had actually quavered when he said that, and whenever Ellsworth replayed the incident in his head, that was the thing that enraged him most of all. Sometimes he imagined the slimy scoundrel in a smoky dive, flush with the thousand dollars, bragging to his lowlife buddies in between hee-haws and buying rounds for the house exactly how he had weaved the tight web around the country hick, one slick and deceitful strand at a time. Because, as it turned out, the man never had any claim to the cattle in the first place.

But that was to come later, learning that he'd been rooked. Over the next two days, he and Eddie drove nearly half the herd the seven miles back to their place, four or five head at a time. Then, on the third morning, just as they started through the gate with another bunch, the real owner of the farm showed up, after being away at a family gathering in Yellow Springs for the past week. Fortunately, Abe McAdams was a reasonable man. Though the law was sent for and a shotgun calmly directed at Ellsworth's head while they waited, it could have been worse. Nobody would have blamed McAdams if he had killed them both. The constable finally arrived in a Model T with a white star painted on the door. By that time, McAdams really didn't believe the pair intentionally meant to steal from him, but Constable Sykes, a man who'd heard enough false cries of innocence to blow the roof off a concert hall, insisted that they be taken into custody just the same, at least until he had made some inquiries. Neither of them had ridden in an automobile before, and Ellsworth, already sick over being duped, splattered the running boards with vomit several times before they got to the Pike County jailhouse. Everyone, from the toothless wife-beater in the next cell to the crowd of curious citizens who gathered outside their barred window, wondered how the farmer could have been so dumb. More than a few offered to sell him things: a mansion on a hill for fifty cents, a genuine lock of Jesus's hair for two stogies, the Baltimore & Ohio Railroad for a dozen brown eggs. Listening to their jokes was bad enough, but even worse had been watching Eddie, who hadn't said a word since they'd been arrested, curl up on a bunk and turn away to face the wall, as if he couldn't bear to look at him. Finally, an hour or so before sundown, they were released. "What about the man who stole my money?" Ellsworth asked on his way out.

The constable shrugged. "I wouldn't hardly get my hopes up. I'll keep my eye out, but I figure that ol' boy's long gone by now. You just make sure you get those cattle back to their rightful owner."

Going back to face Eula that night was the hardest thing he had ever done in his life. If only she had beat him with her fists, screamed curses at him, spit in his face. But no; except for a barely audible gasp when she realized what he was telling her, she said nothing. For weeks afterward, she walked about in a stupor, not eating or sleeping or barely, it seemed at times, even breathing. He began to fear she might do herself in. Every afternoon, he came into the house from the fields or the barn filled with dread at what he might find. But then one November morning, two months after the swindle, he overheard her say to herself, "Just have to start over, that's all." She was standing at the stove fixing breakfast, and she pursed her lips and nodded her head, as if she were agreeing with something someone else had said. After that, she began to come around, and although he knew she might never forgive him for being so reckless and stupid, at least he no longer had to worry about her going cuckoo or choking down a cupful of rat poison.

He scraped the last of the oatmeal from the bowl and stood up. Eula hadn't said a word while he was eating, just sat there staring out the window sipping her coffee. "Well," Ellsworth told her, "when he gets home, you tell him to meet me at the field across from Mrs. Chester's place. And to bring a hoe."

"And what if he don't show up?"

"By God, he better," Ellsworth said. "The weeds have damn near taken over."

3

LIFE HADN'T ALWAYS been so hard for Pearl Jewett. At one time, he'd had a farm of his own back in North Carolina, just a few acres, but big enough for a man to get by on if he was willing to bust his ass. Life was as good as an illiterate farmer with no birthright could hope for in those days, and Pearl made sure to give the Almighty credit for that. He'd been quite a drinker and hell-raiser in his youth, but he turned over a new leaf when he met Lucille, and the only times he fell off the wagon after they married were whenever she went into labor. Hence, the rather odd names bestowed upon his sons didn't signify anything of great importance, but were simply the result of what happens when a man who's been off the sauce for a while consumes too much whiskey and then insists on having his way. With Cane, he had drawn his inspiration from a walking stick that someone had beaten him over the head with in a rowdy tavern; in the case of Cob, it turned out to be a half-eaten roasting ear he discovered in his back pocket after coming to under the porch of a boardinghouse called the Rebel Inn; while in regard to Chimney, it was a stovepipe that he was fairly certain he had helped a neighbor fashion from a sheet of tin in return for a cup of liquor that tasted like muddy kerosene and left him without any feeling in his fingers and toes for several days. And though Lucille would have preferred Christian names such as John and Luke and Adam, she figured the damage could have been worse, and she just counted her blessings that he was back home and walking a straight line again. He sacrificed much, even giving up tobacco, to pay for a pew in the First Baptist Church of Righteous Revelation in nearby Hazelwood, and every Sunday morning for the next few years, no matter what the weather, he and his young family walked the three miles there to worship. Pearl was especially proud that his wife was one of the few people in the congregation besides the minister who could read the lessons, and so, despite the fact that Lucille's shyness sometimes made it hard for her to look even him in the eye, he had quickly volunteered her after the last lay reader, a silken-voiced, holier-than-thou man named Sorghum Simmons, backslid and ran off with a deacon's wife and a business partner's money. Every week he had to coax her into walking to the front of the church, telling himself it was for her own good. Thus, when she first started staying in bed on the Sabbath, complaining of feeling weak and light-headed, he couldn't help but think she was faking it, and several months passed before he realized she really was sick.

By that time, Lucille had lost a considerable amount of weight, and her sagging skin had turned the dreary gray color of a rain cloud. Taking out a lien against the land, Pearl sent for doctors. One of them bled her and another prescribed expensive tonics while a third put her on a diet of curds and raw onions, but nothing seemed to help. Then the money ran out and all he could do was watch her slowly wither away. What struck her down remained a mystery until the night of her wake. As he sat alone keeping company with her corpse in the dim, flickering light of a single candle, Pearl noticed that the tip of her tongue was sticking out from between her lips. Leaning over to set it right, he saw a slight movement. My God, he thought, his heart quickening, can it be that she's still alive? "Lord Jesus," he started to pray, just before a worm, no wider than a ring finger and no thicker than a few sheets of paper, pushed forward several inches out of her mouth. Pearl lurched back and knocked the chair over in his rush to get away from the bed, but managed to stop himself at the doorway. He stood listening to the soft breathing of his sons sleeping in the next room while trying to still the frantic pounding in his chest. With a shudder, he thought of some of the words he had heard Lucille read the last time she was well enough to do the lessons: "Where their worm dieth not and the fire is not quenched." Though he couldn't recall any more of the passage, he was certain that Reverend Hornsby had explained in his sermon that it was an apt description of hell. He debated what to do. To bury his wife with that thing still inside her was out of the question, but he had no idea how to go about removing it other than to cut her open, and he couldn't bear the thought of doing something like that. Stepping forward, he saw another two inches of the worm emerge, and the blind head rise up and move back and forth as if trying to get a bearing on this new world it was about to enter. Pearl paced around the room, fighting the urge to crush it with his hands. For the first time in several years, he craved a drink. The only thing to do, he finally decided, was to wait it out, and so he sat back down and spent the next several hours watching the creature slowly work its way out of her.

Not long after sunrise, the last of the worm slid from Lucille's mouth and dropped onto her chest with a soft, almost imperceptible *plop*. Pearl looked out the window and beyond the yard to his fields barren of crops and overgrown with weeds. Lucille's dying had begun in the spring and taken up the entire summer. Soon the man from the bank would be coming for his money, and Pearl didn't have it. He stood and repeated the lesson words aloud: "Where their worm dieth not and the fire is not quenched." He studied on this for a while, then turned to the bed and gathered up the worm like a spool of wet rope and carried it outside. Unrolling it along the ground in front of the house, he pinned each pulsing end of it down with rocks he took from the border of one of Lucille's flower beds. Two peahens, all that remained of his livestock, darted out from around the house and began pecking furiously at it. He grabbed them up, one in each hand, and bashed their heads bloody against a porch post. Then he went back inside and drank a cold cup of coffee before shaking his sons awake. Later that morning, he and Cane carried Lucille out of the house and buried her in the shady spot under a magnolia tree where she used to sit and shell beans and read her Bible. For the next several days, the boys gnawed on chicken bones and decorated the grave with whatever pretty things they could find while Pearl sat silently watching the scalding Carolina sun turn the worm into a silver, leathery strip. When he was finally satisfied with the cure, he stuffed the remains into an empty coffee-bean sack along with some of the peahen feathers and sewed it shut like a shroud. Ever since then, and that had been nearly fourteen years ago, he had used it to rest his head on at night, and to remind him, lest he ever forget, that nothing is certain in this earthly life except the end of it.

4

WHEN EDDIE DIDN'T return home by suppertime that evening, Ellsworth knew something was amiss. The boy never stayed away this long, no matter how shit-faced he got. The farmer stood on the porch puffing on his cob pipe and listening to Eula bang around in the kitchen. He prayed to God the fool hadn't gotten drunk and drowned in a pond, or made his way over the hill and caught a dose of the syph off one of those Slab Holler girls that the men who loitered over at Parker's store were always warning the young bucks about. What a mess. Though he had always tried his best to hide the extent of Eddie's screwups from Eula, it was getting harder and harder to come up with excuses. He didn't even know why he kept doing it, other than to save her from the worries. For just a second, he wondered which would be worse, finding him floating facedown in somebody's mud hole or watching him go blind and crazy from a sick peter.

"I can't figure it out," he said when he finally mustered up the courage to go in the house. "Think maybe he went fishin' with those Hess boys?" Without bothering to reply, Eula wiped her red hands on the front of her apron and went back to the stove. Ellsworth sat down and nervously drummed his fingers on the table. Looking about the room, he noticed that she had rearranged the two faded pictures on the far wall, tropical island scenes cut from a magazine that Eddie had brought home one Friday from school when he was ten, explaining that Mr. Slater, the teacher, had tossed it in the trash. The first time he ever caught him in a lie, Ellsworth recalled. He had met Slater on the road the next afternoon, on his way to question Eddie about the *National Geographic* that had turned up missing from his desk drawer. Another student claimed he had seen him with it. "I don't know if he's the one who took it, Mr. Fiddler," Slater said, "but—"

"It was him," Ellsworth said, his face turning crimson from embarrassment.

"Oh," the teacher said, "so you knew he stole it?"

"No, but I do now," Ellsworth answered. And what had he done? Nothing. Handed Slater a quarter for the goddamn magazine and kept it a secret from Eula, thinking she would be better off not knowing. Just like he'd been doing with the wine.

A few minutes later Eula put out his supper, a meatless stew that she had been serving every Tuesday and Friday since last fall, and sat down across from him. Except for a rather prominent overbite, she had been almost pretty when they married, with her bright blue eyes and smooth, milky complexion, and her looks had held up well over the years, but it was clear that the last year had been hard on her. Although she had rallied in most ways after the loss of the money, she no longer seemed to care about her appearance. Her thin cotton dress was stained with various splatters, and her hair was just a greasy brown ball pinned atop her head. Even from the other end of the table, it was hard for him to ignore the strong odor of her sweat. "Ain't you gonna eat?" he said, as he began buttering a slice of bread.

"You need to dump that wine," Eula said, her voice calm but definite. "What's left of it anyway." Her mind was made up. Something had to be done about Eddie before it was too late. Just two weeks ago, after spending the morning in his bedroom supposedly nursing another one of his bellyaches, he had slipped out of the house with the shotgun and blown a hole through Pickles, the cat that had been her closest companion for the past ten years. Of course, he swore right off it was an accident, and though she was fairly sure that was true, she'd still felt he needed to be taught a lesson. But all Ellsworth had done was get more inventive with the allowances he made for the boy. Looking back on it, she didn't know why she had expected anything else. He had always been too softhearted and trusting for his own good, and Eddie had learned over the years to take advantage of that good nature any chance he got.

Laying the bread down, Ellsworth looked away as he took a drink of buttermilk. At age fifty-two, he had a friendly, somewhat meek face, and thinning gray hair that Eula kept trimmed with a pair of sewing scissors. He could still outwork most men in the township, though sometimes now he woke up in the morning wondering how long he could keep it up. Since the embarrassment suffered last fall, he had grown heavier in the belly and jowls, even with Eula's rationing, and had recently developed a slight stoop that often made him look as if he were searching the ground for a nail that had dropped out of his pocket, or the clue to a mystery he was forever trying to solve. In many ways, the con man had stolen more than just money from them.

On the afternoon that he came in from the fields and Eula told him Pickles had been shot, he went straight to Eddie's room. When he flung the door open, the boy jumped up from his bed, and a book lying beside him fell to the floor. He had just finished digging the cat's grave a few minutes before, and was still shiny with sweat. "What the hell's wrong with you?" Ellsworth had yelled.

"It was an accident, I swear," Eddie said.

"An accident? How could such a thing be an accident?"

"I tripped and the gun went off. I didn't mean to do it." To an extent, anyway, Eddie was telling the truth. After spending the morning secretly sipping on some of his father's wine and searching fruitlessly through a tattered book called *Tom Jones* for the juicy parts that Corky Routt had promised were in it, he had grown bored and decided to sneak the shotgun out of the closet and go blast a couple of birds. He was staggering across the backyard with Pickles sashaying along a few feet in front of him when he stumbled and fell. The gun, which had a loose trigger, went off when it hit the ground, and he lay there cursing for a minute before he raised up and saw that the blast had split the cat nearly in half.

"You been drinking again, ain't ye?" Ellsworth said, looking at the boy's bloodshot eyes.

"No," Eddie answered nervously, "but with the way Mom carried on, I almost wish I had been."

Ellsworth shook his head. Though he tried his best to love his son and accept him for who he was, he found himself wishing yet again that he was more like Tom Taylor's boy, Tuck, big and rawboned and shoeing mules by the time he was ten years old. He felt guilty whenever he had such thoughts, but he had been waiting years for the boy to straighten up and be of some use. Not once had he ever given Eddie a proper thrashing, and though he had no stomach for any kind of cruelty—be it kicking dogs or whipping horses or drowning kittens or beating children—he regretted his soft touch now. Farming fifty acres by himself was hard work, and he wasn't getting any younger. Now he was beginning to wonder if Eddie, with his lazy ways and thin wrists and that shaggy mop of blondish hair always hanging in his eyes, might have been better off a girl. At least then there might have been a chance of landing a stout son-in-law who could help out. But everything was a trade-off, and so whatever a man did, he usually ended up wishing he had done the other. "What's that book you got there?" he asked.

"Uh, well," Eddie stammered, "it's about a guy who—"

"I don't give a hoot what it's about. Where'd ye get it?"

"Corky loaned it to me."

"Well, you go on over to his house right now and give it back."

"Yes, sir."

"I mean it," Ellsworth said. "Won't be no more readin' around here till you straighten up." Eula had insisted that Eddie finish the sixth grade before he was allowed to quit school, and the farmer was convinced that a big part of the boy's problem had to do with his education. In other words, he had gotten just enough of it to fuck him up for the real world. Ellsworth had seen it happen before, mostly to flighty types like horny spinsters and weak-eyed store clerks with a lot of time to kill. They would stick their noses in a book and then all of a sudden Ross County, Ohio, wasn't good enough for them. The next thing you knew, they either got caught up in some perversion, like the old Wilkins woman who somehow managed to split herself open on a bedpost, or they lit out for some big city like Dayton or Toledo, in search of their "destiny." Sometimes the line that divided those two impulses blurred until they amounted to pretty much the same thing, as in the case of the Fletcher boy the police found butchered in a hotel room in

Cincinnati with a woman's wig glued to his head and his pecker tossed under the bed like a cast-off shoe.

Ellsworth could sense his wife staring at him from across the table, waiting on an answer about the wine. He set his glass down and cleared his throat. "I don't see what that's got to do with Eddie takin' off," he finally said.

"Your side of the family's always been too partial to drink, you know that," Eula pointed out.

"That ain't true. Uncle Peanut was fine until his woman ran off with that tinker."

"Fine? My God, Ells, you're talkin' about a man who once ate a dog turd at Jack Eliot's fish fry for a pint of moonshine, and that happened long before he ever hooked up with Jolene Carter. No, I mean it. Eddie might turn out to be a drunkard, but it's not going to be with our help. Get rid of that wine and that will be the end of it."

The buttermilk rose back up into his throat like hot lava, and Ellsworth had to swallow several times to keep it down. All the work he had put into it, his finest batch, and her making it sound as if dumping those barrels was no bigger deal than emptying grandma's piss pot. He knew she had a right to be upset, but, Jesus Lord, there had to be another way. The two cups he drank in the evening were the only thing he had left to look forward to most days. He looked over at the cellar door cut into the floor in the corner of the kitchen. "What if I was to put a lock on it?" he asked, after he was fairly sure he wasn't going to upchuck buttermilk all over the table.

"A lock? On what?"

"On the cellar door," he explained quickly. "That would keep him out of it. Parker's got some over at the store. Padlocks."

Eula noted the slight tremor of desperation in his voice, and, for a moment, she started to weaken. Maybe something like that would work, she thought, rubbing her forehead. She was right on the verge of giving in when she glanced out the window and her eyes landed on Pickles's grave in the backyard. The boy was drunk when he shot her; she didn't doubt that for a minute. She knew it was partly her fault, too; perhaps if she had spoken up sooner, Pickles would still be alive. But still, if Ellsworth had wanted to save his wine, he should have considered something like a lock long before now. "No," she said, "I'm not changing my mind."

"Why not?"

She sighed and said, "Because it's our boy we're talking about. Just do it and get it over with." Taking a sip of coffee, she looked over at the mostly bare shelves where she kept her staples. "But now that you mentioned the store—"

"Yeah?"

"Well, you did remind me of something."

"What's that?"

"We're nearly out of sugar and salt," she said, "and I got to get ready for the canning. The way things is looking, that garden might be the only thing that keeps us alive this winter." She stood and started out of the kitchen. "You might as well go over to Parker's tomorrow and take care of it."

"But what about Eddie?" Ellsworth asked. "Don't ye figure I should go out lookin' for him?"

Eula stopped and put her hand against the doorway. She leaned there for a moment with her back turned, feeling dizzy. A wave of intense emotion ran through her body, and she began to tremble. Her son had disappeared and her cat was dead, and on top of that, it suddenly occurred to her that the sugar and salt would take what little money they had left. To think that this time last year they had a thousand dollars put aside. She bit her lip and fought the urge to cry out.

From where he sat, Ellsworth watched her narrow shoulders start to shake. An awkward silence filled the room, and he wondered if he should get up and hold her. But just as he was scooting his chair back, she wiped at her eyes and said, "I reckon Eddie will come home when he's ready. He's probably just out playin' around." Then she continued on into the bedroom. For a long time, Ellsworth sat staring at the stew congealing on his plate, and when he finally figured she was asleep, he slipped down into the cellar with the lantern. He looked about and found five empty jugs, then removed the wooden tops from the two wine barrels. After he filled them, he carried the jugs out to the barn and hid them in the loft. Then he went back to the cellar again. There were at least three or four gallons left. He dipped out a cup and drank it fast, then sat down at the bottom of the stairs with another.

5

AFTER HE LOST his wife and the bank took the farm, Pearl and his sons wandered aimlessly like nomads across a harsh, impoverished South still broken by a war that even he was too young to remember. They encountered corruption and decay at every turn, and their luck shifted from bad to worse. He prayed to God to smooth the way a bit, but no matter how hard they worked, their pockets remained empty and the best the four of them could do was stay one step ahead of starvation. He couldn't understand it. Sitting by the fire in whatever meager camp they had made for the night, Pearl supped on parched corn and moldy bread and went back over his life, trying to recall something he might have done to deserve such a fate. He knew that he had sinned on occasion, yet no more than most, and certainly not as much as some. Pride had always been his biggest defect, and he knew that forcing Lucille to read those church lessons had been a vain and selfish act, but still, wasn't God supposed to forgive? If not for him, then at least for his sons? And so, doubts began to creep into his mind, and that worried him even more than where their next meal was coming from.

By the time Pearl met the hermit along the Foggy River, Lucille had been gone ten years and the worm that killed her had turned to powder in his pillow. He was sitting on the bank in a daze that afternoon while the boys fished the water with their hands. They hadn't eaten anything in several days, but he didn't have the strength to help them. An occasional sparking sound that had started up in his head a few months ago had recently turned into an unrelenting sizzle, as if his brains were being sautéed in a frying pan, and he hadn't slept more than a minute or two at a time in weeks.

The man came out of the woods and sat down beside Pearl without a word, as if they had known each other for years. Suddenly aware of a presence, he roused himself and looked over, saw a bent and mis-shapen stranger carrying a rod made of ash and wearing nothing but a grimy, torn sackcloth. On his forehead, a red canker the size of a silver dollar seethed like a hot coal. Pearl was reminded of a picture card he had once seen of a heathen who had lived his entire life chained to a tree sitting in a pile of his own slops, his eyes turned to black bubbles from staring into the sun. A pockmarked missionary just returned from some foreign land had passed it around the First Baptist Church of Righteous Revelation while grubbing for donations. Pearl wondered if he was dreaming. "Looks like you been on the road a long time," he finally said to the man.

The stranger nodded. "See that little white bird over yonder in that cypress?" he said, pointing with his rod.

Shading his eyes with his hand, Pearl squinted across the river. "Yeah, I see him."

"I been following him for fifty years now. He takes me wherever I need to go."

"I had no idy a bird lived that long," Pearl said.

"Oh, that one will never die."

"How do ye figure?" said Pearl.

"Well," the hermit said, "I've seen him blown to pieces with a four-gauge scattergun, and split in two by a panther's claws, and even set on fire by a gang of no-goods over around Turlington a couple year ago, and yet there he is, a-sittin' in that tree just as pretty as you please. He always comes back."

Pearl thought for a minute, then asked, "You some kind of preacher?"

The man shrugged his bony shoulders. "God speaks to me from time to time, and His bird shows me the way. Not much else to it."

Before he realized it, Pearl was telling the man about Lucille and the worm and all the ill fortune that had come after. He confessed that he was even beginning to wonder if God existed, for why would He treat some so badly and let others off the hook completely? It didn't add up. There was no way his paltry sins were equal to the tribulations that had befallen him and his family. After Pearl finished, the man sat quietly for a long time stroking his long, matted beard. Then he glanced down at his callused feet. He leaned over and began tugging on one of his big toenails with his knotty fingers. Without so much as a wince, he tore it off and held it up for Pearl to see.

"You got it all wrong, my friend," the man said. "The truth is you been chosen. God's giving you the chance for a better resurrection, just like he did your old woman. Without taking hold of some of the misery in the world, there can't be no redemption. Nor will there be any grace. That shouldn't come as no surprise if you study on it. Look what He let them Jews do to His own son. Most of us got it damned easy compared to the suffering that went on that day. But what they call 'preachers' nowadays, they don't want to tell people the truth. Ol' Satan's tricked them into believing the way to salvation can be had for a little bit of nothing. Why, some of them even go around in their fancy clothes claiming that the Lord wants us all to be rich. How does such a man sleep at night, telling lies like that? Using God to fatten his own pockets? Pure sacrilege, that's what it is. You wait and see, those kind will burn the hottest come the Judgment Day. It's just a shame their flocks will end up roastin' with 'em. No, you got to welcome all the suffering that comes your way if you want to be redeemed."

"You really believe that?" Pearl said, staring down at the man's bloody toe while recalling the beaver hat and calfskin gloves the Reverend Hornsby back at the church in Hazelwood used to wear a bit too proudly.

"Friend, you and those boys of yours could drown me in that river right now and it would be the most blessed thing ever happened to me."

"I don't know," Pearl said. "I can see where sleepin' out in the cold and goin' hungry from time to time might do a man some good, but, mister, we're about starved clear out."

The hermit smiled. "I ain't et nothing in over a week except a few tadpoles and the creatures I've found in this beard of mine. I wouldn't want no more than that."

"If that's so," Pearl said, "what is it I get for all this redeeming you talkin' about?"

"Why, one day you'll get to eat at the heavenly table," the man said. "Won't be no scrounging for scraps after that, I guarantee ye."

"The heavenly table?" Pearl repeated. He hadn't heard of such a thing before, and wondered if maybe he had been dozing on whatever Sunday morning Reverend Hornsby preached on it.

"That's right," the hermit said, dropping the toenail to the ground. "But keep in mind, only them that shun the temptations of this world will ever sit there."

"So what you're a-sayin' is that them that has it good down here don't ever get to see the Promised Land?"

"Their chances are slim to none, I reckon. Too many spots on their garments, too many wants in their hearts."

Gathering up some sandy dirt in his hand, Pearl let it trickle through his fingers. It was obvious the old man was a thinker. "Well, let me ask you this then," he said. "What about this here noise I got in my head? I'd give the rest of my life for just one night without it."

"Lean over here," the man said. He put his ear against Pearl's and held his breath. From a distance, they looked like two spent lovers watching the water pass by. A blue-winged dragonfly hovered above their gray heads, then darted off into a bunch of brown cattails. "Mercy," the hermit said, after listening to the buzzing inside Pearl's head for several minutes, "sounds like you gettin' ready to hatch you a star in there."

"You think it will ever go away?"

"Oh, I expect so," the man said. "That's the one good thing about this here life. Nothin' in it lasts for long." Then he glanced over at the bird in the cypress tree and reached for his staff. "Well, it's been nice talkin' to ye, brother, but I see my little friend is ready to go. Who knows? Maybe one of these days we'll have us some wings, too." Just as he stood, a loud commotion erupted down at the water and Cane whooped and slung a large catfish up onto the bank. The man shook his head as he watched it flop around in the mud. "Best you tell them to throw that thing back in," he said to Pearl.

"I can't do that, mister. That's their supper."

"Mark my word," the man said, "you let them eat that cat, before long them boys will be wantin' everything the easy way." Then he stepped down into the river and started to make his way across. At its deepest point, the water rose above his chest, and his beard suddenly popped up to float along in front of his face like a buoy. A mass of insects scurried to the top of the nest of whiskers to keep from drowning, and Pearl watched as the white bird swooped down from the tree and began plucking them off one by one and placing them on the hermit's outstretched tongue.

No sooner had the man disappeared into the tree line than the sizzle in Pearl's head sputtered to a stop, never to start up again. He entered briefly into a complete and profound silence, and in that glorious moment, he began to see God in a new light. If life was going to be hard, at least the hermit had provided a good reason for it, even a great one. From then on, Pearl seemed to intentionally follow the road that promised the most misery, and the only thing that brought him satisfaction was the worst that could happen. Hoping to replicate that perfect moment again, he plugged his ears with sawdust and clay and chewing tobacco and pebbles and chunks of wood, but the outside world always managed to seep through. He even considered piercing the thin tympanums with a thorn, but he worried that God might look upon such a selfish act as the desecration of a holy temple. Slowly, after countless failed experiments, he came to realize that he wouldn't know the great silence again until he went down into his grave. That moment by the Foggy River had been just a preview of the eternal peace to come if he stayed the course and didn't weaken. "I will be redeemed," he kept repeating to himself. He wished for it more than anything, more than food or land or love, or even life itself.

6

EDDIE STILL WASN'T back the next morning when Eula came into the kitchen and found Ellsworth standing by the counter drinking his fourth dipper of water. Her eyes were puffy and she was still in her nightdress, a shapeless gray sack she had slept in as long as he could remember. She handed him five dollars for the store. "Whatever you do, don't lose it," she said. "It's all we got left."

He nodded his throbbing head ever so slightly, then took another gulp. His pipes hadn't felt this dried-out in years. After carrying the five gallons of wine over to the barn, he had stayed up trying to finish off what was left in the barrels. By the time he'd lurched and groped his way back up the stairs, it was nearly three o'clock in the morning. Looking down at the money in his hand, the old guilty ache started up again, and he thought back on all the years it had taken Eula to save the thousand dollars he had lost. Jesus, the patience it had taken, one quarter at a time, one dime, one penny even. And now here he was hiding wine behind her back. Shit, he was no better than his Uncle Peanut. Might as well go out and hunt up a dog turd to nibble on.

"Remember," she went on, as she turned away to light the stove, "twenty pounds of salt and the rest in sugar. No, wait. Get five pounds of Folgers, too. You might as well shoot me if we run out of coffee. And try not to stay away all day, either."

Without another word, or any breakfast for that matter, Ellsworth went to the barn and hitched the mule to the wagon and made his way out to the road. He wanted to get away before she started in about Eddie and the drinking again. She was probably right, he had to admit. He thought about the way his uncle used to flop around on the floor whenever he ran dry, his eyes damn near popped out of his head and the sweat pouring off of him like rain. He debated the problem all the way to Nipgen, pointing out the pros and the cons to Buck the mule, and trying to be as rational as he could be under the circumstances. Finally, just as the little burg came into view, he made his decision. Though he couldn't do much about the way he'd spoiled his son or the book learning Eula had insisted upon, he could get rid of those barrels, and, yes, by God, even the jugs if he had to, before Eddie came back home. It was an awful sacrifice to make, but if he did it now, before the boy got any worse, maybe he'd never have to clamp a stick in his mouth to keep him from chewing off his tongue, like his grandmother used to do with Uncle Peanut.

Pulling into the dusty lot of Parker's store, he set the brake on the wagon and climbed down. He recalled that the last time he had been here the ground was still frozen. Ever since the cattle ruse, he had avoided people as much as possible, hoping none of his neighbors found out about it. As he pushed the screen door open, he saw the two bachelor brothers named Ovid and Augustus Singleton leaned over a checkerboard set atop a stack of wooden crates. It was rumored that they ate from the same plate and still slept together in the same bed they had been born in some fifty-odd years ago. They spent the majority of their days riding around the neighboring townships in a squeaky black carriage pulled by a pair of bony, dilapidated nags, searching through trash piles and abandoned houses for junk to sell, and as far as Ellsworth was concerned, they were as worthless as teats on a tater. He nodded to them stiffly, then turned and waited for Parker to finish tallying some numbers on a piece of cardboard. He hadn't even placed his order yet when the storekeeper mentioned the army training camp the government was building on the edge of Meade, the county seat fifteen miles to the east. "Why they doing that?" Ellsworth asked.

"'Cause of the war," Parker said. In all the years Ellsworth had known the storekeeper, he had never seen him without something stuck in his mouth, and today he was sucking on what appeared to be a pink rubber eraser, but could just as easily have been the tongue of some small animal. He took off the green eyeshade he wore and scratched at his head. A few flakes of dandruff floated down onto the counter.

"What war?" Ellsworth said.

Behind him, Ovid spoke up. "Hell, Fiddler, the country declared war on Germany back in April. You didn't know that?"

"Well, I knew they was fightin' going on somewhere, but I didn't know we was in on it."

"Sure we are," Augustus said. "A couple of them Baker boys have already signed up."

Then Parker put his pencil down and said, looking at the farmer and shaking his head, "Ells, you need to quit gettin' all your news off that jackass out there and start talkin' to us regular folks once in a while. Shit, he probably don't even know where Germany is."

The Singletons got a kick out of that, and Ellsworth's sunburned face turned an even deeper shade of red as he stood by the counter and listened to them hoot and cackle. He had always been at least vaguely aware of his limitations, but the thought of being bested in anything, even worldly affairs he had never heard of, by a pair of yahoos who had never, as far as anybody knew, done an honest day's work in their lives, was almost more than he could stand. He had wanted to inquire about Eddie, ask if anyone had spotted him around, but figured that would just open up the door to another insult and so he let it go. However, on the way back home, nodding to himself and occasionally spitting great wads of phlegm that stuck like glue to Buck's wide, sweaty rump, Ellsworth put two and two together in his own slow way. Somehow, Eddie had heard about that army camp.

"Why do you think that?" Eula asked when he told her that afternoon what he figured Eddie might be up to. She was bent over the kitchen table rolling a cylinder of dumpling dough back and forth while a pot of water heated on the stove.

"I don't know," Ellsworth said. "I just got a feeling."

Eula dabbed at the sweat on her face with her apron, then looked over at the sacks of salt and sugar he had set on the counter. Being a bit more realistic than her husband ever was when it came to their son, she had a hard time seeing Eddie as the type to voluntarily join something as strict and harsh as she imagined the military was, but then again, stranger things had happened, like the time Uncle Peanut got saved over in Jimmy Beulah's shanty and didn't touch a drop for nearly six months. "So where in the world is Germany anyway?" she said, as she picked up a knife and started cutting the round tube of yellow dough into half-inch pieces.

Ellsworth's face reddened again. He had no idea, but, still smarting from the abuse hurled at him earlier at the store, there was no way he was going to admit it. Going to the water bucket, he drew himself a drink, then sipped slowly while considering various responses. Finally, trying to sound both as nonchalant and convincing as possible, he said, "Hell's fire, Eula, even ol' Buck probably knows where Germany is."

"I don't," she said.

Holy Christ on a cross, Ellsworth thought, the woman could be a sister to that damn bunch over at the store. "Well, fetch me a map," he said, "and I'll show ye."

"Map? Ells, you know we don't have no—" Then Eula stopped and turned to look at him. "Wait a minute," she said. "You don't know, either, do ye?"

Ellsworth took a deep breath. Though he had never, not once, struck Eula in all the time they had been married, he now fought the urge to throw the dipper at her head. He had listened to more than a few of his neighbors, usually after they'd had a drink or two in the back room of Parker's store, brag about beating their wives for some infraction or other, and he had always looked upon such men as cowards and bullies. But standing there in the hot kitchen with the past days and weeks and months of frustrations and setbacks simmering inside him, he could almost understand why some of them yielded to it. He took another drink of water and thought longingly of the jugs of wine hidden in the hayloft. No, he and Eula had been through too much together to allow a little thing like geography drive him to do something he would regret for the rest of his life. And so, without another word, he hung the dipper back on the bucket and headed out to the barn.

7

By THE TIME they ended up working for Major Tardweller, Pearl's sons figured their father had racked up enough hardships for them all to sit at the head of the goddamn heavenly table he had been blabbering about for the past three years. Just a couple of days after Cane advised that they cut back their biscuit ration, they discovered that the cache of potatoes they had buried in the ground to last them the rest of the summer was full of rot. They had woken up that morning to rain, and it being a Sunday anyway, Pearl had decided they would take the day off from clearing the swamp. It was the first break they'd had in several weeks. For a few minutes, the old man stood watching as the others sorted the bad from the good. "How does it look?" he finally asked.

"Like we're gonna go hungry," Cane replied.

"Well, they's worse things. Remember that ol' boy I met on the Foggy River? Shoot, he didn't eat nothin' but tadpoles and bugs and he seemed to be doin' all right. If'n he can do it, I reckon we can, too."

"It might come to that 'fore it's over with," said Cane.

"No need to worry," Pearl said. "The Lord will give us our reward someday."

"I ain't eatin' no goddamn tadpoles," Chimney muttered.

"What say?"

After taking a deep breath to steady himself, Chimney replied in a loud voice, "I said I'd gobble down frog shit and thistles if that's what it takes to stay on His good side."

"That's right," Pearl said, nodding his head. "As would I." Then he pulled up his pants and tightened his belt another notch before walking away, whistling the first few notes of some half-forgotten hymn that Lucille used to sing to herself.

"Me, too," Cob said after the old man was out of earshot. "Why, I'd eat me a pile of rocks if that's what it took." Ever since he had first heard Pearl describe heaven as some sort of celestial banquet hall where the food was piled high forever and you just helped yourself whenever you took a notion, Cob had become obsessed with gaining entry to it. The only other thing that had impressed him as much in all his nineteen years was Willy the Whale, a huge retarded oaf they had once seen in a stall at a county fair in Hancock County. Said to have been discovered living on pinecones and bat guano in a cave in the Smoky Mountains, Willy was so fat he used a woman's petticoat for a napkin. His manager was taking bets that he could eat half a hogshead of raw crawdads in an hour. Though they were supposed to be alive, anyone could see that a good three or four inches of dead ones were floating around on top of the greasy brown water. It wasn't until that day, when he saw the manager, with just a minute to go, cram the last of the bottom-feeders down Willy's throat with a long wooden spatula as if he were priming a cannon, that Cob realized such a thing as a truly full belly was even possible anywhere else but in the Promised Land. And although something crucial had burst inside Willy and he died right in front of the crowd while the wagers were being collected, Cob was still a little upset that Cane hadn't let him audition for the job when the carny came around later looking for someone with a healthy appetite to fill in for the evening show.

Chimney tossed another moldy spud across the yard, then turned to look at Cane. "What was it Bloody Bill said? 'I'd rather rob and kill and be free for just one day than be stuck under some bastard's thumb for a hundred years'?"

"That Bloody Bill," Cob said, "he a bad one."

Cane sat back in the dirt. "I believe he said 'under some *Yankee's* thumb,' but you quoted him fairly right." By then, he had read to his brothers from *The Life and Times of Bloody Bill Bucket* so often that Chimney could recite practically every word of it by memory. Even Cob was able to remember certain lines if prompted, at least a few that dealt with food and drink. Perhaps because their lives had been so empty of anything but hardship and toil, it had made quite an impression on them. The author, Charles Foster Winthrop III, a failed poet from Brooklyn who had once dreamed of becoming the next Robert Browning, had centered the plot of the novel around one Colonel William Buchet's insatiable need to avenge himself against the Northerners who had pillaged his plantation during the Civil War and left him without even a single cotton ball to wipe his ass on; and Winthrop had filled the book with every act of rape, robbery, and murder that his indignant, syphilitic brain could possibly conceive. For this, his twentieth such potboiler in less than three years, he was paid the niggardly sum of thirty dollars. By the time he settled with his creditors, and spent an hour passing diseases back and forth with the foul and wrinkled whore who lived across the hall in his building, Winthrop didn't have enough money left over to buy a loaf of bread. "Well," he said that night to the vermin living behind the cracked plaster in his dank room, "I gave it my best, and that's all a man can do." He waited until morning, and then, with the same cool steadiness he had conferred upon Bloody Bill, his final creation, the hack brushed the rat turds off his one good suit and chugged down enough turpentine to peel the paint off a two-story house. By the time the Jewetts discovered the book in a cast-off carpetbag near Oxford, Mississippi, poor Winthrop had been moldering in a soggy, unmarked grave on an island in the East River for nearly seventeen years, another forgotten casualty of the callous and fickle literary world he had once hoped to conquer.

"Come on," Chimney said, "let's quit fiddle-fuckin' around here and make a break for it. Shit, this ain't no way to live."

"Pap ain't gonna put up with something like that," Cob warned. He grew nervous whenever his younger brother started talking about leaving, and he'd been doing a lot of it lately. Why couldn't he just be thankful that they were all still together and had a place to stay? Granted, the shack leaked a little and a wood floor would have been nice, but compared to some of the places they had slept in over the years, it was practically cozy. And why did he think things would be better somewhere else? They never had been. Not one time.

"Hell, he wouldn't even know we were gone," Chimney said. "He pays more attention to his nigger ghosts than he does us."

"Well, then . . . well, then . . ." Cob stammered.

"Well, then what?" Chimney said.

Cob furrowed his brow, tried to think of a response. As he did so, he squeezed a large squishy potato into a hard glob the size of a walnut. Just as he was ready to give up, his eyes landed on the shovel the Major had loaned them the other day, and he suddenly remembered his little brother's one weakness. "What about Penelope?" he said. "You just gonna take off and leave her behind, too?"

Cane snorted, trying to stifle a laugh, and Chimney's face flushed with blood. He started to reach for a rock that was half-buried in the bottom of the hole, but then stopped himself. It wasn't Cob's fault that he had brought up the bitch's name; it was his own for being so goddamn stupid in the first place. From time to time, Tardweller had borrowed Pearl's youngest to groom his horses and clean out the stables. Because he was the only one ever sent for, Chimney had started to believe that the squire looked upon him with favor. He had even gotten it into his head that the man's daughter, Penelope, a shapely but spoiled fifteen-year-old with strawberry blond hair and icy green eyes, was developing romantic feelings for him; and he had foolishly bragged to his brothers that he spent most of his time in the barn romancing her on a pile of feed sacks while they slaved away in the fields. For a few weeks, Penelope was all he thought about; and he ceased dreaming of gun battles and wild pussy and began fantasizing wedding bells and undying love.

But then one afternoon near the end of May, as he loaded manure from one of the stalls into a wheelbarrow, he overheard the girl complaining to her father that she'd rather see anybody, even a nigger, handling her horse than that ugly piece of white trash who was always hanging around spying on her. "Oh, don't you worry about that little inbred bastard," the Major had told her. "They's not a one of them Jewetts got the grit to mess with one of mine. I could work 'em to death and that dumb ol' daddy of theirs would still pucker up and kiss my ass like I done give him the keys to the kingdom. No, sweetheart, that boy even think of touchin' you, he'll be one sorry sonofabitch." Just then, two of Penelope's girlfriends arrived, and she retreated to the front porch to sip ice tea with them, and Tardweller lay down under a shade tree in the front yard to take his afternoon nap. However, he couldn't shake off the thought of the Jewett boy ogling his daughter. It kept circling around in his mind until soon he was in a rage. He finally got to his feet and stomped across the yard. When he entered the barn, he found Chimney currying one of the horses. Tardweller was a big man, and he grabbed the boy by the scruff of the neck and dragged him outside with ease, kicking his ass several times with the toe of his boot and making a big show of running him off in front of the ladies. "I ever catch you around my house again, I'll cut the nuts right off ye," he had yelled as Chimney broke loose and ran.

Straightening up from the potato pile, Chimney looked toward the thinning woods on the far side of the cotton patch. Even after almost three months, he could still hear those women laughing at him. He'd been too ashamed to tell his brothers what had happened, though he was sure Cane knew there had never been any fucking or anything else going on between him and Penelope. Only he and Cob were dumb enough to believe something like that could ever happen. And what the Major said was true. Tomorrow, they would be back over there in the swamp killing themselves for damn near nothing. The keys to the fuckin' kingdom, all right. Hell, they still owed the mutton-chopped tyrant for the hog they were eating on. He ignored Cob's question, and instead glanced over at Cane. "What about it, brother? You had enough yet?"

Wiping some sweat from his brow, Cane looked toward the cabin. They'd had this discussion a hundred times or more since they'd first come across the Bloody Bill book, and it was always the same, Cob afraid of changing anything and Chimney burning to change it all. Of course, Chimney was right, nothing was ever going to get any better as long as they stayed with Pearl. And though Cane knew the book was fictitious, sometimes it still seemed closer to the truth than anything he had read in his mother's Bible. According to Charles Foster Winthrop III, the world was an unjust, despicable place lorded over by a select pack of the rich and ruthless, and the only way for a poor man to get ahead was to ignore the laws that they enforced on everybody but themselves. And from what Cane had seen in his twenty-three years of barely surviving, how could he disagree? Of course, he couldn't go along with rape or murder, but, he had to admit, the idea of robbing a bank did possess a certain appeal. Just a few minutes of daring could possibly change their lives forever. Still, out of some old-fashioned loyalty or deep-seated superstition he was unable to shake, Cane was loath to desert their dotty old father. To do so might curse him and his brothers for the rest of their lives. No, it would be better just to wait it out. He watched Pearl stumble on the two steps leading up to the door of the shack. "Ain't no reason to get in a hurry now," he told Chimney. "You best stick with me and Cob. Our day's comin' soon enough."

"You mean for the heavenly table?" Cob asked.

"Well, not exactly," Cane said in a patient voice, "but don't worry. You'll get there one of these days."

Chimney let out an exasperated groan. "Jesus Christ, you're startin' to sound like Pap." Standing up, he wiped his hands on the front of his pants. "All right then," he said, "I'll give it a little longer." He started off toward the water bucket sitting in the shade of the tulip tree, then stopped in his tracks. Cane and Cob watched him tilt his head and stare for a moment at the blanched and cloudless sky, his wet rag of a shirt clinging to his bony back. The only sound to be heard was Pearl's faint whistling inside the cabin. Chimney spat in the dust and shook his head. "The heavenly table," he said loudly over his shoulder as he began walking again. "Pork chops thick as a bull's cock, beefsteaks the size of wagon wheels, buttered biscuits as hot and fluffy as the tits on . . ."

Cane smiled to himself and reached down. He picked up another potato and looked it over, then placed it on top of the good pile.

8

THE DAY AFTER returning from Parker's store, Ellsworth hitched up the wagon around noon and started down the road toward Meade. He had made up his mind during the night. It had occurred to him, as he lay in bed digesting his supper and wondering how many miles away Germany might be, that he also had no idea what the war was even about. He rolled over in bed and stared out the window into the darkness on the other side of the rippled pane. He had once shucked corn with an old man named Garnet Quick who had lost an ear in the War Between the States, the one they fought over freeing the slaves, and Ellsworth had harbored a sneaking suspicion ever since he'd talked to the man that a war could get started over the least little thing. And if the fight wasn't worth fighting, he had reasoned, as he lay there listening to Eula call out to Pickles in her sleep, then how could he sit by without raising a finger and allow his only son to take a chance on getting maimed or even killed?

By that evening, Ellsworth was standing on a hill overlooking the army camp splayed out north of the town on the other side of the Scioto River. It was much larger than he'd expected, as big as most cities, he reckoned, and for the first time all day, he began to have doubts that he could get Eddie back even if he did find him. Ellsworth had been to Meade a few times in his life, and though he had been confident when he left home, he had forgotten about the lonely, insecure feeling that always came over him when he was among a crowd of complete strangers. Now, staring across at the huge camp, still under construction but already filled with hundreds of soldiers and trucks and horses—even a flying machine, only the second one the farmer had ever seen in his life, circling like a buzzard above it all—he grew nervous. There were forces at work down there along the river that would intimidate almost anybody. And not just there, either. Why, just a couple of hours ago, he had seen a woman dressed in men's trousers driving a Ford Coupe out along the Huntington Pike all by herself. As he watched the airplane make one more pass over the camp and then land on a flat strip of ground outlined in whitewash, Ellsworth rubbed his chin and recalled standing around the stove in Parker's store one night last winter and someone, maybe Tick Osborne, saying that these were what people called "modern times." Most of those gathered there were in agreement that the world now seemed head over heels in love with what the tycoons and politicians kept referring to as "progress," but before they could begin arguing the pros and cons of exactly what that was going to mean in the long run, Jimmy Beulah spoke up and said, "'End times' is more like it." Then he spat on the stove, and Kermit Saunders passed him a bottle and said, "Amen," and the only sound you could hear in the store after that was the crackle of Jimmy's spit on the black metal lid.

Suddenly, Ellsworth wished he had followed Eula's advice and given the boy a couple of more days to come back on his own before he went looking for him. When the sun began to sink in the west, he gathered up an armful of corn husks from the bed of the wagon and dumped them on the ground for the mule, then ate a hunk of fried bread and two turnips for his own supper. He washed it down with water from a gourd jug, and wished he had remembered to bring along a jar of wine to keep him company. Unhitching his suspenders, he took off his shirt and loosened his pants, then lay down with a corn knife at his side. As the darkness settled in, a few stars began to appear above him and an owl hooted its lonely call from a nearby tree. He would make his way, he thought, to the army camp first thing in the morning. He hoped to Christ, if Eddie was there, that he hadn't sworn any oaths or made his mark on any papers yet. Though Ellsworth didn't have any proof other than his word, he would argue that the boy had just turned sixteen. That alone should be enough, he figured, though he could also add that Eddie was needed at home to help with the farm. But what if they still wouldn't turn loose of him? He stared at the kite-shaped outline of Boötes as he tallied up the boy's defects. All right then, if nothing else worked, he'd swallow his pride and tell them his son was as lazy a drunkard and thief as any in the country, and that an army that would take someone like that must already be on the verge of losing the battle. True, there were plenty of men around who could outdrink the boy ten to one, and, as far as he knew, the only thing Eddie had stolen in his life was that damn magazine from the schoolteacher, but the people running the camp wouldn't know that. Ellsworth ran these arguments over and over in his head until the lids of his eyes grew heavy as stones, and he finally began to snore along with the mule, both of them dreaming, on that warm and moonless night, of nothing in particular.

He awakened early the next morning and splashed some water on his face, rubbed a bluebell leaf over the few teeth he had left. Unwrapping a piece of linen that contained two hard-boiled eggs, he peeled the shells off with his thumbnail. He ate them slowly while longing for a cup of coffee and gazing over at the army base. Then he watered the mule and started down the hill toward Meade along a dirt lane shaded by box elder and sweet gum. Half an hour later, he came out into the sunlight and the main road. Off in the distance, he saw a black man stripped to the waist and pulling weeds out of a row of beans. Ellsworth wondered how much one like that would cost him if he couldn't get his son back. A big one, he figured, would charge plenty, but perhaps he could find something smaller—hell, even a sick one could probably outdo Eddie—who would still put in a good day's work for a fair price.

He had just started up again when he saw what appeared to be a caravan headed toward him, taking up most of the road. In the lead was a motorcar driven by a swarthy, toothsome man dressed in a paisley vest and a frilly white shirt. A jewel big as an eyeball glinted from a ring on one of his hands. Following him was a canvas-covered dray refitted with rubber tires and pulled by four horses. A frightful-looking woman with massive thighs puffed on a cigarillo while holding the reins loosely. Beside her on the cushioned wagon seat was another girl, with a bruised face that reminded Ellsworth of a windfall apple left too long on the ground. She had her skirts hiked up and her skinny legs gaped apart, airing her privates. A few feet behind them was a second man, riding a red roan. He was dressed in dusty black clothes and had two pistols strapped to his thick waist. Glancing back after they passed,

Ellsworth saw another woman through an opening in the back of the wagon. She was seated on a wooden chair running a brush through her long yellow hair. Not a one of them had acknowledged the farmer, and he traveled on to Meade listening to the creaking of the leather harness and the steady dull *plop* of the mule's hooves against the hard-packed road, pondering what in the world such people might be about.

9

THE JEWETTS WERE working frantically to finish clearing off the swamp before the offer of the chicken bonus expired. Just that morning, Tardweller had stopped by to remind them they had only two days left. They actually had three, but he was a little pissed off by the progress they had made. He figured if any of them argued about it, he'd just tell them the deal was off. A few hens weren't anything to him, but he'd bet a couple of his hunting buddies fifty dollars each that they'd never get done in time. Still, no matter how it turned out, he'd definitely gotten his money's worth out of these idiots. Regular men would have charged him ten times as much and taken twice as long for the work they were doing. Sitting in his canopied buggy, he glanced at Pearl out of the corner of his eye, then casually mentioned that he was on his way to Farleigh to get more ice for his wife and daughter. "Be glad when it cools off some," he said. "I can't hardly keep up with 'em, they go through it so fast."

The Major waited on the old man to say something, but Pearl just slowly nodded. Though even breathing the thick, humid air required extra effort, he hardly broke a sweat anymore. It was as if he were drying up and turning into worm dust himself. He stood beside the buggy and waited to be dismissed while Tardweller watched Cob and Chimney drag some brush to the edge of the clearing. For several minutes, the only sounds to be heard were the steady *chunk, chunk, chunk* of Cane's ax against a soft pine, and the airy swish of the paper fan the Major was waving at his fat face. "By God," he finally said to Pearl, "even if ye don't win them hens, you sure give it a good try." Then he drove off laughing.

That afternoon, Pearl's stomach started acting up and he threw down his ax and hurried behind a bush, his hands fumbling with the knot he had tied in his rope belt. Ever since they'd started eating on that sick hog, he'd been prone to the squirts. He was squatted down with his pants around his knees when he suddenly emitted a high-pitched cry and toppled forward on his face. His sons, scattered across the clearing, all turned and looked at one another. Cob began to run in Pearl's direction. "Keep an eye out," Cane yelled. "He probably been bit." The rotting carcasses of at least twenty rattlers and cottonmouths they had killed over the last several weeks hung from the lower branches of a huge oak standing alone in the middle of the hacked acres. Tardweller had ordered them not to touch the tree because it held, as he put it, "sentimental value," and the brothers had whiled away hours speculating on what he might mean, Cane and Chimney finally agreeing that under that blue shade was probably where the man had gotten his first piece of ass. Such a spot, they figured, would be memorable to anyone, even that arrogant skinflint. Cob stopped and grabbed the rusty saber, then took off again. By that time, the others were only a few feet behind him.

After looking about for a snake, they turned Pearl over and searched for a bite mark, but found no sign of one. Although his eyes were open, they were fixed blankly on something that only he could see. A thin web of spittle hung from his chin whiskers to his Adam's apple. Cob scratched his head and said, "I think he's takin' a nap." He and Cane were on their knees on either side of the old man.

"No, he's sick," Chimney said. "I saw him puke up his biscuit this morning." He stepped back a couple of feet, started trying to squeeze a splinter out of the palm of his hand.

Cane leaned over and put his ear against Pearl's chest. He listened for a minute, then raised up. "Jesus," he said. He grabbed hold of the old man's bony shoulders and shook him.

"What ye doin'?" Chimney asked.

"Pap?" Cane said. "Hey, Pap." He shook him again, but not so hard this time.

"Well?"

"I think his ol' heart's give out."

"No way," Chimney said. "Hell, I couldn't keep up with him five minutes ago."

"He sleeps pretty hard sometimes," Cob said, gently smoothing his hand over Pearl's forehead. "Poor ol' Pap, he's just tired, is all."

"No," Cane said, "that's not it." He turned and looked at Chimney. "I hate to say it, but I think he's gone."

Cob's brow wrinkled and his hand moved down to pick a burr off Pearl's shirt. For a moment, his brothers wondered if he understood, but then he said, as casually as if he were talking about the weather, "Well, that makes sense, I reckon. Remember what he said this morning?"

"No," Cane said, "I don't recall."

"He said he could see someone a-settin' a plate out for him. I just thought he was goin' on about them ghosts again, but I bet he was talkin' about the heavenly table, wasn't he?"

"Shit, that don't mean nothin'," Chimney said. "That's all he ever talked about."

"Yeah, but still . . ."

Nothing else was said for several minutes, and Cane pushed Pearl's muddy brown eyes closed with his thumbs, his living hands framing the wasted face for a moment like a picture hanging on a wall. Then he raised up and looked about the clearing. To his disgust, he found himself thinking that there was no way they would ever finish in time to get the chicken bonus now. The least he could have done was speak up this morning when Tardweller lied through his goddamn teeth about how many days they had left. That would have been something anyway, taking up for the old feller one last time. He fought down a sick feeling rising in his throat and said quietly to Cob, "Help me get his pants back up."

As he stood watching, Chimney spat on his hands, then ran them through his hair. He wondered what Penelope was doing, hating her more than ever just then. From what he had seen those weeks he had worked in the barn, all she ever did was ride around in her college beau's automobile and drink lemonade on the front porch. Well, whatever it was, she sure as hell wasn't standing soaked with sweat in a field staring down at a dark, bloody lump behind her father's feet, green bottle flies already buzzing around it. An anxious feeling swept over him just then, a wild desire to take off running and never look back, and he turned about in a circle several times before he could get settled down. Goddamn, he thought, just takin' a shit. What a lousy way to go. Snake bit would have been a hundred times better.

Cob finished tying the belt and looked up at the sky. Somewhere out there beyond that blue expanse was the new country his father would soon be entering, one blessed with goodness and cool breezes and an everlasting repast. He smiled. There was nothing to be sad about. As he had heard Pearl say many times since his meeting with the hermit, a certain amount of suffering was called for to gain entry into paradise, and now that trial was over with for him. "Just think," Cob said. "The heavenly table. He's got it made now, don't he?"

"He sure does," said Chimney. "Shame we couldn't have hitched a ride with him. Hell, they probably already fittin' him for his feed bag."

"This ain't the time to be jokin' around," Cane told him.

"Maybe not," Chimney said, "but I think Cob's right. That poor old sonofabitch lying there just got the only thing he's wanted for years. Christ, we should be happy for him."

Although Cane couldn't dispute the logic in his brother's argument, such an attitude was still, to his way of thinking, a little too swift and coldhearted for the occasion. It was only right that a tear or two be shed, or, at the very least, some kind words spoken, before you started poking fun at someone's passing. He stood up and walked over to the water bucket to retrieve his shirt. As he did so, he heard Cob say, "Well, I know I am. Heck, he'll be eatin' steaks big around as wagon wheels, and tender as . . . as . . . Oh, shoot, how tender was them steaks again, Chimney?"

"Tender as a young girl's kitty-cat."

"An' the biscuits? What was it you said about them?"

"Oh, they'll be hot and fluffy as—"

"Enough," Cane said. He looked toward the shack on the other side of the cotton field. "You gather up the tools and me and Cob will carry him back to the house."

"Where we gonna bury him?"

"Back there by the hog pen," Cane said, as he finished buttoning his shirt. "At least that way he'll have some company."

10

BEFORE ELLSWORTH WAS halfway across town, he saw, coming toward him on Paint Street, a group of soldiers on horseback, their new leather saddles squeaking and the polished tack shining brightly in the morning sun. He pulled Buck off to the side and studied the procession closely, but he didn't see any sign of Eddie. After they turned and headed down Main in the direction of the train depot, he continued on. He was amazed at how much Meade had grown since his last visit, and nearly overwhelmed by the racket coming from the automobiles and horse-drawn carriages and throngs of people on the sidewalks. "And this a weekday!" he exclaimed to himself. He looked about for something familiar, and as the mule plodded by Spetnagel's Hardware with its ears bobbing, he recalled that he had bought Eula a nice dress there once, a blue and white print with pearly-looking buttons and a lacy collar. Even after all these years, he could still see the surprised look on her face when she opened the box. They had been married only a short time and were still getting to know each other. She had worn it to church the next week, and as they started to drive home afterward, he heard her start softly singing the hymn the preacher had chosen to close the services with. "What you so happy about?" he asked.

Eula stopped singing and glanced shyly at him, then looked away. "I know it's silly," she said, "but ain't nobody ever bought me anything as nice as this dress before."

Ellsworth had felt a lump start to form in his throat. Though Eula didn't talk much about her past, and he didn't ask, he'd heard a little about how she had been raised on the edge of Bourneville. Her father had been born deformed, without any fingers, and his arms hung helplessly at his sides like a pair of clubs, while her mother, when she was in the grips of what people called one of her "spells," walked the roads at night wrapped in nothing but a bedsheet and talking nonsense about being of royal blood. Nine times out of ten, someone would usually find her the next morning lying violated in a ditch or under a tree somewhere, the older boys around Bourneville, and even some of the men, not caring one iota about who the crazy bitch married to Crip Sims claimed to know in Buckingham Palace. Throughout Eula's childhood, every spoon of slop put out on the banana crate they used as a table was due to somebody's charity. By the time she met Ellsworth in 1897, she was twenty-two, keeping house for an old man named Wheeler in Bainbridge in return for fifteen dollars a month and a bed in a windowless back room. Her parents were long dead, and her lone surviving relative, an older brother who had left home on his twelfth birthday, was a tramp who used to come through every two or three years to bum a buck or two. "Well, shoot, you're my wife, ain't ye?" Ellsworth finally managed to say.

"Until the day I die," she had answered, then leaned over and kissed him quickly on the cheek. The dress, along with a pair of stockings and a petticoat, had set him back four dollars, but it was the best money he ever spent in his life.

When he finally arrived at the entrance to the army camp, Ellsworth swung down off the wagon and approached the three guards warily, explained that he was looking for his son. "Been gone three days now," he said.

"Was he called up?" asked a man with a corporal stripe and a nose shaped like a sharp blade.

"What?"

"Did he get a draft notice?"

"No, not that I know of."

"So he enlisted?"

"Maybe," Ellsworth said.

"Well, if you don't know, why do you think he's here then? He could be anywhere."

Just as Ellsworth had begun to suspect last night, they were going to make it hard for him. That's just the way it was with the government; he had heard it said a hundred times over at Parker's store. They were incapable of doing anything in a forthright, sensible way. But Christ Almighty, he couldn't just turn around and head home without knowing for sure. What would he tell Eula? He looked the man straight in the eye and said, "I'd be much obliged if you'd check anyway. It took me most of a day to get here."

The corporal stared off into the distance while pulling at his chin, looking as if he were about to make a momentous decision that could affect the entire outcome of the war. His name was Alfred Zimmerman, and he had paid a flunky draft-board doctor ten dollars to overlook his flat feet so that he might finally escape his father's print shop in Akron and embark on what he truly believed was going to be a glorious career in the military. He wasn't sure yet what special talent he possessed that would pave the way for his advancement, but in his view, compared to the two imbeciles he'd been stuck with on gate duty, he was virtually another Napoleon Bonaparte. "What's his name?" he finally asked the farmer with a deep sigh.

"Eddie."

"What about his last name?"

"Same as mine," Ellsworth said.

Zimmerman's face began to turn red, and the other two soldiers elbowed each other and chuckled. "So what the hell might that be?"

"Fiddler."

Turning to one of the others, a stocky man with a head shaped like a bean can and thick, sun-bleached eyebrows that birds occasionally mistook for a pair of dead caterpillars, Zimmerman said, "Private Ballard, you'll be responsible for the gate while I run this down. Just remember, like Lieutenant Bovard told us the other day, the enemy could be anywhere." Then he wheeled around and marched off, his nose pointed skyward like a rudder and his back ramrod straight, toward a group of canvas huts off in the distance.

"Jesus, Ballard," Ellsworth heard the third soldier say, a thin, bookish-looking man with wire-rimmed spectacles and a pale, triangular face who went by the name of Crank, "that Zimmerman needs to ease up a little. What's his problem anyway?" An only child, he'd lived with his elderly parents in a neat, ivy-covered brick house in Martins

Ferry, and had made a comfortable living keeping the books for several businesses before being called up. He had many quirks, among them an absolute rigidity when it came to the manner in which his food was laid out on his plate, and a maddening inability to sleep anywhere but in his own tiny bedroom. Because of the sloppy ineptness of the mess-hall workers, he hadn't eaten anything but candy bars in over a week, and the insomnia he had suffered from since his first night in the barracks continued unabated. The fervent desire to make it home and never have to eat a chicken leg that had accidently brushed up against the mashed potatoes, or sleep in the same room with another human being ever again, was the only thing that kept him going.

"Don't pay him no attention," Ballard said. "The Jew got him a stripe, and now he thinks he's Colonel Custard." Unlike Crank, Ballard, a local boy who had been born and raised in a shotgun shack at the bottom of Porter Holler, considered his draft notice the luckiest thing that had ever happened to him, chiefly because it allowed him to escape the clutches of a pie-faced country woman whom he had managed to impregnate two years in a row behind the makeshift bandstand at the annual Lattaville Coon Hunters' Dance. The way he saw it, even getting ground into mincemeat on a foreign field was better than playing daddy to a couple of hillbilly bastards and hubby to a floozy who didn't think twice about spreading her legs for a glass of cider and a cake doughnut.

"You mean *General Custer*, don't you?" Crank said.

"Shit, what difference does it make?" Ballard replied. "He's a prick, that's what I'm saying."

Ellsworth stood waiting for a long time in the hot sun. The guards ignored him and he studied their brown uniforms and campaign hats out of the corner of his eye, trying to picture Eddie wearing one. He overheard Ballard tell a joke about a queer who set up house in a cucumber patch, but he couldn't make heads or tails out of it. He wondered if either of them knew where Germany was located.

When Zimmerman finally returned, his spine was even straighter than before. Unfortunately, in the time it took him to reach the office where the records were kept, he had allowed his mind to drift for a minute or two, first daydreaming about his next promotion and then worrying about what Ballard and Crank were saying behind his back, and he had forgotten the name the farmer had given him. "Who are you looking for?" the private behind the desk asked. Zimmerman had shut his eyes for a moment and strained his memory. The last name started with an "F," of that he was sure. "Franklin," he guessed. The private scrolled through several pages, then said, "Don't see any Franklin, but we got a Wesley Franks signed in two days ago." "That's him," Zimmerman said, and out the door he went.

"Well, you were right," he told Ellsworth. "They got a new one on the list goes by that name."

"Good," the farmer said. "How do I get him back?"

"You can't," Zimmerman said, shaking his head. "He's already been inducted."

"But he's only sixteen years old. That's too young to be fightin' the Germans, ain't it?"

"Too young!" Ballard spoke up. "Ain't you heard? Them Huns got newborn babies chained to machine guns. They either fight or get dumped in the stew pot with the horse apples. Don't worry, your boy's plenty old enough."

"Good God, Ballard," Zimmerman said, "you've been talkin' to Sergeant Malone again." The sergeant he referred to was a great spinner of horrific war stories, and much admired among some of the new recruits at Camp Pritchard. As a youth, he had fought in Cuba in 1898, and then, ever nostalgic for what he considered the "best three weeks of his life," had quit his job in a glove factory in upstate New York and joined up with the Red Cross in the summer of 1915, it being the only way an American could get to the war at that time. Although he soon found out that the conflict in Europe was no horsey lark in the tropical boonies, to his credit he endured eighteen months of hell with an ambulance crew around Verdun before he began to go haywire and ended up in a loony bin down near Marseille. Despite his protestations, he was judged unfit for further service and sent home just a few weeks before the United States entered the fray. By then he was twitchy and gray and thirty-eight years old, a mere shell of the boy who once rode with Roosevelt, and though he didn't think they would take him, he showed up at the recruiting station in Albany anyway. To his surprise, because of his experience at the Front, the whiskey on his breath had been ignored and he'd quickly been offered a sergeant's rank. Now he was training doughboys how to take a shit in the mud without getting their heads blown off, and practicing a self-prescribed form of controlled drinking that kept him from diving to the ground every time a bird flew over.

"So? I guarantee you Malone knows more about what's goin' on over there than your Lieutenant Bovard ever will."

"He's a bad one to drink, my boy is," Ellsworth interrupted. It was embarrassing to admit, but what did it matter? He would never see these men again anyway. "And dumb, too," he added, figuring he might as well lay it on as thick as possible. "You don't want to be a-fightin' along someone like that, do you? Hell, he's as liable to shoot the wrong man as the right one. Believe me, fellers, he ain't fit to be in your army."

"Mister," Crank said, "if being stupid kept men out of the army, there wouldn't be enough left in Camp Pritchard to wash the dishes in the chow hall."

"Don't listen to the bookkeeper," Ballard told the farmer. "He's just pissed because—"

Throwing up his hands in frustration, Ellsworth said, "What if I talked to the boss?"

Both the privates laughed, but before either could make another smart remark, Corporal Zimmerman silenced them with an upraised hand. He had allowed this foolishness to go on too long and he needed to reinforce his authority. Turning to Ellsworth, he began speaking slowly, as if he were talking to someone who had just awoken from a long coma. Zimmerman had discovered, over the course of manning the gate eight hours a day for the past couple of weeks, that many people, soldiers and private citizens alike, have a hard time taking no for an answer. They're like little children who have been spared the rod and trust that, by yowling long enough and loud enough, they will eventually get their way. He was convinced that any parent who didn't beat their offspring within an inch of their lives at least once a week was doing the world a great disservice, and he was thankful now that his own father had followed that line of thinking. Sure, it might have hurt at the time, but if it hadn't been for his old man's leather strap, Zimmerman thought, he might have turned out like that sniveling whiner Crank, or, God forbid, that mouthy, fatheaded Ballard. "Now," he told Ellsworth, as he finished explaining the situation in short declarative sentences that even a cretin might understand, "the best thing for you to do is go back home. Don't worry, you'll see your son in a year or two." He held up one finger, then another, in front of the farmer's face.

Ellsworth's eyes widened. "A year or two!" he sputtered. Why, he couldn't imagine it taking more than a few weeks to kill every human being on the planet if you had someone overseeing things who knew what they were doing. But then again, with the government in charge, it might go on forever without anything to show for it. There was no way he was going to get Eddie back. He realized that now. "What's this war about anyway?" he asked.

The soldiers glanced at one another uneasily. In all their hours of manning the gate, and answering a thousand questions, nobody had ever asked them that one before. "It's complicated," Zimmerman said.

"What's that mean?"

"Some bastard shot some other bastard," Crank said. "Over around Russia somewhere."

"That's pretty much the crack of it, from what I hear," Ballard chimed in.

"You mean the *crux* of it."

"Actually," Zimmerman said, "it started in Austria. I ought to know. I've still got family living there."

"I'll bet you do," Ballard said snidely. "I'll bet ol' Australia's full of your kind."

Crank rolled his eyes. "He said *Austria*, not Australia."

"Well, if that's the reason they started this war, the politicians must be clear out of their minds," Ellsworth said, raising his voice. "Either that, or they're a-lyin' to ye."

The soldiers all stared silently at the farmer for a moment. Regardless of how they felt about each other, they all believed, deep down, that there was nothing nobler than being a courageous patriot defending his country against the savage Germanic hordes. Even Crank, as much as he missed his parents and French toast on Sunday mornings and his peaceful bedchamber overlooking the sugar maple in the backyard, would have agreed with that if push came to shove. "Sir, you could be arrested for that kind of talk," Zimmerman finally said.

"Yeah, what the hell are you, buddy?" Ballard added. "One of them damn Wobblies?"

Ellsworth didn't know what a Wobbly was, but from the way the guard spat the word out of his mouth, he figured it couldn't be a good thing. Lately, it seemed that wherever he turned, something beyond his comprehension was lying in wait to make him look like a fool. He decided not to say anything else. Even if the reason they gave for the war sounded like one of the dumbest things he had ever heard in his life, there was no way he was going to give these guards any more ammunition to use against him. As soon as he did, they'd have him playing house in a pickle patch with that other poor bastard they had joked about. He turned away and climbed back on his wagon.

Reaching for the gourd under the seat, he took a drink of water, then looked over at the camp again. In a field far off to the left, a row of soldiers stood at attention near the edge of a freshly dug trench. A thick-chested man with skinny legs paced back and forth in front of them, giving a speech. His voice was loud and gruff, but Ellsworth was still too far away to hear what he was saying. He gripped a rifle with a gleaming bayonet attached to the end of the barrel. Every so often, he stopped talking and gave a bloodcurdling cry, then stabbed the bayonet into what appeared to be a feed sack filled with sand. Ellsworth wondered if Eddie was standing in the line of soldiers, and if he had helped dig the ditch. As hard as it was getting him to do a few chores around the farm, it would serve him right if the army had stuck a pick and shovel in his hands first thing. He'd ask Eddie about that the next time he saw him. He would probably be wearing one of those brown uniforms, have a story or two to tell. Maybe he would even know the whereabouts of Germany. It suddenly occurred to him that perhaps the army was a good thing, especially if it toughened the boy up. Hell, he might turn out to be a halfway decent farmer after all.

He sat watching the man attack the feed bag until there wasn't anything left but a few shreds of burlap, and then he turned the mule and headed back toward town. Glancing over at the gate, he saw a glowering Ballard drop to the ground and start doing pushups while Zimmerman stood over him counting, the hint of a smile creasing his otherwise stony face. At least now, Ellsworth thought, as he passed a huge cairn of stinking slops and discarded civilian rags, the wheels of the wagon squeaking and black flies swarming over man and mule alike, he could tell Eula for certain where their boy had run off to.

II

IT TOOK THE Jewett brothers the rest of the afternoon to dig a grave in the dry, hard earth on the other side of the hog pen, just a few feet away from the sunken area that contained the mulattoes. When they were done, they washed Pearl's face and hands, then went through his pockets. Besides his pocketknife, which Chimney had already called dibs on, all they found was seventeen American cents and a Canadian nickel along with half a plug of linty tobacco and a sales receipt for a handful of nails purchased over two years ago. After wrapping him tightly in his blanket and lowering him into the hole, Cob climbed down and slipped the worm pillow under his head. They took turns filling in the grave, then Chimney walked over to the porch and returned with the rusty saber. "Remember when we found this fuckin' thing?" he said.

Cane nodded and smiled. They had discovered the sword one windy autumn day in a woods a few miles outside of Atlanta, unaware that over fifty years before, some Northern soldiers working point for Sherman's army had used it to mark the spot where they had buried one of their comrades, a fat and jolly shoemaker from Boston who was singing an aria from *The Barber of Seville* when the top of his head was sheared off by a sniper's minié ball. The blade was standing up in the dirt, and Pearl had jerked it from the ground without thinking, then he and the boys had moved on. Two days later, though, while searching through a garden patch hoping to find something edible the owner might have overlooked, it suddenly occurred to him that the sword might be more than just another cast-off remnant of the Civil War. Hadn't he heard once of a man in Tennessee who had found an ordnance box filled with silver bullion while digging a footer for a house? The more he scratched about in the empty garden with the saber, the more he began to imagine that it had indicated the spot where a cache of war booty was hidden. "Gather up yer brothers," he finally said to Cane. "We're headin' back into them woods."

"What for?" the boy had asked warily. Although he was only thirteen years old at the time, Cane was already beginning to doubt much of what came out of Pearl's mouth, not because he was a liar, but because it was evident that he was slowly losing his mind, and had been ever since Lucille died and he started sleeping with the worm under his head.

"Goin' back to where we found this sword."

"What about Mississippi? You said we'd—"

"Back when the war was a-goin' on, people hid stuff from the Yankees all the time. Their gold and jewels and what have ye."

"Okay," Cane said, "but that don't—"

"And I'd bet anything somebody used this sword to mark the spot where he buried his valuables," Pearl went on. "Probably got killed before he could get back to it, the poor bastard. It just makes sense. Why else would it been stuck in the ground like that?"

Though Cane figured there were at least a dozen other explanations for why the saber had ended up in the woods, any of them more logical than the one his old man was proposing, for the life of him he couldn't think of one just then. "I don't know," he said, "maybe . . . maybe . . ."

"Maybe quit yer stutterin' and get them boys rounded up," Pearl had ordered.

They had been homeless and barely making it for almost three years at that point, but on their way back to the woods, Pearl began talking of the grand meals they would soon be eating and the land they would buy and the new duds they would sport. He even made up a marching song to keep Cob and Chimney moving along at a steady pace. To pacify Cane, he mentioned sending him to one of those universities where smart people loafed about talking bullshit; that is, if he still thought book learning was something he wanted to waste his time on once he got his share of the treasure. His enthusiasm was infectious, and even Cane slowly allowed himself to start dreaming that just maybe their luck was about to change.

It took four days to figure out the approximate location where they had come across the sword, and they then spent another week digging a series of deep pits, searching for what Pearl kept referring to as the "sweet spot." Finally, on their twenty-third attempt, Chimney hit something with the shovel blade that didn't sound like the usual root or rock. Pearl jerked the boy out of the hole and jumped in. He began slinging dirt into the air with his hands, working like a madman for several minutes before he suddenly stopped and uttered a sickly, frustrated moan. When the dust cleared, the boys walked up to the edge of the hole and looked down upon the remains of the shoemaker, no longer fat and certainly no longer jolly, wrapped in a rotten horse blanket.

"Pap," Cob said, after his father climbed out, "how we gonna trade them old bones for a new farm?" Before he could stop himself, Pearl whirled around and backhanded the boy, knocking him over a pile of dirt. Then he stalked off, disappearing into the trees. When he returned several hours later, looking nearly as lifeless as the skeleton, he was carrying two dead rabbits and had his coat pockets filled with windfall apples—his way, Cane figured, of asking forgiveness. Pearl decided to hang on to the sword. "Ye never know," he had said, "it might come in handy someday." And so it did, eleven years later, as Chimney shoved it down into the loose soil at the head of his grave.

Standing around the red clay mound, Cane flipped through the pages of the Bible, finally coming to a passage in the Hebrews that their mother had marked with a pencil. "I reckon you should bow your heads," he said. Then he cleared his throat and began to read:

"And what shall I more say? For the time would fail me to tell of Gedeon, and of Barak, and of Samson, and of Jephthae; of David also, and Samuel, and of the prophets: Who through faith subdued kingdoms, wrought righteousness, obtained promises, stopped the mouths of lions, quenched the violence of fire, escaped the edge of the sword, out of weakness were made strong, waxed valiant in fight, turned to flight the armies of the aliens. Women received their dead raised to life again: and others were tortured, not accepting deliverance; that they might obtain a better resurrection: And others had trial of cruel mockings and scourgings, yea, moreover

*of bonds and imprisonment: They were stoned, they were sawn
asunder, were tempted, were slain with the sword: they wandered
about in sheepskins and goatskins: being destitute, afflicted,
tormented; of whom the world was not worthy: they wandered in
deserts, and in mountains, and in dens and caves of the earth."*

"Amen."

"By God, that hit the nail on the head," Chimney said. He squatted
down and picked up a pebble, tossed it on top of the mound. "He probably would've give anything for one of them sawings."

"The man had a need for pain, that's for sure," Cane said.

Cob stared at the sword stuck in the ground, his brow lined with
worry. "Cane?" he finally said.

"Yeah?"

"Now that Pap's gone, who's gonna fix the biscuits?"

With a loud hoot, Chimney sprang up. Behind him, the evening
sun seemed to be halted on the blue and orange horizon, as if it, too,
were paying the old man some last respects. "What now, boss?" he said.

Cane glanced over at his youngest brother. Standing there dressed
in rags with his thin arms hanging at his sides and his ribs showing
through his shirt, Chimney seemed more wretched than he could ever
recall seeing him. Even Cob, who could usually go two or three days
without eating and not lose an ounce, was beginning to look a little
poorly. It was time to leave this place before they all ended up planted
around the hog pen. "People most always have a big feed after a funeral,
don't they?" Cane said.

Chimney shrugged his shoulders and spat. "I reckon most do, yeah."

"Well, then, what say we eat the rest of that pig."

"All of it?" Cob asked excitedly.

"Hell, yes," Cane said. "Who's gonna stop us?"

12

ON HIS WAY back across Meade from the army camp, Ellsworth remembered that Eula's birthday was coming up soon. Perhaps a little present would help ease the news about Eddie, maybe even get her to forget about the wine. Now that he knew the boy was safely ensconced in the military, he was having second thoughts about dumping it. The gift would have to be cheap, though. Maybe a broom, he thought. He had noticed the other day that the straws on her old one were worn clear down to the handle. Not as nice as a new dress, but it would still surprise her. He stopped Buck on a street lined with elm trees and pulled his purse out. He was counting the coins that he kept back for pipe tobacco when he heard some whistling and looked up. A short, wiry man wearing a pith helmet and knee-high gumboots stepped out from between two houses. He carried a long wooden pole over his shoulder and a dead rat by the tail. A blackjack smeared with blood hung from a cord on his wide leather belt. With his small head and bowlegged walk, he bore a strong resemblance to a Floyd Odell who used to witch water for people out in Twin Township.

As the man started to pass by, he smiled and nodded at Ellsworth. His was the first friendly face the farmer had seen since he had left home the morning before. "Mister," Ellsworth said quickly, "you wouldn't have any idy where I could buy a good broom, would ye?" He noted that the pole the man carried was marked at regular intervals with dabs of black paint like a measuring stick and looked to be about eight feet long. The bottom third of it was coated with wet, dark matter, and a ball of flies buzzed around the tip of it like bees around a fragrant flower.

The man stopped. "A broom? I sure do. I got an uncle that makes 'em. Old boy's blind as a bat, but I guarantee you his sweepers are ten times better than anything you'll find in the stores." He pointed the rat down the street. "Just make ye a left at that house up yonder with the white fence and go down a block or so. You'll see his sign right across from Antoine's barbershop. You can't miss it. His name is Cone."

"Cone," Ellsworth repeated. "That your name, too?"

"Yes, sir, it is. Jasper Cone."

"Reason I ask is you look an awful lot like an Odell I used to know."

The man shook his head. "No, I been a Cone all my life."

Though a little leery of making himself look like a fool yet again, Ellsworth's curiosity got the better of him. He hesitated a moment, then asked, "What ye doin' with that rat?"

"Oh, I haul them out to the dump," Jasper explained. "Nothing worse than a rodent when it comes to spreadin' diseases."

"That your job? Go around killin' rats?"

"Well, not exactly," Jasper said. "Mostly I check the levels on the outhouses, but if'n I run into, say, a black snake while I'm in there, or a spider's nest, or a possum, or what have ye, I go ahead and take care of it." He set the end of the pole down on the sidewalk and leaned against it. "Yes, sir, they's a lot more to being the sanitation inspector than most folks realize."

Though Ellsworth couldn't begin to imagine why anyone would pay a man to go around poking a stick in people's privies, or why a man would want such a job in the first place, he nodded and said, "I bet ye seen some sights, ain't ye?"

"I surely have," Jasper said. "Ye'd be surprised at what goes on in a shithouse." He looked about, then moved toward the wagon and lowered his voice. "Husbands a-cheatin' on their wives, wives a-cheatin' on their husbands. And that's not nearly the worst of it. I've come across people doin' things that would make your hair stand on end. It's the privacy, see? That's what attracts them. Ye step in and latch the door and everybody thinks you're just takin' a dump. Why, I bet ye half the girls in this town have lost their cherry in somebody's johnny." He took another step closer. "Then there's other stuff, too. A couple months back I rescued a newborn out of one over on Hickory Street. The mother thought she was just havin' pains from some cabbage she'd et for supper, but as soon as she started to strain, out plopped a baby right down in the slop. Didn't even know she was expecting, or so she claimed anyway."

"Good Lord," Ellsworth said.

"Oh, it turned out fine," Jasper said. "I ran him straight over to Doc Hamm's once I pulled him out. They put my name in the newspaper and everything. Heck, the mother even said she was goin' to name him after me, but then her old man, he got jealous, started claiming that I'd been spying on her, and, well, that put the stops to that. But you can ask Mr. Rawlings, the city engineer, I don't need nobody's permission. I got a legal right to check any outhouse in this town." Then Jasper's face turned dark and he lowered his voice even more, to the point where Ellsworth could barely hear him. "Found me another one, too, over on the south side, but it was already dead. Nothin' but his little feet stickin' up like a couple of peckerhead mushrooms. They never did find out who put him there." He shook his head sadly and glanced down at the rat in his hand. A drop of blood dripped from its crushed skull and landed on the toe of his boot.

"Sounds like a helluva job," Ellsworth said.

"It's an awful of a thing to say, but hogs is cleaner than a lot of the people around here. And since they started building Camp Pritchard, the town's nearly doubled in size. That's a fair amount of fecal matter when you think about it." Anytime he found himself in a conversation with someone, especially a stranger, Jasper liked to throw in a technical phrase if given the opportunity, so that the person would know he truly was a professional. "Fecal matter" was one of his favorites.

"I imagine so," Ellsworth said.

"Right now the drinking water's the main worry," Jasper went on. "I find effluent running into a well, I got no choice but to shut it down."

Ellsworth wasn't sure how to respond, but he was damn glad he lived out in the country where a man had room to shit all he wanted. Clearly he was in the presence of an official who wielded a lot of power.

After all, he thought, only someone with substantial pull could shut down a man's water supply, no matter what sort of filth was floating in it. Taking a chance that the man might be in agreement, he said, "Well, these are modern times, I guess."

Jasper's face lit up and he gave the rat a good shake. "Yes, sir, they are," he said, his voice rising with excitement, "but you still got a lot of people set in their ways. As Mr. Rawlings says, they want to hang on to their slop jars and corncobs and privies and jakes no matter what. Hell, I think half of them would do their business right out in the street if they could get by with it. You mark my word, though, if'n we don't kill ourselves off first, someday everybody in the country will have indoor facilities, and I don't just mean some hole sawed in the floor, either, like Chester Dotson's got in his parlor." He took a deep breath and wiped his nose with the same hand that held the rat. "Well, it's been nice talkin' to ye, mister, but I better get back to it. Last time I counted, there were still over eighteen hundred outhouses in this town, and I'd bet my buffalo gun at least one of them is causin' trouble today." Then he turned on his rubber heels and headed across the redbrick street, swinging the rat by the tail like a whirligig.

A FEW MINUTES later, Ellsworth halted the mule in front of a small white house. From a porch post hung a wooden sign that had a broom painted on it with a careful hand. Across the street, several men were squeezed together on a bench in front of the barbershop smoking, while another stood reading them a story from a newspaper in a theatrical manner, with much hand-waving and fist-clenching and verbal emphasis on certain words. The farmer set the brake on the wagon, then walked up to the porch. He knocked on the door and a voice inside called out, "It's open." He stepped inside a dark and musty room that smelled of stale sweat and straw and bacon grease. Hanging in one corner from a hook in the ceiling was a birdcage that contained what appeared to be a mummified parakeet. An old man with long white hair sat in a rocking chair in the opposite corner. Even though the air was stifling inside the closed-up room, he wore a thick woolen sweater underneath a butcher's apron stained with spills from a hundred dinners. His eyes were covered with a translucent film that reminded Ellsworth of egg whites. The man leaned forward and sniffed the air. "You got a mule?" he asked.

"Yeah."

"Thought so," the man said, tapping a crooked finger to his nose. "Mules got a smell all their own. I used to have a team of 'em back when I could see."

"That right?" Ellsworth said. He found that he couldn't stop staring at the dried-up bird in the cage. He wondered if the man had forgotten it, or just couldn't bear to part with it. This room, he thought, must get awful lonely at times.

"Well," the man said, "what you need?"

"The sanitation inspector mentioned you got brooms for sale."

"You mean Jasper?"

"He told me you was his uncle," Ellsworth said.

"Is he still wearing that goddamn helmet?"

"He had one on, yeah."

The old man laughed. "Don't get me wrong, Jasper's all right, but sometimes I think that job might have gone to his head." He paused and spat into a tin cup he held in his lap. Then a sly grin spread over his face. "I don't reckon he mentioned his dick, did he?"

"What?" Ellsworth asked, a little startled.

"Didn't think so," the broom maker said. "If ye ask me, that's what he should be proud of. Hell, anybody can count turds, but there's few men alive hung like ol' Jasper. He'd give one of them bull elephants a run for their money."

"Well, I only talked to him for a minute or two."

"Yeah," the man said, "he's right ashamed of it, and I blame his mother for that, her and that goddamn religion of hers. She did everything in her power to ruin that boy. Why, I had me a cock like that, I'd have the women a-crawlin' around here on the floor begging for it."

Ellsworth coughed and cleared his throat. "So, about the brooms," he said.

"Yes, sir," the old man continued, ignoring him, "they'd think they'd had a log chain drug through 'em by the time I got done, by God. I'd put . . ."

The broom maker was still talking when Ellsworth slipped out the door. Thankfully, the men sitting on the bench across the street now seemed to be in a deep discussion, and he managed to get away without being noticed. He was almost out of town when he saw the saloon across from the paper mill, a shabby hole in the wall called the Blind Owl. Ellsworth pulled the mule over and thought for a minute. Though he wasn't in the mood to talk to anyone else today, a drink surely would do him good after all the aggravation he had been through. Of course, there were bound to be people in there telling tales and spreading lies, but what if he just kept his mouth shut and minded his own business? That would work, he told himself, and he set the brake on the wagon and went inside.

The room was dark, and he'd already laid a quarter on the bar before he realized to his surprise that he was the only customer in the place. The keep set a glass of warm beer and a shot down in front of the farmer, then went to the other end of the bar and reached his hand down into a gallon jar. All the while Ellsworth sat there, the man stood silently looking out the window at the street with a scowl on his face, crunching pig's feet and spitting the gristle out on the floor. Not a single word was said. His name was Frank Pollard, and he had been a hateful bully for as long as anyone could remember. He had grown up believing that he was something special, and the discovery, around the time of his fourteenth birthday, that this was not the case had ruined him for any sort of happiness that didn't involve making other people miserable. Pollard's father had left him a little house and twelve acres when he passed ten years ago, but the son despised country life even more than people, and so he sold the place the morning of the old man's funeral and moved to Meade that afternoon. He bought the Blind Owl three days later. He slept on a cot in the back room, and barely made enough to keep the bills paid—nobody in their right mind would have ever hired Pollard to run a business of any kind—but he didn't care. He'd discovered the first week he owned the joint that it was perfect for attracting the kind of scum he could feel superior to, which was a feeling he needed much more than any amount of money. Drunks were weak-minded and careless and apt to let their emotions get the best of them. He loved to goad them into saying something stupid or taking a swing at him so that he had an excuse to take them out back in the alley and beat them senseless; and for many years that had been enough.

13

UNBEKNOWN TO COB, his brothers had already decided his fate and theirs by the time they sat down that evening and proceeded to eat up everything in the shack: a quarter of a hog and several dozen mealy potatoes and a partial bag of buggy flour and two rusty cans of peaches they found in Pearl's winter coat. Using Bloody Bill as inspiration, the plan they'd quickly put together while Cob was out fetching a bucket of water involved stealing three of the Major's horses, then riding to Farleigh, the nearest town, and robbing the bank there. After that, they would head north to Canada and start over. Cane wasn't sure—hell, he'd never even been inside a bank before—but he guessed the haul would be worth a few thousand dollars at the very least. But for it to work, they needed to leave tonight, before Tardweller discovered that Pearl was dead and they lost what Bloody Bill called "the element of surprise." On all of these things, Cane and Chimney had been in total agreement.

However, deciding how to deal with Cob had been a different story. Chimney believed that, because of his thickheaded nature and his obsession with all that heavenly table bullshit, he would prove to be a liability when it came to taking a bank, or even stealing a goddamn horse for that matter. As dumb as he was, he might get killed, or even get one of them killed. "He'd be better off with some farmer," Chimney said. "Hell, he wouldn't mind, long as they feed him. We could even send for him once we get to where we're going."

Cane realized, of course, that what Chimney said made sense, but it didn't matter. He couldn't leave either of them behind. Though he had never mentioned it, not once in all the years they'd been together, Lucille had called him to her bedside when she was sick and made him promise to look after his brothers. "Especially Cob," she had said. "He's always going to be slow." It was just a day or two before she passed, and as far as he knew, it was the last thing she ever said to anyone. "We can't do that," he told Chimney. "For Christ's sakes, he ain't some dog you can kick out when you get tired of takin' care of him. He's our brother."

Yearning to get started, Chimney decided it best not to press the issue, at least for now. Besides, he figured Cane would realize his mistake the first time Cob fucked up. "Well, if you say so, but how the hell you going to talk him into it?" he asked. "He's not gonna like it, you know that."

Cane got down on one knee in front of the fireplace and lit some kindling under a couple of pine logs, then replied, "The first thing we do is get his belly full."

And that they had, even holding themselves back, as hungry as they were, so that Cob could have more. When all that remained was a greasy potato or two, Cane casually suggested that they take an inventory of their inheritance.

"Inheritance?" Cob said. "What's that?"

"Everything Pap's left us."

"Why ye want to do that?" Cob asked a little suspiciously. He already had a vague feeling that something was up. Why else would they have let him have a whole can of peaches to himself? And nearly half the pork that was left?

"Just to see what kind of shape we're in, that's all."

"Oh."

Lighting the lantern, they laid everything they owned out on a blanket: a 12-gauge shotgun with a busted stock and three slightly damp shells, seven dollars in gold pieces along with the change from Pearl's pocket, their mother's Bible and *The Life and Times of Bloody Bill Bucket*, a nearly full bottle of Morning Dew whiskey that Pearl kept strictly for medicinal purposes, a straight razor, two pots and one blackened skillet, their bedrolls and a cracked mirror, a hammer, a butcher knife, four plates and three tin cups, their coats, and a pencil stub.

After that, they sat silently for a while, resting with their backs leaned against the wall. Cob still didn't understand the purpose of dragging all their junk out into the center of the room, but it didn't matter; he felt more contented than he had in a long time. No wonder people had a big supper after a funeral. It occurred to him that this was what he would feel like all the time once he got to heaven. An image of Willie the Whale stuffed to the gills with crawdads floated through his head, and he yawned. Though there was still a little light left outside, the smoke that lingered in the shack from the cook fire, along with the shadows cast across the room by the sputtering lamp, created the illusion in his mind of it being later than it really was. He reached over for the last potato in the skillet and stuck it in his mouth, then said with a sigh, "Well, fellers, if we're gonna get any work done tomorrow, we better be gettin' some sleep."

Cane looked over at Chimney and winked, then pointed at the trash heap that was their earthly possessions. "Just look at that," he said. "You ever seen such a sad sight? We been working like dogs our whole lives and I bet the poorest cracker sonofabitch in Georgia's got more in his poke than we do."

"Oh, I don't know," Cob said. "Like Pap always said, it could be worse."

"Maybe," Cane replied, "but I'd hate to think what that would be like." He reached for the whiskey bottle and twisted off the cap. "Well, at least we got our bellies full for once."

"We sure did," Cob said. "Lord, I'm about to bust."

"And just think, people like that damn Tardweller eat like this every day," said Chimney.

Cane took a sip from the bottle, then said, "I reckon we could, too, if we put our minds to it."

"How do ye figure that?" Cob said. "Shoot, we don't even have enough flour left over for biscuits in the morning. I'll tell ye one thing, it's gonna be a long day in the field tomorrow."

"Well, that's something we need to talk about," Cane said. He passed the bottle to Chimney, and then proceeded to explain their intentions. Though he started out aiming to be honest, his own desire to escape, which, after all, was dependent on convincing Cob the plan was a good idea, soon took over, and he ended up greatly minimizing the risks and embellishing the rewards instead. The more he went on, the better it sounded, and by the time he was finished, half the people in the country would probably have been clamoring to join up with them. He ended his spiel, sounding more coldhearted than he meant to, by saying, "Look, we're not gonna force you to do anything you don't want to do. As far as I'm concerned, you your own man now. But you need to understand, me and Chimney's leavin' out of here tonight."

Cob looked away toward the window. So it was finally going to happen after all. He thought about all those times his brothers had argued about quitting Pap and taking off on their own. But it was just talk then, Chimney blowing off about all the women he was going to fuck, and Cane dreaming about living like those fancy people that always looked down their noses at them whenever they had to walk through a town. Even he knew that as long as the old man was still alive, he didn't have to worry about such things. But now everything was about to change, in ways he couldn't begin to comprehend. It was all too much to take in, Pap dying and the big supper, stealing horses and robbing a bank. A panicky feeling rose up inside him. What the hell did that even mean, his own man? He had never had to decide anything in his life.

"Well?" Chimney said impatiently.

"I ain't smart enough to be no outlaw."

"You won't get no argument from—" Chimney started to say.

"Don't worry," Cane broke in. "I'll watch out for ye."

Cob scratched his head and tried to think. A sudden urge to sleep came over him, and he fought to suppress another yawn. Oh, how he wanted to just lie down and forget about everything, wake up in the morning and go chop some more brush. Why couldn't things stay the same? He had always done whatever was required of him, never once questioning or complaining, but nobody had ever asked him to give up his soul before. Why, there probably wasn't a second went by that the ol' Devil didn't make Bloody Bill regret what he'd done. Still, what choice did he have? He couldn't imagine a life without his brothers any more than he could imagine being his own man. They had never been apart, not for a single night. And that wasn't the only thing troubling him; now that they'd had their big feed, all that was left to eat was the rat that ran around in the shack at night, and he'd be a hard one to catch. Cob rubbed his hands roughly over his face. "Shoot, I got no idy what to do," he finally said.

"Stick with us," Cane said, and after a moment's hesitation, Cob agreed with a nod of his head, though it was obvious his heart wasn't in it.

"Okay, at least we got that shit out of the way," Chimney said, taking another hit off the bottle.

"But why Farleigh?" Cob said. "They some bad people in that town. Don't you remember what they did the last time we went through there?"

"Sure, I do," Cane said. "I reckon I remember everything about that goddamn place." The year before, when they were looking for work, a man gutting a turtle under a railroad trestle had told them about a farmer named Tardweller on the other side of Farleigh who might be hiring. It was a Sunday and they were on their way to talk to him. Just a hundred yards or so before the rutted clay road turned into a smooth graveled street, they passed a corpse hanging from an elm tree, a white man with a piece of cardboard pinned to his bloody long johns that said RAPEST. Some citizens loitering around a fountain in the square, admiring someone's new automobile, told them to keep moving when Pearl asked if they might get a sup of water. He commenced to preaching to them about charity and the life in the world to come and the heavenly table, and somebody in the crowd bounced a rock off his forehead. By the time they made it out of there, even the women gathered in front of the brick church were hurling stones at them.

"That was a sight, wasn't it?" Chimney said. "The way they'd clipped that ol' boy's pecker off?"

"I ain't a-killin' nobody, though," said Cob.

"You won't have to," Cane assured him. "If there's any trouble, me and Chimney will take care of it. I promise ye."

14

WITH STILL SEVERAL miles to go before he made it home, Ellsworth came to a pasture that brought back a distant memory. Since he felt the need to take a leak anyway, he stopped the mule and stepped off the wagon onto the dirt road. As he unbuttoned his fly, he looked down into the field, and thought back on an evening when he was a young boy. It was in the early part of the winter and he was with his father. They had spent the day cutting firewood for a widow woman over on Storm Station Road; and they were on their way home, tired and hungry. The old lady had offered them part of her dinner, some moldy bread smeared with lard, and it had bothered his father the rest of the afternoon, trying to decide if he should take a dollar from someone who was obviously even poorer than they were. In the end, he had allowed to Ellsworth that fifty cents was plenty for chopping two ricks of wood, and that's what he had charged her.

His father was puffing on his pipe and talking about something, probably the weather or what he planned to plant in the spring, Ellsworth couldn't recall what now. A snow was beginning to fall. In the gray twilight, he had seen a rabbit poke its head out of a burrowed place in the dead brown leaves along the edge of a ditch that ran down the middle of the field. Though nearly forty years had passed since that day, the culvert was still there, still overgrown. Thinking now of that rabbit, all alone on that cold winter night with the snow starting to cover the ground, a sweet and sorrowful feeling overcame him. Of course, he knew that that creature had died long ago, just as his father did a few winters later. But with a swelling in his throat, he wondered, almost desperately it felt like, if he might find some sign of that rabbit were he to go down there and search among the weeds and brambles. His eyes began to water. So many had passed on in his lifetime, and so much had happened or not happened that had taken him further and further away from the boy he was back then. No, he thought, as he wiped his sleeve across his face, he wouldn't find anything, not a sliver of bone or a shred of fur, not if he hunted for a week. The rabbit was gone forever, and that saddened him in much the same way the stars sometimes did at night, the way they kept shifting in the same abiding patterns, as regular as clockwork, year after year, century after century, regardless of what went on down here on this godforsaken ball of rock and clay, be it young men getting butchered in another war, or some crazy blind man living with a dead bird, or an innocent babe drowning in a rat-infested outhouse, or even some poor shivering rabbit sticking his head out of the weeds to watch a farm boy making his way home with his father.

A couple of hours later, he unhitched Buck from the wagon and led him into the barn. After making sure he had water and feed, Ellsworth climbed into the hayloft and took a couple of pulls from one of the jugs he had hidden there. Then he headed for the house, still half lost in the bittersweet nostalgia brought on by the pasture.

Eula was sitting barefoot on the front steps in the dusk, sucking on a piece of bacon rind and trying not to think about Pickles. In her hand was an orange bloom she'd pulled off the trumpet vine that filled a trellis at the end of the porch. The last day and a half had been the longest time she'd ever spent entirely alone since her marriage, and she had missed having the cat around more than ever. There had been a moment this morning when her grief nearly overwhelmed her, and she had hurt so much she would have almost traded her husband and son both for the chance to spend even just one more hour with Pickles. "So you didn't find him?" she asked.

Ellsworth stopped and looked up, a little startled by her voice. For a brief moment, he believed she was talking about the rabbit in the ditch, but then he remembered Eddie and the purpose of his trip. "Well, I did and I didn't," he said. He wished now he'd gone ahead and bought a broom at the Woolworth's. Now that he thought about it, Parker would probably charge him twice as much for one.

"Did ye see him?"

"No, they wouldn't allow it."

"Who?" she asked. "Who wouldn't?"

"The army. He'd already signed the papers by the time I got there."

"So you was right after all."

"At least we know where he is now," Ellsworth said. He turned and watched some purple martins darting and pirouetting in the darkening air across the road. "Who knows? Maybe this will be good for him."

Biting the bacon rind in two, Eula tossed the flower into the yard and started to stand. "Well, go ahead and get washed up while I put out your supper. Then you can tell me all about it."

15

IT WAS AFTER midnight when they left the shack and started
through the piney woods toward Tardweller's manse. They had decided
to leave most of their belongings behind, and so, besides the two books
and their blankets, they carried only Pearl's old shotgun and his straight
razor and the two machetes. A sickly yellow half-moon lit their way.
When they arrived at the edge of the yard, they stood in a copse of
evergreens and watched for signs of life inside the dark two-story
house. Except for the chirping of the crickets and the gurgling of their
guts, everything was quiet.

"I ain't never stole nothing in my life," Cob said miserably. He
wished more than anything that his brothers would change their minds,
and just head back to the shack. If they got some sleep, maybe tomorrow they wouldn't be so gung-ho about turning outlaw. And wait a
minute, what about the chicken bonus? Why, he bet they hadn't even
thought of that.

He was just getting ready to mention it when Cane said suddenly,
"Come on, let's go," and they were hurrying across the open ground to
the barn, stooped over like apes. Chimney unlatched the door quietly
and pulled it open just enough for them to slip inside. They stood there
for a minute while their eyes adjusted to the darkness, and then Cane
handed Cob the shotgun. "Keep an eye on the house," he whispered.

"No, I already told ye, I ain't a-killin' nobody," Cob said loudly, trying to give the gun back.

"Jesus Christ," Chimney hissed, "keep it down."

"You don't have to," Cane said. "Just let us know if you see someone
coming, that's all." Then he and Chimney set the machetes by the door
and went feeling their way among the stalls, the horses now snuffling
and stamping their feet nervously.

Inside the house, Thaddeus Tardweller was slouched in the parlor in his favorite chair when he heard a noise through the open window that made him sit up. His wife and daughter were spending the night at a cousin's house on the other side of the county, and he had enjoyed a comfortable evening alone drinking brandy in the dark and idly thinking of all the women he had molested over the years. Almost like a man's voice, he thought as he reached under the chair for his revolver. Draped in a long white nightshirt, he stepped out onto the porch and stood listening with his head cocked toward the barn. Goddamn, he almost wished somebody was out there, just to liven things up a bit. Only once in his life had anyone dared to steal from him, and he had made that whole pack of mulattoes pay for the one's mistake. He had killed all the men and boys in a flurry, but then his lust got the better of him; and while he was fucking the prettiest of the wenches, the other three he had locked in the shack got away. It wasn't until he was finished with her that he realized he should have made them dig their own graves first. Not being accustomed to labor, it had taken him two days to cover up all those niggers, and he'd nearly lost his mind, what with all the flies and the stink. When he was done, he told everyone that the fever had wiped them out, and, since the ones who escaped never showed their faces again, nobody even questioned it. Thank God for the memories, he thought. Sometimes they were all that kept him going these days. Staggering off the porch, he pulled back the hammer on the pistol and began crossing the yard, the hem of his nightshirt dragging through the dewy grass.

Cob, unfortunately, was much too tired for the task he'd been assigned. It had been, to his reckoning, the longest day of his life; and as soon as his brothers turned away, he had set the shotgun down, pressed one blurry eye against a crack in the siding, and promptly nodded off. As he dreamed of Pearl walking through clouds with a white napkin tied around his neck, Cane and Chimney finished choosing three horses from among the six in the stalls, two brown thoroughbreds and a gray Arabian. They had just started to bridle them when they heard Tardweller yell in a drunken voice, "Come on out now, you sonofabitch, and I'll let you go." A moment or two later he added with a snicker, "I give you my word as a God-fearin' Christian."

Dropping the bridles, Cane and Chimney hurried past a still sleeping Cob to the door and peered out. The Major was no more than a few feet from them, weaving a little as he awaited a response. "Goddamn," Chimney whispered, as they bent down and picked up the machetes. If by some miracle they got out of this alive, he thought, he would strangle Cob with his bare hands. Cane should have known better than to trust him with anything. The stupid sonofabitch— Just then, one of the horses kicked against the side of its stall, sounding like a cannon going off, and Tardweller jerked the door open. "Well," he said, as he started to step inside, "I give you a chance, you thievin' piece of shit, but you—"

When Cane grabbed for the pistol, Chimney brought the corn cutter down on top of the man's skull with as much force as he could muster. A splinter of bone flew sideways through the air and bounced off his cheek. As the Major dropped to his knees, a stream of blood sputtered out of the top of his head like a small geyser. Chimney stepped back and swung the machete again, burying the blade in the back of the man's thick, meaty neck, but he remained upright, his eyes blinking rapidly and his mouth opening and closing like a landed fish sucking air. The boy tried to jerk the knife loose, but it was wedged tight between two vertebrae. "Jesus Christ, do something," he yelled to Cane, as the big man let out a bellow and slowly, miraculously, started to get back up.

Cane stood with a shocked expression on his face, the pistol in one hand, a machete in the other. In all the months of imagining their escape, nobody had gotten hurt. At least not on the first goddamn night. How could he have been so stupid? He heard Chimney yell, "Shoot the sonofabitch," then watched him step back out of the way. Raising the revolver, Cane pointed it in the direction of Tardweller's head. He drew a deep breath and tried to steady his aim. But just before he pressed the trigger, a blast exploded off to the side of him, lighting up the entire scene in reddish orange for a second, and something wet splattered against the wall. He whirled around, saw a grim-faced Cob standing in the shadows with the shotgun, a gray wisp of smoke rising from the barrel.

For maybe a minute, they stood silently looking down at the Major in his bloody nightshirt, sprawled out on the floor with the top of his head gone. "Holy shit," Chimney finally said in an awed voice. "I never saw that coming."

"Me, neither," Cane managed to say.

"Goddamn, Cob, you did good," Chimney said. Then, placing one foot on the dead man's lower back for leverage, he bent down and grabbed hold of the machete's wooden handle.

Cob was still standing there with the shotgun raised to his shoulder. Everything had happened so fast. Why, just this morning, he had seen the Major and Pearl talking together, as alive as any two people could be. He heard Cane call his name in a faraway voice. He was vaguely aware of the horses, upset over the commotion, nickering and bumping against the stalls. For a moment, he couldn't move, and wondered if maybe he was still dreaming, but when he saw his brother yank the machete loose from Tardweller's neck, he flung the shotgun down and turned away just as most of his funeral supper sprayed from his mouth onto the straw-strewn floor.

Cane waited until he finished being sick, then started out the door with the pistol. "Get them horses ready," he ordered in an urgent voice.

"Where you going?" Chimney said.

"Up to the house."

"You sure you don't want me to take care of them?"

"No," Cane said. "I'll handle it." He looked over at Cob wiping the vomit off his chin. "You two did enough already."

FINDING THE DOOR ajar, he entered the house trembling, still unhinged by what had just happened in the barn. He moved from room to room in the dark looking for Tardweller's wife and daughter, so relieved when he didn't find them that he almost got down on his knees and thanked God. He hoped they were off somewhere visiting, something Chimney had mentioned they did on occasion, and not already halfway over to the next farm after hearing the shotgun blast.

The house smelled faintly of perfume and spices and tobacco, and he was suddenly aware of the stink roiling off his filthy body, a mix of shit and sweat and fear. Lighting a candle, he began searching hurriedly through closets and drawers. He found another 12-gauge and a box of shells. He took a black frock coat hanging from a door and three white shirts folded on top of a polished bureau and a gold pocket watch lying on a nightstand. He hunted all over for the purse he knew the squire carried, but it was not to be found. In the kitchen, he came across a bar of soap and a box of cartridges for the pistol and two bottles of brandy in a sideboard, along with a large smoked ham barely nibbled on and a pan of light rolls covered with a cloth. Wrapping everything up in the coat, he started out the front door, then stopped. He had never been in a house this fine before, and after what had just happened in the barn, it might be the only chance he'd ever get to experience one. Going into the parlor, he sat down carefully in a soft upholstered chair. He was disappointed not to see any books. A box on a side table was filled with cigars, and he stuck a handful of them and some matches in his shirt pocket. Just for a minute, he tried to enjoy the flowered wallpaper, the painting of the fox hunt above the mantel, the spinet piano in the corner, but he was suddenly overwhelmed with shame. He had lost his nerve back there in the barn, broke his promise to Cob to take care of everything. As he went out, he quietly shut the door behind him.

"Well, I didn't hear no shots," Chimney said when Cane returned to the barn. "What'd ye do, strangle 'em or slit their throats?" A lantern had been lit, and he was standing next to one of the thoroughbreds showing Cob how to cinch the girth straps on the saddle.

"I went all over," Cane said, "but they ain't there."

Chimney stopped and studied his brother for a moment. Satisfied that he was telling the truth, he spat and said, "Ah, they probably out fucking somewhere, knowin' them two whores."

Spreading the coat out on the floor, Cane began passing out the supplies for them to stick into their saddlebags. As he handed Cob the ham, he cleared his throat and said, "I owe you an apology, brother. I should have been the one killed him. It's my fault you got your hands bloody."

"Aw, don't worry about it," Chimney said. "Hell, even ol' Bloody Bill fucked up a time or two, right?" He threw a saddle on the Arabian and reached under its belly for one of the straps. "But I reckon it's a good thing we had Cob backing us up. Jesus, I still can't get over it. Him a-snorin' one minute and then BAM! Talk about blowin' somebody's brains out. He's a goddamn natural, that's what he is."

"Well, anyway," Cane said, "it won't happen again. I guarantee both of ye that."

Cob didn't say anything. In fact, it is doubtful that he heard a word that was being said, for he was now holding a ham the size of a new-born infant. It was like something he'd imagine you'd find on the heavenly table, in between the roast beef and the spare ribs, but instead it was right here, in his dirty hands. He had heard Pearl talk about sin and gluttony and false riches enough to know he should toss it to the ground and stomp it, but, shit, what would be the sense of doing that now? He had just killed a man. He was going to hell anyway. Raising it up to his mouth, he tore a big hunk off with his teeth and began to chew.

"Jesus," Chimney said, prying the ham loose from Cob and sticking it in a saddlebag, "what do ye think you're doing? You just puked your guts out."

Cane looked over at them as he lifted himself onto the other thoroughbred. "Come on, boys, this ain't no time to be fuckin' around."

"How long you think 'fore they catch us?" Cob asked.

"Pretty damn soon if we don't get to moving."

When they came out to the main road, they stopped and looked behind them. It was only then that Cane, with just a corner of the barn's pine-shingled roof visible in the moonlight, realized they should have brought Tardweller with them, hid his body where no one would ever find it. For a moment, he considered turning back, but quickly dismissed the idea. He told himself that at least this way the man's wife could give him a proper burial, though the real reason wasn't quite so compassionate. In truth, he wasn't sure he could handle looking at it again. "Well, brothers," he said, "ain't nothing ever gonna be the same now."

"That's for goddamn sure," said Chimney, then he gouged his horse in the flanks and the others followed. Moving northward at a canter, the hooves of the animals pounding against the hard-packed earth, the enormity of their crime slowly began to pale in contrast to the feeling of freedom that grew inside them with each passing mile. From time to time they saw a midnight lamp glowing like a tiny star in a distant farmhouse or settlement, but met nobody on the dark strip of road. Finally, just before dawn a mile or so outside of Farleigh, their bodies aching and the insides of their thighs rubbed raw from riding and the horses slathered with foamy sweat, they cut off into a woods where they found a shallow, rocky creek. They took their first bath in over a year, then sat naked in the soft, green grass under a sycamore tree and ate most of the ham and bread while the horses gazed at them stupidly.

"Heck, this is a regular picnic," Chimney said, stretching out his skinny legs and wiggling his toes. "Just think, this time yesterday, we was gaggin' down another one of them damn biscuits and gettin' ready to go cut brush."

Cane got up and went to his horse. He came back with the three shirts he had stolen, handed each of his brothers one. "I don't reckon they'll fit, but at least they're clean."

"You know," Chimney said, "it was almost like he was a-waitin' on us."

"Well, that's the trouble with owning property," Cane replied. "A man can't sleep at night for worrying about it." He finished buttoning his new shirt, then picked up the frock coat and shook the dust off it.

Cob wiped his greasy fingers on his hairy belly, then tore another piece off the ham. "Wonder what Pap's doin' right about now?" he said.

"Probably the same thing the Major's doing," Chimney said.

"What's that?"

Chimney smiled as he reached for his grimy overalls. "Standin' at the gate, getting ready to meet his Maker."

16

Lieutenant Vincent Bovard of the newly formed 343rd Machine Gun Battalion stepped out onto the porch of the long, low building he shared with two dozen other junior officers at Camp Pritchard. He had just finished another pile of asinine paperwork, and was looking forward to his first smoke of the day. It was still morning, but already the August sun was beating down upon the flat, treeless army base with the same harsh relentlessness that Colonel Garland Pritchard, the obscure, half-crazed Union commander for whom the camp was named, had led his guerrilla forces across the South in the shadow of Sherman's great march to the sea, supposedly doing cleanup, but mostly taking potshots at anything that had been lucky enough to survive. Settling into a rattan chair, Bovard looked about with satisfaction. Though the construction was still going on from sunrise to sunset, the sweltering air filled with the sounds of hammering and sawing, the cantonment already resembled a well-designed town. And to think that just a couple of months ago there had been nothing here but cornfields and cow patties. Being even a small part of such a vast operation was something to be proud of.

For a brief moment, though, as he sat in his scratchy uniform listening to the racket going on around him, Bovard almost wished he was sipping a glass of ice tea at the Sandcastle Inn on the breezy Atlantic seashore, or lying in a shady hammock at his parents' summer cottage in the Adirondacks. But then he heard Sergeant Malone's hoarse voice in the distance screaming obscenities at a couple of unlucky privates. No, he reminded himself, this was exactly where he wanted to be, among men preparing to go to war. The old life of soft, mindless pleasures was over with. From here on out, he would take his comforts in the mess halls and barracks and trenches smelling of sweat and burned coffee and gun grease. It was his destiny, he could see that as clearly as he had seen anything in his twenty-two years of living.

Even so, it had taken him several weeks to get used to Camp Pritchard. At six foot two, with wavy brown hair and sea-green eyes flecked with tiny blue deposits and a perfectly straight nose passed down from his great-grandfather, a minor French aristocrat who had been lucky enough to escape to America with his head during the Reign of Terror, Bovard stood out among the crude Midwestern farmers and store clerks and mill hands that made up the bulk of the camp's troops like a polished stone sitting atop a pile of coal clinkers. A large part of his initial problem with handling the harsh realities of camp life was owing to his education. Trained in classics, he had entered the military with abnormally high expectations, but unfortunately, the men he had encountered so far were a far cry from the muscle-bound sackers of Troy or the disciplined defenders of Sparta that he had been infatuated with since the age of twelve. Still, even though the draftees had been a sore disappointment, both physically and mentally, he had quickly learned to deal with them. It was simply a matter of lowering one's standards to fit the circumstances. After all, how could one expect any of these poor, awkward, illiterate brutes to have even heard of Cicero or Tacitus when at least half of them had difficulty comprehending a simple order? In just a matter of days, he went from trying to form a Latin reading club to thinking that a lowly private who still had most of his teeth and could name the presidents was practically a paragon of good breeding and sophistication.

Stretching out his legs, Bovard pulled a small leather case from his pocket and took out a cigar. His father had sent him a box of them last week, along with a carved walking stick and the last known copy of Colonel Pritchard's memoir, a musty tome called *A Great Man Looks Back,* which he'd found completely unreadable and had passed on to the camp library. He cut off the end of the golden brown Cuban with a small pair of snips and reached for a match. He still found it hard to believe that just three months ago he was sitting in a hotel room in Columbus, Ohio, drunk and filled with self-loathing, mulling over the best way to kill himself. As he puffed, he thought again about the initial cause of his despair, his former fiancée, Elizabeth Shadwell. Just as he was finishing his degree at Kenyon College, and turning his thoughts to their upcoming wedding, she had suddenly jilted him, explaining in her Dear John letter that she had fallen in love with somebody else, an attorney already moving up in a well-respected firm in New York that worked chiefly on behalf of several major industrialists with war contracts amounting to millions. Looking back on it now, Bovard knew that he shouldn't have been so surprised at her desertion. Ever since he had left Harvard at the end of his second year to go study at Kenyon with Professor Hubert Lattimore, a world-renowned expert on ancient Greek and Roman board games, Elizabeth had hinted that she was having doubts about his choice of study, even referring to it on several occasions as nothing more than "a frivolous pastime." To think that he had worked himself half to death to become one of the only five people on the planet who understood the convoluted and seemingly nonsensical rules of *divide et impera,* only to have her call it a hobby! "Again, I am sorry," she had added in a postscript to that last missive, "but I have to think of the future. I wish you the very best of luck with whatever you finally decide to do with your life." He had sensed her oil tycoon father's influence behind the entire thing, it being no secret that Bernard Shadwell was revolted by his potential son-in-law's apparent lack of interest in moneymaking. And so, in just a few lines of delicate script, Elizabeth had violently altered the course of his life, a life that seemed, in the immediate aftermath of her betrayal, to have been wasted on ancient ideals and traditions that couldn't even begin to compete with the ego-driven, cannibalistic forces of twentieth-century capitalism.

Though he had put on a brave front when his parents arrived from Philadelphia for his graduation ceremony, as soon as he saw them back onto the train, he'd packed a bag and fled to a hotel in nearby Columbus. After ordering a case of brandy brought up to his room, he had stripped down to his underwear and proceeded to get completely soused, his plan being to slit his veins open in the bathtub upon finishing the last bottle, just as the noblest of Romans had done. However, near the end of his third day, something began to bother him. Perhaps it was some vague sense of manly completeness he was after, or, more likely, just plain old revenge, but he suddenly felt the need to lose his virginity before committing himself to the Great Beyond. With a faithfulness that now seemed downright comical, he had kept himself pure for his wedding night, but now there would be no such night. How many times, he drunkenly wondered, as he cracked open another bottle, had that little slut been untrue while he walked around the Kenyon campus at two in the morning with a throbbing pair of blue balls?

But how to go about it? He knew nobody in Columbus except a distant aunt, and the only thing he remembered about that overly pious woman was that she owned a vast collection of hair shirts and was allergic to sunlight. Too, he wanted to get the matter over with as quickly as possible, and hated the thought of wasting time on wining and dining and drawn-out seductions. Of course, there had to be prostitutes about; according to some of his school chums, such women were everywhere, even in the dreariest sectors of the Corn Belt. Drawing the window blinds, he lay down on the bed and entertained images of a sophisticated, dark-eyed Italian courtesan tapping shyly on his door. Their one night of passion would be so intense that later, unable to bear the thought of living without him, she would weigh herself down with stones and throw herself off a bridge into one of the muddy, carp-infested rivers that flowed through the Buckeye State in the same ponderous way sap seeps from a tapped maple. Then things got fuzzy, and after a time, he passed out again.

In the end, after being holed up in the hotel room for over a week, he offered a slatternly, red-haired Irish chambermaid fifty dollars to sleep with him. Although she readily agreed to the exchange—after all, it was probably more money than she earned in a month—to his surprise, the little hussy had the audacity to insist on certain conditions. Studying him with eyes that resembled cold, green marbles, she said, "First off, ain't nothin' happens till the ol' mouse is warmed up good and proper."

"Excuse me?" Bovard said, a puzzled look on his unshaven face. "The mouse?"

"Me privates," she said, rolling her eyes at his ignorance. "I love a man's tongue on my puss, but my old man, he's too old-fashioned for it. Says it always make him feel like a hog eatin' from a trough."

"Good God!"

"And I'd need a nice lunch before we get down to the bizness."

Completely rattled, Bovard reached for a bottle on the nightstand and took a long drink.

"And cake and ice cream for dessert," she went on. "I crave the sweets even more than a good screw."

"I can't believe what I'm hearing," Bovard said in a faint voice, more to himself than to the maid.

"And another thing, too," she said, waving a finger in the air. "The fifty don't count for anything extra."

"Extra?"

"Yeah," she said. "If'n, say, you force me to swaller your wad, or you get the notion to poke me in the bunghole. Each of them filthy acts is another fiver."

The maid said all of this without the slightest embarrassment, and the full extent of Bovard's reversal of fortune struck him just then like a knife in the pit of his queasy stomach. To think that a fortnight ago he was engaged to one of the most beautiful and sought-after young women in Philadelphia, and now here he was, about to surrender his virtue to a gutter-minded domestic with a bubbly rash on her neck and a smear of what appeared to be egg yolk on her pointy, somewhat bristly chin. But he was growing afraid that he would lose the nerve to kill himself if he kept putting it off. She would have to do. He picked up the phone and ordered the lunch.

When the desk clerk, a beer-bellied, liver-spotted sad sack, knocked at the door, the maid rushed to the closet and hid. Just pushing the cart into the room, loaded with enough food to feed a family of six, seemed to leave the poor bastard exhausted, and an uncomfortable minute or two went by while he leaned one hand against the wall and panted. Finally, after recovering from his labors and making sure everything was to Bovard's satisfaction, he started out, but then turned and asked in a wheezy, apologetic voice, "Beg your pardon, sir, but you haven't seen Myrtle around, have you?"

"Myrtle?"

"Yes, sir, the maid who takes care of this floor."

"No," Bovard said hurriedly, "I haven't seen anyone."

"I was just wondering, sir. She's left her things right outside your door."

"Her things?"

"Yes, sir, her mop and linens and such." The man glanced at the closet, then started to step out into the hall. "That's all right, sir," he mumbled, as he closed the door. "She was having tummy troubles this morning, so she's probably gone off to the terlet."

As he listened to the maid chomp and chew and slurp—he'd turned away toward the window when she dipped a fat, green pickle into the gravy boat and then licked it clean—Bovard wondered, with more than a little trepidation, what he had gotten himself into. After consuming half a chicken and a mound of mashed potatoes and a relish tray and four buttered rolls, she heaped a pint of chocolate ice cream on top of a three-layer coconut cake and did her best to finish it off, too. For several minutes, she sat looking a bit nauseated, but then grabbed the brandy bottle Bovard was nursing. She took a long swig and belched forth a thunderous, full-throated yawp, such as an enraged donkey might make. He shuddered, thinking again of his former fiancée. In all the years he had known her, not once had Elizabeth ever emitted such a gross sound in his presence. Why, he doubted very much if she had ever passed a whiff of gas outside the privacy of her water closet. He was just about to tell the maid that he'd changed his mind when she stood and quickly shucked off her uniform and undergarments, all of which were stained and tattered beyond description. Then, with a long, lazy sigh, she laid back on the bed and parted her stubby, purple-mottled legs. She looked over at him and patted the place beside her, smiling with teeth that reminded him of kernels of decayed Indian corn. It was too late to back out now without hurting her feelings, he told himself, and he was too much of a gentleman to do that, even to such a vile and loathsome creature. He got up from the chair by the window and staggered toward her.

After a few clumsy, halfhearted caresses on his part, the maid quickly took over, displaying the same unbridled zeal for lovemaking that she had shown for eating. She forced his head between her thighs with her red, calloused hands and ground her thickly thatched privates, the orange hair as rough as a wire brush, against his face. Five minutes of this and she exploded like a water balloon, squalling like a mashed cat and filling his mouth with what she referred to in a gasp as her "nectar." Then she twisted around and pushed him back on the bed. She chewed on his knob and tickled his balls and tugged on his shaft until it was raw, but alas, he remained as soft as a sock in a laundry basket. Finally, after employing every trick she could think of—and it seemed to Bovard that the woman knew every dirty one in the book—she raised up and gave him a knowing look. "I could send a boy up, guvner, if that's the problem," she said. "Long as I still get me fifty, that is."

"A boy!" Bovard yelled, frustrated beyond measure with his cock's lack of response. "You dirty whore! What do you think I am?"

"I got no idy," she said, rolling off the bed, "but a regular man you're not. And who do you think you are anyway, callin' me a whore? I got half a mind to send me old man up to kick the shit out of ye."

"Oh, so your husband is hanging around here somewhere, is he? What, lurking in a closet? Hiding under some bed? What is he, your pimp?"

"No, he works the desk downstairs," she said matter-of-factly.

Bovard stared at her for a second, a puzzled look on his face. "Him? The old fellow who brought up the cart?" Oh, God, he thought, could this frightful mess get any worse? What a mistake he'd made.

"Ol' Taylor might not look like much," she said, "but at least he knows what to do when the hinges is greased and the door's ready for entry. Why, he's like a young bull when it comes to—"

"Out!" Bovard screamed. "Get out!"

"Would ye like your sheets changed before I leave?"

"No, damn it to hell."

"There's a lad I know who—"

Bovard lurched from the bed with a look of insane fury on his face, and the maid grabbed her uniform off the floor and the money from the dresser and ran out of the room, slamming the door behind her. He stopped and stared into the mirror hanging over the mahogany dresser. There he stood, twenty-two years old and naked except for a crusty nightshirt, the sour taste of some scullery maid's unwashed vagina in his mouth, his tongue blistered and quite possibly bleeding, his manhood shriveled with shame and defeat, his brain soaked with alcohol, at the end of his tether in a hotel room in the middle of Ohio, when he realized with a jolt the awful truth about himself. And the truth was that he, Vincent Claremont Bovard, had never had any more interest in the female body than a woodchuck has in learning the particulars of Latin verb conjugation. Feeling himself getting sick, he stumbled into the bathroom and retched up the sliver of chicken the maid had pushed down his gullet in a playful mood. Then he went back into the room and flopped down on the bed. How could he have been so blind? So ignorant and full of self-denial? After all, his revered Greeks and Romans had written so much about it. Buggery. Pederasty. Homosexuality. Tears began to run down his face. Thank God Elizabeth had called off their engagement. Cold chills ran over his body as he thought about the embarrassing fiasco the wedding night might have been. Then he leaned over and vomited again, this time on the braided rug, before falling into a fitful, nightmarish sleep.

The next afternoon, after deciding that leaving this world unsullied by lust was the more honorable thing to do after all, he looked by chance out the window and saw, down below on High Street, a military parade made up of Spanish American veterans showing their support for the war and carrying a banner advertising Liberty Bonds. He reached for a bottle and sat down to watch. Citizens of all ages were lined up on the sidewalk waving paper flags, tossing flowers and confetti. Though his head was fairly pounding, it was the most soul-stirring scene he had witnessed in ages, brimming over as it was with patriotism and excitement and the feeling that something world-changing was about to take place. Something much bigger and important than he, anyway.

It was that moment that he was thinking of now, as he sat on the porch smoking and looking out over the camp. To die on the Western Front, he had realized that day as he watched the old soldiers marching by, would be a far better way to leave this world than slitting his wrists in a tub of hot water. Once the procession passed and the crowd began to drift away, he had dozed off again and awakened the next morning filled with energy and purpose. After a bath and a shave, he packed his trunk and took a cab to the nearest armory. Though the draft hadn't officially started yet, he was quickly sent, for no other reason than he had a college degree, to the Plattsburgh Barracks in New York for officer training. And now here he was, back in Ohio and on the verge of realizing his true destiny. War-ravaged Europe, with its inbred rulers and long-standing prejudices, was going to provide him, Lieutenant Vincent Bovard, with a death worth fighting for.

17

THANKS TO A beaten-down bank manager named Leonard Spindler who had actually been praying for the past several weeks that such an event might happen, Cane and his brothers took the Farleigh Savings & Trust without firing a single shot. For the past nine years, Leonard had been ensnared in an increasingly unhappy marriage to the daughter of Francis Gilbert, a moneyed and maniacal bully who also happened to own the bank, along with most everything else in the town and the surrounding area. Ironically, he even had a hold on the property of Thaddeus Tardweller, a despised second cousin from his mother's side of the family. For Leonard, it wasn't so much that Mirabelle was hard to get along with—from the first time he'd met her, he had found the poor girl as easy to manipulate as a cud-chewing cow—but that her father wouldn't back off in his demand that they start turning out babies. However, no matter how many times a day they had intercourse, sometimes with Gilbert standing right outside the bedroom door urging them on with a snappy rhythm he beat on a snare drum, the results were nil. What had once looked like a golden opportunity for advancement—Leonard had grown up on a chicken farm out in the country, but had fled to Farleigh on his eighteenth birthday with aspirations of becoming a dandy—had slowly turned into an unremitting nightmare, and the bank manager's nerves had become so overwrought that he now suffered from interminable crying jags that he had no control over. And the longer his father-in-law clamored for an offshoot, the worse the affliction became. Just that morning, standing in the kitchen sipping a cup of tea and dabbing at his eyes with a dish towel while Mirabelle frantically did her fertility exercises in the parlor, he heard the man say loudly, "Girl, I realize anybody can make a mistake, but I still can't understand why you hang on to that no-account fool. When in the hell is he ever going to plant his seed in ye? I can't wait around forever for a grandson, though God only knows what kind of pinheaded cretin that might turn out to be with ol' Bucket of Tears as the father. I'm tellin' you, Mirabelle, honey, you'd be best to go ahead and cut your losses now before he saps all your youth. I know one or two men over in Atlanta who still ask about ye."

Leonard had endured a thousand such insults and harangues in silence over the years, but, as many tyrants realize too late, even a spineless toady sometimes has his limits. Although Francis Gilbert would have never dreamed that his son-in-law had the grit for such a scheme, Leonard had been slowly and methodically draining the bank coffers for the past eleven months, in preparation for his escape to gaudy, wideopen San Francisco. Once there, he planned, in no particular order, to become a complete fop, seek out the best ophthalmologist on the West Coast, and knock up the first woman with a good set of childbearing hips who'd spread her legs for him. Only one more thing was needed to perfect his plan, and that was a scapegoat.

And so, when the awkward and grubby trio entered the bank just a few minutes after Leonard unlocked the door, and announced their felonious intentions, it was all he could do not to welcome them with open arms. In fact, he almost felt sorry for them, as he watched the short fat one trip on the doorjamb, and the youngest accidently spill over a spittoon on his way to guard the front window with a shotgun. It was obvious to the bank manager that the oldest, tall and serious in a black frock coat a bit too big for him, was the brains behind the operation, but even he, after pulling a pistol from the waist of his ragged overalls, seemed at a loss over what to do next. Afraid that some customer might walk in and spoil everything, Leonard took it upon himself to hurry the heist along, first showing them the empty vault, and then dumping the money from the two cash drawers into a bag and setting it on the counter. After that, to give them time to make their getaway and also to cover his own ass, he pretended to faint.

The Jewetts were already two miles out of town by the time Leonard moseyed up the street to the sheriff's office. On the way there, he went over the story he planned to tell one more time in his head, and then squeezed his eyes shut in front of Ollie's Livery until the tears were practically cascading down his pale cheeks. Everyone in Farleigh knew that he bawled like a baby over the slightest upset, and he figured that anything less than full-scale blubbering might arouse suspicion. And what did it matter? After nine years of ridicule, what were one or two more embarrassments? He had thirty thousand dollars hidden under the floorboards on the back porch at home, and only he and the robbers knew how little cash had actually been in the bank that morning. Within a few days, he would be on a train bound for the West Coast with a suitcase of money and the last laugh.

The sheriff, Earl Cotter, a potbellied man with greasy gray hair and a vein-streaked nose shaped like a cork, was sitting at his desk leafing through a seed catalog when Leonard walked in wiping at his eyes. He shook his head at the powder-blue parasol the bank manager carried and the white carnation stuck in his buttonhole. Cotter was just about to ask Leonard why he was carrying a goddamn umbrella when there hadn't been a drop of rain in three weeks, when it suddenly occurred to him that the man never left his post before lunchtime. Never. "What are you doin' over here?" he said, furrowing his brow.

Leonard took several deep breaths as he wiped at his face with a handkerchief, then let out a sigh and whimpered, "It was awful. I thought for sure I was a dead man."

Before the bank manager could finish his report, Cotter leaped up from his desk and grabbed a shotgun from the rack behind him. Hurrying to the door, he stepped out warily and pointed the gun up and down the street. But there wasn't a sign of anything out there except for the Phillips boy bouncing on his damn pogo stick on the wooden walkway in front of Cinderella Vanbibber's house. After the way she had harassed him since spring about birds landing on her fence posts, he was a little surprised the old bitch hadn't already sent her maid over with a complaint about it. "How long since this happened?" he shouted at Leonard through the open doorway.

"Oh, fifteen, twenty minutes ago. No more than thirty."

The sheriff walked back into the office, a dumbfounded look on his face. "And you just now tellin' me!"

"Well, Earl, it takes a while to count to a thousand, even for a banker."

"Count to a thousand? What the hell you talkin' about?"

"That's what I was told to do and I did it," Leonard said. "You weren't there, Sheriff. They were killers if I ever saw one."

Cotter rolled his eyes. "I doubt very much if you've seen many killers in your lifetime, Leonard."

"Well, I seen three this morning, I can tell you that."

"So they was packin' guns, was they?"

"Had 'em pointed right at me," Leonard said, as he watched the sheriff pull open a desk drawer and rummage around for his pistol and holster.

"Anybody else see them?"

"No, I'd just unlocked the door when they barged in threatening to murder me."

"How much they get?"

"All of it."

"Jesus Christ, boy, how much was that?"

"Thirty thousand," Leonard replied without batting an eye. "Thirty thousand, three hundred, and fifty-four, to be exact."

"Lord, have mercy!" Cotter shrieked. "Ol' Gib will probably cry his own self when he hears about this." He hurried to load the gun. His fingers started to tremble just thinking about how Francis Gilbert would react if the thieves got away; he'd once seen him, over the course of several weeks, drive a clerk named Henry Loomis to suicide over an accounting mistake that amounted to sixteen cents. Outside, the sound of the pogo stick got a little closer. He dropped a bullet and dug in the drawer for another one.

"Yeah, Earl," Leonard said, fighting to suppress a smile, "I reckon he might."

"We'll be damn lucky if he don't fire the both of us," the sheriff said. By this time, sweat was running down his face, dripping onto the desk. In his seventeen years of being Gilbert's lawman, he'd never had to deal with anything this bad before, and he was already thinking the worst. If it ended up that he had to kill himself, he swore to God he'd take Leonard with him. And that goddamn pogo stick, too, while he was at it. He holstered the pistol and thrust the shotgun into the banker's hands, then grabbed a rifle from the rack and turned toward the door. "Well, come on, boy, let's go. Thanks to your sorry ass, they done got a good start on us."

"You go on ahead," Leonard said.

"What?"

"I need to go home and change first. Do you realize how much this suit cost?"

"Oh, no, you don't," Cotter said, shaking his head. "We got us some robbers to catch."

Staying off the main road, the Jewetts rode north for several hours before finally stopping in a thicket to give the horses a rest. Cane opened the green cloth bag the bank manager had provided them with and counted the money while they finished eating the rest of Tardweller's ham. "Three hundred and fifty-four dollars," he finally said.

Though Cob had never been able to comprehend exactly how numbers worked—three hundred and fifty-four didn't mean any more to him than a million—he detected disappointment in his brother's voice. But if the old boy at the bank wasn't upset, then why should they be? Heck, he had been one of the nicest fellers they had ever met. He swallowed a piece of meat and said, "Well, heck, that ain't bad."

"Shit, that ain't nothing but chickenfeed," Chimney said. "Especially once you go to splittin' it three ways. Why, a good whore probably costs two or three dollars."

Cane began putting the money back in the bag. "I got a feeling that fancy boy pulled one over on us," he said.

"How do ye figure?"

"Things just seemed a little too easy in there. Hell, he seemed almost glad to see us. I'm bettin' he had the biggest part of it hid somewhere else."

"I knew I should've killed the bastard," Chimney spat.

"Fuck, that won't work. How's he gonna tell us where the money is if he's dead?" Cane wiped some sweat from his forehead with his sleeve and squinted up at the huge yellow sun bearing down on them. In less than twenty-four hours they had become murderers, horse thieves, and bank robbers, and all they had to show for it was three hundred dollars? Christ Almighty, he'd planned on that safe being stuffed with more money than they could carry away.

"Yeah," Chimney said, "I see what you mean. Just need to scare 'em a little. Like when Bloody Bill chopped that ol' boy's fingers off that claimed he couldn't open the safe."

"Well, maybe not quite . . ."

"But I thought we only had to rob the one?" Cob said. "Wasn't that the—"

"I made a mistake," said Cane.

"Don't you worry," Chimney went on. "Next bank we come across, I'll have the boss man squeezin' silver dollars out of his ass by the time I'm done with him."

A couple of hours later, as they made their way through a thorny brake in single file, Cob turned in his saddle and looked back at Chimney. "Can I ask ye something?" he said.

"What's that?"

"If'n one of them whores you talk about is worth two or three dollars, how much ye figure a good ham cost?"

"Oh, probably about the same, I reckon. They wouldn't be much difference between a whore and a ham."

"Well, then," Cob said, "how many of them could we buy with the money we got?"

"Oh, I don't know. Maybe a hundred."

"Whew," Cob exclaimed. "That sounds like a lot."

"Yeah, it'd take a day or two to fuck that many."

"No, I mean, that's a lot of hams, ain't it?"

Chimney laughed. "You're goddamn right it is. Why, if ye was to eat that many hams, ye'd probably turn into a pig yourself."

"Oh, that'd be fine with me," Cob said. "All they do is lay around in the mud all day while somebody feeds 'em horseweeds and slop. Shoot, what more could a feller want out of life than that?"

18

ALONG WITH THE establishment of the army camp at Meade that summer came a vast array of people from all over hoping to reap monetary gain from it, including a pimp who called himself Blackie Beeler, but whose real name was Philo Wilkinson. After making a number of inquiries, he finally found a place to set up business half a mile or so outside of town on the Huntington Pike. A house would have been preferable, but there wasn't a single empty room left to rent by the time he and his girls arrived; and so the long leaky pole barn that had once sheltered Virgil Brandon's goat herd was the best he could do. The retired farmer agreed to let the pimp have it for three dollars a week along with the understanding that he was entitled to a free piece of Esther, the fat one, whenever he felt the need. Hers was the body type he'd been raised on and the one that he still preferred. Why risk filleting your dick on a bag of bones when you could dip into something as soft and fluffy as a cloud? Virgil's late wife had weighed three hundred pounds, and he still missed the way she'd made the bed roll like an ocean every time she attempted to turn over in her sleep.

As soon as they had shaken hands on the deal, the farmer headed home with a new spring in his step, and Blackie began handing out tools and barking orders. He had all of his hopes pinned on the new army base; the way he saw it, Camp Pritchard was his last chance to turn things around. For the past several years, ever since he'd had a falling-out with the police chief in St. Louis and fled the city with a price on his head, he had traveled around the Midwest like a nomad with three girls and his bodyguard, Henry, selling pussy for peanuts and barely making enough to keep going. Now he was down to petty cash and a worn-out Hudson and his ruby ring. To think that he had once been the go-to man for a state rep from Missouri who had a predilection for mother-and-daughter combos, and had shared a bucket of cold oysters and a Swedish opera diva with an Iowa congressman. And everything that he'd worked ten years for ruined just because he was in a rotten mood one night and refused to contribute another dime to the weekend getaway the chief was building on a lake outside of town! The vagaries of life and fate. He had thought about that a lot lately; if only this, if only that. There were just too many ifs in the fucking world. He rolled up his sleeves and went to work.

By that evening, most of the manure had been shoveled from the dirt floor of the pole barn and the weeds cut down. A fire pit had been dug out front and some logs placed around it to sit on. Three canvas tents had been set up in a row under the shed roof, and strings of Chinese lanterns hung between the termite-riddled support posts. The wagon was parked off to the side and the horses corralled behind it in an old rusty-wired pen that Virgil had built years ago to keep a pair of prize Angora nannies separated from his Nubian bucks during breeding season. Though they still had to dig a latrine and set up a bar, Blackie called it a night, satisfied with the progress they had made. Henry lit some kindling and put the coffee pot on, and the women walked down to the creek in their underwear to wash off before supper.

No sooner had they finished eating than Virgil Brandon returned wearing his false teeth and a clean shirt. He had consumed a dozen raw eggs over the past several hours, and had it in his head that he was going to ravage Esther all night long. He followed her to one of the tents swaggering a little, his chest puffed out. Everything was a blur after that. Lord Jesus, he had never experienced anything like it. His dentures had flown out of his mouth and bounced against the canvas wall when he shot his load. The big girl was like one of those new-fangled milking machines that Carl Mendenhall was replacing all his help with, and he couldn't have held back if his life depended on it. After she helped him put his teeth back in and get his pants back up, he stumbled out of the tent without a word and past the campfire, where the rest of them sat drinking coffee.

He was lying on his bed staring up at the dark ceiling when he remembered that Esther had nibbled on an apple core the entire sixty seconds he was on top of her. With an anguished groan, he rolled over and pulled the sheet up over his head. Jesus, what had he been thinking? A damn bushel of eggs wouldn't have done him any good. Why, sometimes at night he could barely make it to the piss jar in the corner without having an accident. They were probably over there having a good laugh about him right now. Shamed in his own goat shed. For the first time since he'd buried his wife, he had to fight back tears. But after a while, he became aware of the fishy smell wafting up from his damp, gray crotch, and it was long after midnight before he finally quit imagining a different outcome the next time he walked over for his free piece, and drifted off to sleep.

The next morning Blackie handed Henry his last fifty dollars and sent him into town to find some musicians and a barrel of cheap whiskey. From his many years of peddling flesh, he had learned that music, combined with the right amount of liquor, often made men just as free-handed with their money as the women did, and he was determined to siphon off as much soldier pay as possible before somebody figured out that war was not the answer. "Go around and spread the word as best ye can," he said. "Tell 'em we'll be open for business tomorrow night."

"What about the law?" Henry asked.

"Let's make some money first. No sense talking to 'em with empty pockets."

Several hours later, the bodyguard returned with a duo in the back of the wagon, an ancient, toothless banjo player and a shaggy-haired, barefoot boy with a harmonica. Though everything about them, from their puke-splattered rags to their bloodshot eyeballs, indicated a serious problem with alcohol, Henry hadn't thought twice about bringing them back to the camp. He had never met anyone who played music for a living who wasn't fucked-up in some sad or depraved way, the same as those who painted pictures or wrote books or traipsed about spouting lines on a stage from the latest melodrama. In his opinion, only the truly miserable were really any good at artistic endeavors of any kind.

"Jesus, where did ye find these two?" Blackie asked, as he pulled a plug of tobacco from the pocket of his brocaded vest and bit a chew off.

"Some dive," the bodyguard replied. Henry was built like a middle-weight pugilist, with big hands and thick shoulders and a wide back. A Remington Model 1888 revolver hung from a leather holster around his waist and a little Stevens pocket pistol was strapped to his left calf. But even though his job sometimes required him to be brutal, Henry was by no means an unfeeling person. When he was a young man in Erie, Pennsylvania, he'd entertained ambitions of entering a religious order, but the old priest at his church, Father Hamilton, a man turned cynical and mean from years of being exiled to a land of lake-effect snow and sour wine and illiterate parishioners who smelled like cooked cabbage, had scoffed at such an idea. Instead, he had recommended the new steel mill that had just opened up. It had been a great disap-pointment, and the only way Henry was able to accept it was to remind himself that everything happened for a reason, which was something his grandfather used to say whenever things turned to shit. Of course, not knowing what else to do, he hired on, but two years later, walk-ing home after finishing a twelve-hour shift in the furnaces, he came upon a man beating a mutt with a garden spade. Words were said, and one thing led to another; and as he tried to explain to his mother that night when he slipped in the back door to tell her goodbye, he'd had no choice. A bastard who would do such a thing to a poor, defenseless ani-mal deserved to die, he hoped even God would understand that. By the time he met Blackie trying without success to build a fire under a rail-way trestle in the middle of Iowa during a cold rainstorm, he had been on the run for several years. Although the pimp had only one whore at the time, a pockmarked farm girl named Vera who he'd grown up with in Nebraska, he claimed, with an air of confidence that belied his cheap suit and rundown shoes, that he was on his way to St. Louis to make his fortune. Within a couple of minutes, Henry had the fire lit and was sharing his last can of stew with them. "You religious?" Blackie had asked, pointing at the small wooden cross that hung from the stranger's neck. "Not really," Henry said. He'd stopped going to Mass right after the old priest consigned him to the steel mill. "My mother give it to me the last time I saw her." "Good," the pimp had said. "I could use a man like you." They had been together ever since, had seen a hundred girls like Vera come and go over the years.

"And what about the whiskey?" Blackie asked, as he looked the musicians over.

"It'll be here this afternoon."

The pimp made a beckoning motion with his hand. "Well, come on, boys, let me hear something."

Climbing down off the wagon, the pair nodded to each other, and began awkwardly trying to find some sort of matching rhythm, the old man picking at the strings of the banjo with his arthritic fingers, and the boy shyly doing a little shuffle with his feet while trying to follow along with the mouth harp. Unfortunately, the longer they played, the worse they sounded, and before they could finish the first song—Blackie couldn't figure out if it was supposed to be "Dixie" or "Camptown Races" or possibly even some deranged version of "Onward, Christian Soldiers"—the girls had emerged from their respective tents and were bent over double, cackling with laughter. When the final notes died away, they all clapped and sat down around the campfire. Still giggling, they passed the coffee pot around and began rolling cigarettes.

Henry looked at Blackie and shrugged. "Hell, boss, once them soldiers get liquored up, they'll sound all right."

"Christ, Henry, they'd give a dead man a headache," the pimp said. He spat a stream of black juice on the banjo player's shoe and walked away without another word.

After Blackie disappeared around the last of the tents, the bodyguard turned and asked the boy, "What'd you say your name was again?"

"Eddie. Eddie Fiddler."

"Well, tell me now, how many songs you know, Eddie?" Henry hoped that perhaps they had just gotten off to a bad start. Stage fright maybe. He had heard it happened to the best of them on occasion. Even Esther, probably the least self-conscious person he'd ever met, occasionally got the jitters if too many voyeurs crowded into her tent to watch her play a tune on some john's skin flute.

The boy looked at the banjo picker for help, but the old man had his eyes glued on the women. "Oh, hard to say, really," Eddie said weakly. "A few, I reckon." Last evening, out of their minds on a bottle of moonshine called Knockemstiff that he had traded his shoes for, they had stolen a dozen baby chicks from a coop in somebody's backyard and ate them alive for dinner. He had awoken this morning tangled up in a patch of ivy with a raging headache and a tiny beak stuck between his two front teeth.

With the tip of his finger, Henry tapped the boy's forehead hard several times. "Do I look like someone you wants to be a-lyin' to?"

"No, sir," Eddie mumbled, afraid to move. Staring at the cross hanging from the big man's neck, the realization of how low he had sunk since leaving home suddenly brought on a wave of nausea, and he had to swallow several times rapidly to keep from blowing feathers and booze all over the man's shiny black boots.

"So, goddamn it, how many do ye know?"

"Two," the boy answered. "The one we just played, plus'n another one. We ain't been together all that long."

"Now why in the hell didn't you tell me that before I brought you all the way out here? You and that ol' soak done wasted my whole morning."

"You didn't ask. Besides, Johnny says all music sounds pretty much the same anyway."

"Lord Almighty!" Henry cried. "That's got to be one of the dumbest fuckin' things I ever heard in my life. How long you been playin' that harp anyway?"

"Uh, I don't know," Eddie said, trying to remember just how many days it had been since he and the old man had met. "Maybe a week?"

"Sonofabitch," Henry muttered as he turned and headed toward the wagon.

The banjo player made a great show of bowing to the women and smiling with his gum ridges, then asked the boy, "Did we get the job?"

"I don't think so," Eddie answered as he watched Henry climb up on the wagon seat and unwrap the reins from the brake handle.

"Well, shit, ask him."

"Johnny wants to know if we got the job?" the boy called out.

"Fuck, no," Henry yelled. "Now get your asses in the wagon so I can haul you back to town."

"Come on, Johnny," Eddie said. "Looks like he's in a hurry."

"You go on," the old man said. "I'm a-thinkin' I'll just stick around here awhile." He winked at the whores, then eased himself down on a stump and began strumming the banjo slowly, as if he was about to serenade them with a love ballad.

As the boy climbed into the wagon, Henry said, "What the hell does he think he's doing?"

"Oh, it's hard to tell with Johnny. Sometimes he gets a little crazy if there's a woman around."

Henry stared at the old man for a minute, then cursed and jumped down off the wagon. Stomping across the campsite, he grabbed the banjo picker by the back of his frayed shirt collar and started dragging him away.

"Don't you hurt him, Henry," one of the girls warned. "He don't mean no harm." Her name was Matilda, and with her freckled pug nose and pigtails and tiny tits, Blackie was often able to pass her off to older men as a fourteen-year-old runaway fresh off the farm. She was also the most likely of the three women to cause trouble. Her father, a coal miner in West Virginia, had coughed up the last black shreds of his lungs on her eighth birthday, and she had nursed an abiding sense of injustice ever since when it came to workers' rights. Her face was still recovering from a bruising Blackie had given her last week after an argument over menstrual cycle pay.

"Shut the hell up, Matilda," the bodyguard said. "This don't concern you."

"Oh, yes, it does," she said. "You lured that poor old man out here with the promise of work, and then you turn around and treat him like that? It ain't fair, is it, girls?"

Emboldened by the prostitute's sympathetic remarks, Johnny decided to resist. First he dug his heels into the ground, then tried to jerk out of Henry's grasp. When that didn't work, he swung the banjo around and clipped the end of the bodyguard's nose with it. A loud twang reverberated through the air.

"Oh, shit," Esther said, a cigarette dangling from her chapped lips. "That's probably the last song that ol' coot will ever play." She was wrapped in a thin Oriental robe and had a thick layer of pancake makeup spread over her face like putty. Her corpulence had gone down in value lately, as thinner bodies became more and more the vogue among the younger clients, so nowadays Blackie advertised her in much the same way a diner did their blue plate special, in that, though it wasn't the best fare on the menu, it was by far the cheapest and would satisfy any hunger if you ate enough of it. A long column of gray ash dropped from the end of her smoke into the damp crevasse between her two sagging breasts.

His eyes now bulging with rage, the bodyguard snatched the banjo out of the old man's hands and beat him with it about the head like a flyswatter until it lay scattered on the ground in a dozen broken pieces. By the time he finished, Johnny was sobbing like a baby. Disgusted, Henry tossed him into the back of the wagon, then climbed back up on the seat. Eddie wondered if he should try to blow a little tune to help calm the situation, then decided against it. One wrong note and the big man was liable to murder them both. Instead, he reached over and tenderly patted the top of his partner's bloody scalp.

"I can't stand watching this," Matilda said. She stood up and began walking toward the creek.

Ignoring the commotion around her, Peaches, the third and by far the most striking of Blackie's offerings, with her long bleached-blond hair and ability to speak certain words in French, said to Esther, "I remember this one house I worked in up in Chicago. They had a regular orchestra. Played every night in tuxedos. I slept in a bed with silk sheets, had a colored girl named Lucy woke me up every afternoon with a breakfast tray and a little vase of flowers." She took a sip of her coffee and swiped at a fly buzzing around her face. "Now look at me. Three-dollar screws in a pup tent. In Michigan, no less. Sometimes I wake up and wonder what the hell ever happened."

"You're in Ohio," Esther told her.

"Oh, Jesus," Peaches said. "And I thought it couldn't get any worse. I swore to God I'd never step foot in this state again after that week I spent in Akron with the rubber man."

"You know," Esther said, as she watched the wagon turn out onto the main road, "they really didn't sound that bad to me."

19

AFTER THEIR SECOND robbery, a bungled affair in Danville, Georgia, in which Cane's pistol went off accidently as they fled out the bank door with six hundred dollars, and Cob fell off his horse as they galloped out of town, it was decided that, if they were going to survive, they needed to spend some time focused on marksmanship and staying in the saddle. That same night they broke into a hardware store in a nearby hamlet and stole three Springfield rifles and five Smith & Wesson Schofield pistols and several cases of ammunition, along with enough pork and beans and oyster crackers and chocolate bars to last them a week. They rode deep into the hills the next morning and set up camp in an isolated valley rimmed with limestone outcroppings and dotted with patches of lush green grass.

Over the next several days, they went through over a thousand rounds of ammunition and burned out the barrels on two of the pistols. If it hadn't been for Cob's idea of sticking chewed-up wads of licorice in their ears, prompted by memories of Pearl and his efforts to regain the Great Silence, the repetitive blasts would have probably destroyed their hearing, as well. Though Chimney turned out to be by far the best shot—able to knock the head off a crow with the Springfield at a hundred yards after only a couple of hours of practice—Cane, and occasionally even Cob, were soon blowing tin cans and ground squirrels into the air at a respectable fifty. Getting the hang of shooting and reloading on horseback at anything faster than a walk proved more daunting, and Cob nearly broke his neck several times before he was allowed to quit. Still, by the time they broke open the last box of bullets, Cane and Chimney felt confident that they could hold their own in a fight.

They were packing up, getting ready to ride out of the valley, when they heard the buzzing sound. "There it is," Chimney said, pointing at what looked like a giant mosquito high up in the sky coming toward them. As it got closer, the airplane began to descend, and by the time it passed over them, it was close enough that they could make out two goggled men inside. They saw the one in the seat behind the cockpit lean out a little and look down at them. Cob raised his hand and waved. "I bet there's one of them carnivals or county fairs goin' on around here somewhere," he said. "I wish we could go."

At the other end of the valley, the plane turned and began to circle back. The pilot, Reese Montgomery, was a golden-haired playboy who had spent the last two years traveling around the country spending his tycoon father's money like water and looking for adventure and unique items of interest. Three months ago, he had leased a private coach from the B&O for himself and his butler and cook, and another rail car to carry two of his latest acquisitions: a German-built Fokker two-seater biplane he found on the Brownsville black market, and the Eau Claire County Nut Cracker, a burly cage-fighter raised in the Wisconsin logging camps who had recently gained a certain notoriety for castrating several of his opponents with his teeth. Also traveling in the second car was Arnold Whistler, the playboy's mechanic and go-to man in an emergency. A former maintenance supervisor at one of the Montgomery textile mills, he had been an employee of the family since before Reese's birth. There had been a time when he thought, if he demonstrated enough diligence and loyalty, he might be made head manager at one of the bigger factories, but that time had passed, and his primary duties these days consisted of covering up felonies and filth and secretly wiring back reports to John Montgomery from time to time, informing him of his brat's whereabouts and latest erratic behavior. Still a little wary of the Nut Cracker's mood swings, he slept in the cockpit of the Fokker with a small five-shot Colt within easy reach; and every morning he reminded himself that if he could put up with their shit just a few more months he could retire to a little cottage he had purchased on a hill overlooking Camden, Maine, and never again have to negotiate a payment plan with a battered woman or end another telegram to Montgomery senior with "Your Faithful Servant."

The train had just arrived in Atlanta when Reese heard about the three outlaws who had robbed the banks in Farleigh and Danville and were also accused of murdering some hick squire named Tardweller. Though the reward, a pitiful two hundred and fifty dollars, didn't interest him in the slightest, the DEAD OR ALIVE notice at the bottom of the wanted poster was too good to resist. If nothing else, he told Whistler, hunting them down might be good sport. And besides, he was bored, bored shitless with life as well as with the woman who was this summer's companion, a raven-haired English tart advertised by her bankrupt brother-in-law as the most titillating piece of romance this side of the Mississippi, but who had turned out to be just another brainless suction pump looking for a rich husband. Indeed, though her pedigree supposedly extended as far back as Charlemagne, her entire bag of tricks could have easily been replicated by half a dozen other mammals. Just that morning he had said so, comparing her to a baby calf, and then left her bawling like one on the marble floor. God, she was boring.

He had his train cars parked at the first siding outside Atlanta, then unloaded his plane and flew to Danville with the mechanic and several firearms. After talking to the local constable, he had several caches of fuel sent ahead to various towns within a hundred-mile radius, and set off looking for the bandits, described as three dipshit farm boys in dirty white shirts riding horses. Landing that evening in a small junction called Coon Crossing to top off his petrol tank and find some shelter for the night, he was picking at a supper of overdone quail in the local boardinghouse when he heard about a young berry picker who had told about an almost constant barrage of shooting in the hills to the northeast just that afternoon. At sunrise the next morning, after downing several cups of chicory coffee laced with brandy, he and Whistler flew off in that direction.

And lo and behold, there they were, right out in the middle of an open field. This was going to be almost as easy as the time he shot the muzzled lion in a cage over in New Jersey. As he turned the plane to make a second pass, Montgomery indicated to the mechanic with shouts and hand signals to hold his fire until he got as close as possible. The three men down below were still looking up, their mouths gaped open in curiosity. Whistler leaned out over the fuselage and fired several times as the plane got within a hundred yards of the ground. After passing them, Montgomery pulled back on the joy stick and the plane ascended sharply, then banked to the left and began still another swoop.

"Jesus Christ, let's get out of here," Cane yelled, as the next round of bullets pinged about them, one ricocheting off a rock and clipping a few strands off his horse's matted tail.

"Ain't no time for that," Chimney said, jerking his Springfield from the scabbard on his saddle. "The sonofabitch is already comin' back around." They were ratcheting shells into the chambers of their guns when Montgomery swooped over again, sending the horses and Cob into a panic as several more bullets splatted in the dirt around them. As the plane began to make yet another circle, Chimney told Cane, "Just aim for the front."

Montgomery, at that moment, was growing enraged with Whistler, who was struggling to reload. An entire magazine emptied and not a single hit. He decided that he was going to have to shoot the bastards himself. Though there was a machine gun mounted on the front of the plane, the synchronization was out of whack and Whistler had been at a loss as to how to fix it. If Reese engaged it, there was a good chance he'd shoot the wooden propeller off. He was bored, but not that bored. Berating the grease monkey with every curse word he could think of, he leaned heavy on the stick and pulled a Colt .22 out of his coveralls. To do any good with it, he was going to have to get close enough to count their goddamn teeth, assuming the ingrates even had any. He looked down and saw two of them raise rifles and point them at the plane, which only incensed him even more. In all the time he'd been alive, nobody had ever had the audacity to raise their voice to him, let alone threaten him with a gun. For Christ's sake, he was a Montgomery; his father played bridge with the Rockefellers, his mother had served as Grand Madam of the Heirloom Ball!

The mechanic yelled a warning just as Montgomery heard the *whap* of the bullet, felt it rip through his neck and exit the other side below his ear. More surprised than hurt, at least for a brief second, he dropped the pistol to the floor of the cockpit and reached for his throat with both hands. Behind him, he heard Whistler fire off another round just before the plane shot upward and then leveled out for a few seconds, seeming to nearly come to a stop a thousand feet in the air. Hot blood gushed from the holes in his neck and poured over the front of his coveralls. Everything was happening too quickly. He tried to take a breath and choked. Another clot of blood gushed from his mouth, and he pitched forward as the plane began to nosedive, banging his face against the front panel. He heard the mechanic yell something, felt him pounding frantically on his back. He thought about how the girl he'd left in the club car would probably fuck the butler and the cook out of pure joy when she heard about his demise; and he felt a little regret roll over him just then, because, really, she hadn't been so bad. It was he who had—

"Poor fellers," Cob said, as they watched the plane smash into the ground a few hundred yards away, scooping out a short trench with its nose before bursting into a ball of flames. "I guess they wasn't from no fair, was they?" Then they heard a scream, and Cane jumped on his horse and started to ride toward the wreck. "What the fuck are ye doing?" Chimney yelled, just before the plane exploded again, tossing bits of burning flesh and canvas into the air. The funnel of black smoke was visible for miles around, but it didn't matter. They were long gone by the time the law got there.

20

Back at Camp Pritchard, Lieutenant Bovard was standing weak-kneed and hungover outside a barracks, watching Sergeant Malone demonstrate some exercises to a group of fresh recruits. Last night, he had bypassed the usual cocktails and small talk at the officers' club in Meade and accepted the sergeant's halfhearted invitation to have a drink at the Blind Owl, a tavern a few blocks farther down Paint Street across from the foul-smelling paper mill. Imagining the place would be jumping with all manner of sordid characters, from knife-wielding ex-convicts to pasty-faced gamblers to alcoholic adulterers to perhaps even a fallen woman whose sleazy talents included picking up coins off the floor with her nether parts, Bovard found himself instead in a dreary, piss-smelling room lit by a couple of sooty, rusted lanterns watching Malone stare silently into the fly-specked mirror behind the bar while the only other customers, a decrepit banjo player and his young harp-playing sidekick, sat in the corner nursing mugs of flat, musty-tasting beer and debating where they were going to make their bed come closing time. A bit disappointed, the lieutenant was just getting ready to call it a night when the sergeant, sometime around his fifth whiskey, suddenly began talking about his experiences with the Red Cross on the Western Front. Malone spoke in a low, somber voice for the next two hours, his eyes never straying from his reflection in the glass, as if he were a priest watching a stranger spill his guts in a sanctuary. At midnight, the bartender, a burly, wooden-faced oaf who hadn't emitted a single sound the entire evening, turned out the lamps; and the sergeant, in mid-sentence, shut up and never said another word, not even during the taxi ride back to the base.

After slipping past the guards at the gate, Bovard had stumbled to his quarters so aroused from what Malone had said that he was still awake at reveille, his handkerchief stiff with ejaculate and his hand cramped so badly that he had a difficult time lacing up his boots. Two cups of strong coffee had revived him somewhat, and now, watching the new soldiers break out in a sweat, he felt himself growing hard again. One boy in particular had caught his eye, a slim, olive-skinned youth named Wesley Franks. Thankfully, his erection quickly subsided when he heard Malone call out, "At ease!" Wiping some sweat from his brow, he glanced at the men as they collapsed to the ground, gasping and moaning. He watched a tubby boy named Meecham roll over on his hands and knees and puke in the dirt. Jesus, he thought, a few leg raises and jumping jacks and they're crying like schoolgirls. No, this wouldn't do. A single second-rate gladiator working weekends on the coliseum circuit for a few extra denarii could have wiped out the entire fucking platoon with a butter knife.

He then looked over at Malone, and suddenly became aware of the wheezing in his lungs, the rivulets of whiskey residue streaming from his pores. Built like a blacksmith, with a thick, black mustache and a long jagged scar running along his jawline, the sergeant was certainly an imposing figure, but, shit, he was also nearly twice as old as any of them. Perhaps because of a strange sort of camaraderie he now felt with the man after listening to his confessions in the Blind Owl, or maybe because he was ashamed that he had spent the night jacking himself into a frenzy over what he'd heard, it suddenly didn't feel right to just stand around, as he had been doing the last couple of weeks, and allow Malone to handle everything. Bovard thought for a minute. Though he'd never seen a man gutted with a bayonet or slept standing up in a pit swimming with rats, he did still hold the record at the Hill School for the mile, had been captain of the rowing team at Kenyon. Tossing his cap to the ground, he told Malone to go sit in the shade. He ordered the men to line up and tighten their boot laces. My God, they could barely stand. What they needed, he thought, was something inspirational, a short speech aimed to get them focused. "A soldier of the Roman Empire," he began, "could jog all day long at a steady pace with a full pack that weighed somewhere between thirty-five and forty pounds." Pleased with his opening, he paused for a moment to let that bit of information sink in. He was about to continue when someone in the back mumbled, "What the hell's he talkin' about? Fuck, we ain't Romans. You a Roman, Davy?"

Bovard's face quickly flushed crimson with anger and embarrassment. Oh, you've got that right, you dumb hillbilly, he thought to himself. Not a one of you sorry bastards would make a good pimple on a legionnaire's ass. He was on the verge of blurting out such an insult when he glanced at Malone, still standing at his side, a passive look on his face, ready to take over again whenever his superior had had enough of playing leader for the day. He steadied himself. "No, we're not," he said instead, "but we are Americans." Then he turned and pointed at a tall oak that stood half a mile away at the eastern edge of the base. "Three times to the tree and back, gentlemen. Follow me."

After he'd run them into the ground—a quarter of the men lay practically helpless in various spots along the route—Bovard casually walked over to where a shaky Wesley Franks was sprawled out in the grass attempting to uncap his canteen. "Here," he said, crouching down on his haunches, "let me help you with that."

"Thank you, sir," the boy managed to say between gulps of air.

Bovard twisted the top off and handed the canteen back; and Wesley sat up and proceeded to drain it. Resisting the urge to tell him to slow down, the lieutenant waited until he was finished, then asked, "Where are you from, Private?"

"Place called Veto, sir."

"Is that in Ohio?" Bovard said, as he tried not to stare at the sweat dripping off the boy's smooth handsome chin onto the crotch of his brown pants.

"Yes, sir, over near Belpre. It's just a little place."

Bovard was about to ask the boy about his family when, out of the corner of his eye, he saw Malone start walking toward him. "Keep up the good work, Private," he said instead. Then he stood and jogged effortlessly across the field to meet the sergeant as several of the men lying nearby watched him with hatred in their eyes.

"I think that's about all they can take this morning, sir," Malone said. "Looks like you wiped 'em out."

"Whatever you think best, Sergeant. I guess maybe I did go a bit overboard."

"Not at all, sir. Not at all. There won't be anybody holdin' their hand when they get to the Front."

They waited silently for the men to recover, watched a crew push a borrowed French SPAD out of an airplane hangar and point it toward the gravel runway. Bovard thought again about what Malone had told him in the bar last night. Of course, he knew that most of it was nothing but lies and bullshit and myths perpetuated by soldiers who were bored or superstitious or terrified, but hadn't Homer and Virgil once sought inspiration out of the same bloody timeworn cloth? Standing in the early morning sun, relaxed by the run, he felt his eyelids growing heavy, and then ... and then ... and then he and Wesley are pinned down in a funk hole in the middle of No Man's Land near a section of the Hindenburg Line. Night finally falls and they sleep in each other's arms, exhausted and smeared with other men's blood and guts and skin. An ugly, jaundiced-looking moon casts a sinister glow over the smoking landscape. Just as dawn breaks, a whistle sounds a long, paralyzing note from a sector of the German trenches, and, in what seems like no more than a few seconds, he and Wesley are overrun by a company of enemy soldiers, screaming savages with pointed helmets and fat, piggish faces. Though they put up a valiant fight, and Bovard imagines it as the most glorious few minutes a man could ever hope for in this world, the two don't stand a chance against such overwhelming odds. After the Huns shoot and hack and bludgeon their bodies beyond recognition, they quickly become food, first for the swarms of flies and rats, and then, a few hours later, for the tribe of deserters that Malone claimed live in the tunnels and caves beneath No Man's Land and prowl the battle-fields under cover of darkness, robbing and cannibalizing corpses. The sergeant swore—this was sometime around whiskey number eight—that he and another stretcher-bearer had come across such a group of ghouls one night while out searching for the wounded after a particularly bloody skirmish, English and French and Russian and Italian and even a Turk, all banded together, mad as hatters and feasting on a cadaver, gibbering in some new language they had formed underground. The lieutenant was just beginning to imagine Wesley and himself being eaten, bones and all, by some nefarious monster dressed in a slop-encrusted uniform of many colors, when he became aware that someone was talking to him. His eyes flew open. Malone was looking at him curiously. "Are you all right, sir?" he repeated.

"What's that?" Bovard said, looking a little dazed.

"I asked if you were all right, sir. You seemed—"

"No, no, I'm fine," the lieutenant said, quickly regaining his composure. "In fact, Sergeant, I don't believe I've ever felt better in my entire life."

21

Ten days or so after Ellsworth returned from Meade, Eula told him that she wanted to go see Mr. Slater, the teacher at the schoolhouse in Nipgen. "Why would you wanta do something like that?" he asked.

"Well, if Germany's where they're a-sendin' Eddie, I'd like to have an idy of where it is, and I figure if there's anyone around here who could show us, it will be him."

Ellsworth frowned. Ever since the embarrassment with the stolen magazine six years ago, he had done his best to avoid Slater, but he couldn't think of a good excuse not to take her; the man didn't live but a couple of miles away. It was only after he'd agreed that Ellsworth began to see it as an opportunity. He could let him know that the boy had turned out all right after all, that he wasn't locked up in a hoosegow somewhere for larceny or something even worse. It was the first time in ages that he actually had something to be proud of when it came to Eddie, and by the time they left for the teacher's house the next afternoon, he was actually looking forward to doing a little bragging.

They found Slater, a pale, skinny man with wiry red hair, lounging in a hammock tied between two chestnut trees in his front yard. He was playing a wooden flute, one much the same as a shepherd stuck with his flock on a lonely hillside might have passed the time with in olden days. A wide-brimmed straw hat covered his rather small head.

When he saw them approaching, he rolled out of the hammock and set the flute atop a rusty overturned washtub. "Mr. and Mrs. Fiddler," he said, taking off his hat as he walked up to their wagon. "What a surprise." Ellsworth noted a little disdainfully that he was barefoot and had a yellow dandelion stuck behind his ear. Not only that, he didn't appear to have on any underclothes beneath the baggy nightshirt he was wearing.

"I hope we're not botherin' ye," Eula said.

"No, no, not at all. What can I do for you?"

"Well, we was wonderin' if you might have a map of Germany."

Slater thought for a moment as he fanned himself with the hat and scratched at a deerfly welt on his neck. "Not Germany specifically," he said, "but I do have a map of the world, if that would do you any good."

"Does it have a picture of Germany on it?"

"Well, it's more like an outline, Mrs. Fiddler. Showing the boundaries."

"Do you think we could see it?"

"Yes, of course, but if you don't mind my asking, why the interest?"

"That's where Eddie's a-goin' to fight," Ellsworth said, puffing out his chest a little.

"Eddie? My God, is he in the military? I wouldn't have thought he'd be old enough."

"Neither did I, but they took him just the same."

"Have you tried to get him back?"

"He'd already signed his name by the time I found out."

"Yes, but Eddie can't be more than . . . what is he, fifteen?"

"Sixteen this past spring."

Slater was surprised. He certainly would have never thought Eddie Fiddler the type to run off and join the army. Immature for his age, that's how he would have described him. Except for the time he'd stolen a magazine from his desk drawer, he had never really been any trouble, but then he had never been anything else, either. When he didn't return after his sixth year, Slater hardly gave it a second thought. Most of the boys around here just bided their time until they could quit. Only Tommy Fletcher had had the makings of a scholar, and he had thrown everything away to become some homosexual's plaything for a year or so in Cincinnati before he was discovered mutilated and murdered in a fleabag down along the river. Thank God the boy's parents had never found out that he was the one who had given Tommy the money for the train ticket. But Slater had learned his lesson, and it was the last time he ever got personally involved with one of his students, no matter how sorry he felt for them. Well, bravo for Eddie. Maybe the war would be good for him.

He led them into the house and through a small, messy parlor toward the kitchen. Dog-eared books and journals were strewn about the floor, stacked high on the two battered easy chairs that sat in front of the fireplace. A layer of dust that Eula later described as an inch thick covered the oak mantel. A white hen sat clucking softly on a soiled red pillow in one corner of the room, and a mound of dirt and feathers had been swept carelessly into another. The house used to be part of the Culver farm, but it had been in Slater's name for some time now. Though most of the teachers who had taught at the Nipgen schoolhouse in the past barely knew more than the students, he had shown up for the job interview with a bona fide bachelor's degree in English Literature from Ohio University; and Mrs. Culver, who pretty much had her hand in everything that went on in the township, was determined to keep him, whatever the cost. Stay and get my son, Albert, into college, she had told Slater, and I'll give you a house and five acres. He had refused at first, said he only needed the job for a year or two. He had dreams of becoming a famous playwright, of winning acclaim in the theater and traveling the world accompanied by an ever-changing entourage of beautiful lovers and bootlicking parasites. But after several summers of filling notebook after notebook with what he eventually came to realize was tepid, empty fluff that quite frankly would have made a dog sick, the idea of living out his life in quiet obscurity slowly took hold, began to seem more and more attractive. By then, Albert was ten years old. "Wonder whatever happened to ol' Shakespeare Slater?" he could imagine some of his former classmates saying when they ran into each other. "Remember him?" There was nothing tragic or noble or self-sacrificing about it. It had felt right, that's all. If asked, he would have said that he had finally come to the realization that he didn't have what it takes. Better to find out early than torture yourself for a lifetime. But, of course, nobody asked. And Albert Culver? Without Slater coaching him, the poor numskull hadn't lasted one year at the University of Toledo.

"There it is," he said to the Fiddlers, pointing to a cracked, sun-bleached map hanging in a lacquered frame on the wall above the kitchen table where tiny black gnats swarmed about some dirty dishes. The map had been donated to the school by Mrs. Culver's grandfather probably around the same time that John Wilkes Booth was making his final curtain call, but it was so obsolete by the year Slater started working there that he bought a new one with money out of his own pocket and took the old one home.

Eula and Ellsworth stepped forward, peered at all the different colored shapes. They were staring at the South Pole region when Slater realized that neither of them could read. He moved between them, stuck his finger on the map. "This is Germany, but when they send Eddie overseas, he'll probably go to France first. From what I've read in the newspapers, that's pretty much where all of our soldiers will end up."

"That's somewhere over there, too, ain't it?" Eula asked.

"Yes," Slater said, as he slid his finger an inch or two southward. "This is France."

"So then . . . where would we be?"

"Right about here," the teacher said, tapping the approximate location of Ohio.

"Well, heck, Eula, that don't seem very far away," Ellsworth said.

Slater cast a puzzled look at the farmer, but then, after a brief hesitation, started to explain, in the same patient voice he tried to maintain when he was talking to his slower students, "Oh, it's quite a distance really. The world is a big place. You have to understand that the map just makes it look smaller. Everything is scaled down so that it can fit."

"And what's this?" Eula said, pointing at the broad expanse of blue that separated America from Europe while waving gnats away from her face.

"That's the Atlantic Ocean."

Ellsworth leaned in for a closer look. "Why, that don't look no bigger than Clancy's pond," he said.

Now Slater wasn't sure how to respond. Although the ignorance of some of the locals didn't surprise him at all anymore, he now wondered if perhaps Ellsworth was pulling his leg. To not know the location of a foreign country was one thing, but to confuse a great ocean with a Huntington Township fishing hole was something entirely different. Even that crazy-ass preacher, Jimmy Beulah, one of the most backward-thinking men that Slater had ever met, had a rudimentary knowledge of the vastness of the earth, though he did still believe it to be as flat as a griddle cake. Oh, well, either way, the sooner he took care of their questions, the sooner he could get back to his music. He was right on the verge of finishing his first original composition, a slow, mournful piece in eight movements meant to capture the educator's dread of returning to the classroom after the bliss of the summer break. Tentatively titled "Might as Well Hang Myself," he had been working on it off and on for the past several years. "Anything else I can help you with?" he asked the couple.

"No," Eula said. "I just wanted to see where they're sending my boy, that's all. We appreciate ye takin' the time."

A few minutes later, as they were driving home in the wagon, Ellsworth asked her, "What are ye thinkin' about?"

"Oh, nothing much," she said. "Eddie, I guess. Wondering why Mr. Slater don't get himself a wife or at least hire a housekeeper. What about you?"

Ellsworth was also curious as to why Slater didn't have a woman. Even a man who put flowers in his hair should be able to find some kind of mate. Then again, maybe the teacher just didn't want the worries and responsibilities that came with being hitched. He and Eula had a better marriage than most he knew about, even with all the troubles they had gone through the past few months, but there were still occasional moments when he caught himself recalling with fondness the years when he was a single man. He didn't know how he had done it, staying out all night running with Uncle Peanut or coon hunting with the Holcomb twins or hanging out in Parker's back room, then working all day and doing it again the next night. Heck, these days he could hardly stay awake long enough after supper to finish a pipe. Age had finally caught up with him, as it did with everyone eventually. Even his memories were beginning to feel tired. He gave a little sigh, then said, "Do you think he's read all them books?"

"Probably," Eula said. "Why else would he clutter up his house with 'em if'n he wasn't going to?"

"Well, I'll tell ye this, after seeing him a-layin' under that tree half-naked like that, I'm damn glad Eddie decided to take up soldiering. I bet they don't put up with any of that silly horseshit in there, by God."

"I don't care nothin' about that," Eula said. "I just want him to come back in one piece." She started to sniffle, and from somewhere out of her dress she took out a hankie to wipe her nose.

"Ah, don't you worry," Ellsworth said, wrapping his arm around her and pulling her close. "He'll be fine. Shoot, the next time we see him we'll probably have to salute and call him General Eddie. Now wouldn't that be something?"

22

ON HIS WAY to the Senate Grill for his usual afternoon pick-me-up, Benjamin Hamm, a longtime physician in Meade, turned the corner at Paint and Second Street and saw Jasper Cone a few yards ahead, bent over in the middle of the sidewalk, wiping the crud off his measuring stick with the ragged remains of an old shirt. The doctor stopped in mid-step, then backed away and crossed the street, hoping to avoid him. It wasn't that he didn't like the young man; he was just too busy today to get into another tedious discussion about Emerald Hollister's intestinal worms or Jasper's suspicions that Mrs. Castle over on Caldwell Street might be suffering from hemorrhoids. Because of his access to everyone's privy, Jasper could at times be spot-on when it came to diagnosing certain health problems among the citizenry, but it was still, Hamm thought, an invasion of privacy if he discussed them, even with somebody in the medical field. So, for example, if the Appleby girl that lived on Piatt Avenue wanted to puke up every morsel of food she ate, or Mule Miller took up eating glass again, that was, ultimately, their own business.

The doctor had known Jasper ever since moving from Baltimore to start his medical practice. He'd no sooner hung up his shingle when the boy's mother, a high-strung, intensely devout Catholic with a pinched face and brown, puffy eyes, sent for him. He'd had a couple of walk-ins that morning with minor ailments, but this was his first house call, and he was, to say the least, a little nervous. "What seems to be the problem, Mrs. Cone?" Hamm had asked, looking around the cramped parlor. Religious icons made of plaster sat in a neat row on the mantel; a few Bibles and prayer books lay open on a table in front of the horsehair sofa. A wooden shrine to the Virgin Mary, illuminated by several candles, was set up in the corner.

"It's my son," the woman said, a sob catching in her throat as she looked toward the narrow stairs leading to the second floor. "He's . . . he's . . ." she stuttered.

"Well?" Hamm said, hoping it was something easy, like constipation or a stomachache. With the ink on his medical degree barely dry, he didn't think he was quite ready to tackle something life-threatening yet. He was sure his lack of confidence would soon go away, but a few more days to settle in before he confronted something complicated or ghastly would be a blessing.

"It's not something a lady can talk about," she said, wiping delicately at a tear running down her powdered cheeks. "Just look him over and you'll see. An adjustment, that's what he needs."

"A what?"

"An adjustment," she repeated. "So he's normal."

Shit, this must be bad, Hamm thought, as he looked down at the string of rosary beads she was squeezing in her hand. "What's his name?" he asked.

"Jasper," she managed to whisper right before she gave a little swoon and carefully crumpled onto the horsehair sofa.

Hamm climbed the stairway with a sense of dread. Though he really didn't believe in a divine being anymore, he stopped near the top and crossed himself anyway, hoping for some guidance and preparing for the worst. It was inevitable, he had been told in medical school, that he would lose a patient now and then, but why did the first one have to be a child? "Just do your best," he told himself, as he walked toward the open door at the end of the hall. However, when he entered the room he found a boy standing rigidly in front of a bed, looking quite healthy except for a frightened look on his rather plain, bony face.

"Well, lad," Hamm said, after introducing himself, "can you tell me what's wrong? I can't make heads or tails out of what your—"

"I don't want you cuttin' on it," Jasper interrupted.

"On what?" Hamm asked, figuring the boy must be suffering from a cyst or tumor of some kind.

After a moment's hesitation, Jasper unbuckled his pants and let them drop to the floor. He wasn't wearing any drawers. Hamm stood there speechless for a minute, staring at the long slab of meat hanging between the boy's skinny legs. "So this is what your mother was talking about?" he finally said. "Your penis?"

Jasper nodded grimly, then reached down and pulled his pants back up over it. "She wants you to whack some of it off, but I'd rather you maybe tried to shrink it like those Africans do with the heads and stuff."

Only then did the doctor realize what the woman meant by "an adjustment." Lord, could she be serious? He glanced about the room, bare except for a small dresser and a plain wooden cross hanging on the wall above the neatly made bed and a long rifle leaning in the corner. "But why?" Hamm asked.

"To make me normal," the boy replied. "Just like she told ye." Then he began to tremble and a single tear flushed from one of his brown eyes and dripped off his chin onto the floor.

"Now don't worry, son," Hamm said. "I'm not going to touch it, let alone operate on it, I promise. How old are you?"

"Be twelve my next birthday."

"So you're still in school?"

The boy shook his head. "Mother won't allow it. She says freaks shouldn't be seen in public."

"What about your father?"

"He got killed right after I was born," Jasper said. "Over at the paper mill." He turned then and pointed at the rifle. "He bought that buffalo gun just for me. You ever seen one before?"

"No, can't say that I have."

"Mother won't let me shoot it, but one of these days I will."

Hamm looked out the window into the backyard, saw a couple of chickens pecking in the dirt, a mangy cat stretched out on a low hanging limb in a mulberry tree. Once, as part of his surgical training, he and several classmates had dissected a cadaver. The man on the table had been found frozen to death on a bench in downtown Baltimore in the middle of the day. Just a tramp with no name, no next of kin. Other than that, the only thing Hamm remembered about the poor fellow was that he'd had the biggest cock any of them had ever seen. Pumped up, it would have been the length of a hatchet handle and as big around as a specimen cup. They had all gone out for a beer afterward, and, of course, there had been much joking about it, most of them finding it hard to believe that a man who possessed something so magnificent could have ever ended up alone in the gutter. And by the time Jasper's quit growing, Hamm estimated, as he watched the cat suddenly drop from the tree and slink off through the grass, his would be even larger than the one they had removed from the bum, the one that had ended up pickled in a jar of alcohol in a dark closet alongside some mutated embryos and a three-headed mouse.

"Your mother," the doctor told Jasper, "just doesn't understand. There's nothing wrong with you. Certainly not anything we can *fix* anyway. You're just going to have to live with it. My God, son, probably ninety percent of the men the world over would give anything to have your problem."

That had been sixteen years ago, and now Jasper was twenty-seven. But what most men would have looked upon as a great gift, he had always considered a curse. Of course, his mother was to blame, with her insane, unrelenting tirades about Devil's spawn, perverted desires, and hellish retributions. Growing up in such a house, Jasper became half-mad himself. It was a lonely life, filled with shame and guilt. As far as the doctor knew, he had never been with a woman. If he had, she would have probably ended up in the hospital a medical emergency, needing stitches at the very least. Not long after Hamm examined him, Jasper started keeping his penis bound up in a homemade truss constructed from a swatch of coarse canvas and strips of leather cord and a pair of silk bloomers he found lying behind the Blind Owl Saloon on one of those few nights when his mother forgot to lock him in his bedroom. But then, when he was eighteen, Cassandra Cone died from a heart attack while walking home with one of her chickens from a Blessing of the Animals service. Suddenly, Jasper's world opened up in ways he'd never dreamed of. Within days of her passing, his uncle, the broom maker, got him a job emptying outhouses with a scavenger named Itchy Ingham, and every evening after they shoveled the last load of shit off the honey wagon, they took turns shooting rats out at the city dump with the buffalo gun. For someone whose life had been as joyless and stunted as Jasper's, every day with the easygoing Itchy was like a holiday. He and the old man worked and ate and murdered rodents together six days a week. Then one blazing hot afternoon in the summer of 1915, Itchy keeled over and died in the middle of scooping out a particularly odious crapper at a boardinghouse over on Chestnut Street that catered to men who worked at the Old Capitol Brewery. Besides Jasper, the only other person who attended the funeral was Ernie Bagshaw, the dump keeper. The next day, Jasper made a place in the shed behind his house for Gyp, the donkey that pulled the honey wagon, and went back to work by himself.

A year later, after a spring flood sent a hundred shithouses floating down Mulberry Street into the Scioto, and six people died of cholera after drinking water from a fountain in the city park, water suspected of being tainted by the nearby jakes, the city engineer, a man by the name of Rawlings, convinced the mayor to call an emergency meeting of the city council to discuss the raw sewage situation. The engineer, fresh out of Wabash College, was brimming with modern ideas, and though he didn't come right out and say it, for fear of being pegged a crackpot or, even worse, a Socialist, his hope was that somehow they could start pressuring citizens to install indoor plumbing. The debate went on for several hours, but in the end the city leaders reluctantly voted 5 to 1, with one abstainer, that they should hire what Rawlings referred to as a "sanitation inspector." He admitted it was a new concept, but one he felt was necessary if they wanted to avoid any more disasters like the one that had occurred in the spring. "Good," he said after the votes were tallied. "I've got just the man in mind."

"Who might that be?" Bus Davenport, the school superintendent, asked suspiciously. After being involved professionally with children for so many years, he found it difficult to trust anyone who might possibly have been one in the past.

"Jasper Cone."

The howls of protest could be heard three blocks away. "At least hire someone who's qualified!" Sandy Saunders, an insurance salesman and the one nay voter, yelled, banging the silver-headed cane he always carried on the varnished floor.

"There's not a soul in this county who knows more about filth than that boy," the engineer said.

"And could you remind us again exactly what he'd be doing?" queried Homer Hasbro, the mayor and sole abstainer, quietly, as he poured himself a drink of water from a pitcher on the table. Though Homer was inept in almost every way, he had still somehow learned that the single best thing a politician could do to survive was absolutely nothing, and he had won his last four elections by expertly riding the fence. Privately, he was in favor of any modern convenience, but he wasn't about to sacrifice his cushy job by becoming actually involved in pushing for one. The majority of people hated change more than anything.

"Going around and checking privies."

"That's it?" Saunders said incredulously.

"Of course not. If he finds one that's in danger of overflowing and polluting a well, either their own or their neighbors'," Rawlings explained, "he'll issue a warning ticket. Then they'll have a few days to set things right before the city starts fining them three dollars a week. Gentlemen, I can't stress enough the need for immediate action. Right now there are approximately nineteen hundred outhouses within the city limits."

"Wait a minute," Henry Tatman, the new owner of Lange's Grocery, said. "Who's going to be doing the emptying? Since Cone's a scavenger, wouldn't this be a . . . a . . ."

"Conflict of interest?" Biff Landers said. Twenty years ago, Landers had been a law student at the University of Michigan, but a hazing incident turned deadly had gotten him expelled and seemingly stuck forever in a low-level supervisory position in the boiler house at the paper mill. Now his lungs were full of coal dust and the closest he'd ever come to realizing his dream of arguing a case in a courtroom was when he was summoned as a material witness in a former friend's divorce proceedings. There wasn't a day went by when he didn't regret tying the noose around that little freshman's neck.

"Yeah," Herman Matthews, the real estate agent, chimed in, "he'll be making money hand over fist. Maybe we should think this over some more." Though he'd just voted for the measure, he was already beginning to have a change of heart. As the owner of at least a dozen rental properties, none of which had indoor plumbing, it had just occurred to him that he might be held responsible if his tenants didn't abide by the new law.

"No," Rawlings said, "that won't happen. I've already talked to him about it. He understands he'll have to quit the honey-dipping if he takes the inspection job."

"But calling him an inspector?" said Saunders. "Jesus Christ, Rawlings, we're talking about Jasper Cone. Does he even know how to read? People will think we've lost our goddamn minds."

"It's just a job title," the city engineer replied. "Call him what you want."

"Well, then, who's going to take over his business?" Edgar Blaine asked. A Presbyterian minister by trade, he had recently retired, and it had taken him most of the evening to figure out exactly what was being discussed. Up until just a few minutes ago, he thought they were planning some sort of celebration. He had told his wife again this morning that his brain wasn't working right, that it would be better if he let someone else have his seat on the council, but she wouldn't hear of it. For some reason, no matter how many times he came down to breakfast wearing nothing but socks on his hands, or tried to butter his bread with a coffee cup, she still refused to believe that his best years were behind him. Why couldn't she see that he just wanted to spend his time in the garden with a blanket covering his cold legs, reading through his old sermons and reflecting on the number of souls his words might have saved before he forgot what words were actually used for?

"I don't know yet. Anybody here interested in cleaning out privies?" Rawlings said. He looked over at Saunders. "What about you, Sandy? Pays two dollars a cubic yard."

23

AFTER SHOOTING DOWN Reese Montgomery's airplane, the Jewett brothers started traveling mostly at night. Since they had to stay off the roads most of the time, it was slow going in the dark. During the day they camped along brushy creeks and snaky swamps, hid in hollowed-out caves and deserted homesteads, with one always standing guard while the other two slept. They lived mostly on hardtack and candy and tins of stew and evaporated milk, but it was still the best fare they had eaten since before their mother died. Continuing their way northward, they robbed several general stores, collecting up various firearms and boxes of ammunition—along with a *Webster's International* dictionary and a teakwood box of silver flatware—to the point where they finally had to steal an extra horse just to haul their arsenal. Inspired, at least in part, by *The Life and Times of Bloody Bill Bucket,* Chimney and Cob started dressing in cowboy garb, ten-gallon hats and dungarees and hand-tooled pointy-toed boots, while Cane, with the black frock coat and new white shirt, his hair greased back with pomade, took on the same look of shady refinement favored by riverboat gamblers and dissipated men of the cloth. Crossing into Tennessee, they held up three more banks, finally hitting the jackpot in a little town called Wayward. That night, after Cane finished counting the $29,000 in hundred-dollar bills the trembling bank clerk had pulled out of the vault and tossed onto the coat Chimney had spread on the floor, he looked at his brothers and said, "That's it, we're done."

"What do ye mean?" Chimney said.

"No more robbing. There's enough cash here we don't need to take any more chances."

"You swear?" Cob said. By this point he was sick to death of running all night and hurting people and stealing their property. Sometimes the only thing that kept him from slipping off and giving himself up at the nearest post office or calaboose was Cane's promise that they would buy a farm, a home, a place to call their own, as soon as they made it across the border into Canada.

Cane nodded. "All we got to do now is disappear."

Unfortunately, that wasn't going to be as easy as it sounded. The big haul in Wayward had come with a heavy price. While Cane was sitting on his horse acting as lookout during the holdup, a deputy in a motorcar had spun around the corner, ramming the steel bumper into the animal's front legs and snapping them like twigs. Tumbling backward out of his saddle, Cane hit the ground hard, but managed to hold on to his Smith & Wesson. Just as the deputy raised his rifle, Cane fired two shots at him, the first one ripping his chin off and the second puncturing his right lung. Townspeople ran to their windows and watched as the tall man in the black coat put the screaming horse out of its misery before emptying another pistol into the still-sputtering engine of the automobile.

Though they managed to escape and steal another horse that night, the very next day they encountered still more trouble. While looking for a place to relieve himself, Bill Wilson, the leader of a posse from Wayward, accidentally wandered upon them hiding in a thick, tangled stand of pine trees. He was unbuttoning his trousers when he looked up and saw Cane pointing a gun at him. To the outlaw's surprise, Wilson smiled with an air of complete confidence. He was the constable in Henderson County, and had been, over the course of a twenty-year career, in a number of fixes just as bad as this one. Most criminals, he had often told people, were essentially gutless cowards, and if you didn't show any fear, they'd usually lose their nerve and slither away like snakes. He'd shot a number of them hightailing it for some hidey hole after he'd stared them down. But even men as dedicated and tough as Bill needed a break now and then, and he had been fishing the riffles on the Beech River when all hell broke loose in Wayward, or he would have probably already had these bastards either locked up or in their graves. "You better think twice about that, buster," Wilson said coolly. "I got a whole pack of men right over the hill waitin' on me." From the witnesses he'd talked to, he was fairly certain this dirty thug was the one who had blasted half of Deputy Lamar's face off.

"Keep quiet," Cane said.

"And what if I don't?" asked Wilson loudly, shifting his eyes over to the fat one someone had described as a half-wit, sitting on a log in the gloomy shade in a cowboy outfit with what appeared to be a paper bag of Circus Peanuts in his lap. He wondered where the third one might be. Probably passed out in his bedroll, he figured. That was another thing about such scum; within a few hours of committing a crime, they usually got liquored up, either to celebrate their haul or to keep from dwelling on the fate that awaited them once they were apprehended. He was about to say as much when he heard a footstep behind him and the swish of something cutting through the air. There was no chance to call out to his comrades over the hill or draw his weapon or even utter a final prayer. As he landed with a soft thump on the pine needle floor, the last thing he saw was a skinny boy bend down in front of him and wipe blood off a machete; and the last thought that went through his partially detached head was that today was a Thursday, and tomorrow would be a Friday.

Just a few hours after the posse brought Bill Wilson's body back to Wayward, the attorney general of Tennessee, Ezra Powys, consulted with his most trusted political advisers and upped the reward for the brothers dead or alive from $750 to $5,000 American dollars. It was an outrageous amount to offer, even for cop killers, but he had run on a platform pledging to clean up corruption, and recent allegations that he was in the pocket of a consortium of Memphis moonshiners were steadily gaining traction throughout the state. But, as his consultants told him, if he played this right, and showed the people that he was willing to do whatever it took to bring the criminals to justice, the murder of Bill Wilson might just save his career. Within hours of making the announcement, he realized he had made a mistake ever listening to the dumb bastards. According to several editorials that ran in that evening's papers, the majority of taxpayers of Tennessee didn't think there were more than three or four people walking the globe worth five thousand dollars, and certainly not a self-deluded, two-bit constable from Henderson County who had a reputation for shooting misdemeanors and old drunks in the back. Too, many of these same taxpayers lived on collard greens and corn pone six or seven days a week; and a great percentage of them were beginning to view the robbing of a bank as a just blow against the system that helped keep them in poverty. One of the writers even speculated that the reason the attorney general was so eager to offer such an outlandish reward was because the money the Jewett boys had stolen in Wayward belonged to one of his Memphis cronies! Even worse than that, Powys found out that the funeral for Bill Wilson was to be held on Sunday at noon, and he had a tee time scheduled for one o'clock at the newly opened Happy Valley Golf Course. Though he had only recently taken up the game, it was already becoming an obsession. One of his underlings discreetly tried to get the service changed to an earlier time, or perhaps even moved to Monday, but Mrs. Wilson insisted that her husband be buried on the Sabbath at the same time of day that he had entered this world forty-two years ago. "Sorry, Chief, she won't budge."

"Well, shit" was all Powys said. He glanced regretfully over at his clubs sitting by the door of his office. All week, the only thing he'd had to look forward to was spending some time practicing his swing. By the time he was photographed kneeling in prayer beside the coffin, and sat through three hours of pompous preaching and teary accolades, and walked the widow through the cemetery, he almost hated Bill more for getting killed than he did the outlaws for killing him.

Even so, he woke up Monday morning looking forward to seeing the hard-earned publicity that his advisers had guaranteed him on the front pages of the papers, only to discover that John Herbert Montgomery had stolen his thunder. Yesterday evening, the tycoon had suddenly broken his silence about his son's killers, informing a group of newsmen gathered outside his Long Island estate that he was willing to pay three times what Tennessee was offering to whoever brought him their heads. Except for brief notices in a couple of the local rags, Bill's funeral wasn't even mentioned. Photographs showed Montgomery barely able to control his grief, and the attorney general vaguely wondered whether he could ever summon such emotion—if, for example, his old mother passed away, or his wife ran off with a better man. He doubted it. As blind as he was to most of his defects, even Powys knew that the first thing a man lost when he entered politics was his humanity.

Of course, the story Montgomery fed the journalists was not the real story at all, which was something the attorney general, as many times as he had manipulated the press himself, should have realized. As for the tears in the photographs, all the eighty-year-old tycoon had to do was recall the afternoon long, long ago when he'd told a young, impoverished Tom Edison to go fly a kite, and they fell like rain. And as far as Reese went, the outlaws had actually done him a favor by blowing his spoiled, rotten son out of the air—by his accountant's calculations, the lazy little whoremonger had cost him close to a million dollars in the past year alone—but still, as several of his cronies had reminded him repeatedly in the days since the boy's death, you couldn't let the hoi polloi think they could murder the privileged class without repercussions, or you'd end up with another Russia on your hands. The sooner this Jewett trash was tracked down and dealt with, the sooner he could forget about the entire mess and get back to the business of the day, which was making as much money as possible off the clusterfuck in Europe before somebody threw in the towel.

On the heels of Montgomery's pronouncement, reporters from all the big news organizations on the East Coast were quickly dispatched south to get in on the story before it was too late. Every newspaper in America featured tales written about the outlaws and their crimes. From time to time, the brothers managed to get hold of one lying around somewhere, and the black-and-white drawings of their faces nearly drove Chimney crazy the first few times he saw them, since he was made to look like a sneaky, bucktoothed rodent, and Cob a fat, goofy baby, while Cane was always portrayed as some sort of devilish ladies' man. Disregarding the facts, several of the more liberal publications began to twist the crime spree into a romantic saga, due in part to a hysterical widow's claim that the oldest had handed her a bouquet of sweet williams and a fifty-dollar gold piece after they watered their horses at her well in Chapel Hill. More conservative journalists, however, chose to ignore the heartthrobs and moonbeams, and put a different spin on the tale. Thus, on the same day that a Socialist weekly in Boston ran an editorial stating that the brothers were just humble, illiterate sharecroppers who had killed their tyrannical overseer after he refused to allow them time off to bury their dead father, a staunchly right-wing daily out of New York City compared the outlaws to a band of ungodly savages who were possibly even worse than the Huns, going so far as to claim that they had robbed and left for dead a half-dozen good Christians along a highway in Arkansas who were on their way to a revival. And things were just getting warmed up. Crimes as far away as Idaho and Arizona were soon attributed to the trio. A fruit farmer in Vermont, sensing that his nosy wife was beginning to sus-pect his own sick behavior, and viewing the brothers as the perfect fall guys, walked into the Montpelier police station and swore that he had come upon them burying a woman's nude body in his orchard. For-tunately, the detective on duty, a man by the name of Abe Abramson, was blessed with an uncanny ability to detect when someone was lying, mostly by observing the manner in which they held the cup of coffee or tea he thrust upon them while they were being interrogated; and within hours the farmer was arrested for the slayings of nine females who had disappeared from the Green Mountains over the past decade. Still, even though that grisly incident received much attention nation-wide and should have served as a wake-up call that perhaps the outlaws were being blamed for crimes they hadn't committed, the reporting became more and more tawdry and unbalanced, and the telegraph and phone wires fairly sang with contradicting lies and outlandish bullshit. But there was one thing that everyone seemed to be in agreement on, and it was this: with deputized posses in six states now searching for them, along with a great number of independent bounty hunters, it was only a matter of days or even hours before the brothers now known as the Jewett Gang would be no more.

24

ALTHOUGH BLACKIE TRIED to promote his new place as the "Celestial Harem of Earthly Delights," it was hard for anyone to accept Virgil Brandon's goat shed as being anything close to an exotic playground; and, to his dismay, it quickly became known simply as the "Whore Barn." Too, it wasn't quite as successful as he had initially hoped. He had planned on the girls having more johns than they could handle, but it turned out that the soldiers at Camp Pritchard were kept on a fairly tight leash, at least through the week. Mandatory classes on the horrors of venereal disease also put a damper on business. The physician who conducted the classes, a Dr. Eugene Eisner, scoured the county looking for the most ravaged victims of gonorrhea and syphilis he could find to parade and sometimes even treat in front of the recruits. He often had to pay them out of his own pocket, but he didn't care; the look on the soldiers' faces as they watched him knock the clap snot out of some hilljack's pizzle with a rubber hammer was priceless. Since Eisner, who was also an ordained Methodist minister, believed that such diseases were a useful, even God-sanctioned deterrent against sex outside the marriage bed, he didn't condone the use of condoms. As he had told various colleagues over the years, he would rather die than help promote anything that allowed the promiscuous to continue their licentious lifestyles with impunity. No, with the rubber hammer act, he was trying to achieve a more permanent psychological effect, something a man would automatically recall every time he thought about sticking his prick in some casual acquaintance. As he boasted at the little gatherings the general occasionally held for privileged members of his staff, half the men who sat in on his lectures took vows of chastity at some point or other, even those who were already betrothed. As one captain quipped to his buddies, the crazy bastard's enthusiasm was "infectious."

However, if someone had asked Jasper Cone, he would have said that business was booming for the pimp. Ever since Blackie and the girls had set up shop in Virgil's shed, he had been watching them at night from the weedy perimeter of the lot. At times he wondered why he tortured himself so. In addition to walking around half-numb from lack of sleep, the insects nearly ate him alive, and he sometimes witnessed things that sickened his stomach, not an easy feat when you consider that this was a man who spent hours every day mucking about in shithouses without the slightest qualms. Too, wasn't it useless to pine over something you could never have? Because of his size, Jasper hadn't had an erection since before he quit growing around the age of seventeen, not a full-blown one anyway. "Not enough blood in your body," Doc Hamm had told him a couple of years ago. "Even if it was to happen, you'd probably pass out before you could do anything with it." But though he knew the doctor was right—he had grappled with his cock enough times to know it would never stand at attention—he still had desires; he could feel them coursing through his body whenever he came upon a woman, whether it be on the street, or in an outhouse during a surprise inspection, or looking through some neighbor's carelessly curtained window late at night. He was to a great extent like a man without a stomach who nonetheless can't resist spending all of his free time hanging around a chophouse buffet.

Along with unrequited lust, another part of Jasper's fascination with the Whore Barn was just being able to see how the women operated. There had always been a prostitute or two in Meade—old Midge Daniels with her varicose veins and flabby honkers, and a colored girl named Jellybean who lived over on White Heaven—but they did their dealings behind closed doors. Here, everything was out in the open. The number of men who went in and out of the tents astounded him. The weekdays were sometimes slow, but on Friday and Saturday nights he often counted seventy or eighty. Young bucks, too, determined to get their money's worth. Jasper had heard that you couldn't wear one of those woman things out, but, Lord, that was a lot of pounding when you added it all up. And there were other things to be had, too, besides just what the pimp called a "straight fuck," which, even to the virginal

Jasper, began to sound a little boring after a while. For an additional dollar, the blonde would speak strange words in a foreign accent, and the skinny one would dress up like a schoolgirl, while the ugly one, if properly aroused, would swallow a man's spunk just for the hell of it. No wonder she was so fat, Jasper thought. Just the other night when that wagonload of boys from Monkey Town tore into her, she must have slurped down a quart of the stuff. Oh, yes, it was such a clamoring, festive, noisy place, with the lighted lanterns hanging between the posts, and the pimp serving drinks at the little plank bar, and the bodyguard taking the money and keeping the lines moving in an orderly fashion. They even had a jug band playing on the weekends, a trio from Kingston that called themselves the Ginseng Gang. True, there was sometimes trouble, like the other evening when they had to pistolwhip the big-boned country boy from Clarksburg off the one called Matilda. For one reason or another, he'd decided that he was going to make her moo like a cow, and when she refused, he went a little crazy. You could still see his handprints around her throat the next night in the campfire light. But the way Jasper figured it, at an average of three dollars a shot, the Whore Barn was making more than enough money, no matter how much he heard Blackie bitch to Henry on slow nights about the clap doctor out at the army base cutting into their profits with his rubber hammer trick.

25

SERGEANT MALONE WAS sitting on a stool in front of the camp post office, his nose stuck in the *Scioto Gazette,* when, out of the corner of his eye, he saw Bovard approaching. Jesus Christ, he moaned to himself, not a minute's peace. It wasn't so much that he disliked the lieutenant; hell, he was nicer than most of the college boys he had come across. At least he didn't walk around like he had a broomstick shoved up his ass and his nose stuck high in the air like the Yale brats, Benchley and Smothers. And he had gotten Malone drunker than Katy's cunt again two nights ago, so there was that, too. No, it was something else. He reminded the sergeant of those Englishmen he had watched with a telescope from a distant field hospital kicking a football out into No Man's Land just as they began an attack, their heads swollen with glory and honor and all that other bullshit they were taught in their public schools. By the time the sortie was over, the only thing left of the entire regiment was that damn ball, bobbing around in a shell hole filled with bloody water and body parts. You might have gotten by with that sort of bravado in the past, but not anymore. Now there were machine guns that fired three hundred rounds a minute and mustard gas that turned the lungs to pink froth and generals who thought that if they only lost a few thousand men gaining an extra yard or two, why, they had achieved some great victory. Maybe it really would be, as some people predicted, the last war that would ever be fought.

"Anything interesting in the paper?" Bovard asked as he stepped up onto the porch.

"Not really, sir," Malone said. "I just been reading about this Jewett Gang." The lieutenant's eyes, he noticed, were even more bloodshot than yesterday morning, and his face was flushed and sweaty, but he looked damn happy for a man who was so obviously hungover. In fact, he was practically beaming. Malone wondered if maybe he had visited the whore camp last night, perhaps gotten laid by the blonde the pimp billed as a genuine Parisian fashion model. From what he had heard, she was quite a hit with some of the officers. He held the newspaper up for Bovard to see. The main headline proclaimed in big black letters: SEARCH STILL ON FOR KILLER OUTLAWS. An interview with the local city engineer discussing the mental, physical, and spiritual benefits of indoor plumbing was the only other front-page story. The war wasn't even mentioned.

"Yes, I heard something about them," Bovard replied. Leaning against a porch beam, he pulled his cigar case from his pocket and offered the sergeant one. The Jewett Gang had come up in a conversation he'd had last night with an effeminate theater manager named Lucas Charles. They had bumped into each other in the Candlelight Supper Club, a quiet establishment that carried a decent brandy and was quickly becoming the lieutenant's favorite watering hole. Lucas was girlishly slender and small-boned, with soft delicate hands and purplish bags under his rather corrupt-looking gray eyes. They had talked about this and that, and then sometime around eleven o'clock, he had invited Bovard to a room he kept above the Majestic Theater, just a bed with an unwashed sheet thrown over it and a red upholstered chair and scattered bouquets of dead flowers and half-empty jars of cold cream. A torn and faded poster of a once famous actor, twinkly-eyed and sporting a top hat and monocle, was tacked to the wall. "Ol' boy performed here once," Lucas said, nodding at the picture as he poured them a drink. "Fell in the orchestra pit twice, he was so plastered." He shook his head. "Poor bastard. Couldn't remember his lines anymore."

"Whatever . . . whatever happened to him?" Bovard had asked nervously, glancing again at the bed. It had become apparent to him over an hour ago that he was being seduced, but now that push was about to become shove, he wasn't so sure he wanted to have his first sexual experience with such an obvious sissy. Wasn't being queer bad enough without being so damn blatant about it?

"Cut his throat in Cleveland a week later during an intermission.

Made a real mess of the dressing room, from what I heard. I guess they booed him off the stage for the last time."

The lieutenant took a drink from the glass Lucas handed him as he thought back on his own dark time in the hotel room in Columbus. Fortunately, before he slipped up and mentioned it, there was a knock on the door, and a man named Caldwell entered. He was even more disheveled and limp-wristed than the theater manager. A druggist by trade, he was dressed in a wrinkled white suit and carried a battered straw boater in his hand. A half-smoked cigarette was stuck behind his ear, and his blue tie looked as if it had been dipped in a mustard pot. Tossing the hat in the corner, he kicked off his shoes and produced a vial of tincture of opium from his pocket with a grand flourish. "Damn it, Clarence," Lucas said, as he locked the door, "I told you to quit bringing that stuff over here."

"Yeah, but you like it, don't you?" Caldwell said, as he uncapped the bottle.

"That's the problem," Lucas said. "I like it too much."

Bovard glanced uneasily at the bottle. Jesus Christ, not only were they homos, they were dope fiends, too. From what he had heard, just one little taste of that poison and you were forever after crawling the walls for it. A panicky urge to flee the room swept over him, but, in the end, the greater fear of being viewed as some sort of cowardly boor won out. And so he had stayed, and within thirty minutes of slugging down the drink Caldwell doctored up for him, there wasn't another place in the world he would have rather been than in that filthy hole with his two new pals.

Malone lit the cigar and dropped the match into a dented helmet that served as an ashtray next to his stool. "According to this," he told Bovard, "they might be in Ohio now."

"And isn't there an outlandish reward being offered for their capture?"

"Five thousand dollars. Or fifteen thousand if you take their heads to this Montgomery tycoon. Lot of jack for three sharecroppers."

"I just don't understand people like that."

The sergeant shrugged, set the paper on his knee. "I expect somewhere along the line they got tired of being shit on. That's what usually happens. It don't take much to turn a man into an animal." He leaned over and spat in the helmet. "You'll see what I'm talking about when you get to the Front."

The lieutenant blanched a little, took his handkerchief from his pocket and wiped his face. Last night, all of them drugged and naked and slick as pigs, Lucas had donned Bovard's service cap and suggested that they play a game. After a little coaxing, Caldwell agreed to play a captured German officer, and they tied him to a chair with strips of cloth torn from a sweat-stained pillowcase. They had done all sorts of things to extract information from the dirty Hun. It had been great fun for a while, a bit reminiscent for Bovard of his boarding school days, until Lucas stuffed a sock in the pharmacist's mouth and pulled the leather whip out from under the bed. Caldwell's eyes grew big as saucers then, and he fought like the dickens trying to break loose from his bonds, but all he succeeded in doing was toppling the chair and knocking himself unconscious when his head hit the hard oak floor. "Christ," Lucas said, "I don't know what got into him. He usually likes this sort of thing."

"Shouldn't we do something?" Bovard had asked as he watched a trickle of blood run from Caldwell's nose into his open mouth.

"Absolutely," Lucas said, nonchalantly tossing the whip into the corner on top of the druggist's straw hat and climbing over him onto the bed. "There's all sorts of things we should do." He settled back against the headboard and smiled. "I can't wait to show you a couple of them."

"No, I mean about Caldwell."

"Oh, hell, don't worry about him," Lucas had said. "Clarence is tougher than he looks. Just stick that candle up his ass and get over here."

Lighting his cigar, Bovard realized, as he inhaled the smoke, that he could still taste the theater manager in his mouth. He turned away and pretended to study a column of soldiers from the 157th marching past, listened to the sergeant carefully tear out the article about the outlaws and stick it in his pocket. Last night had been the strangest and most exhilarating experience of his life, and though he still felt essentially the same disgust and shame with himself as he had on that bleary afternoon in the hotel room when the Irish trollop revealed to him his true nature, at least he no longer had to fret about whether or not he was going to die a virgin.

26

Ellsworth came up out of one of his fields and started down the road toward home. He'd been checking the corn again, trying to judge how much yield to expect. The summer had been hotter than usual, and there hadn't been a decent rain in weeks; and so, from the looks of things, they'd be lucky to make enough money to get through the winter and spring. They had a hog they could butcher, and Eula had her chickens, but once you figured in taxes and coal and other essentials, they still needed, at the very least, a hundred dollars cash. He was damning the cattle swindler to hell again when he looked up and saw the Taylor boy coming toward him carrying a little bundle over his shoulder. "Howdy, Tuck," Ellsworth said when he got closer. "What you up to?"

"I went to Meade to join the army," the boy said, wiping a bead of sweat from his upper lip, "but they wouldn't have me."

"Why not?" Ellsworth said. "You got something wrong with ye?"

"They said I was too young," Tuck said. "Said you got to be at least eighteen to volunteer."

"Why, that don't make no sense," Ellsworth said, "them taking Eddie and not you. He ain't no older than you are, is he?"

"Eddie?" the boy said.

"Sure, he's been a-soldierin' almost a month now. Hadn't you heard?" Ellsworth watched as a puzzled look came over Tuck's face. "You know something I don't know?" he asked the boy.

Tuck swallowed, then said, "Mr. Fiddler, Eddie ain't in the army."

"What? Why do you say that?"

"I seen him down in Waverly just last week."

"No, you must be mistaken. I had a man at the camp tell me he was there."

"Well, I don't know why the man would've told ye that, but it was Eddie I saw in Waverly. Maybe he got kicked out or something."

Ellsworth suddenly felt a little light-headed. "Was he with anybody?" he asked.

"Yeah, one of them Newsome girls. The one they call Spit Job. She was hangin' all over him. And some old feller playin' music."

"Music?"

"Yeah, he was blowin' on a harmonica."

"Was he drunk?"

"You mean Eddie? Probably. I doubt if he'd let himself be seen dancing a jig out in public with Spit Job unless he was loaded."

"You don't know Eddie then," Ellsworth said, a bitter taste rising in his throat. "He's went clear off the rails here lately."

"I'm sorry," the boy said.

"No, no, I'm glad you told me. Leastways now I won't have to worry about him getting his fool head shot off in Germany."

"I wish they would've let me in," Tuck said. "I'd give anything to go."

"Well, you'll get your chance, I expect."

"I don't know. Pap heard someone at Parker's say this might be the last war that ever gets fit."

"Aw, you liable to hear anything over there. Crazy as people are, they'll probably be plenty more of 'em."

Tuck nodded his head, then said, "Well, I better get on home and let them know."

After the boy left, Ellsworth sat down under an old hickory that stood beside the road, a tree that had been there when his father was a boy, and leaned back against it. He again went over the conversation he had had with the man at the gate, wondered why he had lied. All the pride he'd been feeling for his son was gone, wiped away in less time than it takes to tie a shoelace. He felt deflated, as if someone had squeezed all the air, all the life, out of him. He should have known better than to get his hopes up, thinking Eddie would return from the army someday a man, ready to take over the farm. Thank God, except for Slater, he hadn't told anyone about it. For a minute, he considered walking back to the house and hitching up the wagon, going to

Waverly to hunt the little bastard down, but then realized that wouldn't do any good. What was the sense of dragging him back? He thought about Uncle Peanut, of how he'd disappear for weeks at a time and then return shaky and near death to let his mother heal him up again, just so he could take off again and break her heart into more pieces. No, he wasn't going to allow Eddie to do that to Eula. He'd give him one more chance if he came home, but that was all. As Jimmy Beulah once told his grandmother after he found Peanut seized up in a ditch over on Hartley Road and reluctantly dragged him home to her, sometimes you just have to let go.

When Ellsworth finally returned to the house that evening, he walked into the kitchen with his hands behind his back. "Look what I found," he said to Eula.

"What is it?" she asked. She was bent down pulling a pan of cornbread out of the oven.

"Just take a look."

"Can't ye see I'm busy?"

"C'mon."

"Oh, my," she said, when she turned around and saw the furry ball in his hands.

"It's a female. Looks a lot like Pickles, don't it?"

Setting the hot pan on top of the stove, she took the kitten from him and held it up to look into its green eyes. "Where did you find her?"

"The ol' momma's got 'em hid in a dead tree over on the widow's place. I been watchin' her awhile now."

"Who?" Eula said with a grin. "The cat or the widow?"

"Ha!"

"Can I keep her?"

"Course you can."

Later that night, as they were getting ready for bed, Eula said, "I'm going to name her Josephine, after my mother."

"That's good," Ellsworth said. He hung his bibs on a peg and turned out the lamp.

They had been lying in the dark for several minutes when Eula said, "I still wonder why we haven't got a letter yet."

"Letter?"

"Yeah," she said. "From Eddie. At least one to let us know how he's doing."

"They probably got him busy," he told her. "I wouldn't worry about that. Besides, we couldn't read it anyway."

"Maybe so, but Mr. Slater could."

Ellsworth decided the best thing to do was try to steer the conversation in another direction. He thought for a moment, then said, "Oh, I see what's goin' on now."

"What do you mean?"

"That damn schoolmarm. You're stuck on him, ain't ye?"

"Don't be silly," Eula said, then giggled and swatted at his shoulder.

"Must have been that flute he was a-playing. Or maybe that dandelion stuck in his ear."

"You're crazy," she said.

"Yep," he said, as he rolled over to face the wall, "I knew I should have never took you over there to see him."

"Go to sleep," she said, "before you get into trouble."

Ellsworth closed his eyes, but images of Eddie twirling some little strumpet around in a circle kept him awake long into the night, and it was nearly sunrise before they finally spun off into the shadows.

27

ON A COOL, cloudy morning four weeks to the day after committing their first crime, the Jewett Gang made their way into a small, quiet village they had been observing for close to an hour from a dried-up creek bed. After spending three days ducking a group of assassins accompanied by a supply truck flying a flag that had the Montgomery family crest sewn on it, they were down to their last saltine and desperate to replenish their supplies before moving back into the brush. By that time various explanations were being tossed about across the nation—in newspapers, saloons, parlors, town hall meetings, churches, and courthouses—as to how they could have committed all of their crimes without getting caught or even sustaining a single scratch. Thanks in part to a tabloid story that claimed the gang was traveling with a Haitian voodoo priestess named Sylvia who had been chased out of Texas for casting a spell on her landlord, a good portion of the public had come to believe that their run of luck was the result of supernatural forces. Others, being somewhat more rational, considered it evidence that they were either the most brilliant criminals to ever come down the pike, or that the South was in bad need of retraining its police departments. The vast majority, however, held firm to the belief that the brothers would eventually make a mistake, in much the same way that even the most skilled of gamblers will eventually draw a bad hand if he keeps on playing; and that was exactly what was about to happen in Russell, Kentucky.

As they approached the general store, Cane tried to hand Chimney some money for the groceries.

Chimney looked over at the wad of dollar bills and sneered. "Shit, I don't need that," he said, patting the pistol hanging on his side.

"Look, goddamn it, we can't be takin' any chances over some lousy canned goods," Cane said. "I thought we done went over this."

Even though Chimney had been able to see the merits in Cane's argument that it was time to lie low and focus on making it to Canada, he wasn't quite as keen as his brothers were on completely giving up the outlaw life when, in his opinion, they were just starting to get good at it. Besides that, he was in a foul mood. He still hadn't gotten a chance to fuck a woman yet, and lately it had been preying on his mind something awful that he was going to die before getting a chance to shoot his jizz into something other than his hand. "Don't worry," he said, as he slid down off his horse, "this won't take a minute. C'mon, Cob."

"Do I have to?" Cob asked.

Cane spat and looked up and down the street. Except for a kid playing with a dog a few doors down, there wasn't another soul to be seen. "Yeah, fuck, you better go on in with him," he said, "just to be on the safe side."

As Cane sat out front keeping watch, and Chimney pilfered the cash register and loaded up two gunnysacks with provisions from the shelves and a stack of old newspapers lying on the counter, the bony, spectacled storekeeper wrung his hands and cried like an old woman, his boo-hoos getting louder by the minute. "Knock that whiny bastard in the head!" Chimney yelled, but instead Cob tried conversing with him about the price of hams and the need for rain. It was no use, the clerk kept up his racket. Though the store was drearier and more poorly stocked than any they had come across, just as they were getting ready to leave, Chimney found a long unopened packing crate hidden under the counter. "What we got here?" he said.

The man quit bawling immediately. "You don't want to mess with that," he said, sucking in his snot and wiping at his eyes. "That's a special order for Mr. Haskins."

"What's so special about it?" Chimney said, as he started to pry the box open.

"Mr. Haskins is not a man you want to—"

"I'll be damned," Chimney said. Inside the crate, wrapped in oiled paper, lay a new Lee-Enfield and two wooden boxes of cartridges. He tore the paper off and picked the rifle up, aimed it at the storekeeper's head.

"You take that gun," the man said, swallowing hard, "Mr. Haskins is going to make me pay for it. It came clear from England. Please, boys, I'm just barely makin' ends meet now."

"Well, that's between you and this Mister feller you keep going on about," Chimney said, as he turned and walked out the door, loaded down with groceries and the Enfield and one of the shell boxes, the heels of his new cowboy boots clicking loudly on the scarred wooden floor, the few dollars he'd taken from the register sticking out of his front pocket. "Come on, Cob, let's go. And don't forget that other sack. I got some peaches in there for you and Cane."

Cob looked at the clerk and shrugged his shoulders and put his pistol back in his holster. Then he picked up the gunnysack and started out, the cans clanging against each other. The man stared after him grimly, his spectacles a little crooked on his long, narrow face, thinking there was more food in those two pokes than his wife and seven children sometimes got to eat in a month. Again this morning, breakfast had been a corn cake so thin you could have read the fine print on one of Mr. Haskins's loan agreements through it. He realized suddenly that he had finally arrived at his own personal crossroads, just as his grandpa had said would happen someday if he lived long enough, and that what he did in the next few seconds mattered more than anything else he'd ever done in his life. For once, his fate was in his own hands and not somebody else's, and though his hands were trembling with fear, he reached under the counter.

At the door, Cob stopped and said, "Well, been nice talkin' to you about the rain and all." Because the man seemed to be in such a bad mood over Chimney taking the gun, he didn't really expect a response, but he turned and looked back at the clerk anyway, just in time to see him bringing a Winchester repeater to his shoulder. Dropping the sack, Cob ran for his horse. Bullets started flying through the open doorway and crashing through the windows, the sounds of rifle blasts and glass shattering echoing down the street. He was throwing his leg over the saddle when he got hit. As Cane emptied his pistol into the front of the store, Chimney grabbed the reins of Cob's horse and led him out of town at a gallop. Within two hours, after poring over the blood drops in the dirt and the wanted poster the sheriff passed around, a group of citizens, including the store clerk, gathered together a few supplies and horses and headed out of town to make their fortunes.

Luckily, the slug that tore into Cob's thigh hadn't hit an artery or the bone, but because of the constant jostling from the horse, he kept losing blood, and eventually his boot was overflowing with it. He became so woozy he couldn't keep his eyes open, but whenever they stopped to rest, the posse from Russell appeared in the distance; and they had to tie him to the saddle to keep him from falling off. By the time they came across an abandoned farm the following afternoon, his brothers were beginning to worry they might lose him. "Well," Cane said, as he looked at the overgrown yard around the house, "this might be the end of it."

"How you figure?" Chimney asked.

"We can't ride no more till he gets better, so if they track us here, we're fucked."

Leaning over the horn of his saddle, Chimney spat and then said, "Well, I don't know who those ol' boys are back there, but I don't figure they can shoot any better than we can."

"Maybe, but there must be fifteen of them in that pack."

"So?" Chimney said. "That many don't even amount to one box of shells."

Cane shook his head and started to climb off his horse. "You're quite the optimist, ain't ye?"

"What's that? One of them words you got out of your dictionary?"

"Means someone who's always lookin' on the bright side of things."

"Well, might as well, the way I figure it," Chimney said. "A man gets to thinkin' he's beat, he just as well hang it up. Besides, they'll be enough of that doom and gloom shit when we're dead."

They loosened Cob from the saddle and eased him down, then packed him to the house, through tall patches of milkweed and broomstraw and past a few blighted stalks of corn growing out of the top of an ancient rubbish pile. Thick vines infested with tiny brown spiders draped across the front of the rotting porch, and Chimney hacked a path to the door with one of the machetes. Kicking it open, he watched a long black snake slither across the rough pine floor in the summer shadows and disappear through a crack in one of the walls, leaving a winding imprint of itself in the soft dust. He spread a blanket near a fireplace made of clay bricks, and they carried Cob inside and laid him down. "I'll take care of the horses," he told Cane. He found a large black pot in the kitchen, covered with a lid and half full of a dried-up lump that had probably once been a soup or perhaps a stew. After banging out the mess on top of a rough pine counter, he carried it back outside. He tethered the animals in the shell of an old lean-to and unsaddled them and began hauling guns and supplies into the house. Then he walked about the property until he discovered a caved-in well, hidden in a thicket of wild roses. Even though it was dark by the time he finished cutting a way to it through the briars, he carried water to the horses in the pot, and by the time he came back inside the house, it was long after midnight. In the light from a candle stub, he watched Cane pour some whiskey into the bullet hole in Cob's leg and then wrap it in a fresh bandage. "How's he doing?" he asked.

"Hard to say," Cane said. "At least the bleeding's stopped for now. That's the main thing." He stood up and took a drink from the whiskey bottle, then passed it to Chimney.

"What about the bullet?"

"It'll have to stay. We start diggin' around for it, we might make things worse."

"Well, I don't reckon it matters much. Hell, Bloody Bill carried fifteen or twenty around inside him, and it didn't hurt him any."

Cane was quiet for a moment, then said, "You do know somebody just made him up, right?" It was a question he'd thought of asking several times over the last couple of weeks, whenever his brother spoke of Bloody Bill as if he were a real person, but he'd kept putting it off, partly because he feared what Chimney's answer might be, and partly because he wasn't sure it made any difference in the long run anyway.

"Course I do," Chimney replied, handing the bottle back. "I'm not that fuckin' stupid. Still don't mean it can't be true. The ol' boy that wrote the book had to get his ideas somewhere." He sat down and leaned his back against the wall, looked over at Cob passed out flat on his back on the floor, breathing loudly through his mouth. "You and me was lucky, wasn't we?"

"What, that we didn't get shot?"

"No," Chimney said, "that we weren't born like him. I mean, hell, even if he lives, he don't have much to look forward to, does he?"

"I don't know," Cane said. "Before the old man died, he was probably the happiest one of us."

"Only thing that proves is how dumb he is."

Cane shook his head and took another drink, then capped the bottle. He debated if he should remind Chimney that the only reason they were in this predicament in the first place was because he'd insisted on stealing a few cans of beans instead of paying for them, but decided that keeping the peace was more important right now. And besides, if Cob lived through the night, tomorrow Chimney would probably be bragging on him for being such a tough bastard. "Well, what about you?" Cane asked. "What is it you look forward to if we get away with this?"

"Me?" Chimney said. "I'm gonna drink and fuck and carry on for ten or fifteen years, then meet me some nice girl and settle down. Maybe have a couple brats."

"Ten or fifteen years?"

"Sure," Chimney said. "Shit, I'm only seventeen."

"Well, that's true."

"How about you?"

Cane hesitated. He was sure his brother wouldn't understand what he looked upon as a life worth having, but what did it matter? Hell, they could all be dead tomorrow, and all of their dreams gone with them. Pulling a cigar from his pocket, he lit it, then said, "I remember one night we was walkin' through this town with Pap. I think it was in Tennessee. I was maybe fifteen, I reckon. Cold, rainy ol' night. We were hungry as hell, been on the move all day. We passed by this big house that was all lit up inside, and I saw a man leaned back in an easy chair with his feet propped up by a fire. And on the wall behind him was more books than I ever imagined there was in the world. Rows of 'em. Then some woman came into the room and—"

"What'd he do then?" Chimney asked. "I bet he fucked her, didn't he?"

"No, it wasn't like that."

"So was she too old or ugly or what?"

"Like I said, it wasn't like that," repeated Cane, regretting now that he'd even mentioned it in the first place.

"What the fuck?" Chimney said. "A bunch of books and some puss walkin' in on ye? That's as crazy as Cob and his heavenly table horseshit. I don't know about you sometimes, brother." He moved over to the empty window frame and peered out at the dark tree line across from the house. "Better go ahead and get ye some sleep. Sounds like you need it. I'll keep the first watch."

Cob came to the next morning, a bit surprised that he wasn't still on his horse. He tried to raise up, but he'd never felt this tired in his life. He saw Cane sitting on a warped and splintered wood floor covered with dust and grit and purplish balls of coon scat, his back leaned against the wall, reading one of the newspapers Chimney had taken from the store. A small pile of feathers from where a bird had been eaten by some animal lay over by the entrance to the other room. "Where are we?" he asked.

Cane looked up. "Some old house we found." He set the paper aside and picked up a canteen.

"So them men quit chasin' us?"

"Maybe," Cane said. "We ain't sure yet." He held the canteen to Cob's lips with one hand and lifted his head with the other.

"Where's Chimney?" Cob asked after he had drunk his fill.

"I'm right here," Chimney said. Swiveling his head to the left, Cob saw his other brother squatted down, looking out the front window. Beside him was the rifle they had stolen from the storekeeper. Other guns had been placed on either side of the door, and a wad of bloody rags was tossed in the corner.

"How long we been here?" Cob said.

"Since last night."

"Boy, when I first woke up, I thought for sure we was back at the shack on the Major's place."

"Yeah," Cane said, glancing around. "I guess it does have the same ambiance."

"*Ambiance?* I've heard that word before, ain't I?"

"Sure you have," Cane said. "Remember that line in the book about Bloody Bill? Talkin' about the sportin' house? 'The elegant, subdued ambiance of the gilded room was—'"

Then Chimney, still staring out the window, cut in and finished the sentence: "'. . . suddenly shattered by the forced entry of a lustful, liquor-soaked Bloody Bill, his side-arms rattling in their tooled-leather holsters and his gold tooth gleaming in the light from the candelabras like the rarest of Satan's jewels.'"

"What the heck does 'gilded' mean?" Cob asked.

"Well, I think it's like 'shiny,'" Cane said. Then he remembered the story he'd come across in the paper. "Hey, listen to this." He commenced to reading aloud about a night watchman in Savannah who claimed that he fired six rounds point-blank into one of the Jewett Gang, the chubby one with the moon head, and watched as the criminal laughed them off as if the bullets weren't any more lethal than mosquito bites or the good-night kisses of some sweet, innocent child.

"Damn, I wish it were so," Cob said, craning his neck to look down at his throbbing leg.

"Jesus Christ, we never been within a hundred miles of there our whole lives," Chimney complained. He walked from his post at the window over to the coffee pot sitting at the edge of the fireplace. Although Cane was usually against risking the smoke of a fire when they had men trailing them, Chimney had let him sleep all night, and he didn't have the heart to tell him no when he said he'd like a cup of coffee. "And where do they get the rest of that bullshit? Skeeter bites. Fuck, look at him. He's lucky that ol' boy back there couldn't shoot worth a damn or we'd probably be a-plantin' him right about now."

After that, they lapsed into silence, listened to the snake slither around inside the walls. Cob dozed off again and Chimney went out to check on the horses. Cane opened the newspaper, and on the third page he found an article about German soldiers roasting young children over a spit for their dinner in some place called Belgium. He shook his head when he finished reading it. At least he and his brothers weren't the only ones being lied about.

28

JASPER CAME INTO the Blind Owl right after Pollard opened up and stood by the door with his hand on the handle. "What the fuck do you want?" the bartender asked. He was wiping out some glasses with a rag he'd blown his nose in a few minutes ago, setting them on a shelf under the bar. Unlike the cook who strives to maintain a semblance of cleanliness in his kitchen for the most part, but occasionally can't resist sticking a dead fly or two in some whiny customer's meal, Pollard didn't discriminate; in one way or another, he passed on a taste of his grossness to each and every one of his patrons.

"It's about your outhouse," Jasper said. "It's runnin' clear over in Mrs. Grady's yard, it's so full."

"Had a couple boys in here last night had the flux," Pollard replied. "They musta filled it up."

"That's what you said last week," said Jasper.

"So?" Pollard said. "I can't help it they came back. What do you want me to do, start turning payin' customers away just cause they got the runs?"

"Well, you got one week to get it cleaned up, or the city's gonna take action."

"What the hell's that supposed to mean?"

"I told ye before, they're gonna start fining ye," Jasper said. "Three dollars a week."

Pollard's fat face turned crimson and he threw the rag down, started to come around the end of the bar. "I'll tell ye what, you little bastard, you turn me in, I'll—"

"Mrs. Grady's already done that," Jasper blurted out. "I'm just deliverin' the message." Then he fled out the door and sprinted a block down the street before he slowed down. He hadn't trusted Pollard since the night a few years back when Itchy brought him to the Blind Owl to buy him his first beer, and then proceeded to get loaded himself, as if it were his birthday and not Jasper's. He'd always felt guilty about leaving the old man there that night, but he could hardly keep his eyes open after finishing off the second mug of First Capital somebody forced upon him; and besides that, within minutes of their arrival, Itchy had started pursuing a gray-haired crone dressed in a long shift sewn together out of a couple of mismatched parlor curtains. The next day, when he didn't show up to help clean Mrs. Fetter's johnny out, Jasper went on the hunt of him. Not finding him at home, he walked down to the bar and asked Pollard if he had any idea where he might have gone.

The barkeep had glanced up briefly from the newspaper he was reading, then turned a page. "I think he left with that ol' hag he was playin' kissy-face with."

"Any idy where she lives?"

"No, but from the looks of her, I'd say she lives under a bridge somewhere. Like one of them trolls. Hell, she might be cookin' him up in a pot right now, though I can't imagine that ol' fucker would be very tasty."

"Well, what time you figure—" Jasper started to ask.

"Jesus Christ, you little shit, I'm not his goddamn babysitter," Pollard yelled. "Now, unless you want a drink, get the fuck out of here and quit botherin' me."

After checking the rest of Itchy's usual haunts, Jasper had gone back and finished the job at Mrs. Fetter's. He didn't have any choice, really; the woman's daughter was getting married over the weekend, and they had promised that the shithouse would be in tip-top shape for the guests. Just by luck, Paint Street was closed off at the paper mill because of a gas leak, and the only way to get through to the dump with Gyp and the honey wagon was to take the alley that ran behind the Blind Owl. And that's how he finally found Itchy, an old tarp slung over him and beaten to a pulp just a few feet from the bar's back door. Jasper had taken him back to his own house, put him to bed in his mother's old room. Doc Hamm did his best to patch him up, but it was touch and go there for a while. For the entire four days he was unconscious, Jasper never left his side except to feed and water Gyp. And then, on the fifth morning, the old man opened his eyes and asked for a drink of water. He never did remember anything about that night, though Jasper was fairly certain he knew what had happened, and it didn't have anything to do with a troll camped out under a bridge.

After the sanitation inspector delivered the warning and ran out the door, Pollard locked up and went to the back room to check on the man he'd had chained to the floor next to his cot for the past four days. He'd pried his nose off with a bottle opener an hour ago; and he sat down on the bed and told him it wouldn't be much longer, that he was going to finish him off with an axe tonight. He went on talking, though he wasn't sure the man was capable of listening anymore. "You make number seven," Pollard said. "A lot of people consider that a lucky number, but I bet they'd change their minds if they saw you right now, wouldn't they?" He lingered awhile longer, eating a can of bully beef while he looked over his work. Then he went back out front, served a few drinks to some winder boys getting primed to start the second shift over at the paper mill.

As far as the man in the back room went, he'd been beyond caring after the second day in the chains. His name was Johansson, and he was a carpenter from Indiana who specialized in fine joinery and loved to square dance, but after tonight, he would just be a pile of dumb pieces. Around three or four in the morning, Pollard would bag up everything he wasn't keeping and carry it over to Paint Creek. Standing on the bank shaking out the bloody burlap sacks and watching the slop float away in the dark water, he would picture some of it making it via the Ohio all the way to Cairo, Illinois, and from there down the Mississippi to the Gulf of Mexico, the soft parts eventually passing through a hundred fish guts, the bones scattered perhaps as far as the cold, deep Atlantic. And for just a few minutes, with the stars ticking in his ears like bombs and the air rubbing against his skin like sandpaper, he would find himself slowly building to an ecstatic orgasm, as if some beautiful angel was reaching down out of the heavens and touching him with a knowing hand in all the right places.

29

THE POSSE FROM Russell, their horses wrung out and the last of their liquor gone and the storekeeper getting on their nerves with his countless retelling of his brazen confrontation with the outlaws, returned to town two days later, half drunk and empty-handed. No sooner had the bleary and disappointed clerk walked into his house than his wife showed him a new poster issued just that morning stating that Kentucky was upping the reward for the Jewett Gang an additional five hundred dollars. "God Almighty," he said, "I better go get the boys rounded back up."

"Now wait a minute, Wilbur," she said. "Why let any of those fools have a share of it? There's only the three of them, and you done winged the one, right?" She grabbed his hands and looked pleadingly into his eyes. "Just think about it, the new life all that money could buy." He stood for a long moment looking past her out the window at his brood of rickety brats playing listlessly around the front stoop. One of them, his namesake no less, was eating dirt again, and he was the healthiest one of the bunch. How would he ever pay Mr. Haskins for his rifle when he couldn't even keep his own family fed? He remembered again what the sonofabitch had said as he strutted out the door: "That's between you and this Mister feller you keep going on about." His wife was right. To share an opportunity like this when he was in such wretched straits would be downright madness. Townsfolk would talk about him for years, about how he went back out on his own to hunt the bandits down that very same afternoon, barely taking the time to swallow some cold hash and trade in his old plug for a fresh one at Jim Flannery's livery, talking gibberish about having an important appointment at some crossroads somewhere.

—

It wasn't long before the Jewetts were on the move again. Hardly believing his luck that he'd found them, the storekeeper had managed to get within a hundred feet of the house before Chimney spied him over the rim of his coffee cup through the porch vines. Now he lay sprawled in the mass of rosebushes around the well, his spectacles still cocked crooked on his face, a .303 bullet from the Lee-Enfield having split his brave but foolish heart into two nearly equal pieces of pulpy muscle. He had toppled into the briars just as a light rain began to fall. Cane and Chimney then circled the perimeter of the property searching for other members of the posse, but all they found was a lone horse covered with sores tied to a tree fifty yards into the woods. The animal had been on its way to the glue factory when the clerk rushed into Flannery's yelling that he needed a new mount. "Not worth keeping," Chimney said, looking the spindly nag over. He pulled off the saddle and bridle and cut it loose. Then they headed back to where the dead man lay. Inside one of his pockets, along with a handful of shells and two dirty hoecakes, they found the updated wanted poster.

Cane kept glancing up to scan the tree line as he read the latest offer. They were now accused of three times as many murders as they had actually committed, and robbing twice as many banks. As if that wasn't bad enough, the torching of an old folks' home in Gainesville, Florida, and the vicious defilement of two virgin sisters with a wooden crucifix outside of Waynesboro, Virginia, had also been added to their list of crimes. He folded the paper and stuck it in his pocket. The rain picked up a little more. "I'd say we better get out of here tonight," he said. "If some damn store clerk can find us, it's hard to tell what's comin' next." Passing Chimney one of the corn cakes, he started to bite into the other one before he realized what he was doing. He slung it to the ground and stepped on it; and for a brief second he was recalling the time that Pearl stomped Chimney's biscuit on the floor, not long before he passed.

"But what about Cob?"

"Don't have no choice," Cane said. "We'll just have to take it slow."

Chimney stuffed the corn cake into his mouth and bent down to pry the Winchester from the clerk's hands. "I think I'll hang on to this."

"Jesus Christ, brother, we already got enough guns to start a goddamn army."

"We might need to before this is over."

"Well, I hope that poor bastard took better care of it than he did his
horse," Cane said.

"I doubt it," Chimney said. "You'd have to be an idiot to try what
he did."

"Aw, you can't blame him," Cane said, just as a loud clap of thunder
shook the air and the rain turned into a steady downpour. "Fifty-five
hundred dollars, that much money would fuck any man's head up."

Thirty minutes later, as they started away from the farmhouse in the
gray storm light, Cob looked down with feverish eyes from his horse
at the storekeeper's wet corpse caught in the briars, his face turned
up at the sky, and his open mouth overflowing with rainwater like some
obscene fountain. "It's funny," he muttered.

"What's that?" Cane asked.

"I was just a-thinkin' that one of the very last things I said to that
man 'fore he shot me was I hoped we got some rain. And now look at
him."

30

FROM TIME TO time during that period, Jasper saw a couple of the men who sat on the city council stop by the Whore Barn, men who were always casting complaints about him shutting down this or that well or shithouse like he was some sort of despot lording it over the citizenry, when all he was trying to do was the job he'd been assigned. He had met up with the worst one of them just yesterday, Sandy Saunders. Dressed in a tailored blue serge suit and swinging a new cane, the insurance salesman started to pass by silently, with a look of disdain bordering on revulsion, as if the sanitation inspector were nothing but a maggot or a bit of offal stuck to the bottom of one of his custom-made shoes. However, when Jasper stopped in the middle of the sidewalk three or four feet in front of him and grinned, Saunders couldn't resist a smart remark. "What say, shit scooper?" He tapped his cane on the sidewalk, then struck a rakish pose as he saw a couple of young ladies approaching.

"I wouldn't call me that no more if I was you," Jasper replied, the smile plastered on his face growing even wider.

"Oh," Saunders said with a laugh, "and why not, you little turd?"

Moving closer, Jasper waited until the women walked on by, then said, "Because I saw you over at the Whore Barn the other night. Sucking on the toes of the fat one got the grease dabbed all over her face. And you a-courtin' that nice daughter of Mr. Chapman's and blowin' off to everyone about how you're gonna run for mayor next fall. That's why, Sandy. From now on, you either start calling me Mr. Cone, or I'll tell the whole goddamn town about ye."

For at least a minute, Saunders stood speechless, staring open-mouthed at the inspector. His face turned a ghostly white, then a bright red, and finally a deep angry purple. "You're . . . you're crazy," he finally managed to sputter.

Jasper winked and started to move on. "I might be," he said over his shoulder, "but at least I'm not payin' money to lick a whore's dirty feet."

Even though he had finally turned the tables on Saunders, his most vocal critic and one of the snootiest pricks to ever come out of Ross County, Jasper was still rattled by the encounter. Because it was the only thing that soothed him when he became upset, he hurried home right after work and took his buffalo gun out of the closet in his bedroom, where he kept it wrapped in an old quilt. Sitting down on the bed in front of a tall mirror, he wiped the long, heavy rifle down with a rag dampened with Hoppe's Solvent. He began talking to himself as he did so, glancing in the mirror from time to time, pretending that someone was seated across from him listening. "So this Jasper feller," he said to his reflection, "he decided his town had been dirty long enough and it was time to clean it up, and the first thing he did was go over to Sandy Saunders's office on Paint Street and, BOOM, he shot the dirty snake's head off with a buffalo gun his daddy bought at an auction one time up in Frankfort, and, by God, you should have seen the look on the sonofabitch's face right before ol' Jasper pulled the trigger, and his brains splattered like red mud against the wall. And then he walked over to the jail and killed both those Wallingford boys and their old man just because they'd let everything go to hell, and then he blasted a hole the size of a . . ." He talked on and on like this for quite a while, assassinating various city leaders and other higher-ups, ridding the town of filth and corruption once and for all. He was being hailed a hero when he realized he was at it again, losing himself in a fantasy that he kept wishing he had the courage to carry out. Though he did so with regret, he stopped abruptly in the middle of a speech being given by some big-breasted matron in which she was extolling his high morals and princely virtues. She was standing on a stage in the newly renamed Cone Park. Draped behind her was a banner that had the image of a buffalo gun sewn on it, and in the front row sat his father, alive and well and hardly aged at all.

After sitting for a few minutes staring at his now silent image in the mirror, he wrapped the gun in the blanket and stuck it back in the closet. Then he dropped his pants, undid his truss. A thin shaft of yellow sunlight swirling with dust motes shone through a crack in the curtains. Taking out his cock, the bane of his existence and his cross to carry for as long as he walked the earth, he wrapped both hands around it and whipped it against the side of the oak dresser until he wept. He finally quit beating it and took a bloody leak in a bucket sitting in the corner and bunched it back up in his pants. Exhausted by his efforts, he went downstairs and drank a glass of water, then curled up on his mother's couch and went to sleep with all her old plaster saints watching over him with sadness and understanding and compassion, as saints are wont to do.

31

TWO DAYS AFTER killing the store clerk from Russell, the brothers came to a high granite bluff overlooking a wide river. A mile or so to the west, they could just make out, in the early morning fog, a train crossing over the water on a covered bridge; and to the east, they watched a coal-fired barge come around a curve, pulling a load of raw lumber. They had been riding hard all night. To Chimney's dismay, most of the arsenal they had collected had to be dumped in a pond after the packhorse split a hoof and couldn't keep up. A group of men, a dozen or more in number, had been gaining on them steadily. Yesterday evening Cane had caught a whiff of their cook fire as they came up out of a steep, rocky ravine they had hidden in all day. While he pushed forward with a weak and feverish Cob, Chimney had slipped up close to their camp and listened to them as they ate and drunkenly bragged about what they would do with the criminals after they killed them. From what he could gather, a bearded man that the others called Captain was the leader. Sitting on a campstool, he wore an old blue coat with tarnished braids on the shoulders, and a tall hat decorated with shiny bits of foil and a plume of peacock feathers. "As long as we got their heads as proof for the bounty, I don't give a good goddamn what you do," he heard him say. "Fuck 'em in the ass for all I care."

"By God, Cap, that's a grand idea," another man said. "Many women as they've raped, them sonsofbitches deserve a good cornholing."

"But do we cut their heads off *before* we fuck 'em, or *after* we fuck 'em?" someone else asked.

"Well," Captain said, as he rooted loose a piece of meat stuck between his teeth with a finger, "the way I see it, if'n you want them to squirm around a bit and not just lay there like some ol' cold housewife, then ye'd best keep 'em alive until after you've had your fill."

As Chimney listened to several others voice their opinions about the pros and cons of live fucks versus dead ones, he settled a bead on Captain's head with the Enfield. He wondered how much cornholing they'd be up for if he blew the old boy's gummy brains all over their hot vittles. His heart started beating faster, and he felt his finger slowly begin to squeeze the trigger, but then he recalled Cane saying, "Whatever you do, don't start nothing. The shape Cob's in, we'd never be able to outrun 'em." Letting out a sigh, he turned away and sneaked back to his horse. It had taken him half the night to find them in the dark.

"So that's the Ohio?" Chimney asked.

"Far as I can figure, it is," Cane said.

"Jesus, I never thought it'd be that big."

"Looks like the bridge is the only way across."

"Well, let's get to it then," Chimney said. "If they didn't get too drunk last night, those bastards probably ain't more than an hour or so behind us."

Cane shook his head. "No, we'll have to wait till the sun goes down. We get caught in the middle of that thing in the daylight it'd be a goddamn turkey shoot." He looked around at the thin trees and patchy grass growing out of the rocky soil. "At least here we got the high ground."

"But there's nowhere to run if they find us," Chimney argued. "Unless we do what Bloody Bill did, and I'll say right now I'd just as soon shoot it out."

Looking over the edge of the steep bluff, at least two hundred feet above the river, Cane thought about how Bill Bucket, with a small army closing in on him from three sides, had chosen to leap to his death with his horse off a high cliff in some windblown New Mexico desert. "A modern-day Icarus" was the way Charles Winthrop III described him in that last flowery paragraph, "harried and hemmed in on all sides by a cruel and unjust world, making a final glorious attempt to break free of all his earthly bonds." Though they didn't have any notion as to who this Icarus feller was, they had speculated he was probably some robber who had come to a bad end in some bygone time. Cane rubbed the back of his neck, glanced over at Cob. "What do ye think, brother? Can ye go a little farther?"

Cob was slumped over in his saddle, a thin string of drool hanging from his bottom lip. His skin was pale and greasy with sweat. When he heard Cane speaking to him, he straightened up a little and opened his dull eyes. "Remember them peaches the old man had hid?" he said.

"What about them?"

"I got one a-growin' inside me. I can feel it."

"No, buddy, you just got a fever," Cane said.

"I wish I'd never ate them damn things. They was rotten and now I'm a-rotten, too."

"Maybe you got one of them worms in ye like mama had," Chimney joked.

"Jesus Christ, shut up," Cane said. "He don't need to hear that shit."

"And why does he keep followin' me?" Cob said. He turned his head as if he were looking at something behind them.

"Who?"

"Tardweller. No matter what I give him, he won't go away."

"Well, that settles it," Cane said. "We stay here for now."

They laid Cob on his blanket under a gnarled crabapple tree, hobbled the horses in the grassiest spots they could find. Then Chimney climbed with the Enfield twenty feet or so into a tall spruce at the southern edge of the promontory and propped himself between two thick branches. He reached in his back pocket for a strand of licorice and leaned back against the sticky trunk to keep an eye out for the band of sodomites that were on their heels.

Cane was searching through the saddlebags, trying to figure out if they had any food left, when he realized with a start that *The Life and Times of Bloody Bill Bucket* was missing. He thought for a minute, recalled that the last place he had seen it was back at the farmhouse where they had hid out from the Russell posse. Evidently, in the rush to get away after Chimney killed the clerk, he must have forgotten it. "Bloody Bill," he said to himself. How many times, he wondered, had he read that book to his brothers? He had lost track, but it had to be fifteen, maybe twenty. Though he had always known it was just an outlandish tale written by someone (and maybe Charles Foster Winthrop III wasn't even his real name) who probably didn't know any more about killing people and robbing banks than an old maid who'd spent all her life hidden away in a bedroom of her father's house, it had still given them hope when there was none, something to aim for that was bigger than the life they'd been handed, even if it was crazy to think they'd ever get away with it. And where would they be right now if they'd never found it that day in that moldy-ass carpetbag? Or, for that matter, if he hadn't been able to read. Still be poor as dirt, doing Tardweller's bidding and trying to stretch another meal or two out of a sick hog.

Up until now, he reckoned that the only period in his life when he had truly felt like he was worth something was when his mother was teaching him his letters. She used to brag on the easy way that he picked up words, said that someday he would be a schoolteacher. After she died, he used to put himself to sleep at night thinking about those hours they spent together at the kitchen table, but after four or five years of wandering around half-starved with Pearl, they started to fade away, just like her face did. He glanced into the saddlebag they carried the money in, then cinched it closed. After the way that they had lived, he couldn't hold it against Chimney for simply wanting good times and women, but he desired something more for Cob and himself. Nothing fancy, just a decent life. A sturdy house with polished floors and a good woman and clean clothes and books on a shelf. Like he'd seen that rainy night in Tennessee.

He raised his head and saw two young boys fishing on the other side of the river, the leaves on the trees behind them already turning, vivid splashes of orange and red and yellow. A flock of starlings swooped down along the water, then rose up and scattered in different directions across the blue sky. He leaned against his horse and closed his eyes, and though he knew it was way too much to expect after all the awful things they had done, he asked God in a whisper to help them get to Canada. And in return, he vowed, he would try to live right the rest of his time on earth. Then he went over and sat beside Cob. In the shade, the air had a slight chill to it. He yawned and cocked his pistol, laid it on the ground beside him.

The sun was setting when Chimney shook him awake. "Come on, we better get to it."

Though the fever had subsided, Cob was still weak as a cat. What they needed, Cane thought, was to find somewhere to put up for a few days and rest once they got across the river. As Chimney gathered up the guns and got the horses ready, he poured more whiskey on Cob's wound, then tied a clean rag around it. "So is that Canada over yonder?" Cob asked.

"No, that's Ohio," Cane replied, handing him the canteen. "But we're gettin' close."

Before they left, they split the last of some jerky and a chocolate bar. As they mounted their horses, Cane remembered looking through the saddlebags earlier. "I think I lost Bloody Bill's book," he said.

"What?" Cob asked.

"I can't find it, and the last time I recall seeing it was back there at that farmhouse. I must've forgot to pack it."

For a moment, Chimney looked disappointed, even a little sad, as if he'd just found out he'd lost a good friend, but then he spat and said, "Aw, we can probably find us another one. I imagine they sell 'em all over the place. Besides, we can damn near recite every word in it anyway."

"It don't matter to me," Cob said. "The way I look at it, that thing's been nothin' but trouble."

They made their way down off the bluff in the dark and traveled west along a gravelly path to the covered bridge. The sky was the color of a crow, and they could hear the water lapping against the girders. There was just a narrow, planked walkway between the two sets of rails, barely wide enough for a man. They stood at the mouth of the tunnel and peered in, but a thick mist made it impossible to see anything. "Let's just hope we don't meet anything in there," Chimney said.

"Like what?" Cob asked.

"Oh, I don't know," Chimney answered. "Could be any number of things. Maybe a train, or a pack of wild dogs, or those ass-fuckin' bounty hunters, or a—"

"Come on," Cane said, "let's just get it over with." Then he nudged his horse lightly and disappeared into the tunnel, his brothers following close behind, the hooves of their animals ringing hollowly on the wooden floor high above the water.

And so, on September 28, 1917, the notorious Jewett Gang entered the state of Ohio at approximately one o'clock in the morning. Just a few hundred yards on the other side of the bridge was a small hamlet known as Sciotoville. They entered it warily, with guns drawn, though not even a single dog was awake to greet them. The only sound to be heard was the creaking of a metal sign hanging in front of the general store, slightly swinging in the dank, fishy-smelling breeze coming off the river. It didn't take them more than five minutes to cross the entire town. As they headed out, they stopped and watched a northbound freight pour out of the tunnel at forty miles an hour, the headlights of the engine looking like yellow smudges in the fog. They were only a couple of yards down the gravel bank from the rails, and, as the train rolled past, the earth began trembling under the horses' hooves. The animals skirted and thrashed their tails nervously, their heads thrown back and their startled eyes bulging in their sockets. Cane saw his brothers mouth some words, but the loud, thumping clatter of the steel wheels drowned them out. They waited until the last of the swaying boxcars blew past them, and then they proceeded on.

32

AGAINST HIS BETTER judgment, Bovard had taken a taxi into town that night and had the driver drop him off in front of the Majestic. Soft and slothful Lucas Charles was the complete opposite of everything the lieutenant respected in this world, but, as so many men throughout the centuries have discovered, a contrary nature often proves the most irresistible. He promised himself, however, that this would be the last time. He was too close to fulfilling his dream—with Pershing now in Chaumont, there were rumors that they might finally be shipping out within the next few weeks—to ruin everything with a sordid scandal. So, one last dalliance and that would be the end of it. He bought a ticket at the booth and endured an utterly stupid performance by some inept vaudevillians who brought out a monkey every time they began to lose the audience. He felt sorry for the poor animal. It was obvious from the way he attacked a stagehand that captivity had driven him insane. As soon as the show was over, Bovard rushed over to the Candlelight and downed two brandies to rid himself of that brainless song the performers kept singing, something about life being as sweet as a cherry pie. When he returned to the theater, he found the crowd gone and the theater manager standing in front of the closed double doors smoking a cigarette. "I wasn't sure you were coming back," Lucas said.

"After that atrocious spectacle, neither was I."

Lucas laughed, then said, "Well, I'm sorry you didn't enjoy it. Would you like a refund?"

"It's hard to believe they get paid for that."

"The Lewis Family is actually quite popular. Didn't you notice? There wasn't an empty seat in the house."

"Yes, but—"

"Look at it this way. Did you think about your problems while you were watching them—that is, if someone like you has any? About the war, say? If not, then they did their job. Sure, those poor bastards can't sing or dance their way out of a paper bag, but being so goddamn awful is part of their appeal."

"But when an ape is the most talented one of the bunch, then—"

"Mr. Bentley is a chimpanzee," Lucas said curtly. "Not an ape." Although he knew that the five brothers who made up the Lewis Family were a stupid, vulgar bunch—and, Lord knows, they were almost impossible to deal with at times—criticism of any of the acts he brought to the Majestic always rubbed him the wrong way. For sure, he'd rather be booking someone with class, say, one of the famed Barrymores or the juggler W. C. Fields, but he did his best with what he'd been handed. He flipped his cigarette out into the street where it landed in a pile of fresh manure. "Come on, let's go upstairs and have a drink."

As soon as he locked the door to the room, Lucas began shedding his clothes. "Hold up," Bovard said. "Let's not get in a hurry."

"Don't worry," Lucas replied with a smirk, "I'm not going to defile you. I just need to get this goddamn suit off." He reached for a silk kimono hanging on a hook. Then he poured some Kentucky Tavern into two dirty glasses, and handed one to the lieutenant. It had a bit of dry lipstick on the rim. Probably Caldwell's, Bovard figured. The druggist had found a tube of red in the nightstand drawer the other night, had it smeared all over himself by the time they tied him to the chair. "Cheers," Lucas said, as he sank back on the bed.

Bovard sat down on the chair and took a drink. He was beginning to regret his decision to come here tonight. He looked about the room, the wrinkled sheet stained and crusty, the smashed crackers scattered on the rug, the leather whip curled up like a viper in the corner. The smell of a slow, relentless decay hung in the stale air, and he found himself breathing through his mouth as lightly as possible. Silence filled the room and he nervously took another sip. Bovard wondered, for the first time, how Lucas had ended up here in this tomb. He recalled something an uncle had once told him: "Vincent, whenever you find yourself in a situation with nothing to say, just remember that most people love to talk about themselves. A condemned man could probably forestall his execution by fifteen precious minutes just by asking the hangman where he hailed from." And the truth was, he realized, he actually was curious about how Lucas had become overseer to an endless parade of debauched thespians, shameless comedians, and mediocre songbirds hoping for a big break. "Why don't you tell me something about yourself?" he finally said.

The theater manager arched an eyebrow at the lieutenant, then looked into his glass, twirled the amber liquid around. "Sounds like we're getting serious."

"No, I just wonder how you came to be working here."

"You mean at the Majestic?" Lucas said.

"Yes," Bovard said.

Lucas rose up and poured himself another drink. "Well, I grew up in Meade," he began. His family had been well off, the bulk of the money coming from a brewery and a canning factory that his grandfather had built from scratch. He'd always felt that he was a little different from other boys, but he didn't realize why until he went skinny-dipping one summer afternoon when he was thirteen with a couple of older cousins. Their nakedness aroused him so much that he cramped up and nearly drowned in three feet of water. Lucky for him, they'd thought his erection was caused by a story one of them told about seeing a neighbor's housekeeper through the fence one night in the backyard, sitting astraddle a drummer who'd been canvassing their street that day selling magazine subscriptions, pumping up and down on him like a piston while the moon shined on her round, white ass.

"That's quite a detailed description for something you heard so long ago," Bovard said.

"Well," Lucas replied, "it *was* a memorable day." Anyway, not knowing what else to do, he'd tried to fit in, even dated a couple of girls from the better families in high school, but it was hopeless. All he could think about whenever he was with them was their brothers. Sometimes the only thing that kept him from killing himself was knowing that someday he'd be leaving, taking his secret with him. "It was the best thing that ever happened to me," Lucas said, "going off to William and Mary." On campus, he quickly became acquainted with a shadowy group of his own kind. They were so secretive and paranoid that they didn't even acknowledge each other's presence in public, but by the end of his first semester, he'd been to bed with all of them, even a fat one with a clubfoot and an addiction to sweets who lost his mind over the winter break and ended up entering a Trappist monastery in Kentucky. And then, one evening in the library, he happened across a reproduction of Géricault's *The Raft of the Medusa* and decided he wanted to be an artist. He dropped out of school the next fall, spent the next several years wandering around Europe, supposedly searching for inspiration. "Of course," he told Bovard, "that didn't make my old man happy, but he went ahead and paid for everything anyway. I think by that time he had things figured out, and was just relieved he didn't have to look at me anymore."

He stopped for a moment and put out his cigarette in an ashtray, then settled back on the bed again. "I was getting ready to board a train for Berlin with an Italian boy I'd fallen in love with, a street cleaner, of all things," he said wistfully, "when I got a telegram that he was dying." But by the time he arrived back in Ohio, his father was already in the ground, and Lucas soon discovered that the old patriarch, as sensible and prudent a man as ever lived, had lost almost everything investing in a rubber plantation in Bolivia that, as it turned out, existed only on a sheet of worthless paper. That was over eight years ago.

"He didn't check it out first?" Bovard said.

"Well, he had lost most of his marbles by that time," Lucas explained. "Old-timer's or thick blood or whatever."

"That must have been quite a blow."

"Oh, it was, but looking back on it now, I suppose it could have been worse. I missed Giuseppe for a while, but I was lucky that the theater job opened up. I'll be the first to confess that I have no skills whatso-ever. By the time the taxes were settled and the funeral paid for, Mother didn't have anything left but the house and some jewelry."

They sat there for a while without speaking, and then, through the open window, Bovard heard some men passing by in the alley below. They were talking loudly and he thought he heard Wesley Franks's voice among them. He stepped over and pushed the dirty curtain back just enough to peek out, but they had already disappeared around the corner.

"Something wrong?" Lucas asked.

"No, I just thought I heard a familiar voice. One of my men."

Lucas smiled and pulled open the drawer on the nightstand. He withdrew the small brown bottle the pharmacist had brought over the other night. "Some of this will help you forget all about him," he said. "At least for tonight."

The lieutenant hesitated. He was already a little drunk. "Not too much," he said. "I damn near missed reveille the other morning."

Lucas spilled a little into both their glasses and they drank. Then he stretched out on the narrow bed and lit another cigarette. Taking a drag, he patted the empty place beside him, and Bovard thought of the ugly slattern in the hotel room in Columbus. She had done exactly the same thing. Lucas blew smoke rings at the ceiling while he watched the lieutenant fumble with the buttons of his uniform. After dropping his pants, Bovard happened to glance over at the dead actor's face on the wall, and was suddenly stricken by his merry, eternal gaze. Evidently, the old boy was still having a ball when he had posed for the poster. Bovard stared back at him for a long moment, vaguely wondering if he had been up to this room, too, then stepped unsteadily to the edge of the smelly mattress. Time seemed to slow down, and he thought of Odysseus's men, drugged by the lotus-eaters. Perhaps, he thought dreamily, if he survived the war by some quirk of fate, he and Wesley could settle down on an island somewhere in the Aegean Sea. They could become simple farmers or fishermen, live in a stone house filled with golden sunlight. He heard Lucas sigh, felt a hand come to rest on his leg. His mouth felt dry, and the last thing he remembered was wetting his lips with his tongue.

In the middle of the night, he awoke feeling as if he had been wrapped in gauze, his head as dull as a wedge of cheese. Lucas had rolled off the bed and lay passed out on the floor. He dressed hurriedly, and then, after taking one last glance around the shabby room, made his way down the dark stairs. He found a cab parked at the corner of Paint and Second, and had the driver let him out a block from the foggy camp entrance. As he sneaked past the three sleeping guards, that stupid song comparing life to a fucking pie started up in his head again, but now it didn't sound quite so bad. In fact, he was humming it softly to himself a few minutes later when he tripped over a boot that some bastard had left in the aisle of the barracks and damn near broke his neck.

33

AT THE EDGE of a sandbar along the Scioto River, Eddie Fiddler was sitting cross-legged on a blanket he had stolen off a clothesline in Waverly, staring at the black water streaming by a few feet away. Johnny was lying beside him, humming in his sleep. The boy was debating once again about whether or not to take off before the old fucker got them in big trouble, or somebody from back home saw him making a fool out of himself. Thanks to Johnny, half the people in Meade had already witnessed that. After the man at the Whore Barn demolished the banjo, Johnny had stayed shit-faced for several days, woefully claiming that his music career was over with, but as soon as they ran out of liquor, he began to panic. "I'll be goddamned," he said, drawing on all of his inner strength, "if I'm gonna let some two-bit goon destroy everything I've worked for!" Within a couple of hours, he'd come up with a new routine. Now Eddie danced and beat on a tin can with a spoon while the old man blew the harp and sang songs. It was humiliating—they sounded even worse than before—but somehow they got by. Shopkeepers got in the habit of tossing them a nickel just to get them to move on down the street; groups of soldiers looking for a good laugh were sometimes worth a quarter or more, especially if they were drunk themselves; once they were even offered two dollars to perform in a saloon, only to find out too late that the owner had provided all of his customers with rotten eggs to throw at them. Eventually, though, the police ran them out of town, and they had headed south to Waverly.

Eddie straightened out his legs and leaned back on his elbows as he recalled how he had ended up in such sorry straits. It all started the day he killed his mother's cat and his father had made him return *Tom Jones* to that little sex maniac Corky Routt. It was all his fault, Eddie figured; well, at least to an extent. After taking the book back and complaining that he hadn't been able to find even one dirty thing in it, Corky had told him to forget about that baby shit, that he had something a thousand times better than that now. "What do ye mean?" Eddie had asked. "Those Nesser girls over in Slab Holler," Corky replied. "They'll fuck a man silly if he brings their pappy something to drink." And so he had spent the next two weeks thinking about what that would feel like. Finally, he couldn't stand it any longer, and he'd waited one night until his parents went to bed, then slipped off with two jars of Ellsworth's wine. As long as he was back home before sunup, he assured himself, nobody would be the wiser. He was trying to get his nerve up to knock on the Nessers' door when out of the woods came an old man carrying a banjo over his shoulder and singing "The Ol' Black Cat Shit in the Shavings." He was short and rail-thin with an egg-shaped goiter sticking out of the side of his neck and a head of wild gray hair badly in need of a trim.

"What ye got there?" the man had asked when he saw him standing in the shadows near a pile of firewood a few feet beyond the porch. Thinking that he was the girls' daddy, Eddie had passed him the jar of wine. He watched the man drain it in two long gulps, then smack his lips and reach into his back pocket for a pint of blended whiskey. He uncorked the bottle, then stuck out his hand and said, "My name's Johnny. What they call you?"

"Eddie Fiddler."

"I reckon you lookin' for some woolly jaw, ain't ye?"

"Well, I . . . I . . ." Eddie stuttered.

"Don't worry," Johnny said. "I'm good buddies with the old man. I'll get ye fixed up."

"Oh," the boy said. "So you ain't their pap?"

"What! Hell, no. If'n them little bitches was mine, I'd have done killed them all. I don't see how ol' Harold stands it, some of the shit they pull." He took a sip from the bottle, then handed it to Eddie. "Which one ye want?" he asked.

"I don't know," Eddie said. "I ain't never been here before." Then he tipped the bottle up and had his first taste of whiskey.

"Well, if it was me, I'd take the one they call Spit Job. She's still got a tight one, or at least she did the last time I came through here."

"Where you from?" the boy asked, passing the bottle back.

"Nowhere special," Johnny said. "Here and there. I'm on my way to Meade to see that army camp, but figured I'd stop by here first and get my dick wet."

"You going to join up?"

Johnny laughed. "Shit, do I look like a fuckin' soldier? But I am a-thinkin' there might be some money to be made there."

"How's that?"

"Playin' music," Johnny said. "All's I got to do now is find me a partner."

Within an hour, Eddie had fucked Spit Job behind the woodpile and was headed for Meade with Johnny. They passed within a mile of his house, but the whiskey made the whole world glow that night with wondrous possibilities, and he couldn't bear the thought of it ending so soon. He told himself instead that a day or two wouldn't matter, but then it seemed like every time he was ready to go back home they somehow got hold of another jug and he was off to the races again. Then Spit Job had hitched a ride into Waverley last week, acting as if she wanted to be with him, and that made it harder than ever to leave.

Tonight, though, everything seemed hopeless. They'd spent the entire evening singing and dancing, and hadn't even made enough coin to buy a pint of the cheapest stuff. Then Spit Job had ridden off with a couple of rough-looking farmhands, three-hundred-pounders with hands nearly the size of his head, and he and Johnny had finally given up and walked down to the river. It was an awful feeling, being sober and imagining what those two bulls were doing to her in the bed of their truck. Johnny had warned him about her, but Eddie truly thought that all she needed was someone to pay some attention to her, who wasn't talking filth to her all the time and only trying to get in her pants. The hell with her, he thought, and with Johnny, too. Even if he had to walk all the way, he could be home in a day. Of course, his parents would both be pissed, especially his mother, and there would be a lot of bitching and questioning the first few days, but eventually they'd get over it. Nothing they could dish out, he figured, would be any worse than this.

He was just getting ready to take his leave when a rusty clattering Ford came bouncing down the lane and stopped close to the sandbar, maybe thirty feet from where they were lying. When the driver shut the engine off, Eddie reached over and shook Johnny awake, pointed at the vehicle visible in the moonlight. They listened for a minute to a man and woman talking loudly in drunken voices. Then the doors swung open and the pair emerged from the car unsteadily and climbed into the backseat. "That dirty dog," Johnny said. "He gonna get him some."

The man's name was June Easter. He was a former butcher who had cut the pinkie finger off his left hand while trimming out some chops, and had subsequently lost his nerve for the knife and become a baloney salesman. Now he just went around the countryside peddling other men's meat in a frayed, fat-smeared suit that, on a hot day, smelled faintly like a corpse. He lived out of his car most of the time, and knew a hundred different spots where he could park for the night. Usually, if business had been good that day, he'd pick up some broken-down bar floozy to spend the night with; and tonight it was a redhead with a beer belly whose name escaped him, though he was fairly sure he'd fucked her a time or two before. After he got her naked and stretched out in the backseat, he pushed his pants down and started ramming her like he was trying to bust something loose inside. Eddie and Johnny listened to them go at it for several minutes, the woman's head banging against the door and the man huffing and puffing like an old steam engine. Then suddenly, the seat stopped squeaking and one of them let out a groan and everything turned quiet.

After a few minutes, Johnny slipped up to the car cautiously. Looking in on them, he saw the baloney salesman lying on top of the woman with his pants gathered down around his ankles. They were both passed out. He reached inside and moved his hand around until he found the wallet in the man's back pocket, and then discovered a nearly full fifth of gin and half a roll of some sort of lunchmeat in the front of the car. He and Eddie took off up the rutted road and went a mile or so before they stopped and looked through the billfold. There was nearly twenty dollars inside, enough to keep them drunk for a week. They spread their blanket under a tree and drank the gin and gorged on the meat and carried on until dawn. When they came to that afternoon, they walked back to Waverly to buy another jug and see if Spit Job was ready to do some more dancing.

34

As the Jewett Gang slept along the weedy bank of a dried-up stream near Otway, Ohio, a geologist named Arthur Vaughn, originally from New Haven, Connecticut, and now working as a surveyor for a Pennsylvania mining company that was buying up tracts of land all over Kentucky, came across what appeared to be just another deserted homestead, the third in less than a week. For Arthur, each of these places had its own particular sadness—and this one was no exception, as he looked to the right and saw the weather-beaten remains of a little girl's cob doll protruding from a waste heap—but they also shared a common loneliness, more akin to a long-forgotten graveyard than a spot where people had once lived and worked and loved. However, as he led his pack mule up closer to the house, he realized from the look of the slashed vines around the tumbledown porch that someone else had been here recently. Perhaps this place wasn't abandoned after all. "Hello," he called out several times, but got no response. He shaded his eyes with his felt hat and peered through the open doorway. He could see a book lying on the floor near the fireplace. Arthur had brought a copy of *Huckleberry Finn* with him when he started this assignment, but he had finished it over a week ago and was starving for something new to read. He studied the stomped path through the weeds leading away from the porch to a crude shed. "Hello," he yelled again. "Anybody home?" He waited a minute, then tied the mule to a termite-riddled post and stepped cautiously inside the house.

When he turned the book over and saw the title, he said, under his breath, "You've got to be kidding me." Then he let out a little laugh. It was one of those trashy dime novels that he and his brother, William, bedridden with the tuberculosis that would eventually kill him, used to read on the sly when they were young. In fact, of all the books that Arthur had sneaked into the sickroom, this had been his brother's favorite. He swatted the book against his leg, then stood in the middle of the hot room contemplating what remained of the tasteless artwork on the torn and faded cover. A sinister-looking desperado draped in a poncho stood defiantly in the middle of a desert, pointing two pistols the size of cannons at some shadowy figures approaching on horseback in the distance. *"The Life and Times of Bloody Bill Bucket,"* Arthur said aloud, trying to imitate the overly dramatic voice his brother had some-times used jokingly when it was his turn to read. "By Charles Foster Winthrop the Third." Because the doctors had warned their parents that William should avoid all manner of excitement, they had to keep the book hidden behind a loose piece of molding in the closet. And when his brother finally choked to death on his own blood, Arthur had managed to slip it into his coffin without anybody knowing.

He leafed through it, skimmed a few vaguely remembered para-graphs. It was obvious from the smudged fingerprints and dog-eared pages that it had been pored over a number of times. Looking about the room, he saw a couple of bloody dressings tossed in the corner, some empty bean cans in the fireplace, three different sets of boot tracks in the dust. Jesus, he thought, what the hell had went on here? And how did this book, this moldy, crumbling relic from his own familial past, ever end up in an abandoned hovel in the backwoods of Kentucky? For some reason, he suddenly recalled a conversation he'd had with his father last year when he was home for a visit. "Mark my word, Arthur," the old man had told him, "before long there won't be a spot on the globe that hasn't been infected with this *progress* they keep on about."

"But what's wrong with that?" Arthur had said. It was a bright but chilly day right after Thanksgiving. They were sitting in the library and he was staring at his brother's portrait hanging on the wall. By then, William had been dead ten years. Arthur took a sip of the warm wine the maid had brought in and reminded himself to visit the grave before he left the city.

"Because, son," his father had said, lifting his beloved copy of Plato—the leather cover cracked from age and the spine broken from a thousand hours of examination—from the table by his chair, and way-ing it about like a call to arms, "in another hundred years, everything we deem worthwhile, over three thousand years of thought and tradition and learning, won't be considered any more important than what some tribe of dark-skinned savages has to say about a spirit they believe lives in a damn seashell. Don't you see? Everything will be looked upon as equal when really it's not."

Arthur had known well enough not to argue. The old man had practiced law for forty years and had never lost a case, as far as his son knew. Still, the future was coming, whether people liked it or not. Granted, the state of Kentucky certainly wasn't some South Sea island filled with savages cut off from the rest of the world, but this house felt just as isolated and backward as he imagined a place could be, which was maybe why finding this particular book here was such a surprise. Taking one last look around, he wondered again about the cast-off bandages. Then he shoved the book in his pocket and stepped outside.

He was headed into the woods when he noticed sunlight glinting off something in a briar patch on the other side of the house. Dropping the mule's lead, he held his arms aloft and made his way through the tall weeds toward it. As he got closer, he began to smell the rot, could hear the flies buzzing. He covered his nose and mouth with a handkerchief, then pushed forward a few more feet. To his horror, he saw two large crows pecking away in short bursts at a man's upturned face. Arthur lurched back, then stopped himself. What had initially caught his attention was a pair of spectacles hanging from one of the man's ears and shining in the bright light. His swollen limbs had turned a bluish-green color and were about to burst through the seams of his ragged clothes. A clot of maggots boiled forth from a hole in his chest and dripped like raindrops into a muddy well of water right below him. Pulling a .32-caliber Iver Johnson pistol from his pocket that he used to kill snakes with, Arthur cast another look around the perimeter of the property before firing a shot into the air to scare the birds away.

His heart pounding, he watched them flap through the air and land on the roof of the house. Then he turned and stumbled to the mule, waving the gun about wildly. Grabbing the rope, he began tugging and cursing the goddamn dumb beast to get moving, his only thought to flee from this haunted, godforsaken place as fast as possible. And though the crows were already sated, they waited patiently until the intruder disappeared into the trees, then flew back to the briar patch to tear away some more of the softer parts the clerk had left to offer.

35

ON HIS WAY to lunch in the officers' mess, Bovard came around the corner of a building lost in thought and almost tripped over Wesley Franks seated on the ground reading a letter. The lieutenant had learned yesterday that Dr. Lattimore, his adviser at Kenyon, had dropped over dead from an aneurysm a couple of weeks ago, and he'd just realized this morning that the many times the man had brushed up against him when they were alone together in his office were not as "accidental" as he'd claimed. He couldn't believe how naive he'd been. Clearly, the old classicist had wanted to fuck him. Had it been so apparent that he was homosexual? Even before he knew himself? "Pardon me, Private," Bovard said, as Wesley dropped the pages and scrambled to stand up and salute.

"My fault, sir," the private said.

"A letter from home?"

The boy stared straight ahead. "Yes, sir."

Bovard let his eyes wander for a moment over the slim body. Though it didn't make a big difference in the way he imagined he and Wesley might die together, it was nice to know that at least he could read. He wondered if he should offer to loan him the copy of *The Oxford Book of English Verse* that his parents had sent him the other day. Accompanying the book was a note in which his father informed him that they had gone to Elizabeth's wedding in New York, and that she sent her regards. It sounded almost like an apology, the way it was worded, as if the old man were afraid his son might look upon their attendance as a betrayal; and Bovard reminded himself to write and reassure them that he was more content than he'd ever been, that he had no ill feelings whatsoever toward the money-grubbing bitch. If they only knew how happy he was not to be stuck in that life anymore. He looked down at the letter on the ground near Wesley's feet, two sheets of paper covered with a large, childish scrawl, and suddenly realized this was the perfect opportunity to ask a question that had been on his mind ever since he'd first laid eyes on the boy. "Fiancée?"

Wesley twitched a little, but stayed at attention. "Well, sort of, sir."

"At ease, Private."

As the soldier bent down to pick up the letter, the lieutenant sneaked another quick glance, then turned and walked away. So what if Wesley had a girlfriend? As Lucas had told him the other night, half the men he'd fucked over the years wore a wedding ring. Though most of them endured marriage only because it provided a cover-up for their deviant behavior, hating every minute of it, there were some who actually got a thrill out of living a double life. "Think about it," Lucas said. "Sucking a prick one day, knocking up the wife the next. It's like walking a tightrope that never ends, knowing that one little slipup could ruin you forever."

By the time he arrived at the mess hall, most of the men had finished eating, and Bovard settled for just a cup of coffee. "I'm telling you, fatso, that's a bargain," he heard First Lieutenant Waller say to a chubby gunnery officer. "Four dollars a shot for a pretty little wench that speaks French? You can't beat that with a stick." With his black curly hair and pencil mustache and endless talk of sex, Waller had quickly established a reputation around camp as a master fornicator, and quite a few inexperienced men sought out his advice before they made their first trip to the Whore Barn. He claimed to know every crack and crevasse of every working girl within a thirty-mile radius of Meade.

"Yeah, but you could choke it with your hand," another lieutenant joked.

"Ha!" Waller said. "No doubt in my mind, Bryant. You probably try to strangle that snake of yours to death every night, don't you?"

"Why would I do that?" Bryant said. "Just hang out at the Majestic long enough and that ol' boy that runs the place will do it for you."

"Isn't he a friend of yours, Bovard?" Waller asked, winking at a couple of other officers sitting across from him.

"Who are you talking about?"

"The funny boy that runs the theater uptown."

"Oh, him," Bovard said, trying to act casual. "No, I've talked to him a time or two, but I wouldn't call him a friend. I can't even recall his name now."

"Snyder here says he tried to grab his cock in the men's room last night."

Bovard's stomach did a flip, but his face remained calm. "Good Lord," he said. "You mean intentionally?"

"Hell, yes," Snyder said. "He had his hands all over me. I'll give him this, though, the little bastard can take a punch. I must have hit him seven or eight times before he stayed down." He raised his fists up for them all to see the red abrasions on them.

"Looks like you nailed him pretty good," Bovard said weakly.

"Did he ever try any of that stuff with you?" Waller asked. Several men at the next table laughed.

"What stuff?" Bovard said.

"You know, that queer stuff?"

"Certainly not!"

"Well, maybe he thought Snyder was another one of his kind," said an aide named Hurley who worked for Major Willows.

"It's an abomination," said Second Lieutenant Elkins, a teetotaler since birth and head of Camp Pritchard's newly formed Morality Committee. He saw this as an opportunity to let everyone know where the organization stood in regard to faggots and dykes. Granted, only one other man, a little Bible-thumper from Ironton, had showed up at the first meeting, but, as his mentor, the clap doctor Eisner, later reminded him, it takes only a single spark to start a fire.

"I never thought I'd say this, but for once I agree with you, Elkins," Waller said. "Goddamn queers. If they're not going to hang 'em, they ought to at least round them up and stick 'em on an island out in the ocean somewhere away from decent folks. What do you think, Bovard?"

"Well," the lieutenant said, as he sat down at the table and recalled the opiated fantasy he'd had about Wesley the other night, "it sounds to me like you might have hit upon the perfect solution."

36

ELLSWORTH WAS CUTTING corn in a field he rented off Clyde Ferguson's widow when he saw a colored man sporting a light gray bowler hat sauntering down the dirt road. He stopped working and watched the man pause and remove his hat, then proceed to pull a broad-toothed comb through his black, wiry hair. He wore a pair of threadbare pinstripe trousers and a faded yellow shirt. Recalling the black man he had seen working in the field that day outside Meade, Ellsworth decided to look upon the stranger's appearance as a good omen, though he was a bit concerned about the primping. One that liked bright colors and carried a comb was likely to be damn near useless when it came to getting blisters on his hands; and it was a known fact that you could hypnotize some of them with a mirror, although he reckoned you could do that with any fool who thought himself pretty, no matter what the color of his skin might be. He looked around at all the corn that still needed cutting. The way things were going, there would be snow on the ground before he finished. "Yo!" he yelled to the passerby. "Yo!"

The man dove to the ground as if dodging a bullet, the comb still stuck in his hair. He lay there for a minute, a fearful look on his face, then slowly raised his head. He spotted the farmer in baggy bibs and a sweat-soaked linen shirt walking up through the field toward him, gripping a corn knife in one hand.

"Hidy," Ellsworth said, once he had cleared the ditch that ran alongside the road. "Didn't mean to scare ye."

"I ain't scared," the man said defensively, as he stood and dusted off his pants. "Just careful is all." His Christian name was George Milford, but a woman he had once shacked up with in Detroit had dubbed him Sugar because she thought his sperm tasted like taffy, and that's what he had gone by ever since. He was running from a crime he had committed in Mansfield, Ohio, three days ago, and was on his way to Kentucky to see his family. He hadn't seen any of them in over ten years. Pulling the comb from his hair, he slid it into his back pocket, then put his bowler back on. "What you want?"

Ellsworth hesitated. It had just occurred to him that he should probably talk to Eula first before offering the man a job, but it was a good twenty-five-minute walk back to the house from here, and he couldn't expect a stranger to wait around while he went seeking his wife's permission. However, if he let this one get away there might not be another, at least not in time to do him any good with the harvest. Already it was the first day of October. He had to admit that he'd taken on more than he could handle. Hoping to make back some of the money he had lost last fall, he had rented two extra fields off the widow, but he hadn't planned on Eddie not being around to help. "I was wonderin' if you might be lookin' for some work?" he said to the black man.

Sugar spit out the stem of a weed he'd been chewing on. Though he wasn't interested in a job, never had been, for that matter, he had discovered that while most white people tolerated colored folks, to a degree anyway, especially if they found themselves alone with one, damn near all of them looked upon a black man who wouldn't work with the utmost suspicion and contempt. Sugar shrugged and looked down into the field. "Might be," he told Ellsworth, but no sooner had those words popped out of his mouth than he wondered why he'd said them. Fuck the white bastard. There wasn't another soul around that he could see, and he had his razor in his pocket. Why worry about him? "But then again, I might not be."

"Well, which is it?"

"Depends."

Ellsworth blinked several times, then took a rag from his pocket and wiped the sweat from his face and neck. Hell, he thought, this boy is as smart-alecky as those damn gatekeepers back at Camp Pritchard. "Where ye headed for anyway?" he asked. "They ain't nothing down this way."

"They is if you keep walking," Sugar said. "It will take you clear to the river."

"What river?" Ellsworth asked. He turned and looked down the road. He hadn't been any farther south than Waverly in all the years he had lived. Almost everything he knew about the world lay to the east, toward Meade, and that had always been more than enough for him.

"Why, the Ohio," Sugar said. "You never been there? Shoot, it ain't but forty miles from here."

Ellsworth shook his head. Of course, he had heard of the Ohio, but he had never imagined it as being within walking distance. "Never had no need."

"It's a big river, let me tell ye," Sugar said. "A man ought to see it before he dies."

"What makes you think I'm a-dying?" Ellsworth asked. He had heard once, over at Parker's store, that some coloreds, specifically those born at the stroke of midnight, could see into the future, and he wondered if this man might be one of them.

"I didn't mean you in particular," Sugar said. "Anybody is who I meant." He reached into his pocket and laid his hand on his razor. For a second, he weighed the pros and cons of robbing the dumb hillbilly, but then took another look at the long, wooden-handled corn knife he held in his hand and decided against it. The farmer was a stout-looking fucker for his age; and even if he did have any cash, it would be buried in a tin can somewhere or stuck up a cow's ass. All of these country fools were the same when it came to hoarding their pennies.

"Oh," Ellsworth said. He coughed and cleared his throat, then wiped at his mouth with the rag. "Well, you want the job or not?"

"How much you pay?"

"A dollar for a good day's work," Ellsworth said. "Plus'n a good breakfast." He thought about throwing in a jar of wine every evening, but realized that might backfire on him, especially if the man turned out to be anything like Eddie or his Uncle Peanut.

Four quarters and a bowl of mush, Sugar thought. A man who would trade even one day of his short time on earth for that might as well crawl into a cave and be done with it. Still, why not have a little fun with the cheap-ass motherfucker before he headed off? "Last man I worked for," Sugar said, "he paid three dollars a day."

"Three dollars!"

"Yes, sir, he did. And he fed us breakfast, lunch, and dinner, too. Me and another boy didn't have no arms. Sausages and flapjacks and pork chops and mashed taters and corn on the cob. Then on Sundays we laid under a shade tree in his front yard and et on a big ol' chicken his old lady fried up for us. And like I said, the other boy, he had both his arms cut off, so I did most of the work. Couldn't even wipe his own ass. Had to have the farmer do it for him. Lord, though, that boy could sing. He could coax a woman into anything."

"Holy Christ in a manger, I do that I might as well burn the damn field down."

"Pretty women, too," Sugar went on. "Not no dogs. And I mean anything. Why, he spent most of his time laying in the barn trying to think up new stuff for them to do. They flocked to him like hens to a rooster. Don't seem right, does it?" Then he turned and started on down the road without another word, a toothy grin spreading across his face.

Ellsworth stood in the dust for a while and waited on the man to come back, thinking that no matter what he had said, it would be one rich colored boy who would turn down a dollar a day, but Sugar just kept walking until he disappeared over the next rise. He had a hard time believing there was a farmer somewhere who could afford to pay a single man anything close to three greenbacks a day, or feed pork chops and whole chickens to his help. Nor keep a crippled songbird around whose only job was to chase whores all day! He began to worry that this might be another symptom of these modern times, paying a man more than he'd ever be worth, and perhaps even paying him for nothing at all. Why, if he could find someone who would treat him that good, he might chop off his own arms and hire himself out for regular wages.

And who in their right mind would walk forty miles to see some water? Ellsworth swiped at a fly buzzing around his head and looked across the road to the woods. Maybe the boy had just let on that he was going to the river. Perhaps he was hiding over there in the trees right now, watching him. He had heard they could be sneaky like that, slip up behind you and lift your pocketbook right out of your pants without

you feeling a thing. He walked back down into the field and reached
into a groundhog hole for the jar of wine he had hidden there yesterday.
He took a long drink, reminded himself to lock the doors tonight in
case the spying bastard followed him home. Setting the jar back in the
hole, he started cutting on another row of corn. Sweat ran down his
face and stung his eyes, dripped off his nose. By God, he would show
that boy what he meant by a good day's work. He hesitated a moment,
then began to sing.

37

THAT EVENING, JUST as Sugar decided he had walked far enough for one day, three grimy, unshaven men came around a bend in the road on horses and reined to a stop a few feet in front of him. Two of them wore cowboy hats and overalls while the third's attire consisted of a dusty frock coat and black trousers. A bloody piece of a white shirt was tied around the thigh of the heaviest one. Rifles protruded from their saddles and pistols hung from holsters belted around their waists. They looked to Sugar as if they had accidently stepped out of some bygone era and were searching for a way back to where they belonged. It wouldn't have been the first time that someone ended up trapped in a time that didn't quite suit them. He'd lived for a while with a woman who started coming home every night from her job in a millinery and dressing up like an Egyptian princess. Figuring she was just bored, he put up with the crazy costume for a while, but when she began praying to crocodiles and talking about him escorting her into the Underworld, he'd decided it was time to shag ass.

"Well, I'll be goddamned," Chimney said. "What we got here?"

"Gentlemen," Sugar said, nervously tipping his bowler. He swallowed and tried not to stare at their guns. He thought of his razor, but what use would it do to pull it out? These men would have him dead before he could even snap it open.

"Where ye going, boy?" Chimney asked.

"Headed for the river," Sugar said.

"The Ohio?"

"Yes, sir."

"That's quite a ways on foot."

"I don't mind."

"Anything up this road?"

"Not much unless you like lookin' at cows and chickens."

"What's your name?"

"Sugar."

"You hear that, boys? His ol' mama thought he was so sweet she named him Sugar."

"That ain't my real name," Sugar said quickly. Although it didn't make any goddamn difference what these bastards thought of him, he still didn't want them to think that his mother didn't have the sense to give him a proper name. "It's just the one I go by."

"Well, if I was you, I'd start looking for a new one," Chimney said. "Makes ye sound like a pony." He leaned over his saddle and spat, then looked up and down the road. "I bet you got some ol' gal down there on the river, don't ye? That's why you got that fancy hat on."

"No," Sugar said, "just going to see my people is all."

"Come on," Cane said. "We don't have time for this." It was their third day in Ohio, and for the most part they were still riding at night. This morning they had made it as far as Buchanan, and, just before dawn, ended up in a soggy marsh filled with rotten logs. The rib cage of a deer had rested on a small ferny island rising up in the middle of the foul-smelling morass. After breakfasting on Chimney's last two strands of licorice, they'd spread their blankets on a thick bed of pokeweed and nightshade and settled down as best they could. They had endured it until late afternoon, but finally agreed, though there were still several hours of daylight left, that even getting killed or raped by a posse would be better than the torture being inflicted upon them by the hordes of late-season mosquitoes and black gnats swarming over their stinking skin. They were as worn-out and miserable as they had ever been, and Cane was more determined than ever to find somewhere clean and safe to rest up for a couple of days.

"I don't know, I surely do like that hat," Chimney said.

"Well, then, buy ye one," Cane said. "They probably sell lids like that everywhere."

"Not that one, they don't."

Cane let out a long, exasperated sigh. "Then just take the goddamn thing."

"No, I got a better idea," Chimney said. Pulling the Lee-Enfield from a leather scabbard tied with rawhide to his saddle, he ratcheted a shell into the chamber and looked at Sugar. "Here's the way it's gonna work. I'm a-goin' to let you make a run for it. And if I can knock that hat off your head, then it's all mine, understand? And if I can't, well, it's yours to go on wearing down to the river or wherever the fuck it is you're really going."

"Brother, why would ye want that thing?" Cob asked, the first words he had uttered in hours. "It looks like something ye'd take a shit in."

"Ha!" Cane said. "That's a good one."

"Well, I hadn't thought of that, Cob, but maybe I will. Be mine to do with as I please, right?"

Sugar jerked the bowler off his head and attempted to hand it up to Chimney. "Here, mister, I don't want it anyway. It's all yours for the keeping, free of charge."

"There," Cane said. "It's settled."

"No, it's not," Chimney said. He scratched his chin and looked about, then pointed at a woods on the other side of a field overgrown with wild roses and goldenrod and white-flowered asters. "See them trees over there?" he said to the black man. "You put the hat back on and run that way. I promise ye I'll count to thirty before I cut loose."

"Please, mister," Sugar said, "they no need to do this. I don't even want—"

"Better get to moving, boy. One, two, three . . ."

Sugar looked around wildly, then leaped off the side of the road down into the pasture and started running for the tree line, his arms pumping like pistons and his legs stepping high and the sticker bushes ripping at his flesh.

"But this don't make no sense," Cob said. "He tried to give it to ye."

Ignoring his brother, Chimney kept counting, but at twenty he stopped and settled the rifle on his shoulder. Even after the bowler fell off the black man's head, he seemed intent on shooting. He took a deep breath and exhaled slowly. But just as he started to squeeze the trigger, a loud blast went off beside him and his horse lurched sideways, causing his own shot to fly harmlessly into the sky. He watched his target dive into some tall weeds. "What the fuck?"

Cane put his pistol back in his holster. "Don't ever pull no stunt like that again. What the hell's wrong with you?"

"Jesus, no sense in gettin' so excited. I was just going to scare him a little, that's all."

"Yeah," Cane said, "I bet you were. Well, hurry up, it'll be dark before long."

"Hurry up what?" said Chimney.

"Go find that hat."

"Shit, you think I really wanted that goddamn thing?"

"I don't care if you did or not," Cane said. "Get your ass down there."

A few minutes later, as they sat watching Chimney in the field cursing and flailing at the weeds, Cob said to Cane, "I bet that feller's mad that he lost his hat. Ye could tell he was proud of it."

"Yeah, he probably was. Hard to say how long he had to save up for that thing."

"Wonder why he calls himself Sugar, if that ain't his real name?" Cob asked. "That seems kind of dumb to me. How's anybody supposed to know who he really is?"

"Well, maybe he don't like . . ." Cane started to say, but then he stopped. He looked over at Cob, at his cowboy hat and the red bandanna tied around his fat, sweaty neck and the pistol hanging at his side. He was the spitting image of the drawing on the last wanted poster they had seen, the one the store clerk had carried. Jesus Christ, why hadn't he thought of that before? By the time Chimney found the bowler and made it back up to the road, Cane was in the process of changing their names and working on a line they could use. From here on out, he announced, at least until they crossed the border, he and Cob were Tom and Junior Bradford from Milledgeville, Georgia, and Chimney was their cousin, Hollis Stubbs. They were on their way to Canada to find an uncle.

"That's it?" Chimney said. "Seems a little thin to me." He set the bowler between his horse's ears.

"We need to keep it as simple as possible. That way there's less chance of screwing up."

"What brought this on?"

"Something Cob said about the colored boy. I should have thought of it before."

"You must be startin' to slip if you got Cob giving you advice," Chimney said.

"We got to change our looks, too," Cane said, ignoring him. "Get rid of those cowboy hats and the neckerchiefs. And stick your pistols in your saddlebags."

"You mean all of them?"

Cane stopped and considered for a few seconds. "No, you're right. Maybe we better each keep one handy just in case."

As they got ready to leave a few minutes later, Chimney said, "I still don't feel right about you takin' that shot away from me. I need to keep in practice."

Without a word, Cane grabbed the bowler off the horse's head and tossed it to the ground a few feet in front of them. "Go ahead then, have at it." Chimney smirked a little and pulled out his Smith & Wesson. Every time he fired, the hat skidded and tumbled a little farther down the road. He didn't stop until the gun was empty. "There, ye satisfied?" Cane asked.

"I don't know," Chimney said, as he dug some bullets out of his pocket to reload. "But I reckon it'll do till something better comes along."

38

CRAWLING ON HIS belly until he reached the woods, Sugar then ran for another quarter of a mile or so before collapsing behind a fallen tree. He stayed there barely moving a muscle for over an hour. At one point he counted six shots being fired, and he hoped that maybe the motherfuckers had killed one another before one of them picked up his bowler. Finally, he got up the courage to sneak back to the field to look for it, but it was nowhere to be found. He kicked at the weeds and cursed his bad luck. The finest hat he had ever owned and now some sonofabitch dressed like Billy the Kid was going to take a dump in it.

He made his way through the field and back up the bank. Yellow-winged grasshoppers flew up in front of him. He hadn't gone but a few yards down the flat road when he came upon the remains of the bowler, still smoldering a little around the edges of the bullet holes. Goddamn them! What kind of sick sonsofbitches would do something like that? He would have given anything just then, even the rest of his time on earth, for the chance to slit that skinny ferret-looking bastard's throat with his razor. Or, if not that, at least to be shacked up for the night with a whore and a bottle and a good dinner. He didn't think that was asking too much out of life. The thought of it swept over him like a tempest, driving him half insane, and he flung his arms about in frustration and anger. As his rage mounted, he thought again about his people in Kentucky, that poor bunch of God-fearing, Hallelujah-shouting, ass-kissing sharecroppers. Not once had they ever given him credit for anything. Everybody was against him, even his own mother. And when she finally kicked him out, he had made his way across the Ohio and headed for Detroit, telling them all when he left to go fuck themselves, that he was going to get a job building those fancy motor-cars everyone was talking about, and bragging that the next time they saw his black ass, he'd own a whole fleet of them, one for each day of the week. Not only that, he'd have a white man for a chauffeur, and another just to keep them shined up and ready to roll at a moment's notice.

That had been over a decade ago, and he had lasted exactly two weeks working for Mr. Ford. With his first paycheck, he had bought a cheap suit and a toothbrush and went out for a drink. Five days later, he woke up sick with a hangover in a damp basement room curled up next to a woman he'd met in an after-hours club out celebrating her fifty-seventh birthday. She gave him the first blow job of his life that morning while he chewed on a piece of the tough flank steak she fried him for breakfast; and he realized, as he watched her gray head bob up and down in his lap, that with as many women as there were in a city the size of Detroit, a young man could get by without hitting a lick if he wasn't too particular about what he laid with at night. He had stayed with her two months, until he'd spent every last dime she had saved up for her old age, and then he had moved on to a friend of hers whose husband had just died of a heart attack. Over the years he had pretty much stuck to the same strategy, squeezing all he could out of them, and then finding some excuse to leave as soon as they started hinting around that he needed to find a job. But then he met Flora, a pretty woman in her forties with an appetite for young bucks and a big, round ass like two ripe pumpkins fitted together. She made good money managing a laundry over on Beacon Street for a white man, and Sugar decided that maybe it was time to settle down. Every evening for the next eight months she came home to a clean apartment and supper cooking on the stove, and he thought everything was going just fine until one night she appeared in the kitchen with a long-legged, freckle-faced boy who couldn't have been more than fifteen or sixteen years old. "Who this?" Sugar said as he set out the plates on the table, thinking it was probably another one of her goddamn relatives looking for a free meal or a corner to sleep in.

"This here be Winston," she said. "He's my new man."

"Your what?" Sugar said, whirling around to look at the boy again, standing there with a cocky grin on his face. "What you talkin' about, woman?"

"Look, honey, I 'preciate all this moppin' and tater peelin' you been doing, but truth is, I got no use for a maid."

"Maid! I'll show you a goddamn maid." He took a step toward her, brandishing a fork in his hand.

"Oh, no, you won't," she said calmly. "You'll be packing your fuckin' clothes and gettin' out, that's what you be doing. And just in case you think you goin' to start some trouble, you better look out the window first. All's I got to do is say the word and they'll be in here on you like stink on shit."

Sugar stepped over and pushed the curtain back. A pair of squat, burly men he'd seen a few times at Leroy's, a gin joint he and Flora frequented on Saturday nights, were standing on the steps looking back at him. One was tapping a truncheon against his leg as if he were keeping the beat to some song in his head, and the other was peeling an apple with a pig-sticker. Jesus Christ, she was serious. He turned and looked at the brown gravy simmering in the skillet, the pork chops stacked on the platter in the middle of the table. "But why?" he asked, his voice now sounding almost plaintive.

"To be honest, I need somethin' with a little more pep when I crawl under the covers at night, that's all."

"Well, shit, why didn't you say so? You want more meat, by God, let a man give it to you. You don't need this young punk."

"No, you done had your chance, and I done made my decision," she said. She opened her purse and pulled out a five-dollar bill. "Here, you take this and go get your stuff packed up. There's some things me and Winston need to discuss." The boy winked at Sugar, then pulled a chair back at the kitchen table and sat down. After adjusting the bulge in his pants, he reached over and picked up one of the pork chops. Before he took a bite, he ran it back and forth under his nose several times, loudly sniffing it.

Sugar grabbed the money from her hand and stormed out the door past the men. He was three blocks away before he remembered his clothes. Fuck it, he thought. He'd go back after the bastards left, stick a shiv in the boy's guts the first time he dared to step outside Flora's door. But then it started to rain, and he ended up down by the railroad tracks in a dive called the Depot. He spent the next several days drinking and bemoaning his predicament to any barfly who would listen, going on and on about all the cooking and ironing and pussy licking he had done for the bitch; and then, although he couldn't remember doing it or why, he'd hopped a train headed south.

Standing in the road beside his ruined hat, looking down at the hoofprints of the horses in the thick dust, he went over everything that had occurred since he'd left Detroit. When he came to in that empty freight car with no idea of where he was or how long he had slept, the first thing he saw when he looked out the open door was a sign announcing Mansfield, Ohio. The train slowed down long enough as it passed through town for him to jump off, his only intention being to find a bottle or something to eat, whichever came first. He was walking along the tracks when he spied an old white woman sitting on her porch fanning herself with a piece of cardboard. He hid behind a stack of rail ties and bided his time. Finally, just before dark, she got up and shuffled inside. A light popped on and then went off a few minutes later. He waited awhile longer and then climbed through a window into her kitchen. He searched all around, but to his disappointment there was no liquor or meat to be found. He was buttering some stale bread and gulping his third glass of water from a bucket on the table when she awoke in the next room. Fifteen minutes later, and twenty-four dollars richer, he went back to the tracks and caught another freight.

By the next morning, he figured he'd put enough distance between him and Mansfield to be safe, and he got off when the train made a stop in Meade. It only took a couple of breaths of the stinking, sulfurous air emitted by the paper mill for him to realize that he'd passed through here once before, on his way to Detroit years ago. Walking around, he finally found a colored diner on the south side of town. He was halfway through a big breakfast when the old woman's bloody face appeared in his plate and he shoved the food away. "Something wrong?" the waitress asked. He looked up at her. She wasn't as dark-skinned as he liked them, but she had a nice set of cocksucker lips and fine white teeth and a way of swiveling her hips when she walked that he figured probably got her some good tips, even in a dump like this. She smiled and refilled his coffee cup, and he was just beginning to imagine following her home and screwing her little brains out when he noticed the wedding band on her finger. Despite his many faults, Sugar had never lain with a woman whose husband was still living. It was the one rule he stuck by. Even the weakest and most cowardly of men could become outright dangerous if they were cuckolded, and there were too many unattached females out there to risk getting your head blown off in a fit of jealousy. "No," he told the waitress, shaking his head, "just tired is all." He was relieved in a way. In the past few days, he had lost Flora in Detroit and then lost himself in Mansfield, and he needed something more substantial than a quick piece of ass to make him feel better about himself, this time anyway. He finished off the coffee and stood up, laid a dollar on the table.

As he recalled what had happened next, he cursed and stomped what was left of his hat into the dusty road. He had stepped out of the diner and noticed a small shop across the street. A cardboard placard advertising FINERY FOR ALL AGES had hung in the single, flyspecked window. He counted his money, then entered the store. A few minutes later, he purchased the bowler from a bald, hunchbacked man in a white linen suit. He had never owned such a nice hat before, and he immediately felt better, like a different man almost. "What about some new clothes to go with it, young buck?" the cripple had asked him. "Those ye got on are looking pretty rough."

"No," Sugar said, as he looked at himself in the mirror and adjusted the hat's angle, "this is all I need." And it was, at least for the length of time it took him to walk up the street to a joint with no name and rent a room for the night.

After sleeping fitfully through the hot, sticky afternoon, he had gone downstairs and bought two bottles of cheap whiskey and a fat black whore named Mabel. By the time she sucked him down to the nub, he had finished off one of the bottles and was down to his last four dollars; and he wondered, in his insane drunkenness, just how much was a white woman's life worth anyway? Not much, he calculated sadly, as he watched the whore wipe his seed off her chin. A greasy breakfast and a sporty hat and two bottles of rotgut hooch and a fishy-smelling slut with a wart on her lip. That was what a white woman's life amounted to in the end.

He and the girl kept drinking, and around midnight she puked her guts up in the washbasin. The windowless room filled with her stench, and she dropped to her knees and started crying about leaving her sick baby at home by itself, and shit like that always brought Sugar down. He climbed out of bed and punched and kicked her until she rolled over on the filthy brown rug and farted once before passing out. Her impertinence enraged him even more, and he spread her ass cheeks apart and fucked her from behind, the salty sweat pouring off him and splattering like raindrops on her broad, bruised back. When he was finished, he wiped himself off in her nappy hair and got dressed. The sour smell in the room was suddenly overwhelming. He slipped down the back stairs with her comb and the money he had paid her in his pocket. Stumbling down an alley, he curled up on a pile of garbage with his bowler and awoke the next morning with his head pounding and his tongue dry as leather. Lying there in the trash, he looked up at a pigeon perched on a wire and swore to God Almighty that he was going to straighten up. And since he was so close anyway, he thought, why not go down to Kentucky and show his folks his new hat? It wasn't a shiny car driven by a white chauffeur, but it was better than nothing. He could see them now, gathering around and slapping him on the back, asking a million questions, his mother hugging him until he couldn't get his breath. He had picked himself up and begun walking. Two blocks away, he came across an old man on his knees pulling weeds out of a little vegetable patch and asked him for a drink of water. "Got the dry pipes, have ye?" the old man said, looking at Sugar's bloodshot eyes. "I 'member what that was like. Why, I used to wake up so thirsty I'd pay 'bout anything for a nice cool drink."

"I ain't got no money," Sugar remembered telling the man.

"Sho you ain't," the old man said, nodding his head and grinning, his toothless gums a wet pink that made Sugar queasy all over again. "Spent it all last night, I expect. I 'member when—"

"Can I have a drink or not?"

"Sho you can," the old man said. "Got a well right there."

There was a rat swimming around on top of the water when Sugar lifted the wooden top, and the old man scooped it out with a shovel and started beating it to death; and watching him go after it like he did, yipping and bashing and pounding on it like he was getting back at every dirty bastard who had ever done him wrong, made Sugar think about the white woman again. It wasn't his fault he had gone crazy on her; shit, she would still be alive if Flora hadn't kicked him out. She was the one to blame, her and that goddamn baby-faced nigger she was fucking. He watched the old man pick up the bloody gob by the tail and fling it over into a neighbor's yard, and then he got down on his knees and washed the whore's smell off his face and drank until his belly felt like it was going to burst. A few minutes later, he was on his way out of town, heading for Kentucky.

That had been just yesterday morning, and now here he was standing in the middle of a lonely road miles away from the old man's well and staring down at his hat sieved with bullets and flat as a pancake. Insects buzzed madly in the weeds and a bird called out weakly in the heat. He almost wished he had taken the farmer up on his offer. A dollar a day wasn't much, but at least he'd still have his bowler. He began moving again, feeling the most awful pity for himself. As far back as he could remember, there hadn't been a day when he wasn't yearning for something he didn't have. And that wore a man down after so many years, fighting that feeling day after day without any letup. Why couldn't he ever be satisfied? Why did he keep fucking up? Suddenly he stopped and looked up into the sky. "Lawd," he sobbed, "please, Lawd, I don't want to live like this no more. I'm not a-lyin' this time, I swear. I just want to see my folks now. You help ol' Sugar through this one and I promise you . . ." He searched his mind for what he could pledge, but he couldn't imagine what it might be. "I promise you . . ." he began again, but then he stopped. He had nothing of his own to offer. Even the little bit of money in his pocket was somebody else's. A murdered woman's, no less. He was nothing but a bum, a goddamn, worthless bum. Not once in his life had he ever done anything worthwhile. Wiping at his eyes, he took a deep breath to steady himself and continued on.

Before he was around the next curve the cravings kicked in again, and he beat his head with his fists until his nose and lips were bleeding and his clothes soaked with sweat. Exhausted, he dropped his arms to

his sides and cast a hopeless look down the empty road. He was completely and utterly alone. "Lawd, ol' Sugar . . ." he started to implore
again, but then he realized, with a start, what he needed to do to make
a clean break from his old life. It was so clear to him now, what he
had to pledge. He *did* have a proper name, had been baptized with it
in Finfish Creek when he was but three months old. And from this
day forward, he was going to use it again. George. George Milford.
Sugar was just some fool nickname a dirty whore had cursed him with,
but no more. His pace quickened as the idea took hold. "What's your
name?" he asked himself in a strained, high-pitched voice. "George," he
answered in his own deep baritone, "George Milford." He repeated this
a number of times, letting it wrap around him, the old name salvaged
from the past and the saving grace it would surely bring him in the
future. He should have been in jail awaiting the hangman's noose, or,
if not that, lying with a bullet in his head back there in that field. But
no, the Lord had kept him safe, been keeping him safe all along. Then
he stopped and watched openmouthed as the most beautiful sunset he
could ever recall unfurled like a richly colored carpet across the sky. He
had been staring at it for several minutes before he noticed, off in one
corner, a swatch of the golden shore that his mother used to talk about
all the time. Dropping to his knees, he was just getting ready to sing
the Great Redeemer's praises when a hornet as big around as his thumb
smacked him in the face and drove a black stinger deep into the fleshy
tip of his nose; and before he could catch himself, he was clawing at
his stinking skin again and screaming curses at Flora and all the other
dirty motherfuckers who had ever done him wrong and begging the
Devil for just enough liquor—a drop, a spit, a spoonful—to make his
pain, his endless, endless pain, go away, if only for the time it took to
get around the next bend.

39

WHEN ELLSWORTH FINALLY came in from the field, Eula didn't say anything about seeing a colored boy lurking about, and so he decided not to mention his encounter with the one on the road. He was glad now that he hadn't hired him. It would have been just another thing for her to worry about. Even so, harvesting corn by hand was hard work even for a young man, and Ellsworth, being convinced all day that the lazy bastard was watching him from the woods, was completely gutted from trying to show him how it was done. Not only that, his voice was shot to hell from all the singing he had done. Once he'd gotten started, he found that he couldn't stop, and he must have sung "The Old Brown Nag" a hundred times. "What's wrong?" Eula asked. "You catchin' a cold?"

"No," he squeaked softly. "Just wore out is all."

"A summer cold," she said. "They the hardest to get rid of."

"I done told ye, I ain't sick."

"Well, you sure sound like it," she said. "Good thing you don't have to sing for your supper."

After a meal of cornbread and beans and sliced tomatoes, they went out on the porch to sit a bit before bedtime. The day was quickly coming to an end, and the shadows cast across the yard became a little longer with each passing minute. As she had done every evening for the past few days, Eula wondered aloud why they hadn't heard from Eddie yet. "You'd almost think he's done forgot about us."

"No," Ellsworth said softly, "I don't think that's it. Like I told ye before, I imagine he's been too busy." He shifted uncomfortably in his rocking chair, and a feeling of disgust crept over him. He knew that the right thing to do was just go ahead and tell her the truth about Eddie, but whenever he got the chance, he balked. He couldn't figure it out, unless maybe he'd covered for the boy so much he couldn't break the habit now; and every day he kept it up, the harder it was not to do it.

"How about a hot cup of water with honey?" she asked. "That'll soothe your throat some."

"No," Ellsworth said, "just let me rest here a minute." He stretched out his legs and closed his eyes, felt a cool breeze ruffle his sparse hair. He heard Eula get up from her chair and enter the house. Right before he faded off, he heard the door open again, smelled the cup of coffee she'd brought back with her.

Unbeknown to the Fiddlers, the Jewetts had been watching the farmhouse from across the road for the last thirty minutes. This was just the sort of quiet, out-of-the-way place Cane had been looking for ever since they'd entered Ohio. They hadn't had more than a couple of hours' sleep at a time since they'd left the dead grocer in the rain four days ago, and though Cob's leg didn't seem to be getting any worse, it wasn't getting any better, either. And by this point the horses didn't have another canter left in them, so outrunning the law or anyone else was out of the question. Unless they got some rest soon, they'd never make it to Canada, he was sure of that. "Well, what do you think?" Chimney finally asked.

Holding up his hand for him to be quiet, Cane studied the old people sitting on the porch awhile longer before making a decision. "Well, we won't know till we try," he finally said. He turned and looked at Cob. "What's your name?"

Cob thought for a second, then said, "Junior. Junior Bradford."

"That's right," Cane said. He looked over at Chimney. "Hollis, you let me do all the talking."

Ellsworth was slumped over in his rocking chair when Eula awakened him with a shake. When he first opened his eyes, he thought he must be dreaming. Before him were three men, red-eyed and sweaty and caked with dust, mounted on horses. Rearing up in the chair, the farmer rubbed violently at his face, then said, "What the hell?"

"Howdy," Cane said. "Sorry if we scared ye."

Ellsworth's eyes shifted back and forth as he took a hard look at each of the three in the dusk. "That's all right," he replied. "Didn't hear you ride up is all."

"Pardon?" Cane said.

"He's got a cold," Eula said.

"Jesus," Ellsworth muttered under his breath. He turned and hacked up a ball of grit, spit it over the railing. "What can I do for ye?" he said, raising his voice with effort.

"Well, my brother here, he's got a hurt leg, and we're needin' a place to rest up a day or two."

Ellsworth glanced over at the chubby one, a friendly-looking boy with a smile on his round face, a filthy piece of cloth wrapped around his thigh. "What did he do to it?" he asked.

Cane shook his head. "Just a dumb accident. Playing around with a gun and it went off."

"That sounds like something Eddie would do," Eula said.

"Where ye headed?" Ellsworth said. "Going to join the army in Meade, I bet."

"Well, no," Cane said. "We're headed for—"

"Why not?" Eula said. "That's what our boy done, and he ain't but sixteen."

"It's not that we don't want to," Cane said carefully. From what he'd read in the newspapers, he knew that many people weren't taking this war business lightly. In fact, they had become quite nuts about it, going around kicking dachshunds to death, making ninety-year-old Americans with German-sounding names get down on their knees in the streets and kiss the American flag, calling sauerkraut Liberty cabbage and hamburger Salisbury steak. Searching factories and mines for terrorists, and taverns for hidden hordes of pretzels. And if they happened to have a family member in uniform, they were often twice as zealous when it came to sniffing out slackers and potential traitors. Maybe, Cane thought, they figured it wouldn't hurt so much if their son got his ass blown off as long as there was a good chance the neighbor's boy would suffer the same fate. There were few things in the world that put all people, regardless of education or wealth or place in society, on equal footing, but heartache was one of them. "It's just . . . it's just that . . ." He turned and looked at Cob, then back at the farmer and his wife. "Mind if I get down?"

"Go ahead," Ellsworth said.

Cane eased off his horse and stepped up to the porch. "Thing is," he whispered, leaning toward the couple, "my brother there ain't right in the head, so someone's got to watch over him all the time. It's not his fault, he was born that way, but there's no way they'd take him in the army. As ye can see, he can't even handle a gun."

"Oh, my," Eula said, looking over at Cob. Because of her poor dead mother, she had always harbored a soft spot in her heart for the mentally challenged. And she knew how difficult it was to keep one safe. No matter how closely Eula and her father watched over her, Josephine had always found some way to slip out of the house at night. "Well, it's good of you to take care of him. Not a lot of young men would do that."

"Thank you, ma'am."

"And who's the other one?" Ellsworth said.

Cane glanced back at Chimney, then said, barely able to suppress a smile, "That's our cousin, Hollis. He's not quite playin' with a full deck, either, but he ain't as bad off as Junior." He straightened up and looked over at the barn. "So you farm?"

"I try to," Ellsworth said.

"It can be a hard life sometimes."

"You ever done it?"

"Sure," Cane said. "It's all we've ever done."

"Where would that be?" Ellsworth asked.

"Georgia mostly. Then Pap died a while back, and we lost the land."

"How'd you come to lose it?"

"Back taxes mostly," Cane said. "That's why we're going to Canada. We got an uncle lives up there."

"Canada? That's quite a ways off, ain't it?"

"Well, to tell you the truth, I'm not sure. I just know we got to keep heading north."

Ellsworth settled back and nodded approvingly. At least the boy was honest. He figured that owning up that you didn't know the location of Canada was just as embarrassing as admitting that you didn't know the whereabouts of Germany. And having your farm taken away because of back taxes was as bad as losing your life savings to a checkered-suited con man. Maybe even worse. He reckoned they might have quite a bit in common.

"Them your horses?" Ellsworth asked.

"Yes, sir."

"What's their names?"

"How's that?"

"Their names. Even my old mule's got a name."

"Right," Cane said slowly, a slight hesitation in his voice. Of all the questions someone might ask, the old man wanted to know the names of the horses? Shit, Cob was the only one who'd ever called his anything other than "horse," and he gave his a different handle damn near every day. "Well, this one—"

"Thunder, Lightning, and Hurricane," Chimney said quickly, pointing to each.

"Buck's what I call my mule," said Ellsworth.

Chimney nodded. "That's a good name for one. We used to have—"

"We can pay," Cane cut in, trying to get the conversation back on track before his brother said something stupid.

"What?" Eula asked, coming forward in her chair. "What'd you say?"

"I said we can pay."

"Boys, I hate to turn you down," Ellsworth started to say, "but we—"

"Hold on a minute," Eula said, lightly touching his arm to shut him up. All the time Ellsworth had been dozing, she'd been worrying again about how they were going to make it. Everything was tied up in the corn, but, as he kept telling her, with the summer having been so dry, they'd be lucky to get forty bushels an acre. And that was if he could get it all put up by himself. Though she was proud of Eddie for enlisting in the military, he surely couldn't have picked a worse time. They didn't even have a calf to sell this year. Perhaps the strangers' arrival was some sort of sign that the Good Lord hadn't entirely forsaken them. After all, when was the last time anybody rode in and actually offered them money instead of taking it? Never. "How much?" she asked.

"Oh, I don't know," Cane said. "Could you fix us something to eat?"

"Sure, I can cook," Eula said.

"Well," he said, scratching his head, "how about twenty a day? Would that be all right?"

Eula's heart began beating a little faster. "How many days are we talking about?"

"Three, maybe four. Just till Junior's leg gets better."

"But, Eula, where are they going to sleep?" Ellsworth asked. "We don't have—"

"Hold on and let me think for a minute," she said. Good God, man, she thought to herself, who cares where they sleep? We're talking about sixty dollars here, maybe more. They could sleep in her bed for that much money. Of course, feeding them would use up a lot of the food she had stored back for winter, but they'd still come out way ahead, even if she had to kill half the chickens. Wait a minute, though. How could she be sure they weren't just trying to pull one over on a couple of old people? Just looking at them, you wouldn't think they'd have two nickels to rub together. "Can you pay something in advance?" she finally asked.

Cane pulled a small wad of bills out of his pocket and counted out forty dollars and placed it in her hand. "There's two days' worth," he said.

She glanced down at the money. "It's not that I don't trust ye," she said apologetically, "but we been took before."

"I understand," Cane said.

"Well, one of you can stay in our boy's room, but I'm afraid the other two will have to sleep out in the barn. That's the best we can do."

"The barn will be fine for all of us," said Cane.

"All right then," Eula said. She stood up then and started into the house, gripping the money tightly. "There's a well out back if'n you want to wash up. Ells will get you some soap and a lantern. But the first thing I want you to do is bring your brother in the house and let me change that dirty bandage. It's a wonder he don't have blood poisoning."

"TWENTY DOLLARS A day!" Chimney said. "What the hell was you thinking?" They had just had their first decent meal in several weeks—beans and cornbread and fried pork and stewed apples and coffee—and were now lying on their blankets in the barn loft. There was a large hinged door at one end, and they had propped it open to let in a light breeze that was making the leaves whisper on the two oak trees in the front yard. Cob was already snoring down below them in the back of the farmer's wagon. The horses were in a fenced-in lot behind the barn with the mule and a milk cow, and their guns were stashed under some boards behind a rusty plow that looked like it hadn't been moved since the start of the century. At the other end of the loft, the saddlebag with the money was buried deep in some straw. The jugs of wine that Ellsworth had hid up there lay undetected just a few feet from their heads.

"I would have paid twice that," Cane said. He could barely keep his eyes open. The last time he had felt this peaceful, their mother was still alive.

A nightingale let loose several soft, melodious notes, then stopped suddenly. Chimney sat up and looked over toward the house, a worried expression on his face. He was chewing the inside of his mouth, something he always did when he was on edge. After a few seconds, the bird started up again. "Do you really trust them?"

"Jesus, what do you think they're gonna do? Climb up here and cut our throats? Tie us up and go runnin' for the sheriff?"

"Well, what about Cob? He has a hard enough time remembering where he shit last. How you figure he's going to keep that story straight?"

"Don't worry about him," Cane said. "What about you?"

Chimney spat out the door, then lay back down. "Hollis Stubbs, your dashing cousin." He lazily scanned the constellations in the dark sky, but, unlike most men, he had never found much meaning in the stars. They were too remote, too silent. "Headed for Canada in search of my fortune."

40

THAT EVENING, A man in a thin coat named Everett Nunley stumbled out the front door of the Blind Owl and began walking south toward the Whore Barn. Frank Pollard watched him from the window and chuckled to himself. It was the man's first night in Meade, and just by coincidence, he had turned out to be from over around McArthur, where the bartender had grown up. For the last three hours, Nunley had drunkenly recited every goddamn fact and rumor he knew about the place, along with all the births and deaths recorded over the past twenty years, to the point where, if it hadn't been for Pollard's rule of never maiming or killing anyone whom the law might be able to connect him to in even the smallest way, he would have gladly torn the bastard's arms off and thrown him in Paint Creek to drown. So it was easy to imagine his glee when, desperate to get shed of him, he mentioned to Nunley that the pimp gave out free pussy on Thursday nights, and the dumb sonofabitch actually fell for it. After he disappeared over the bridge, Pollard ate a can of sausages with a fork—he was a great believer in preserved food, and had recently been toying with the idea of trying to can a human—then turned out the lights and settled down in the back room on his cot. From time to time he picked up the jar of teeth he'd collected and shook them. The sound always soothed him, reminded him of the rattle his mother had made him out of a gourd when he was just a little chap.

WHEN NUNLEY FINALLY arrived at the Whore Barn, he walked up to Blackie and Henry sitting by the fire and cheerily announced he was there for his free piece. "What the hell you talkin' about?" the pimp said.

"The barkeep said ye give it out every Thursday."

"Barkeep? Which one?"

"Man named Pollard. Over at the Blind Owl."

"Ah, he's just fuckin' with ye," Henry said.

"You mean he lied to me?"

"He did if he told ye it was free."

"I'll be goddamned," the man swore. "And I used to run traps with his daddy."

"Hell," Henry said, "you should've knowed better. You could search the world over and you'll never find such a thing as free pussy."

"Yeah, I guess so," the man said, his face now clouded with disappointment. "Oh, well, he always was a prick, even when he was a kid."

"How much money ye got?" Blackie said.

The man weaved on his feet and reached into his pants pocket. He pulled out a little change and struggled to count it in the campfire light. "Seventy-five cents," he finally said.

"Have ye anything else you could trade? I hate to see a man go away horny, but goddamn, hoss, I got bills to pay."

Nunley looked blank for a moment, then brightened up a little and said, "Got a good penknife."

"Let me see it," the pimp said. The knife was just a plaything with a crack in the handle, but it had been another slow night. Yesterday, he had knocked on the door at the clap doctor's house intending to try to bribe him into easing up a bit on his lectures, but no sooner than he introduced himself, the man jerked a paper mask from his pocket and covered his face with it, then ordered him off his property. As if he, Blackie Beeler, was carrying some vile disease. He looked over at Henry and shrugged his shoulders. "Hand me the money," he told the drunk. After a quick glance at the coins, he nodded toward the tents. "First one back."

Nunley looked toward the barn, wiped his sleeve across his lips. "What's her name?" he asked.

"Esther," Blackie said. "Now go on, you got yourself ten minutes whether you're done or not."

"Ten minutes?"

"What do ye expect for a busted-up knife and three quarters?"

"Well, shit, I—"

"Don't worry," Henry told the man. "You won't want no more than that once Esther wraps them big legs around ye. I guarantee it."

BACK AT THE Blind Owl, Pollard shook the jar one more time, then set it down on the floor. He raised up and reached into his shirt pocket, took out a small brown bottle capped with an eyedropper. Sleep had never come easy to him, and lately the only time it came at all was when he dosed himself with some stuff he'd gotten from Caldwell, the druggist over on Walnut Street. After squeezing three drops onto his tongue, he put the bottle back in his pocket. Free pussy, he said to himself. Ha. Only a stupid sonofabitch from McArthur would ever believe something like that. He lay there awhile with his eyes closed, then reached over and picked up the jar again. Fuck that town. Someday he'd go back there and set fire to the whole goddamn place.

41

THE SUN WAS coming through the loft door when Cane and Chimney finally woke up, a little stiff from having slept so long. They could hear Eula's chickens scratching and clucking below them. Climbing down the ladder, they discovered that Cob was gone. "See?" Chimney said. "I told you. You got to watch the fat-ass every minute."

"He must be in the house," Cane said.

"Yeah," Chimney said, "probably spillin' his guts."

"Nah, he's sharper than you give him credit for. Come on, I'll show ye."

They found Cob at the kitchen table stuffing grits and eggs into his mouth. Eula was sitting across from him drinking a cup of coffee. "Good mornin', Tom," he said. "Mornin', Hollis."

"Just give me a minute and I'll get your breakfast," Eula said, getting up and going to the stove.

"How did ye sleep, Tom?" Cob asked.

"Like a rock."

"What about you, Cousin Hollis?"

"Pretty good, I reckon."

"How's the leg feelin' this morning, Junior?" Cane said.

"A lot better than yesterday, I'll tell you that. Miss Eula's a regular nurse."

Chimney looked into the parlor. "Where's the ol' . . . where's Mr. Fiddler?"

"Oh, he's been gone a couple hours," Eula said, as she cracked some eggs into a bowl.

"Gone?" Chimney asked, shooting a look toward Cane. "Where'd he go?"

"Down the road a ways. He's wantin' to get another five acres of corn cut today."

"By himself?" Cane said.

Eula shrugged. "Well, with Eddie gone, he don't have much choice."

"That's a hard job for one man."

"I know," she said. "You saw him last night. Couldn't hardly stay awake."

An hour later, as they sat on the front porch sipping coffee and staring out upon the road, Cane suddenly said to Chimney, "I think we should help that old man with his crop." From inside the house, they heard Eula ask "Junior" if he wanted another biscuit.

"Oh, no, not me, brother. I've already told ye, my days of slavin' in a field are over with."

Putting down his cup, Cane reached over and grabbed hold of Chimney's hands. "Look at these," he said, turning the palms up. "Soft as a banker's."

"So?"

"Shit, you don't want to get like one of them bastards, do ye?"

"Forget it," Chimney said, jerking his hands away. "We're payin' them good money to stay here. And besides, I thought we was supposed to be resting up."

"What about this," Cane said, glancing around to make sure Eula wasn't within hearing distance. "We give him a couple good days and then we'll take off for this Meade he was talking about and get you a woman. That'll work, won't it?"

"But why should we even give a shit? Heck, sounds to me like his own boy bailed on him."

"I don't know. They just sort of remind me of what Mother and Pap might have been like if she had lived. You don't remember them like I do. Things were different back when she was around."

"Jesus, talk about gettin' soft."

Cane shook his head, then stood up. "All right, you stay here and have a little tea party with Junior and Miss Eula. I'll go help the old man."

"Fuck," Chimney said with a sigh. Chopping corn didn't go along with his idea of the outlaw life, but sitting around on a porch in a god-damn rocking chair didn't, either. At least it would give him something to do until they got to town. "I'll give him the rest of today and two more, but that's it."

"That's plenty. We can get a lot of work done in that amount of time."

"But then we go to this Meade town and have some fun."

"Fair enough," Cane said. He turned and started to walk toward the barn.

"Hold up a minute," Chimney said. "What about guns? We'll be pretty much right out in plain sight."

Cane paused. His brother had a point. If the law caught them in the open without any horses or weapons, they'd be fucked. "Well, what about them Remington .22s we got?" he said. "We could carry them in our pockets."

"Shit," Chimney scoffed, "one of them little things won't stop nothing."

"Aw, hell, as good a shot as you are, you could just knock their eyeballs out."

Chimney gave a little snort. "Now you're braggin' on me. You want this bad, don't ye?"

"Come on," Cane said. "Let's see if we can find a stone or somethin' to sharpen those machetes with."

That afternoon Ellsworth came back to the house for his dinner, and when he finished, they followed him back to the field with their cutters and another roll of twine. For the rest of the day, they took turns chopping the dry stalks right at the ground while the other two gathered them up and tied them into shocks. The sun was going down when Ellsworth finally got them to quit. As they walked back to the house looking forward to supper, he tried in his fumbling way to tell them the joke he'd heard about the queer in the pickle patch, and it surprised him when they laughed. He wanted to ask them what it meant, but he didn't. Cane and Chimney dumped buckets of water on their heads and ate on the front porch, then gathered up Cob from the kitchen and went to the barn. As Ellsworth told Eula that night after they had gone to bed, "I never saw two men work so hard in my life." His voice was still a little hoarse.

"It's a miracle," she said, looking up at the dark ceiling, his hands resting on her stomach. "How much things have turned around in just one day."

"You figure?"

"Maybe," she said. "I hope so."

They lay there for a moment counting their blessings, and then he said, "I almost forgot. How did Junior do?"

"Oh, he's a good boy," Eula said. "He sure does love to eat, I'll tell you that. You know what he told me after you all left this afternoon?"

"No," Ellsworth said. "What?"

"He told me that sitting in my kitchen was better than being at the heavenly table. I have to say, that's about the nicest thing anybody's said to me in a long time." Though she'd tried to get him to stay off his bad leg, the boy had followed her around like a loyal dog. Her life was, for the most part, a solitary one, and she had to admit it felt nice having someone to talk to through the day. At times he seemed to get a little confused when she asked him questions or said his name, a bit like her mother used to do when she was having one of her spells, but not quite the same, either. With Junior, it was more like he was trying to keep a story straight that someone had taught him. Or maybe a lie. She thought for a moment, debating whether or not to bring it up, then turned and whispered so low she could barely hear herself, "Ells, what do you figure them boys have been up to?"

But Ellsworth didn't respond. He had closed his eyes and already taken the fall that he took every night on his way to sleep. Most times it was either off one of the slate cliffs over on Copperas Mountain or from the sharply pitched roof of Jarvis Thacker's three-story house, the biggest one in the township, but tonight it was into a black pit that seemed to have opened up at the bottom of the cellar steps just as he was heading for one of the wine barrels. Often the vividness of the plunge jerked him back to wakefulness for a minute or two, but not tonight. Trying to keep up with the two young men had worn him to a frazzle. Within a few minutes, he was dreaming that he was back in the cornfield swinging his knife while the colored boy who had passed through yesterday morning sat silently on a white-faced cow, watching him. He was wearing a metal pot on his head, and Ellsworth was singing a song at the top of his voice. Somehow he knew the words, even though it was one that he'd never heard before.

42

THAT SAME NIGHT, Sugar arrived at the bridge leading over into Kentucky. He walked through the tunnel in a soupy fog so thick he could barely see his hand in front of his swollen nose. The midnight air was chilly and damp. Coming out on the other side, he nearly ran straight into a group of white men seated around a campfire just a few feet from the railroad tracks. They were passing a bottle around and laughing at something that had just been said. One of them looked up and saw Sugar trying to slip past undetected and yelled at him to halt. Several leaped up and pointed shotguns and rifles at the dark figure half-crouched in the shadows at the edge of the firelight. "Shit, it's just some nigger," one of them said.

"Come over here, boy," a rough voice commanded. There were at least a dozen men around the fire, and they all carried weapons of some sort, including a crossbow and an antique blunderbuss left over from the Pilgrim days. His chances of surviving a run for it, he calculated, were next to nil. He straightened up and walked over to them slowly. Saddles and bedrolls and other gear were scattered here and there. The smell of meat sizzling in a skillet wafted through the air, and he became aware of just how empty and worn-out his body had become in the week or so since Flora had kicked him out. This evening he had dined on a moldy melon and a handful of dried peas. His eyes searched out the bottle, and he watched a brown-toothed country boy stick the neck of it halfway down his throat and guzzle like he was drinking springwater.

"Where ye comin' from?" an older man with a beard asked. He was barefoot and seated on a stool by the fire. An antique hat of some sort, adorned with a couple of long, dirty feathers, sat upon his head at a cocky angle.

"Across the way there," Sugar answered nervously, pointing back toward Ohio.

"Where ye headed?"

"Shadesville. It's over by—"

"We know where fuckin' Shadesville is, nigger," another man said.

"What was ye doin' in Ohio?" the bearded man asked.

"Working," Sugar said.

"Thieving's more like it, Captain," said a fattish boy named Bill Dolly. He had the soft, hairless skin and flushed, jiggling jowls of a child. The biggest disappointment of his life so far had been, in fact, his life so far; and like so many other white do-nothings, luckless simpletons, and paranoid crackpots, he was convinced that somehow the black race was the root cause of all his miserable failures. "I ain't never seen one that didn't like to steal."

"What the hell happened to yer nose? Was ye in a fight?"

"No," Sugar said. "A bee stung me."

"Come closer," Captain said. "Hayfield, show him that poster."

As Sugar stepped into the full light of the fire, a man with a metal hook for a hand unfolded a dirty leaflet with his teeth and held it up to him. Though the drawings on the paper were crudely rendered at best, he immediately recognized the three cowboys he had encountered along the road. "Well, I'll be damned," Sugar said. He could make out only a few of the words, but he'd seen enough wanted posters in Detroit to figure out that someone was offering $5,500 for the bastards, dead or alive.

"What?" Captain said. "You saw them?"

"I sure did," Sugar said. "They stole my hat and tried to kill me." He took another look at the poster, then added, "Took all my money, too."

Some of the men began talking excitely among themselves and Captain raised his hand to silence them. "When?" he asked.

"Two days ago."

"He's a-lying, Captain," Dolly said. "Them Jewetts don't *try* to kill anyone. Shit, they even shot down one of them aeroplanes." Several standing near him concurred with vague mumblings.

"No," Sugar protested. "I swear."

"Where would this have been?" Captain said.

"Outside a town called Meade. 'Bout forty mile or so north of here."

"But that don't make no sense," a voice in the shadows said. "Why in the hell would someone want a nigger's hat?"

"It was a nice hat," Sugar said defensively.

"Lawd God, those sonsofbitches must be worse than we thought," another said.

"Don't believe it, boys," said Dolly. "A nigger will lie when the truth fits better. They can't help it. It's in their blood."

"I ain't a-lying, I swear."

"But just supposing," said another man, a tobacco farmer by the name of Cloyd Atkins, "what he's saying is true. Why, if'n it is, and they're in Ohio, there's no way we'll ever catch them now."

"I swear," Sugar said. "They was the men on your paper."

"Goddamn, Hershel, my wife's gonna kill me if I come back empty-handed again," a sour-smelling hog farmer in tattered bibs said under his breath to a lanky, hollow-eyed man standing beside him. He had followed Captain into action twice before after being promised a big payday, and twice he had returned to his wretched hovel poorer than when he left it.

A young man with a flat nose and hollowed cheeks that had been ravaged by the pox asked, trying to make his nasally voice sound as serious and respectful as possible, "What do you want us to do with him, sir?" He had been sitting on the log all evening spit-shining Captain's boots and trimming the old man's thick yellow toenails with a paring knife in an effort to gain favor, and he saw this as still yet another opportunity to demonstrate his undying allegiance.

The bearded leader glanced over at Sugar one more time, then returned his gaze to the fire, as if studying the crackling flames for an answer. Unfortunately, the nigger's claim was liable to sabotage the rest of the outing if something wasn't done to defuse it. Captain had convinced his men yesterday morning that the Jewett Gang would attempt to cross over the bridge any hour now, and they had been having a fine time drinking whiskey and telling tales, which, in his opinion, were two of the very best ways a man could spend his days. He didn't really care one way or another if they caught the bandits, but he hated like hell to see the party come to an end or his authority be questioned. How he had come by this authority in the first place was a bit of a mystery, though he had allowed some to believe that he had been involved in the capture of several high-ranking chiefs during the last of the Indian Wars out west. In truth, he had never traveled any farther in that direction than Decatur, Illinois, his entire life, and had never seen a full-blooded redskin other than one he met doing a war dance on a table in a roadhouse somewhere in the Smoky Mountains for a free drink, let alone kill one with his bare teeth, which was how he had decided he was going to end the story he was telling just before the nigger showed up. Now, unless he thought of something fast, his hold over the men would be gone, except for maybe Bill Dolly and the pedicurist and one or two others. "Tie the lyin' piece of shit up and throw him in the river," he finally said.

Before Sugar could make a break for it, three of the men grabbed him and another secured his hands behind his back with a piece of cord. Everyone but Captain then gathered round and marched him out onto the bridge. The one in the lead carried a torch and didn't stop until he came to a place in the tunnel where several side boards had been removed. "Over here," he said.

"Wait, fellers," Sugar pleaded. "I swear to God on a stack of—"

"Hell, I can't see a damn thing," someone said, sticking his head through the gap and peering over the side. "You sure we out far enough for him to hit the water?"

"What difference does it make? He'll be dead either way. If he don't drown, the fuckin' fall will kill him."

"Captain specifically said in the river," the toenail-trimmer pointed out.

"On a stack of Bibles," the black man cried, "I swear—"

"Shut that sonofabitch up," someone said, and a hard, bony fist popped out of the dark, smashing Sugar's nose and making him see stars.

"Maybe we should castrate him first," Bill Dolly suggested. "That's how it's done in certain circles."

"There was nothing in the order about cutting his—" the toenail-trimmer started to say.

"No, let's just get it over with," the one with the lantern interrupted, and two men picked Sugar up and roughly shoved him headfirst through the opening. "I want to see how that story turns out ol' Cap was telling."

"Please, misters, please," Sugar cried, as he dangled in the air. "I can't swim."

"Most niggers can't," he heard someone say, just as the men let go of his legs and he hurtled downward through the darkness.

"That'll teach the black bastard," Dolly said after they heard the splash.

As the men headed back to the campfire, Cloyd Atkins said to no one in particular, "But what if he was tellin' the truth? I mean, if'n those Jewetts already got by us, we might as well—"

"Don't worry about it," another with ginger-colored hair said sharply. His name was Tom Fleming, and three weeks ago he had lost everything he owned, including his wife, with one roll of the dice in a stables outside of Lexington. The way he saw it now, his entire future depended on getting a cut of that Jewett reward money.

"Yeah," Cloyd said, "but I got crops that—"

"Like I said, don't worry about it," Fleming repeated. "I've drunk whiskey with Captain a long time now. He'll figure things out."

"Look, Cloyd," the man with the lantern said, "you think a man who fucked Geronimo in the ass is ever gonna be played the fool by those stupid Jewett brothers?"

"Well, I don't know if I'd call them stupid exactly, Jim. I mean, they've been on the run for quite a while now and nobody's—"

"They stole a nigger's hat, didn't they?" Fleming said angrily.

"But that don't make sense. If they took his hat, then that means that boy really did see—"

Without another word, Fleming pulled his pistol out and jammed it under Cloyd's chin. "You shut up about it right now or I'll blow your goddamn head off and toss you over the side, too. Understand?"

The tobacco farmer tried to nod his head in agreement, but it was impossible with the gun barrel pressed against his throat. He cast a desperate look toward the man gripping the lantern and swallowed. "Sure, Tom, sure."

"Ain't no one going to ruin my chances of getting back my property, you hear me?"

"Yeah, Tom. Whatever you say."

"You're goddamn right," Fleming said. "I'll get her back if it's the last thing I do."

43

CHIMNEY WENT AT the corn cutting like a maniac, the promise of good times and women propelling him to get the job over and done with so they could leave. "That cousin of yours might not be the friendliest man in the world," Ellsworth said to Cane, "but damn, he ain't afraid of work, is he?" They were standing under a locust tree at the edge of the field, taking a break and watching him attack another row. Chimney wasn't any bigger than Eddie, but that's where the resemblance ended. Hell, Ellsworth thought, he didn't even think Tuck Taylor could keep up with this one.

"No, sir, he ain't," Cane said. He looked down at the raw place the handle of the machete had rubbed into the meaty part of his right hand between the thumb and fingers, and grinned a little to himself. One thing for sure, there wouldn't be a lawman or reporter in the country expecting to find the Jewett Gang harvesting a cornfield in southern Ohio. He wished he knew what the papers were saying about them. It had been a week since he'd seen a new one.

"No wonder he's so skinny. How old is he anyway?"

"Hollis? Oh, he's around eighteen," Cane said a little warily. He took another drink of water from the jug and set it down on the ground, figured it best to change the subject. "Yeah," he went on, "won't be long and we'll have this field whipped."

"And a couple days ago I was ready to give up," Ellsworth said. "If it hadn't been for lettin' Eula down, I probably would have. Makes a difference, havin' a wife."

"I expect so," Cane said, recalling the way Pearl had gone off the rails after Lucille died. "What do ye think you'd have done if you hadn't married?"

"Oh, I don't know. I guess if I hadn't met her, I'd have probably drunk myself to death. Had an uncle do that. But she keeps me in line. What about you? You got a woman?"

"Uh, no, sir," Cane said. "Not yet anyway." Christ, he hadn't even kissed a girl, let alone done anything else with one. He thought about the newspaper article he had read about the ones who had been coming forth in little towns all over the South, extolling his romantic charms, the gentlemanly way he treated them, each claiming to be his one and only sweetheart. "A twentieth-century Lothario," the reporter had called him.

"Well, you're still young, but take my advice and don't wait as long as I did to get hitched. I was thirty-four, and I wish to Christ I'd done it sooner."

"Why's that?"

"I guess I would have liked for her to've known me when I was at my best. Heck, when I was your age or thereabouts I screwed some gal seven times in one night, but by the time I met Eula, I couldn't have done that for a thousand dollars." Ellsworth thought about the time he was walking home from a church revival one rainy, windblown evening and saw Mrs. Sproat standing out in her yard under a pawpaw tree with an old slicker draped over her head, as if she were waiting just for him. He was nineteen at the time, living with his mother, trying to make a living for them on the fifteen acres his father had left them when he died. Mrs. Sproat asked him if he'd like to come in a spell to get out of the wet, and he, never having been in such a situation before, thought she just wanted to talk, her being a widow woman and probably feeling lonely on such a miserable evening. They hadn't been inside the house more than two minutes when she started stripping off her long black dress. It scared the bejesus out of him, but he didn't turn away from it. Though she was flabby and gray and a few years past her prime, it was all he could do to keep up with her. He'd shoot a load in her and roll over to get his breath; and she would lie there for a spell, and then start back up on him again with her hands and her lips and by the time the first cock crowed the next morning, he was so weak he couldn't have split a bean pod open. He washed up good the next evening and went back to have another go at her, thinking that she considered him quite the stud, but when he presented himself at her door, she acted as if she didn't even know him. He knew something wasn't right, and so he went up the road a ways and circled around. It wasn't fifteen minutes before he saw Gene Humbolt, a married man with five little ones at home, tie his coonhound to a fence post and sneak in the back. Ellsworth remembered that he'd hurt all the way home that night, but then woke up the next morning happy that he'd had his turn with her and glad that it was over with.

"Well, I'll keep that in mind," Cane said.

"Yes, sir," Ellsworth said, watching Chimney start another row and still thinking about all the ways Mrs. Sproat had kept him going. "A few years makes a big difference in a man, I'll tell ye that. Don't matter who he is. So whatever you want to do, you best go ahead and do it before it's too late."

44

IN MEADE, RIGHT before lunchtime, a sputtering, red-faced Mayor Hasbro called the city engineer into his office and commenced to chewing his ass out about Jasper Cone. In the past week, four more women had accused him of trespassing on their property without good reason and spying on them. And as Hasbro pointed out, what if the idiot went off his rocker and actually laid his hands on someone? Now that their complaints were on record, if they were ignored, even a friendly pat on the ass might bankrupt the city in a lawsuit. "I don't give a damn how much good you say he's doing," he told the engineer. "You tell him to back off."

Although Rawlings had never seen the mayor get so upset or vocal about anything before, he had a hard time believing that the meek and hardworking Jasper could be guilty of such acts, at least not intentionally. He immediately suspected that Sandy Saunders, the sneaky little sonofabitch, was somehow behind the accusations, but he kept his mouth shut. Instead, he returned to his own office to mull the situation over. Not only had the city councilman been a pain in his ass ever since Rawlings had taken over as city engineer, it was common knowledge that he absolutely detested Jasper. Still, he needed proof. Realizing that the best way to get to the bottom of things was to interview the women himself, he was just getting ready to walk back over to the mayor's office to ask for their names when there was a loud knock on his door and a plump older woman named Mrs. Lenora Trego barged in. Before he had a chance to ask what she wanted, she loudly informed him that while sitting in her outhouse perusing Miss Bernice Bottelby's new novel, *Dreams of Milk and Honey,* Jasper Cone had flung the door open on her and attempted to enter. It was the first time the engineer had ever heard anyone actually use the word "perusing" in a sentence, and it threw him off for a second, long enough for her to plop down in the chair across from his desk. Being a retired English teacher, she continued, she might expect such nonsense coming from teenage boys, but from a grown man, and a city employee to boot, that was an entirely different matter. Also, as she stressed at least a dozen times during the hour that he had to put up with her, she was a published author in the *Scioto Gazette*—from what Rawlings was able to gather, she wrote poems about birds and trees and shit like that—and it was common knowledge that any sort of traumatic incident could potentially stop the flow of the creative juices. Why, she hadn't written a decent line since he'd busted in on her.

"And when was that?" Rawlings said.

"Almost three hours ago," Mrs. Trego said woefully, as if it might as well have been a lifetime.

Showing her to the door a few minutes later, he casually asked, "Do you happen to know Sandy Saunders?"

"Who?"

"Never mind," Rawlings said. "I'll see what I can do." It was apparent from the puzzled expression on her face that she'd never heard of the bastard. So maybe it was true after all, maybe Jasper was stepping over the line. He sent out a message for him to report to the office as soon as possible. Something had to be done before his underling seriously fucked up and they both lost their jobs.

It was nearly quitting time when Jasper finally showed up. As usual, the day had been one shitty mess after another, and the stench coming off his clothes and rubber boots in the close confines of the office overwhelmed Rawlings to the extent that he nearly forgot why he had summoned him in the first place. It was only after he jerked a window open and sucked down several drafts of fresh air that he regained his bearings. He sheepishly thought of the mustard gas being used on men in Europe. Perhaps his ex-wife had been right after all, maybe he really was a candy-ass. With his head still hanging out over the sill, he told Jasper, "From now on, you only inspect an outhouse if my office gets a complaint, understand?"

"But you told me to crack down on—"

"Yeah, but hell, boy, you're going overboard," Rawlings said. He took one more deep breath of outside air, then cautiously left the window and moved over to his desk. Personally, as far as the engineer was concerned, the push for indoor plumbing in Meade was worth any number of old ladies, but he was beginning to sense that maybe he had picked the wrong man for the job. He fiddled with a pencil for a moment, then asked, "Do you know a Mrs. Trego over on Church Street?"

"Not really," Jasper said a bit hesitantly. "More like I know of her. Why?"

"I think you know what I'm talkin' about," Rawlings said angrily, snapping the pencil in two and throwing it across the room. "My God, Cone, they put people in prison for less than that. It's no more than a step or two away from rape. I'm warning you, if you can't abide by the rules, I'll have to let you go."

"What do ye mean?"

"Just what I said."

"Ye'd actually fire me?"

"I won't have any choice if you don't straighten up."

"Did Sandy Saunders put you up to this?" Jasper said.

"What? Of course not. You think I'd take orders from someone that sells goddamn insurance?"

"So cleanin' up the town was just talk."

"No, of course not, but we've got to use common sense."

"Why? Nobody else does."

"I don't give a damn what anybody else does," Rawlings said. "From now on out, you don't look in anybody's shithouse unless there's a legitimate complaint. And you make sure it's not in use before you even think of opening the door. I was the one that pushed for you to get this job, but if you embarrass me one more time, I'll hang your ass out to dry."

DISAPPOINTED AND SADDENED that his boss would bend so easily in the face of a little opposition, Jasper went out to the city landfill that evening with his buffalo gun, intending to blow off some steam. However, when he arrived, he saw the dump keeper's shanty door open and decided to pay him a visit before he went hunting for any rats. Back when he was working as a scavenger, Jasper had talked to Bagshaw nearly every day, but since taking on the inspection job, he'd barely seen him at all. He set his rifle down outside the door and entered. Bagshaw, a squat, ruddy-faced man with a pitted lump of a nose, was relaxing on a settee that had the horsehair stuffing coming out of it, his feet propped up on a wooden crate. He was eating a black, mushy banana. A barrel stove sat against the back wall, a dented tin chimney running out the roof. A hodgepodge of women's shoes, collected over the course of the last decade, were piled up in one corner, a towering stack of old newspapers and catalogs in another. Children's toys, in various states of decrepitude, hung from the rafters on rusty wires. "Wanta 'nanner?" Bagshaw asked.

"No, thank ye," Jasper said. "I ain't hungry."

"Found a whole sack of 'em a couple days ago. All the years I been doin' this, and I still can't get over the things people throw away. Ye'd think the whole town was made up of millionaires."

"I wish I was one of 'em," Jasper said.

"Why?" Bagshaw said. "What would you do different?"

"I'd quit my job and build the biggest bathroom this country's ever seen."

"What? I thought you loved that job," the dump keeper said, pitching the banana peel out the door.

"Not anymore. Every time I turn around, somebody's complaining."

"I know what that's like," Bagshaw said. "Agnes is always on my ass about something."

"Agnes?" Jasper said. "Who's that?" All the time he'd been coming out here, he'd never heard the dump keeper mention anything about having a woman, but maybe he'd just met her.

"The one hangin' right above your head there with the pretty blue eyes. I'll tell ye, boy, she can be a handful when she's in one of her moods."

Jasper twisted his neck and looked up. The doll had a crack running down the middle of its porcelain face, and half its red hair had been singed off by fire. Probably a kid playing with matches, he figured. The blue eyes were staring back down at him with an air of haughty superiority. "Oh," he said to the dump keeper. "I didn't know who you meant there for a minute." Then he glanced out the door at the pile of banana skins and heaved a sigh.

Bagshaw pulled at his chin and studied his young visitor, the pith helmet in his lap and the gloomy, dejected look on his face. He hadn't seen the boy so down in the mouth since Itchy had croaked. This was one of those situations, he realized, where the wisdom of an older, more experienced man such as himself was called for. Even Agnes asked him for advice on occasion, and she was one of the sharpest people he'd ever met. "You know what you need, Jasper?"

"What's that?"

"A friend," the dump keeper said, nodding sagely, "a real friend. You find you one of them, you won't need no suitcase full of money or fancy shithouse to make you happy. Believe me, it makes a big difference wakin' up every day knowing you got somebody you can talk to, someone you can depend on." Then, with rotten banana oozing thick as paste through the few teeth he had left in his head, he looked up at the doll and smiled.

45

I T   W A S   G E T T I N G late in the day when Chimney looked up
and saw two men sitting in a carriage watching them from the road.
"Friends of yours?" he asked Ellsworth.

The farmer stopped in the middle of wrapping a piece of twine
around a shock of corn and turned to look. It was Ovid and Augustus
Singleton. "Not hardly," he said, just as one of them took off his hat
and waved.

"Wonder what they want then?" Chimney said.

"Nothing," Ellsworth said. "They're just being nosy." He handed
Cane the ball of twine, then started up through the field. "Don't worry.
I'll get rid of them." Right before the boys came in for breakfast this
morning, Eula had mentioned that she thought there might be more
to their situation than what they were letting on. "Don't it seem a little
strange to you," she said, "them willin' to pay all that money to sleep
in a barn?" He had chosen not to tell her about the stubby pistols he
saw in their pockets, or the way they glanced about uneasily whenever they heard the slightest noise. As hard as they worked, he could
tell that they hadn't been lying about all the farming they had done, but
there also wasn't any doubt in his mind that some sort of trouble had
brought them here. "What do ye want me to do? Tell them to leave?"
he'd asked her, resisting the urge to point out that she was the one who
had made the deal with them. "No, no," she said, "I just wondered what
you thought." Since it was the first time she had asked his opinion
about anything since he had lost their savings, he considered carefully
for a minute before answering. "Well, unless they start causin' trouble,"
he told her, "let's just figure it's none of our business." And now, as far
as he was concerned, that went double for the Singleton brothers.

"What the hell did he mean by that?" Chimney asked Cane as they
watched the farmer approach the carriage.

"I don't know," Cane said.

"Think he's got us figured out?"

"If he has, he don't seem too worried about it."

"Maybe Cob's been runnin' his mouth to the old woman," Chimney said.

"Let's just wait and see," Cane said. "Maybe he didn't mean nothing at all."

At the edge of the field, Ellsworth stopped and nodded to the Singletons. Despite it being a rather warm day, they both wore heavy black coats and gloves. "You need something?" he asked them impatiently.

"We noticed you got yourself some help," Augustus said. He was waving a little paper fan in front of his face that advertised Smith's funeral home in Bainbridge.

"So?"

"Well, we were just trying to figure out who they were. From here, they sort of look like Sawyer Brown's boys."

"They're nobody," Ellsworth said. "Just a couple boys from Pike County needin' work."

"Pike County?" Ovid said. He cast a cocky leer over at his brother. "Did ye hear that, Auggie? You'd think ol' Fiddler would have enough sense to stay away from there after what happened last fall."

"Moo," Augustus said, and they elbowed each other and began laughing.

Ellsworth's face turned red and his hands tightened into fists. So they'd found out about the cattle swindle. And if they knew, that meant everybody in the entire goddamn township knew. Since it had happened down in the next county, he had hoped to keep it a secret, and he wondered now if Eddie had betrayed him. The boy had sworn to keep quiet about it, but he had proven time and again that any promises he made sober were easily forgotten once he got some alcohol in him. Jesus Christ, people were probably spending entire evenings over at Parker's store cackling about it. He recalled going over there one night right after Royal Sullivan sent away for a mail-order bride who turned out to be deaf as a stone and dumb as a post. For three hours they'd gone on about it, joke after joke. And she hadn't cost but seventy-five dollars. That was peanuts compared to the thousand he had lost. And at least Royal still had something to show for his money, no matter how useless the woman was when it came to following commands. Ellsworth looked up at the two in the carriage, still poking each other in the ribs and hee-hawing. It seemed like every time he came across them, they tried to cut him down. And he'd been having a damn good day, too. He started to turn away from them when he suddenly remembered something else he had heard over at the store one evening after Ovid and Augustus had taken off for home, the way they always did the minute the evening sun slid behind the big evergreen that stood in front of Dave Moody's house, no matter what the season. He waited until they stopped to catch their breath, then said, "So is it true what people say, that ye hold each other's hand when you go to the shithouse?" He heard them both gasp, watched the blood drain out of their faces. Without another word, Ovid smacked one old nag's hindquarters with a long willow switch, and the rickety carriage heaved forward with a lurch. Good God, Ellsworth thought, as he watched them disappear over the slight rise in the dusty road, he'd always thought the story was just another one of Parker's wild tales, but maybe it was true after all. Even though he didn't give one iota for either of them, he almost wished he hadn't mentioned it. Things had to be tough, being that fucked-up, no matter who you were.

46

FOUR FEET OF water and a muddy bottom had broken Sugar's
fall from the bridge. After the initial shock, he took account of himself
as best he could with his hands tied behind his back and determined
that nothing was broken. He got to his feet and managed to get his
razor from his pocket and cut the ropes that bound him, then struggled
up the riverbank. The campfire glared above him by the tracks, and he
could hear the men laughing, as if what they had done to him was no
different than killing a dog or a possum. Though his legs were wobbly,
he began walking, water dripping from his clothes, squishing from his
shoes. He reached up to feel a knot on the back of his head. His nose
throbbed, and he tasted blood in his mouth. The moon came out from
behind some clouds and showed him a way through the cattails and
brambles. He headed on south.

The next afternoon, he arrived in Shadesville. He walked through
the little burg with its grocery and barbershop and post office, and
went out the other side past the Baptist church. He continued another
quarter mile until he came to the house he had been born in. It was
empty. Sugar stood there for quite a while looking at it, weather-beaten
and leaning a little eastward with two smallish rooms and a wood-
shingled roof. It was hard to believe, he thought, that nine people had
once lived there together. Shit, the apartment he had shared with Flora
was twice as big. He went up the three rotten steps and through the
unlocked door. Except for a rusty hairpin he found lying on one of
the two windowsills, the house was completely bare inside; and judg-
ing from the dust on the floor, he figured nobody had been there in
a long time. He was so tired that he didn't feel anything, not even
disappointment.

An hour later, he went back into town and saw an old man sitting on a bench in front of the post office. "You 'member me?" Sugar asked.

The man examined him for a minute with yellow eyeballs, then cleared his throat. "Can't say I do."

"Don't matter," Sugar said. "Them Milfords that lived down the road there, where'd they all go off to?"

"Oh, they ain't lived around here for several years now," the old man said. "Not since the mother passed. I think maybe they went to Detroit. They always claimed one of their brothers was up there makin' good money buildin' them automobiles, but only a fool would have ever believed that shit. I knew that boy well, and he never was nothing but a liar and a blowhard. George, I think his name was. He'd brag about gettin' up in the morning, that boy. Like he'd done something big, just by cracking his eyes open. Most worthless nigger ever come out of Shadesville, if ye ask me. I warned them others not to go, but they wouldn't listen. Shoot, I'd say they probably all dead or locked up by now."

Sugar scowled and turned away. So his mother was dead. It didn't surprise him really, now that he thought of it; she could barely get out of her chair the day he'd left. He looked up and saw the cemetery on the little knob behind the grocery. Crossing the road, he found her resting place a few minutes later, a rock with her name scratched on it marking the head of it. The only store-bought stone in the entire graveyard belonged to Mrs. Hitchens, whose son, Marcel, had gone to a Negro college in Alabama and made good. Fucking stuck-up bastard, always wearing that goddamn blue tie and carrying a book under his arm. Getting down on his knees, Sugar started clearing the plot of weeds and dead leaves. He was nearly done when a great tiredness overcame him. He stretched out on the ground in the warm sunlight and closed his eyes. When he awoke several hours later, he made his way back down the hill to the grocery and bought three slices of longhorn cheese and a handful of crackers and a bottle of milk from a young girl with a rag tied around her head and a colicky baby balanced on her hip. He ate his supper out front. Across the dirt road, a group of young black men had replaced the old man on the bench in front of the post office. They were talking loudly and passing a bottle around. Bedrolls and carpetbags lay on the ground about them. Sugar finished his meal and walked over. They were from all over the county, from Fish Creek to Sourdough, and they told him they were going to join Uncle Sam's army. A man with a wagon was supposed to pick them up in the morning and take them to Lexington.

Sugar laughed. "They ain't gonna take no niggers in the army," he said.

"Oh, yes, they are, boy," a tall, heavy man with a loud, confident voice said. Sugar glanced over at him coolly. His front teeth were missing and he had no shoes, but he was wearing a new pair of bibs, and it was evident from the way he rocked back and forth on his bare heels with his thumbs hooked under the brass buttons on the shoulder straps that he thought he was hot shit. If you didn't know better, you'd have thought he was a well-to-do land baron standing on a balcony among a bunch of his lackeys, surveying his vast holdings.

For a moment, Sugar thought about how stupid and childish the man looked. He doubted if the poor sonofabitch had fifty cents in his pocket. But then he remembered the smug way he had felt right after purchasing the bowler, and his stomach clenched up a little. King of the world for just $2.95. Christ, he was no better than this fucking clown. "Where'd you hear that?" he asked, swallowing some watery bile.

"Show him, Brownie," the big man said.

A boy with bubbly white blisters around his mouth pulled a flyer from inside his homespun shirt and handed it over. Sugar scanned the drawing of a black man with thick lips and a broad nose dressed in a sharply creased uniform and saluting. Though it looked official, he still doubted the veracity of it. He figured someone was passing them around as a joke, like the ones he had seen in Detroit last winter promising five hundred dollars and twenty acres to any colored person over the age of eighteen who showed up at the courthouse in Fairbanks, Alaska, during the month of February. A dozen had frozen to death trying to make that journey, and several hundred more stranded before someone figured out it was all a hoax. It was just naturally assumed that some white folks were responsible, so imagine everyone's surprise when it was discovered that a colored boy who swept up nights at a printing press was the culprit. His reason? Nobody knew. He disappeared the same night someone ratted him out, and by the time his body was discovered hanging like a side of beef in the back of a meat locker eight weeks later, it was too late to ask.

"You might as well come with us," a voice behind him said.

Sugar passed the paper back. Just as he was getting ready to reply that, providing the poster was even legitimate in the first place, only an ass-kissing Uncle Tom would volunteer to go off and fight a war started by a bunch of rich white motherfuckers clear on the other side of the ocean, he saw one of the men tip the bottle up. "I sure could use a drink," he said instead.

"Give him a taste, Malcolm."

Sugar took a long pull and handed it back. He wiped his mouth just as the whiskey exploded in his belly. A warm, tingling sensation spread over his entire body, from the bottoms of his sore feet to the top of his bruised head, and he immediately wanted more. "Any place around here to get a jug?" he asked.

A squat, husky man wearing a frayed straw boater pointed across the road to a narrow, windowless hut tacked on the side of the store. "Jenksie over there will fix you up if'n you got the money," he said.

"You ain't from around here, are ye?" another asked.

"No," Sugar replied, "I'm comin' from Detroit."

"Detroit? What you doin' in Shadesville then?"

"Oh, I just stopped by to see some people, but they all gone."

"What people?"

"The Milfords."

"The Milfords? Why, that was ol' Susie's name, wasn't it?" Several of them chuckled.

"Lord, I damn near forgot about her," another said.

"Not me," a light-skinned boy with greenish eyes said. "That girl could suck a—"

"That's my sister you're talkin' about," Sugar said, raising his voice and placing his hand on the razor in his pocket.

"Oh," the boy said.

"Well," said another.

They all looked away or down at the ground for a minute, then someone said, "Here ye go," and handed Sugar the bottle again. He forgot about his sister and stayed with them for a while longer, but they didn't pass their liquor around fast enough to suit him. Walking over to the little shed, he tapped on the door and a sweaty, sickly-looking man wearing nothing but a soiled pair of yellow trousers let him in. The man sat down on a wooden crate before he asked Sugar what he wanted. It was dark inside the room. There was something alive inside the crate, moving around in a tight circle, but Sugar couldn't make out what it was. He bought a couple of pints of Old Rose and that left him with a dollar. Avoiding the volunteers, he sneaked around the corner and down the road to his homeplace and sat under a dead apple tree in the backyard. From time to time, he uncapped one of the bottles and took a sip, then screwed the cap back on tightly. He felt guilty about breaking his promise to the Lord, who had obviously saved him once again, this time from drowning back there at the bridge, but he swore that he would never get drunk again, not after this one last time. Who could blame him really? Coming all the way back here just to find his mother dead, and his brothers and sisters gone. What the hell was he going to do now?

He emptied the pint of whiskey and began on the other, willing himself to slow down and make it last. Eventually, he began thinking about Flora. My God, what an ass. Though he had known quite a few women who would go along with getting fucked in the ol' ham flower if they were high enough or forced to or paid extra, Flora was the only one who actually requested it from time to time. His hand drifted down to his crotch and he started rubbing himself, but it was useless; the more he thought about what he had lost, the more despondent and limp-dicked he became. Jesus, he would probably never meet another woman like her again. A picture of that skinny young buck ramming it into her from behind rose up in his mind. He tortured himself with it for a minute, to the point where he could hear Flora moaning and the bed squeaking. "I'll go back and kill 'em both," he said out loud. "Cut their goddamn heads off." He would start back tonight, he told himself. There, it was settled. But then, just as he was draining the last few drops from the second pint, another idea occurred to him, something so simple he wondered why he hadn't thought of it long before now. He would return to Detroit all right, but not to murder anybody. Why take a chance on getting hanged over that old slut and her baby-faced punk? Instead, he would do as he'd always done, find himself a new puss, and he knew exactly which one he was going after. Flora had a friend named Mary or Margaret or something like that who had just bought a little house a couple of doors down from the laundry that Flora managed. She wasn't much to look at, a scrawny, meek little thing with wire-rimmed spectacles, from what he could remember, but he didn't give a damn. He'd fuck a snake if that's what it took to get back at Flora. He could already see himself sitting on the front porch of his new house with a cup of coffee when the bitch walked by on her way to work. And besides, in all honesty, he really didn't know any other way to live except off some woman. Just look at all the shit that had happened to him in the few days he'd been out on his own.

Excited by his new plan, Sugar hurried back to Jenksie's and spent the last of his money on another jug. With any luck, he figured he could be back in Detroit in three or four days, probably be married by the end of next week. He staggered north past the men still gathered in front of the post office. By that time the sun was beginning to set over the big horse farm to the west that the white family named Montclair had owned since before his granddaddy was born. A few of the men hooted and catcalled when they saw him trip over his feet at the edge of town, and he cursed them and waved his razor in the air. Two or three started after him, but when he took off running, they stopped and threw rocks at him until he disappeared between two hills. He had only gone a mile or so when he curled up under a maple tree and uncapped the bottle. The next morning, he awoke more guilt-ridden and miserable than ever, with an army of red ants crawling over him. The plan that had burned so brilliantly in his mind just a few hours ago was barely smoldering now, and Detroit seemed like a million miles away. By the time he arrived back at the bridge that evening, Captain and his posse were gone. All that was left to indicate they had been there at all was a greasy forgotten skillet and a few discarded jugs. Searching madly among them, he found one corked with a chaw of tobacco, two inches of whiskey left in the bottom of it. He pulled out the slimy plug and tipped up the bottle with trembling hands, and as soon as his frayed nerves settled down a little, he crossed the bridge back over into Ohio.

47

ON THE EVENING of the third full day at the Fiddlers', with the corn all cut and standing in neat shocks in the fields, and the wound in Cob's leg healing over nicely thanks to Eula's poultices, Chimney told Cane it was time to go. They were washing off at the well before supper. Cane agreed, though he did so a little reluctantly. For the first time since they'd fled Tardweller's barn, he had seen Cob genuinely happy, and he hated to see that come to an end. But a promise was a promise, and Chimney had more than fulfilled his part of the bargain. Too, though the days were still warm, the nights were now cool and crisp. He didn't know much about Canada, but he suspected they should probably try to get there before winter hit. "I'll tell 'em after we get done eating," he said.

"However you want to do it," Chimney said. "Long as we go."

They had one of the best meals of their lives that evening—fried chicken and mashed potatoes and gravy and green beans and apple pie—and then they all went out to sit on the porch just as the sun was setting. Chimney walked over to the barn and brought back the last of their whiskey to share with Ellsworth, and Eula even allowed him to splash a drop in her coffee. He figured he'd give Cane a few more minutes, but if he didn't say anything by the time the yard turned dark, he'd tell them himself.

"He's lucky, you know," Eula said, nodding at Cob's leg. Then she launched into a story about a Blosser boy just down the road who had died from an infected rat bite two years ago. Just a little nip on the finger, and within a couple of days, his arm turned green with poison. His parents sent for a Doctor Hamm in Meade and he sawed it off, but it was too late by then. "You could hear the mother cryin' and screamin' clear up here when he took his last breath," Ellsworth added, taking another sip from his cup. The boy's parents asked the doctor to sew it back on before they buried him, Eula went on, so that he wouldn't be a cripple when he got to heaven, but then they couldn't find it.

"What do ye mean, they couldn't find it?" Cane said.

Eula shook her head. "Just that," she said. "The doctor, he'd laid it off to the side of the bed in Mrs. Blosser's roaster pan and it just disappeared into thin air."

"You mean like a ghost?" Cob asked.

"Could be."

"We used to have us some ghosts down where—" Cob started to say.

"Maybe a dog got it," Chimney cut in. "Hell, a dog will eat anything."

"Well, they did have one," Ellsworth said, "a little feisty thing. I think they called it Leo or something like that. But he wouldn't have been big enough to carry off something the size of an arm."

"It's a mystery," Eula said, nodding her head.

"They was a worthless bunch," Ellsworth went on, "especially the old man. He didn't do nothing but sit on the porch all day while his wife waited on him hand and foot. I wouldn't have put it past him to have stolen it himself."

"Why would he do that?" Cob asked.

"Well, I figure with her makin' such a big fuss over the boy dying and all, he got jealous. That's the way he was, always had to be the center of attention."

"Ells, now you know—"

It was then that Cane coughed, and Eula stopped talking and looked over. When he stood up and announced that they'd be leaving tonight, Ellsworth said, "Why don't ye wait till tomorrow? You boys got to be wore out, as much work as ye done."

"Yeah," Cob agreed. "We can go tomorrow."

"Well, we'd like to make it to Meade by morning," Cane said.

"But, heck, one more day—"

"Ells," Eula said, "leave it be." She got out of her chair and went into the house. In the kitchen, she lit the oil lamp and started to rid the table, but couldn't stop thinking about how Junior had said that morning that he wished he could live here forever, then picked up Josephine and kissed her on top of the head. Granted, she hadn't expected them to stay any longer than necessary, but she also hadn't expected that she'd start worrying about any of them, either. She thought for a minute, staring at the floor with her lips pursed. No, she had to say something. If she didn't, she'd regret it, just like she regretted keeping silent about Eddie until it was too late. She placed a stack of dirty plates in the sink and went back to the front door. "Tom," she said, "would you mind comin' in here a minute?" Cane glanced over at Ellsworth, but all the old man did was shrug his shoulders.

He followed Eula to the kitchen. Pouring herself the last of the coffee in the pot, she sat down and looked up at him standing in the doorway. "Now I know I'm just an old woman, and it's none of my business what kind of trouble you're all in, but—"

"We're not in—"

"Let me finish," Eula said. "But that boy a-sittin' out there on the porch with a bullet still in his leg don't need to be a part of it. I been around Junior enough these last couple days to know that much. So maybe you should quit doin' whatever it was that got him hurt, and just get to wherever you're going." Then she picked up her cup to take a sip, but her lip began to quiver, and she set it back down. She appeared about to cry, and Cane was touched that she could have such feelings for his brother.

He started to reassure her that everything would turn out fine, but suddenly, as he looked over at the kitten curled up in a tight ball on its bed of rags in the corner, that didn't seem quite good enough. He owed her more than that. "His real name's Cob," he said, and then turned and walked back out to the porch.

They rode away an hour later with Ellsworth standing in the yard waving goodbye. Cob was still whining about staying one more day, but within a few minutes he was asleep, slumped in the saddle, his round head bobbing over the pommel. It was after midnight when they passed through Nipgen. Not a single light burned anywhere. A lone dog was howling somewhere far off in the hills. "So what's the plan when we get there?" Chimney asked as they left the little burg.

"Well, one thing's for sure, we can't all ride in together," Cane began.

"I'll keep Cob with me and you'll be on your own. Need to stable the horses, get some new clothes. We'll stay in different hotels, pick some place to meet now and then."

"Sounds good," Chimney said. "Anything else?"

"Yeah, you think you could learn how to drive an automobile?"

"What?" Chimney said.

"I been thinkin' on it, and it just makes sense. The more we change things, the less chance of gettin' caught."

"Hell, yes, I could. I can't imagine there's a whole lot to it."

"Well, then, once you get to town and get settled, you start lookin' around, see if you can buy one. Just make sure it's big enough to haul all three of us."

"But what about the horses?"

"We'll figure that out later."

"Jesus," Chimney said, shaking his head and grinning, "did ye ever think a few weeks ago that we'd ever be buying an automobile?"

Cane shifted in his saddle and looked back to make sure Cob was still behind them. "No," he said, "I couldn't have imagined any of this, no matter how hard I tried."

48

BOVARD WAS ON his way to breakfast when Malone caught up with him and informed him that Private Franks had been injured in a barroom brawl sometime yesterday evening and was now in the infirmary. Instead of going into town and being tempted to stop by the Majestic to see Lucas, the lieutenant had stayed in his quarters last night with a pot of tea and read over Thucydides's account of the first invasion of Attica in his *History of the Peloponnesian War*. Unfortunately, stirring images of charging an impenetrable German bunker with a group of loyal young lads following behind him kept slipping in and preventing him from generating anything close to the enthusiasm he usually felt for his favorite historian of ancient Greece, and he had finally turned out the lamp in order to better succumb to his fantasies. Still, it was the first morning in a week or more when he hadn't woken up benumbed with a hangover, and if nothing else, he felt well rested. "In the infirmary?" he said to Malone. "How bad did he get hurt?"

"They say he lost an eye."

"Good Lord!" Bovard said, looking a bit startled. "Are you sure it was Wesley? I mean Private Franks?"

Malone nodded. "Oh, yes, sir, it was him all right."

Bovard thought he detected a slight note of self-satisfaction in the sergeant's voice, and it took him a moment to realize the reason for it. Just two days ago, he had told Malone that he had chosen Wesley to be his groom. The sergeant had questioned his choice, said that the boy seemed a bit too immature for such a responsibility. "What about Cooper?" he had suggested. "He's the best I've seen with the horses." Even though he'd already made up his mind, Bovard had been careful with his reply. He didn't want Malone to think he didn't value his opinion. But Cooper, a pudgy, bucktoothed dullard with jugged ears and a perpetual heat rash, was a veritable ogre compared to the dark-eyed and smooth-skinned Wesley. Just the type of beautiful young man, the lieutenant liked to imagine, that fought and died for honor and glory on the sun-drenched Grecian plains twenty-five hundred years ago. He couldn't help it. Even after all his initial dissatisfactions with the caliber of the recruits, and his subsequent acceptance that he was going to be stuck fighting alongside well-meaning but uncouth farm boys and law clerks and shopkeepers, he was still loath to completely surrender certain noble ideals about men and war that he knew the sergeant would never understand. Besides, what did it matter as long as he kept his sentiments to himself? Or if the boy was any good with horses or not? The cavalry would soon be a thing of the past; modern, mechanized warfare had taken care of that. In the first few months of the conflict, thousands of unfortunate bastards had already proven that charging a machine-gun nest on horseback was tantamount to suicide. By the time they arrived in Europe, the majority of the animals would be relegated to hauling boxes of supplies and pulling artillery. "But I don't understand," Bovard said to Malone. "What was he doing in town in the first place? Wasn't he scheduled for guard duty last night?"

"Well, that's the worst part," the sergeant said. "He left his post without tellin' anyone. I know it's no excuse, but a couple of his buddies said he got a Dear John letter yesterday."

"How did it happen?" Bovard asked.

"Probably the same way it always happens," the sergeant said. "She found her some new meat once he—"

"No," Bovard said quickly. "I mean the eye. How did he lose it?"

"Oh, that," Malone said. "Well, from what I heard, he was in a saloon and some preacher started spouting off about the war being nothing but a moneymaker for the fat cats. One thing led to another, and Franks took a swing at him. Before it was over, he had a piece of glass in his eye. Broken bottle, I suspect."

Bovard took a handkerchief from his pocket and wiped his forehead. "Have they arrested the man who did it?"

"I believe so."

Just then, First Lieutenants Waller and Bryant appeared on their way to the dining hall. Bovard waited until they passed on by, then said, "Well, there's not much we can do about it now. I just wish he'd come and talked to one of us before he did something so stupid."

"Ah, sir, he's not the first man to fuck his life up over a letter from home."

"No, I suppose not," Bovard said, thinking of the anguish he'd felt upon first receiving his last one from Elizabeth.

"Over at the Front, I saw a dozen or more go to the firing squad over that silly horseshit. People can get downright crazy when it comes to gettin' dumped."

"Christ, you don't think they'll execute him, do you?"

"No, sir, not over here, but I imagine they'll make it rough on him for a while, then send him home with a dishonorable."

"I suppose I better go see him this afternoon, write up a report," Bovard said. He started to turn away toward the dining hall. He hated to think what that obnoxious loudmouth Waller would say about this. Ever since Lucas's name had come up during lunch that day, the son-ofabitch had been needling him in pissy little ways. Bovard had been thinking a lot about a story Malone had told him that involved some soldiers who had murdered their commanding officer and made it look like he had stepped on a land mine. Five months ago he would have never dreamed of doing such a thing, but if Waller kept it up, well, who knew what might happen once they got to France? "Sir, you still need a groom," he heard the sergeant say.

Bovard stopped. From where he stood he could see the hospital, and, beyond it, the stables. Oh, well, he thought, if he couldn't have his pick, what did it matter who it turned out to be? Maybe the pain of Wesley's absence at his side would make death at the Front even sweeter. "You were right," he said over his shoulder to Malone. "I should have listened to you in the first place."

"Sir?"

"About Cooper. He's by far the best man for the job."

49

AT NINE O'CLOCK, Cane left his brothers sitting on the south bank of Paint Creek and rode into Meade to look around. Within a few minutes, he was satisfied that the town was big enough that they wouldn't attract attention. The sidewalks were overflowing with people of all sorts, and the streets crowded with every type of horse and mule and car and wagon imaginable. A hundred different sounds filled the sour, slightly chemical air. He returned two hours later and printed in block letters on a piece of paper the name of the livery and the hotel that he wanted Chimney to use, told him where they could be found. "Me and Cob will go first," Cane said. "Give us half an hour. Then ride in and stable the horse and rent yourself a room. Buy some clothes and get cleaned up, then go find out what you can about buying that automobile."

"Jesus, anything else?"

"Yeah, there's a park at the north end of the street you'll be going in on. We'll meet you there by the pond this evening at six o'clock. Better buy yourself a watch."

"Did ye see any whores?" Chimney said.

"No, but don't worry about that right now. From the looks of things, I expect there's plenty around." Cane counted out five hundred dollars and placed it in Chimney's hand. "That should buy the car and keep you going for a while."

Crossing over the bridge on South Paint Street, he and Cob passed the paper mill. They veered off into the east end of town a ways and left their horses at Jonson's Livery, slipping an extra dollar to a stable bum named Chester Higgenbotham to make sure they got some grain. Then they walked uptown to the Hotel McCarthy. Inside the two saddlebags they carried nearly $35,000 and three pistols, along with their mother's Bible and the dictionary. Cane asked the clerk, a man named Harlan Dix, for a room with two beds and a bathtub. Dix cast a glance at them, noted their shaggy, unkempt appearance. Though he himself deplored the growing emphasis on personal hygiene as another reason why the country was turning soft, the McCarthy had a reputation for being the premier hotel in town, and his boss kept rates high to discourage clients such as this motley pair. "Five dollars a night," he said. "In advance." Just as he was getting ready to suggest the Warner down the street, Cane handed him twenty dollars for four days. He stared for a moment at the money, then shrugged and gave them two keys. "Second floor," he said, pointing at the stairway. "Number eight."

Though certainly not one of the hotel's best, the room was still the nicest the brothers had ever been in. It contained two narrow beds and a round woven carpet and a cedar bureau, along with some hooks on the wall for hanging clothes. An upholstered chair sat in the corner. White lacy curtains hung from the two long windows that looked out on the busy street. Another door led to a bathroom with a claw-foot tub. Cob kept pulling the chain that turned on the electric light hanging from the ceiling until Cane, worried that he might break it, told him to stop. Of course, neither of them had ever used a commode before, and it took a minute or two to figure out exactly how it worked. Even then, Cob was afraid of it, and if it hadn't been for his brother telling him he'd get arrested, he would have gladly done his business in the alley behind the hotel rather than risk some sort of injury.

A few minutes later, Cane walked down the street alone to a dry goods store called Lange Mercantile. After standing outside for a minute, looking at various items displayed in the windows, he went in through the double wooden doors. He was browsing along the first aisle when he suddenly realized that he could buy anything in the goddamn place if he wanted. He thought about that as he watched a dirty little man in a funny white helmet and knee-high rubber boots crouch down to admire a bathroom display in the plumbing section. He recognized that look. He'd seen it in his brothers' faces whenever they followed Pearl into a store, and stood gazing longingly at everything they couldn't have while he carefully counted out the pennies to buy some little thing they couldn't do without, a few nails, say, or a can of strap oil. Never anything more than that. He took one more glance at the man, then moved on to the next aisle.

He ended up buying Cob a pair of bib overalls and two shirts and a pair of sturdy brogans and a cloth cap; and for himself, a new gray suit and a pair of ankle-high leather boots. He also picked up several pairs of socks and underwear and tooth powder and brushes and a razor and a bottle of perfumed water, along with some gauze and tape and a bottle of alcohol to dress Cob's leg. At the back of the store, in a corner behind the veterinary supplies, he stumbled upon several tall stacks of used books for sale, and his immediate thought was to purchase them all, but then he realized how impractical that would be, at least for now. He wasn't exactly sure why he loved them, but he knew that he did; and someday, he vowed, he'd have that many or more. He ended up choosing a slightly mildewed copy of *Shakespeare's Tragedies*, remembering that a short passage from the playwright in the *McGuffey Reader*, something about time and how it rushes by so quickly, had been one of his mother's favorites. He then began carrying everything to the front of the store.

A tired-looking man in a bow tie took his money and wrapped everything up in brown paper. "You got quite a load there," the clerk said. "Want me to get a boy to help you with it?"

"No, I can manage," Cane replied. "Don't have that far to go." He walked back to the hotel with the packages and found Cob pulling the light chain again. He ran a tub of hot water, and they each took a bath. Then he shaved them both and demonstrated how to use the toothbrush. "I want you to do this at least once every couple days," he told Cob. He poured some alcohol on the wound and taped gauze around it. Dressed in their new clothes, they went downstairs and out the front door, the clerk hardly recognizing them now. They walked about for a while enjoying their new duds and looking in shop windows. Cane bought some cigars and two pints of bonded whiskey at a liquor store and a small ham from a butcher shop and a bag of doughnuts from a bakery called Mannheim's. At a place called the Belleview, they ate their first restaurant meal, and while they waited on their dessert, they saw the stable bum they'd left their horses with hurry past the window. Though they had no way of knowing, Chester's boss, Hog Jonson, had just informed him a few minutes ago that, with the way automobiles were taking over now, he had decided to shut the stable down after Thanksgiving and start a garage with a couple of his nephews. It was the worst piece of news Chester had received since a judge sentenced him to a ten-year term for manslaughter in the Mansfield Reformatory back when he was twenty, and he was on his way to the Mecca Bar to settle his nerves with the dollar Cane had tipped him. All he'd ever done since his release from prison was work with horses; and now, at fifty-seven, he was too old to start over, but he was also too broke to retire. It was happening all over, Hog had told his wife when she asked what his stable hand would do, men and animals being replaced by machines. Nobody gave a shit as long as they weren't the ones losing out. Don't worry about it, he said, ol' Chester will figure something out. And if he don't, he can always go back to the pen.

50

In the meantime, Chimney had settled his horse at Kirk's Stables, four blocks over from Jonson's, and given the livery man an extra two dollars to keep his Enfield safe for him. In the saddlebag he slung over his shoulder were two Smith & Wessons and a box of shells. One of the Remington .22s was stuck inside his grimy overalls. He watched the man lock the rifle in a cabinet, then walked uptown to the Warner, the hotel Cane had written on the piece of paper.

The desk clerk was reading a book when Chimney walked in. "Can I help you?" he asked. His name was Roland Blevins, and, with the exception of the black ink stains on his fingers, he was what his mother proudly called "the most fastidious and upright young man in southern Ohio" whenever she sensed that she might be talking to someone with an unwed daughter or sister. He brushed his woven black suit three or four times a shift, and not a single strand of hair on his rather pointy head was out of place thanks to the creamy gobs of Fussell's Hair Restorer he applied every morning. Everything about Roland pointed to clean and careful living. He wished he worked at a better establishment, one that didn't cater to riffraff like the boy standing before him, but so far he hadn't been able to get his foot in the door at any of the other hotels. Someday, though, he'd be the day manager over at the McCarthy. His mother was sure of it.

"Need a room," Chimney said.

"That would be two dollars a night," Roland replied.

"You got one with a bathtub?"

"Those are three dollars a night."

"I'll take one of them." Chimney pulled out a twenty-dollar gold piece and laid it on the counter.

"How many days do you plan to stay?"

"Not for sure yet. At least a couple."

The clerk opened the guest registry and told Chimney to sign his name. His stomach roiled just a little when he saw the new guest make two sloppy X's. Since he was a small child, Roland's hobby had been penmanship, and though he should have been hardened to it by now, encountering someone this early in the day who couldn't even print his name was almost too much to take. Just last week, a group of wealthy widows had asked him if he'd give a talk about the Palmer Method at one of their monthly soirées. By the end of the current century, he had predicted during the question and answer session that followed, typewriters and other gadgetry would make artful handwriting obsolete. His pronouncement practically sucked all the oxygen out of the room, and two of the oldest ladies had to be revived with smelling salts and tiny dabs of sweet sherry on their dry, crinkled lips. Mrs. Grady, the hostess, had gently admonished him for his negativity, but what he'd said was true all the same. Why, he doubted if even the bare rudiments of cursive would be taught in the classroom in another fifty years or so. He handed the boy his change and a key. "Room thirty-one, on the third floor."

Chimney started for the stairway, then came back to the desk. "Any idy where I might find me a whore?" he asked.

Roland already had his nose buried in the book again, an introduction to French grammar. He looked up with a startled expression on his face, as if he had been caught in some embarrassing act, which was nearly the case. If the old widows who had practically swooned over his talent with pen and ink had known to what depths he had recently sunk, he wouldn't have been allowed on their property, let alone to sit with them and sip tea from a dainty cup all afternoon. Though his wages at the Warner barely kept him afloat, he had taken out what was for him a substantial loan and visited the Whore Barn several times over the past few weeks to lay with a young trollop who spoke French. Peaches had taken his virginity away from him while whispering *"très bien"* over and over into his ear, and now he was infatuated with her. He covered the book with his hand and quickly said to Chimney, "I don't know anything about that." That was the bad thing about falling in love with a whore; anyone with four bits in their pocket was a potential rival. It was driving him crazy, the number of men he imagined rubbing their rough beards and dirty paws over that pale, beautiful body. His plan to win her over by mastering the language of love had seemed brilliant at first, but it was proving more difficult than he'd expected. He had tossed and turned all last night worrying about it, finally deciding, just before his mother called him down to breakfast, that if he hoped to make sense out of the verb conjugations, he was going to have to hire a tutor. It didn't occur to him until later that morning that if he did that, he wouldn't be able to afford to fuck Peaches anymore—that is, unless maybe he got another loan. To be in love, he was beginning to realize, meant being mired in one goddamn mess after another.

"You sure?"

"Of course I'm sure," Roland said. He looked around nervously, then offered Chimney a handbill from a stack on the counter. "Here, if you need something to do, go over to the Majestic and see the Lewis Family."

"What's the Majestic?"

"Only one of the finest theaters in the Midwest," Roland said. "Right up the street and around the corner."

"What do they do, this family you're talkin' about?"

"Sing, dance, tell jokes, you name it," the clerk said. "Good clean fun. They come through here at least three or four times a year. Just seeing Mr. Bentley is worth the price of admission."

"Who's he?"

"He's the monkey," the clerk said.

Chimney studied the picture of the five grinning stooges and the primate dressed in a little sailor suit. Unless that monkey was putting out, he wasn't interested, but it sounded like something Cob might get a kick out of. Hell, he'd probably go nuts over such a thing. He thought about the pet squirrel they'd kept for a week or so that summer they picked cotton in Alabama, and how Cob had bawled like a baby when he woke up one morning to discover Pearl frying it up in a pan. Wouldn't even eat breakfast he was so upset, which was the first time that had ever happened. "Mind if I keep this?" he asked.

"Go ahead."

Chimney stuck the paper in his pocket and went on up the stairs. After taking a glance about the room, he hid the two Smith & Wessons under the mattress and walked down to a store called Burton's that sold men's clothing and accessories. He bought a pair of soft black-and-gray-striped trousers and a lavender shirt and a derby and a new pair of shoes, along with a pair of long johns and some soap and a bottle of rosewater. On the way back to the hotel, he stopped at a barbershop called O'Malley's and got a shave and a haircut for a quarter. An old man, bald as a turtle, sat in a chair by the window, half asleep. "Any idy where I might find me a whore?" Chimney asked as the barber lathered his face.

"Jesus Christ, son, just look around," the barber said as he began scraping some peach fuzz off the boy's skinny neck. "The world's crawling with 'em. I ought to know. I married one, didn't I, Jim?"

The old man by the window jerked up with a startled expression on his face. "Who? What? You mean Nancy? Aw, she's not so bad."

The barber laughed bitterly. "That's my father-in-law," he whispered low in Chimney's ear, the sour smell of his breath nearly making the boy's eyes water. "He don't know shit."

"What'd ye say?" the old man asked.

"Nothing," the barber said. "Not a goddamn thing. Just talkin' to my customer here."

"I'm serious," Chimney said. "Where can I find one?"

The man wiped the remaining lather off the boy's face with a towel and turned to pick up a pair of scissors. "There's two taxis that park down here on the corner every evening after six o'clock. Either one of them can show ye."

Now he was getting somewhere, Chimney thought. Then the barber turned him in the chair, and he saw an automobile drive past the window. "They a place around here sells cars?" he asked.

"Jesus, what'd ye do? Rob a bank?"

"What's that 'sposed to mean?" Chimney said, laying his hand on the butt of the little Remington stuck in his pants.

"Well, first you asking about buyin' whores, and now automobiles. Sounds like he's got money to spend, don't it, Jim?"

"I don't know," the old man muttered. It was obvious that the crack about his daughter had hurt his feelings.

"Oh, don't be mad, Jim," the barber said. "I was just kiddin' about Nancy. You know that."

"Well."

"Besides, it shouldn't be nothing to you anyway. Hell, I'm the one stuck with her now."

"Clarence, you shouldn't talk like that. Nancy's all right."

"Best place to go look at cars is Triplett's," the barber said, turning back to Chimney. "Just make a left when you leave and another left at the first street. You'll see his lot a couple blocks down. I'd go with ye and buy one myself, but that *all right* bitch I'm married to keeps me in the poorhouse. Ain't that right, Jim?"

Chimney got out of the chair and studied himself in the mirror for a moment, then paid the man. Picking up his bundle of new clothes, he walked back to the hotel and took a hot bath. As he soaped himself up, he thought about the barber and his wife, wondered if she was really as bad as he'd let on. She must be, otherwise why would the bald-headed father-in-law put up with such insults? Christ, the slut was probably bent over a chair getting fucked by someone right now. His hand went down between his legs as he tried to imagine what she felt like. By the time he finished, he had water splashed all over the floor around the tub. He hurriedly dried off, then put on his new clothes and went down the stairs and out the door onto the street. The weather was fine, the sky a soft, cloudless blue. Walking past the hotel where Cane and Cob were staying, he entered a joint called the McAdams. It was the first time he'd ever been in a bar, but he sat down on a stool and noncha-lantly ordered a beer and a steak sandwich like he'd hung out in them all his life. He made small talk with the keep while he ate, then went on down the street looking for the car lot.

Chimney knew absolutely nothing when it came to automobiles, but there were at least a dozen parked on the gravel of various years and models. He was walking around looking them over when a man in a pair of greasy coveralls came out of a garage and introduced himself as Tom Triplett. "You looking for a car?"

"Could be," Chimney said. "Ain't decided yet."

"Well, take your time," the man said. "It's probably the most important purchase you'll make in your lifetime. You from around here?"

"No," Chimney said.

"What brings you to Meade?" Triplett asked, wondering, as he looked at the customer's clothes, if he might be a carny, or another one of those entertainers the fruitcake over at the Majestic was always bringing in. Most of the acts he'd seen there over the years weren't worth the quarter admission fee, though he would admit that goddamn bunch called the Lewis Family did put on a hell of a show once they got wound up.

"Oh, nothing much. Thought maybe I'd buy me a whore."

Triplett didn't bat an eye. Ever since the pimp and his women appeared out of nowhere a few weeks ago, half the men in Meade had whores on their mind, one way or another. He didn't approve of them for the most part, but that most part was because Blackie kept sending his bodyguard over with IOUs for services they had provided to his son, Jeffrey. "Buy ye one of these and you won't have to pay for it," he told Chimney.

"What do ye mean?"

"Hell, son, ain't nothing gets a woman hotter than ridin' around in a nice car."

"That right?" Chimney said.

"As God is my witness," Triplett said. "Why, my boy, Jeffrey, he . . ." The salesman felt his stomach begin to fizz, and he clapped his mouth shut. Talking about his son would just set his ulcer on fire again. The lazy sonofabitch had slithered home again this morning past dawn, all scratched to hell and stinking drunk, looking like an animal that should be shot and put out of its misery. He'd fuck anything with two legs. "Take this car, for example," Triplett said to Chimney, pointing at a shiny red Packard. "Why, I guarantee you, you drive this car uptown tonight, you'll have to fight the women off. Let me ask ye something. How is it ye get around now?"

"Horse," Chimney said.

"Horse!" Triplett laughed. "No wonder you have to pay for it. Ain't no young modern woman wants to be seen on a horse these days."

"I don't know how to drive," Chimney said.

"Shoot, there's nothing to it. I can show ye everything you need to know in a couple hours."

"How much?"

"Well, depends on what you want."

"Which one's the fastest?"

"That'd be the Packard. It'll go sixty miles an hour on good road. I could let you have it for two thousand, including the tax. She's the same as brand-new."

"No," Chimney said, shaking his head, "I can't afford nothin' like that."

"Well, how much can ye afford?"

The boy looked around, then pointed at a black Ford touring car. "How much for that one?"

Triplett rubbed his chin. A man from Clarksburg had traded it in two weeks ago, complaining that it was cold-natured, but he hadn't had time to check out the problem yet. "That one I could let go for two-fifty. She's got a few miles on her, but she's been taken good care of."

"And you can show me how to drive it?"

"Sure, I'll take ye out today if you want."

They went into the office and Chimney counted out the money. The man started scribbling in a receipt book. "What's your name?"

"Hollis Stubbs."

"How do ye spell that?"

"I don't know. Nobody ever showed me."

Triplett made a guess at it, then handed over the receipt. "Always keep this with you so you got proof you own it." Then he shucked off the coveralls and put on a pair of goggles and a long duster. "I'll show you how to start it first," he told Chimney. He proceeded to explain pulling out the choke lever and priming the engine with the crank, then setting the throttle and the spark advance before giving it one more crank to fire it up. He went through the whole procedure twice, the first time slowly, the second time quickly. The car started up fine both times, and he wondered, first, if the man from Clarksburg knew what the fuck he was talking about, and second, if he should have charged the boy a little more for it. "Think ye got it?" he said.

"I think so," Chimney said.

"Good," Triplett said, hopping in on the driver's side. "Once we get out of town, I'll put you behind the wheel."

BACK AT THE McCarthy, Cane was sitting in the room trying to make sense out of the first act of *Richard III* when he glanced out the window and saw two men drive by in a black automobile. It wasn't until a few minutes later, as he was telling Cob again to take it easy on the doughnuts, that he realized the dandy sitting in the passenger's seat wearing the purplish shirt had been their little brother.

51

As soon as he finished helping Malone run the men through a drill on gas defense that afternoon, Lieutenant Bovard headed for the infirmary. A nurse in white showed him to the curtained-off area where an anesthetized Wesley was recuperating from his surgery. Other than a white bandage taped over the left side of his face, a cut on his chin and a small bruise on his forehead seemed to be his only other injuries. Pulling up a metal chair, the lieutenant sat down beside the bed. He heard, coming from down the hall, the evangelizing voice of the clap doctor warning another group of new recruits about the connections between syphilis germs and prostitutes and contaminated toilet seats. "Blindness, insanity, and death!" Eisner yelled as he finished the sermon. "Abstinence, gentlemen, that's the only way you'll survive!"

Eventually, Wesley opened his right eye and looked over, saw his lieutenant. In a voice a bit slurry with painkillers, he said slowly, "First darn time I was ever drunk in my life and look what happened."

"Just so you know," Bovard said, "I heard they arrested the man who attacked you."

"Aw, I should have left him alone, him being a preacher and all, but he just kept on about . . . Heck, I can't remember now. Something to do with the war, I think."

"Has anyone been around to talk to you yet?"

"No, sir, I ain't heard nothing other than I lost my eye."

Bovard felt he should say something encouraging, but what could that possibly be? Disappointment filled the room. No chance for a glorious death now, the poor kid. He imagined Wesley going back to whatever dismal farm or hamlet he had come from once he was released from the brig. "I'll ask ol' Lloyd Beavers about hiring you on at the granary," his father would tell him; and a few months later he'd marry some wide-hipped local girl, sealing his fate forever, though, of course, the boy wouldn't think of it like that, at least not for the first couple of weeks. Bovard, however, could see it all: a month or two of wedded bliss wiped out in seconds by the first serious spat over something as trivial as a burned meatloaf; and then the years passing by one after another, the struggle to make ends meet, the burden of a passel of brats to feed and clothe, the inevitable decline. A lifetime after the war has ended, Wesley sitting on his stoop, his black hair turned gray, worn out with niggling worries and constant back pain and the same old same old. He clutches a brown bottle of home brew in his knotty, arthritic hand. He looks toward the horizon, the quiet evening surrounding him in a lonesome, regretful sadness. His children now gone, his wife suffering from yet another ailment. He hears her inside the house, moving about slowly, muttering to herself. His hand reaches up and touches the black eye patch. Back when it happened, everyone had said he was lucky that he didn't have to go fight. But now, looking around his tiny square of yard at the clumps of dead grass and the old, weather-cracked tire swing hanging in the tree, he . . .

"Am I gonna go to prison?" Wesley suddenly said.

Jerked out of his reverie, Bovard cleared his throat. "Well, I'm not sure, but what you did, it's considered a serious offense."

"What if you talked to them for me? I swear the only reason I took off was my girlfriend sent me a letter saying she was gettin' married."

"I'm sorry, Wesley, but I'm afraid that wouldn't do any good."

"No, probably not."

"What about your family?" Bovard said. "Would you like for me to contact them, let them know what's happened?" The nurse, a crabby, thin-lipped woman, came back and looked in at them, then went away.

"Oh, no, sir, I'd rather you didn't. Truth is, the day I signed up was the proudest my old man's ever been of me, and I don't want to ruin that quite yet."

"I understand," Bovard said, standing up to leave. "Well, good luck."

"I still can't believe she's gettin' hitched to ol' Froggy Conway," Wesley said bitterly, a trace of anger starting to surface through the dope haze. "I swear to God, sir, he's damn near as old as my granddaddy."

"Look, I know it might be hard to imagine now, but I'd wager one of these days you'll see it was the best thing that could have happened."

"Well, you might be right about that. Truth is, I ain't had much feeling for her ever since I got in her knickers last spring. For some reason, I thought it would be more fun than it was. But Froggy Conway? I'll be the joke of the town when I go back home. Jesus. The sonofabitch looks like a hoptoad." He bit his lip to keep from crying and looked toward the window. Just then, he almost wished the old preacher had killed him last night. There weren't but four hundred people in Veto, which meant that he'd see her and Froggy every time he turned around. And that wasn't the worst of it; even if people forgot Mary Ann had cheated on him, they would never forget that he'd deserted his post. Maybe he could move away, he thought, find a job in Pomeroy or Gallipolis, some town where people didn't know him. He was getting ready to ask Bovard what he thought he should do when he realized the man was gone. Might as well get used to it, Wesley thought sadly. Nobody wanted anything to do with him now, not even his lieutenant.

52

AROUND FIVE O'CLOCK that evening, Chimney completed his driving lesson and took Triplett back to his office. The salesman climbed out of the car, his stomach in worse shape than ever. The boy was probably the most reckless driver he had ever met, but at the same time he did have a knack for it. At least a dozen times Triplett had thought they were goners, but somehow the little sonofabitch always managed to pull off another miracle. Triplett tore off his goggles and duster and sucked some air down into his lungs. He'd been so tense for the last hour he'd barely been able to breathe. "Where would I find me an outfit like the one you're wearing?" Chimney asked him.

"Go to Wissler's down on Second Street," Triplett said, still a little dizzy. "That's where I buy all my gear."

Chimney made it to the hardware store just before they closed. He bought a pair of tinted goggles and tight leather gloves and a tan-colored duster, then drove back to the hotel and spent ten minutes trying to park along the curb between a roadster with a flat tire and a wagon filled with crates of apples. He rushed upstairs and washed the dust off his face and hands and combed his hair, then put on his new driving ensemble and admired himself in the mirror. Locking the door to his room, he walked past the ink-stained desk clerk and headed for the park.

Cane was seated on a wooden bench by the pond watching Cob throw bits of bread out onto the water for the ducks. He was mulling over the last scene he had read in *Richard III,* in which the cripple has two nephews drowned in a wine cask. Because this Shakespeare fellow used so many words he'd never heard before, it was hard to figure out exactly what was going on at times; but he was thinking Chimney would probably love a story filled with such meanness when he looked up and saw him striding toward them in his new clothes: the striped pants and purple shirt bright against the tan duster, the goggles covering half his face, the derby sitting atop his head like a black egg.

"So you got it?" Cane said. "The automobile?"

"I did. A Ford. 'Coop,' the man called it. The sonofabitch will go thirty-five miles an hour!"

"Where is it?" Cane asked, as Cob slung the rest of the bread into the pond, then walked over and stood silently looking at his younger brother.

"Parked up in front of the hotel. I been driving it around all afternoon with the salesman. Startin' it up's a little tricky, but I almost got the hang of it."

"Good," Cane said. "What'd ye pay for it?"

"Two-fifty."

"You look funny," Cob spoke up.

"Fuck you," Chimney said. "This is what you wear when you're operatin' an automobile. Course, you wouldn't know nothin' about that. Shit, you can barely stay on a horse."

"Well, that might be," Cob said, "but me and Tom's got the biggest dern ham you ever seen up in our room."

"You watch out he don't try to molest it while you're sleeping."

"Huh?" Cob said.

"Never mind," Chimney said. He took the goggles off and stuck them in the pocket of the duster, then sat down on the bench. "Found out about some whores, too. All ye do is get in a taxi and he'll take you right to 'em."

"Boy, you have been busy, haven't ye?" Cane said.

"So I'm thinkin' we go out tonight and get us some."

"Me, too?" Cob said.

"Ah, I don't think you'd care for it, Junior," Cane said. "Besides, we can't all be seen together."

"But what am I gonna do then?"

"How about I buy you some ice cream at that place we passed and then walk you back to the hotel? You got that ham to eat on and there's still some doughnuts left."

"I reckon," Cob said.

"I'll wait for ye at the corner right down from where I'm staying," Chimney said, as he stood up. "You'll see the taxis settin' there. And don't take too long, either."

Forty minutes later, Cane finally showed up at the cab stand. "Jesus Christ," Chimney said, "I was about ready to take off by myself."

"Ah, you know how Cob is. He got started on that ice cream and didn't want to stop."

Just then a taxi pulled up and two soldiers hopped out of the back-seat. They were in a heated argument about something. They paid the driver and walked around the corner still going at it.

"What was that about?" Chimney asked the cabbie as they climbed in the car.

"Ah, they been out to the Whore Barn," the cabbie said. "The one with the glasses, he had trouble getting it up, and the other kept ridin' him about it. I expect they'll be a fight before they get back to camp. You can tell the red-faced fucker's one of those guys that likes to start shit." He turned in the seat and looked back at them. "Is that where you wanting to go, to the Whore Barn?"

"Yeah," Chimney said.

"This your first time?"

"Hell, no," Chimney said, "I've had plenty of women." He pulled a pint of whiskey from his duster pocket, twisted the cap off, and took a sip.

"No, I mean your first time to the Whore Barn."

"We just got into town," Cane said.

"Well, my advice is if Blackie tries to stick the fat one off on you, tell him you'll just wait for one of the others. Just between us, she's full of gonorrhea." Ever since the cabbie had paid Esther to take a leak on his chest and she'd accidently drenched his new toupee instead, he had been informing everyone that she was wracked with various loathsome and incurable diseases. Not only had she ruined the hairpiece, but she'd made a wisecrack about it, as well, saying it looked so much like a muskrat, it should have been waterproof; and if there was anything he hated worse than a woman with poor bladder control, it was one with a smart mouth. Chimney passed him the pint, and he took a pull and handed it back.

"Who's Blackie?"

"He's their pimp."

"What's that?" Chimney asked.

"Why, he's the one you pay."

"Oh, like their madam," Chimney said, recalling Miss Ashley, the red-haired, ivory-skinned woman who ran Bloody Bill's favorite whorehouse back in Denver, Colorado.

"Madam? Uh, yeah. Only he's a man."

"How much they charge for a piece?" Chimney said as the cabbie pulled out and headed the car south down Paint Street.

"Oh, it's cheap enough," the cabbie said. "You can get a shot of pussy and two drinks for less than five bucks. Course it depends on what you want, too. Some things cost a little more."

"What do ye mean?" Chimney said.

"Well, say you want to get pissed on or have your balls blistered with a candle. That'd be extra."

"Pissed on?" Chimney said. "What kind of sick fucker would want something like that?"

"Oh, I don't know," the cabbie said, shifting uncomfortably in his seat. "I'm just tellin' you what I've heard."

"Well, we just want some of the regular," Chimney said. "The freaks can have all that other shit."

The cabbie took them out on the Huntington Pike a quarter of a mile and drove down a lane, pulling up and stopping in front of a long open shed. "This is it?" Chimney said, sounding a little disappointed. He'd been imagining something grand, like the House of Love, a bordello that Bloody Bill once shot up in Kansas City, all stained-glass windows and mahogany woodwork with a string quartet playing on the stone terrace.

"Yep," the cabbie said. "But don't let the looks of it discourage you none. And if you're anything like me, I'd say you've laid with women in places a lot worse than this. Why, one of the best fucks I've ever had was in a coal bin." In front of the shed a man in a white shirt and paisley vest sat alone at a campfire with a tin coffee cup in his hand. Off to the right, an older-model car and a huge wagon were parked alongside a wire pen that held some horses eating from a mound of hay. Three tents were pitched in a row inside the shed. Several soldiers were drinking at a bar made from boards set across two barrels and talking to another man with a holstered pistol on his side. Half a dozen lanterns hung from beams inside the shed, but they weren't lit yet and the place looked more like a camp for migrant workers than a cathouse. "Who do we talk to?" Chimney asked as they got out.

"The man a-sittin' at the fire," the cabbie said. "He'll fix you up."

When Blackie saw them approaching, he stood up and smiled at them with the biggest, whitest teeth they had ever seen. His thick, dark hair was slicked back in a high pompadour that reminded Cane of a rooster's crest. "You boys lookin' for some fun?"

"Yeah," Chimney said.

"Well, you came to the right place," Blackie said. "I got one named Matilda who's free at the moment."

"She ain't the fat one, is she?"

"No, that's Esther. You want her, you'll have to wait in line. Those boys standing at the bar are next. Matilda's a little on the lean side, but she's a wildcat in the sack."

"How much?"

"Matilda's a high-quality four-dollar piece."

"She'll do," Chimney said, pulling out some money. "Maybe I'll try the big one later."

"Last tent down," the pimp said. "Go ahead. She'll be waiting on ye." Then he turned to Cane and looked at his suit. "Now you look like a man who likes something a little more refined. I got a real lady who speaks French. She's with another customer right now, but they should be about finished."

"How much does she cost?" Cane asked, trying to hide the nervousness in his voice. He watched his brother disappear inside the brown canvas tent.

"Peaches is the same as Matilda."

Cane had just handed the man his money when a wheezing old-timer with brown, leathery skin came out of the second tent dragging one leg behind him. He stopped and bent over, hacked a throat-full of yellowish phlegm onto the ground, then continued on until he disappeared into the line of trees beyond the horse pen. "There ye go," Blackie said, "right on time."

As he walked past the soldiers, Cane heard them talking among themselves about Esther. "She'll do anything you want and you don't have to pay extra for it, either. Me and ol' Dugan double-teamed her the other night, worked her over from the front and the back till we damn near met in the middle." With a little trepidation, he pulled back the flap on the tent and stooped down a little as he entered. A woman with long blond tresses and a pretty face was squatted down over a bucket in the corner, but when she saw him, she sprung up and pulled her white slip down. She reached over and picked up a cigarette from a little wooden box on the table, then said with a frown, "Just give me a couple minutes, okay? I need a smoke."

"Take your time," Cane said. "I'm not in any hurry." He was a little surprised at how comfortable the tent looked, almost like a regular room. A padded chair sat in the corner, and on a polished nightstand beside the small bed was a lit candle and some slightly wilted wildflowers in a blue vase.

"I'm supposed to get five minutes between customers."

"I'm sorry, but he told me to come on back. The boss, I mean."

"Yeah, Blackie's a slave driver. That's what Matilda calls him."

"Want me to step back outside until you're ready?"

"No, Jesus, don't do that. He'll wonder what's going on. Just take your pants off and lay down on the bed."

Cane glanced over at the bucket, then sat down in the chair instead. He tried not to think about the old, dirty bastard who had just left the tent a couple of minutes ago, looking like a mummy emerging from his tomb. Christ, if he'd actually been able to get an erection, she probably still had some of his dusty wad up inside her. Though he wanted a woman, he didn't want one this bad. He was trying to figure a way out of it without hurting her feelings when he remembered what the pimp had said. "So, you speak French?" he asked her.

"I do," Peaches said, exhaling a plume of smoke, "but only for money."

"Well, how about you just talk to me for a while? To tell ye the truth, I think I'm too worn out to do anything else."

"You mean in French?"

"Yeah," Cane said. "We built a fence one time for a man whose wife spoke it whenever she was pissed at him. I always did like the sound of it."

"It'll cost you a dollar extra."

"That's all right," Cane said. He took a dollar out of his pocket and laid it beside the flower vase.

Peaches stabbed the cigarette out in an ashtray, then stood up and shook out her hands, as if she were getting ready to perform some great feat. *"Parlez-vous Français?"* she asked with a wink. *"Oui,"* she replied, nodding her head. It turned out that her entire act was composed of perhaps a dozen or so such words and phrases. Then, as far as Cane could tell, she repeated everything two more times before finally stopping and looking down at his crotch. "Did ye get off yet?"

"What?" he asked, a little confused. "No, I was just . . . You mean men actually . . ."

"Well, yeah, that's the point, ain't it?" She reached for another cigarette. "Hold on a minute and I'll start over. Try to pay attention this time."

"No, that's all right," Cane said, relieved that it was over with. "Like I said, I'm wore out." He stood and turned to exit.

"Wait," she said, grabbing his arm. "Look, I don't want you complaining to Blackie, so if you're in the mood for something else, I'd be happy to oblige. As long as it's not too, well, too unnatural. You want something like that, you'll have to see Esther."

"No, no, it's been nice," Cane said. "Don't worry, I got no complaints." He bent through the flap and damn near ran over another customer waiting outside, a big-bellied, middle-aged man sucking on a lollipop and wearing a green eyeshade.

He bought a splash of whiskey for a quarter from the man at the bar, and nursed it while listening to the soldiers yipping and yowling like dogs inside the front tent where the fat lady was stationed. The pimp still sat at the campfire, but now he was slicing an apple with a knife, dabbing each thin piece into some salt sprinkled on a stump beside him before he stuck it in his mouth. It was another thirty minutes before Chimney finally emerged from the last tent, a sheepish grin on his face. He walked over to Blackie and said, "I owe you for two more." He pulled some bills out of his pocket and handed him eight dollars, then motioned for Cane that he was ready to leave.

They walked back toward town, the taxi passing them on its way to the Whore Barn again. It felt nice to be out in the open and not hiding in some dismal swamp or ditch somewhere. Chimney couldn't stop talking about Matilda. How soft and velvety she felt inside, the sweet way she smelled, the manner in which she wrapped her legs around his back and held him tight after he shot his third load. "Third?" Cane said. "You were only in there an hour, if that."

"Shit, I could have gone five or six if I'd known what I was doing at first. What about you?"

"Just one," Cane lied.

"What'd she look like?"

"Oh, she was pretty enough," Cane said. "What about yours?"

"Matilda? She was beautiful."

"Well, I'm glad ye got you a good one," Cane said.

"So, what about tomorrow night?"

"What about it?"

"Go back out, get some more. Maybe you should try the fat one."

"Ah, I don't think so," Cane said. "I'll probably do something with Cob. Wouldn't be right to leave him alone every night."

"Well, that's up to you, but I already told Matilda I'd be back," Chimney said. "And I wouldn't want to break a promise."

"No, you wouldn't want to do that," Cane said, trying his best to sound at least a little sincere.

"And at four dollars a shot, why, hell, you can't beat that."

"No, it's cheap enough, I reckon."

"Matilda's probably worth twice that. And she's nice, too. I mean, for a whore."

"Well, just remember, those girls are apt to say anything for money."

"Oh, you don't need to tell me nothing," Chimney said. "Remember that damn Joletta Bunyan? She fed Bloody Bill enough lies to fill a corncrib." He started to say something else, but then stopped and pulled a flyer out of his pocket instead, handed it over.

"What's this?" Cane said. They were crossing the bridge and a car was headed toward them. He held the paper up in the glare from the headlamps and saw, in bold black letters: **THE LEWIS FAMILY! NOW APPEARING AT THE MAJESTIC THEATER!** Underneath the heading was a picture of some stout men in bow ties and an ape dressed in a sailor costume.

"Guy at the hotel gave it to me. It's like a show or something. I figured Cob might like to see the monkey."

"Yeah, I expect he would."

They were passing by the paper mill when Chimney noticed a saloon across the street. "How about we get us a beer?" he said. "All that lovemaking's got me thirsty."

"I bet it did," Cane said. He was a little worried about what Cob might be up to, but he didn't want to spoil Chimney's big night, either. "All right, but just one. Then I got to get back to the hotel."

The Blind Owl was empty except for the keep and a bearded man sitting alone at a table by the window, eating hog cracklings from a sheet of greasy newspaper. They asked for two beers, and Pollard served them with a grunt, then went back to the other end of the room. For a couple of minutes, they sat looking at their reflections in the mirror and listening to the man behind them crunch the rinds between his teeth. Finally, Chimney lifted his mug and said, "Race ye." Once they were back outside, he spat and said, "Goddamn, a graveyard would be livelier than that fuckin' place. What the hell's that sonofabitch's problem anyway?"

"Maybe he's one of them mutes," Cane suggested.

"Nah, a prick's more like it."

Before parting ways uptown, they walked over to take a look at their new car parked underneath a light around the corner from the Warner. "Like I told ye," Chimney said, "gettin' it started is a little tricky sometimes, but I'll figure it out."

"I hope so," Cane said, watching as his brother leaned over and rubbed the smudge of a handprint off the front fender with his shirt-sleeve. "That thing's our way out of here." He yawned and stretched, then looked down the street toward the McCarthy. "Make sure you make it to the park tomorrow evening, okay?"

"I'll be there."

Back in the hotel room, Cane found Cob flat on his back in bed snoring loudly. He saw that half the ham was gone and all of the dough-nuts. He hung up his suit coat and took off his shoes and sat down in the chair next to the window. Cob muttered something in his sleep, then rolled over on his side. Turning on the lamp, Cane took a sip of whiskey from one of the pints he had bought, then picked up the Shakespeare and turned to the page in *Richard III* he had dog-eared. After a while, he put the book down and looked out the window at the dark store-fronts across the street. It was the end of their first night in Meade. Much had been accomplished, and there hadn't been the slightest sign of trouble.

53

THE NEXT MORNING, Cob awoke early, already thinking about doughnuts. He looked over at Cane, dead to the world, the book opened on his chest and the bottle nearly empty on the nightstand. He put on his new clothes and slipped out, quietly closing the door behind him. He headed first thing to the bakery where they had stopped yesterday. He went inside and laid five dollars that Cane had given him on the counter and asked the lady working if that was enough to buy a dozen doughnuts. Mrs. Mannheim, a thin, nervous woman with a fingerprint of flour on her forehead, immediately suspected that he was testing her. She glowered at him with bloodshot eyes. Two days ago, the city councilman known as Saunders had accused her of shorting him a nickel, even had the nerve to suggest that she was sending the money she cheated honest Americans out of to her relatives over in "Deutschland," as he'd called it. She had lain awake all night worrying about what sort of trouble he might cause for her and Ludwig, her husband.

She looked down at the money on the counter. It was obvious that they had decided to send in one of their flunkies posing as an idiot to see if she would overcharge him. It was all a conspiracy, just because she and Ludwig were of German heritage. She had lived in Meade nearly fifteen years, and was as patriotic as anybody else in Ross County, but ever since America had declared war in April, she sensed that people were casting suspicious looks her way. The newspapers were urging everyone to be on the lookout for enemy spies. One little slipup and she and Ludwig would be on the shit list. After that, who knew what might happen? Burn their business down? Put them on trial for treason? She had shaken Ludwig awake last night, and told him they should start taking turns guarding the place at night. He had groaned and covered his head with his pillow to shut her out, but then he'd always been too

trusting when it came to people. By the time he saw the light, everything they had worked so hard for would be in ruins.

"Of course, of course," Mrs. Mannheim said to Cob. She bagged
up a dozen and handed them to him. He turned and started out before
she could make his change, leaving the five dollars on the counter. That
was all the proof she needed; now she was certain something was going
on. "Stop," she said in a harsh voice just as he reached for the doorknob.
"You forget this."

"What?"

"Come back here," she ordered.

Cob looked down at the money the woman placed in his hand, the
same amount he had laid on the counter. He was confused. "But ain't
you . . . ain't you supposed to . . ." he stammered.

"On de house," she said loudly, slapping her hand on the counter.
That would fix the bastards! Watching him take off his cap and scratch
his head, a look of befuddlement on his round face, she had to admit he
was a hell of an actor. Much better than that bunch of West Virginia
cretins that called themselves the Lewis Family who were performing
at the Majestic again this week. Ludwig was a big fan of theirs, he had
probably seen their show, if that's what you wanted to call it, a dozen
times over the last couple of years. They were always sending over for
a special request, hedge-apple turnovers or squirrel-brain pie or some
other hillbilly treat. As if they were still back in the snaky holler they
had crawled out of to win, by what had to be, she was convinced, some
perverse alignment of the stars, fame and fortune on the stage. Ludwig was always repeating their stupid jokes to the customers. Not a
one of them did she find funny. It made no sense, the way Americans
sometimes went bananas over certain people for absolutely no reason,
as if they were just drawing names out of a hat. She'd watched her own
nephew go insane over his fixation with a doll-faced bimbo whose only
talent was smiling prettily into a camera. How hard would Ludwig
hee-haw, she wondered, when a gang of liquored-up vigilantes pulled
them out into the street and hung them from a lamppost just for being
German? "Patriotic murder," she'd heard they called it. "On de house,"
she repeated to the stunned-looking flunky, pointing at the door.

Detecting the anger in her voice, Cob ducked his head and left the bakery. He walked along until he found a bench to sit on. He was eating doughnuts and mulling over the woman's strange behavior when he saw a man coming toward him wearing a white helmet and carrying a long stick. He was talking to himself and looking down at the sidewalk; and Cob thought he looked like he could use a little cheering up. "Hey, would you want one of these here doughnuts?" he asked. "The lady said they were *on de house.*"

Jasper Cone looked up, saw a stocky, round-headed man in new bib overalls smiling at him. He didn't quite understand at first. Nobody had ever, except maybe Itchy a time or two, offered him a doughnut before, but then he usually didn't partake of breakfast. It was a habit his mother had instilled in him when he was young. She had always stressed a morning fast to clear the head of dirty thoughts, mostly because she was convinced that anyone built like her son was probably oozing with them. "Don't mind if I do," Jasper said. Sticking his hand down into the greasy paper bag, he pulled one out and admired it for a moment, then sat down on the bench. He laid his measuring pole on the sidewalk in front of him and stretched out his legs, crossed one rubber-booted foot over the other.

They sat there for a while chewing in silence and watching the people pass by. Cob noticed that most of them moved over to the other side of the sidewalk as they neared the bench. Granted, the man had a certain ripeness about him, but still, that didn't account for the cold stares and hateful looks they cast his way. Most people, Cob concluded, weren't nearly as decent as they imagined themselves to be. Just look at the way he had turned out. Never in his darkest dreams would he have ever thought himself capable of killing a man, or stealing from one, and yet he had done both. Though he'd gladly give all the hams and pies and five-dollar bills in the state of Ohio just to see Tardweller ride by in his buggy, even he knew you couldn't wish away the past. He looked over and saw the man swallow the last of the doughnut, wipe the grease and sugar off his hand onto his dirty trousers. Cob held the bag out. "This is nice," Jasper said, reaching in for another.

"Yeah, they are good doughnuts," Cob replied.

"Well, not just that," Jasper said, reflecting on what the dump keeper had told him the other day. "Sitting here in the sun with a new friend and watchin' people walking to work or wherever they're a-going this time of the morning. It don't get much better than this, you know what I mean?"

Cob thought for a minute. He didn't know if anyone had ever called him "friend" before. Not that he could remember, anyway. But then he'd never had doughnuts to offer anyone, either. "Yeah, I think so," he said.

Jasper grinned and took another bite. It still amazed him how you could just be plugging along, stuck in the deepest depression, and then something a little bit wonderful happened that suddenly changed your outlook on everything, that turned your world from darkness to light, made you glad you were still walking the earth. Usually it was something that you didn't have anything to do with at all. For example, like when his mother died. She'd berated him all that morning about the same old stuff, then locked him in his room while she went to church to get her favorite chicken blessed; and five days later the flowers were already starting to wilt on her grave, and he was having the best time of his life cleaning out ol' Vern Melchert's jake with Itchy. And what about this? Why, no more than a couple of minutes ago he was feeling like the loneliest poor soul alive, and now he was eating glazed doughnuts from Mannheim's with a man he'd never seen before. It was all just a matter of sticking it out until the miracle happened.

Looking over at the fellow in the bibs, Jasper wondered if he knew anything about the importance of sanitation in a municipality the size of Meade. "Say, if'n you don't have anything else goin' on this morning," he said, "would you like to go with me while I do a couple of inspections?"

"Inspections? What's that?"

"Well, it's sort of like when a doctor gives someone an examination, only the patient is an outhouse instead." He reached down for his measuring pole, then stood up. "Come on, and I'll show ye."

Cob hesitated. He bit into another doughnut as he tried to think. Cane had warned him that talking to strangers was dangerous, but this one seemed all right. And hadn't he and Chimney gone out last night and did whatever they wanted while he sat in the room by himself? Still, he didn't want to get in any trouble. As Cane kept saying, they had come too far to mess things up now. "I don't know," he said. "Maybe I better—"

"Oh, come on," Jasper said. "It'll be fun. Besides, what else you going to do today?"

"Well."

The inspector smiled and stuck out his hand. "My name's Jasper Cone."

Cob looked blank for a second, then replied, "I'm Junior. Bradford. Junior Bradford."

"Nice to meet you, Junior."

At first he'd been a little nervous, but the longer Cob followed Jasper around that morning, the more at ease he began to feel. He listened to him talk on a variety of subjects: his old mentor, Itchy, and his boss, Mr. Rawlings, the art of killing rats, his father's paper mill accident and his mother's religious beliefs, his ongoing disputes with certain members of the city council, and on and on. Cob had never heard a man flap his jaws so much in his life. He watched Jasper conduct several inspections and write up a warning to post on the front door of someone's residence whose shitter was on the verge of toppling over into the neighbor's yard. After a couple of hours, they took another doughnut break, and then walked along an alley until they arrived at a backyard surrounded by a high wooden fence. Jasper pulled out a pocket watch and checked the time, then sat down behind the fence in the dirt and beckoned Cob to do the same. "They's a woman here that's as regular as clockwork," he said. "In two minutes she'll pop out that back door and head straight for the toilet, I guarantee it." They watched through a crack in the fence, and sure enough, in ninety seconds a middle-aged lady in a long blue dress exited the house and hurried across the lawn. After she closed the door to the crapper behind her, Jasper said with an air of authority, "Now, just watch, she'll be in there exactly four minutes." He showed the watch face to Cob. A few minutes later, the door creaked open and the woman went back inside the house. "Pretty good, ain't it, the way I got her figured out?"

"Yeah," Cob said, "I reckon."

"But I will admit," Jasper went on, "she's one of the easy ones. There's people would probably pay a hundred dollars to have a digestive system as regular as Mrs. Jackson's."

"That's a lot of money."

"Yeah, but you wouldn't believe how some of them struggle with it. Take ol' Herb Cutright, for example. The most awful straining and crying and groaning you ever heard, and heck, from the looks of things, he probably eats a handful of prunes with every meal."

"Poor feller," Cob said.

"Well, let's go check the level," Jasper said, opening the back gate quietly.

The sharp odor of the woman still lingered inside the small space, but Jasper didn't seem to mind. He showed Cob again how to measure the level, sticking the pole down the hole until it hit solids, then bringing it back up and examining it. "See," he said, "it's exactly two feet and five inches from the top of the hole to where you hit the excrement"—he'd been coaching his new friend all morning in the terminology: *feces, effluent, fecal matter, solids, liquids,* et cetera—"so she's still got a ways to go before she has to have it emptied. She might even last through the winter at the rate she's discharging."

"Who does that?" Cob asked.

"You mean empty them? Well, they can do it themselves if they want, but most people hire a scavenger if they can afford it. That's what I used to do before the city begged me to take this job. We got two operating in Meade now, Dwight Harris and Elwood Skaggs. I've made those ol' boys a lot of money the past few months, let me tell ye."

It had been a busy morning—seven outhouses inspected, a wasp nest pulled down and burned, two tickets written, and four rats taken out with a blackjack—and the time had flown by, but when the church bell at Saint Mary's struck noon, Cob suddenly remembered Cane back at the hotel. "I got to go," he told Jasper.

"What's your hurry?"

Cob thought the question over. Fortunately, Cane had coached him a little yesterday afternoon in what to say if he found himself in a tight spot, and though he wasn't sure if this qualified as one, he figured he better be careful just the same. "Tom will be wonderin' where I'm at," he finally said.

"Tom? Who's that?"

"My brother. He's at the hotel."

"Hotel?" Jasper said. "What ye do staying there? Are ye just traveling through?"

"Yeah," Cob replied.

"How long you plannin' on staying?"

"I don't know. Maybe a day or two."

A flicker of disappointment passed over Jasper's face, but then he reminded himself it was always better to look on the bright side. "Well, look, if you're still here in the morning and want to get in on some more inspections, just meet me at that bench around the same time, okay?" As he watched Junior turn and hurry off, he vaguely wondered where he and his brother might be going. He'd always wanted to take a trip himself, see how people did things, say, over in Indiana or up in Michigan. He hoped they stuck around for a while; it had been nice having someone to talk to who didn't make fun of him or call him names like Crapper Cop and Shit Bucket. In fact, it was better than nice; he figured it had been the best day he'd had since before Itchy died.

54

SHORTLY AFTER NINE o'clock that morning, Cane had awakened to find Cob missing. He shaved and washed up hurriedly and threw his clothes on, then spent the next two hours walking up and down the streets looking for him and regretting he'd ever drank that pint of whiskey last night. The last thing he remembered was Richard III limping along a gloomy corridor talking crazy shit to himself. What the hell would they do if Cob got lost, or, God forbid, got himself arrested for some trivial offense? Would he be able to keep his story straight? Cane was headed back to the McCarthy to see if his brother might have returned when he came upon a bookstore he had passed by earlier. Fuck it, he thought, ten minutes wouldn't make much difference one way or another. A bell rang when he opened the door, but he didn't see anyone behind the counter. He was looking through the shelves when a pretty, dark-haired woman by the name of Susannah Chapman came out of the back and asked if he needed any help finding something. Cane glanced at her, then quickly returned his gaze to the shelves. His throat constricted a little as he realized he was probably standing as close to a real lady as he ever had in his life, but after a moment, he managed to ask, in a slightly hoarse voice, "You wouldn't happen to have one called *The Life and Times of Bloody Bill Bucket*, would ye?"

"No," Susannah said, "I'm afraid I'm not familiar with that one. Is it something new?" It sounded trashy to her, and her father made it a point not to carry such books, which was a noble idea, but also an impractical one when it came to doing business in a factory town like Meade. Most people here weren't interested in expanding their minds or learning something new or reading the classics; they just wanted to be entertained a little in between another boring supper and another dead sleep.

"No, it's pretty old, I think." He turned and looked around the shop. "Nice place ye got here." The smell of so many books combined with her perfume was more intoxicating than any whiskey he'd ever tasted.

"Thank you," she said. "It's my father's store. I just help out sometimes."

"Ye got anything you'd recommend?"

"Well, what do you like?"

He shrugged. "Stories, I guess. Just started this one called *Richard the Third*."

"Oh, I love Shakespeare," she said. "'A horse, a horse, my kingdom for—'" She broke off then, putting her hand to her mouth and looking slightly embarrassed. "I'm sorry, I guess I got a little carried away. I almost gave away the ending." Even though he had a thick Southern accent and a cheap suit, Susannah noticed that the customer was quite handsome in a rough, manly sort of way. She would have never thought by looking at him that he had any interest in Elizabethan drama, or, for that matter, that he'd ever read anything other than newspapers and maybe a cheap thriller or two. Her current suitor, Sandy Saunders, was the exact opposite of everything this man seemed to be. An insurance salesman for Mutual of Omaha, Sandy spent almost every dime he made from his commissions on the latest fashions and playing big-shot at the Candlelight Supper Club with a couple of his chums on the city council. Anytime he took her out on a date, it seemed as if his main objective was to stick her fingers in his mouth, which she thought was sweet the first time he did it, but had since turned creepy. Though he was attractive enough, his looks had never transcended the boyish stage and now, at thirty, were already starting to fade due to his constant carousing. Too, he was somewhat erratic, and could get angry over the most ridiculous things. For example, he'd been nursing a resentment against the mayor and the city engineer ever since they'd hired Jasper Cone to look over the town's outhouses. Then, a couple of weeks ago, he shut up about them and began focusing all his rage on Jasper instead, saying the most cruel and hateful things about the pathetic little man. Still, that wasn't what stopped her from fully committing herself to Sandy. Books were her greatest passion, and she could never get serious about a man who didn't read, let alone marry one. To do so, she felt, would be like hitching her star to a fence post that just happened to breathe air and draw a paycheck. In the two years he had been courting her, he had yet to finish *Treasure Island,* which was the book he'd bought when he came in the shop to ask her out the first time. She sensed the customer watching her as she glided her fingers along a shelf, and it made her tingle slightly. Had Sandy ever aroused such a feeling in her? No, she thought regretfully, no matter how hard he sucked on her fingers. She pulled out two leather-backed volumes: a slightly scuffed but tight copy of *Great Expectations* and a pristine *Collected Stories of Edgar Allan Poe.* "Try these," she told Cane, "and if you don't like them, you can bring them back."

He glanced at them and nodded (he would have accepted anything she handed him, even a cookbook written in Italian or a walking guide to Great Britain), then followed her to the front of the store, watching her hips slightly sway as she walked. Pulling out a wad of cash, he laid a twenty on the counter, and she began wrapping the books in a sheet of white paper. He glanced around the store again, trying to build up the courage to ask her out to dinner. Wiping his sweaty palms on his trousers, he realized that he was more nervous than he'd been when he and his brothers walked into their first bank back in Farleigh. Just then he saw Cob limping by the window. Christ, looked for him all morning, and now he shows up. "I'm much obliged," he told her, snatching the parcel out of her hands.

"Wait. What about your change?"

"Keep it," he said as he hurried out the door.

"Goddamn it, where have you been?" he asked Cob when he caught up with him. "I thought something happened."

"No, I was just with the sanitation inspector."

"Who?"

"Some guy I met this morning when I sittin' on a bench eatin' doughnuts."

Cane waited until some people passed by, then pulled Cob by the shirtsleeve into an alley. "What did you tell him your name was?" he said urgently.

"Junior Bradford."

"What else?"

"Nothing. He did most of the talking. His name's Jasper."

"So what is he again?"

"The sani . . . the sanitation inspector."

"What the hell's that? Is he some kind of lawman?"

"No, I don't think so. He goes around trying to catch people doin' their business in other people's wells."

"Are you sure?" Cane said. It sounded a bit unbelievable to him; maybe someone had just figured out how gullible his brother was and decided to pull his leg.

"Yeah, I was with him all morning. He's a nice feller."

"Christ, who in the hell would take a shit in somebody's drinking water?"

"I don't know, but there must be a lot of them doin' it, the way he talks."

"And that's a job, what he does?"

"I guess so," Cob said. "He seems to think it is anyway. You ain't mad at me, are ye?"

Cane sighed and shook his head. "No, but next time don't leave without telling me where you're going first. I been looking all over for you. Remember, we got to be careful."

"He wants me to go with him again tomorrow. Is that all right?"

"What, to look in more privies? Why would you want to do that?"

"I don't know," Cob said with a shrug. "He said we was friends. Besides, what else am I gonna do?"

Cane's stomach growled. Looking down the street, he saw a sign hanging over a door that said WHITE'S LUNCHEONETTE. He'd been half sick all morning from the liquor he drank last night, but now he felt ravenous. "You had anything to eat?"

"Just the doughnuts," Cob said. He wanted to ask why the lady would give them away for free, and what "on de house" meant, but his brother already seemed a little upset. Maybe later, he thought.

"Well, let's go get something."

"Did you have a good time out at that whore shed last night?" Cob asked as they started walking toward the diner.

"Ah, not really," Cane said, wishing he'd had enough nerve to ask the bookstore lady her name. "But Chimney sure did."

55

THAT AFTERNOON, A tree buyer for the paper mill named Nesbert Motley let Sugar out of his automobile at the bridge on the south side of town. Motley was coming back from making an offer on a pristine stand of hardwood down below Buchanan when he came around a curve and damn near ran over the black man standing in the middle of the road. He didn't mind at all giving him a ride—some of the best days of his boyhood over in Lancaster had been spent in the company of a colored boy named Smoky Hansberry—but he was a little hesitant about being seen uptown with somebody so ragged and wild-looking. And what if he later caused trouble? It was true that Sugar looked like he was at the end of his rope. He hadn't had a bite of food except walnuts or a drink of anything but water in three days; the loose sole of one of his shoes flapped with every step he took, and he'd had to tie a piece of ivy around his pants to keep them from falling to the ground. Probably the only thing still keeping him upright was his determination to get back to Detroit and start sweet-talking Flora's friend.

Sugar was walking past the reeking, rackety mill wondering why someone would ever voluntarily stick around such a place when he saw a big man in front of a bar motioning him over. Sugar hesitated a moment, then crossed the street and stopped at the edge of the sidewalk. "You want something?" he asked the man.

"You look thirsty," Pollard said. He'd been sitting on the steps pondering the notice that had been stuck inside his door this morning, informing him that the city was hereby fining him three dollars every week until he emptied his outhouse, or at least took it down to an "acceptable level." Just like the fucking shit scooper had threatened.

"You got that right," Sugar replied.

"You looking for a job?"

"I don't know nothin' about tendin' bar."

Pollard laughed. "Don't worry, business is bad enough without me lettin' a nigger take over." He tore the notice into little pieces and tossed them in the air. "No, what I'm lookin' for is someone to clean out the jake in the back. You take her down four feet, I'll give you two dollars and a pint."

Within seconds of hearing the offer, Sugar could already taste the liquor on his parched tongue. A pint! By God, he'd down it in one long drink. And two dollars! That would buy two more. As far as food went, why, he could worry about that later. "Let me see it," he said.

Pollard led him around the side of the building. "There it is," he said, pointing at an outhouse at the edge of the alley, made of rough slabs with a rickety door hanging a little cockeyed from leather straps.

Sugar opened the door and the stench brought tears to his eyes. A cloud of flies emerged into the sunlight, as if even they couldn't stand the smell anymore. He held his breath and looked inside. The contents were bubbling up over the top of the hole, like a volcano ready to erupt. Just as he was on the verge of telling the man no, he thought of the pint again. "How would I go about it?" he asked, once he stepped away from the door.

"Ye'd have to dip it out," Pollard said. "It's easy. The lid lifts up. I usually do it myself, but I hurt my back the other day." He pointed to a dented tin bucket lying near the back door of the bar. "You can use that."

"But where would I put it?" Sugar asked. "That'd be quite a pile by the time I got done."

"Jesus Christ," Pollard said, "what do you want me to do, hold your hand, too?" He looked around, then nodded toward the well-kept yard that belonged to the Grady bitch on the other side of the alley. "Just toss it over the fence there."

"Two dollars and a pint, right?"

"That's what I said."

"Could I have a snort 'fore I get started?"

"Ha!" Pollard said. "I might be dumb, but I ain't plumb dumb. I'll pay ye when you finish the job."

For the next three hours, Sugar dipped shit from the hole with the leaky bucket and carried it across the alley, dumped it over the other side of the fence. By the time he finished, there was a pile of waste standing four feet high in Mrs. Grady's backyard, the edge of it sliding slowly toward the meticulously maintained plot bordered with seashells and white pebbles that contained her prizewinning rosebushes. He was just getting ready to knock on the back door of the bar to ask for his pay when a policeman sped up the alley in a car and stopped. "What the hell do you think you're doing?" the cop asked in a sharp voice.

"Just got done cleanin' out that jake," Sugar explained. The thin coat of excrement that covered his clothes and hands and arms was already beginning to harden in the sunlit air.

"No, I mean why the fuck are you dumping it in Mrs. Grady's yard?" the cop said. His name was Lester Wallingford, and his father was the chief of police in Meade. He and his brother, Luther, were the only two full-time employees on the force, and in their sibling rivalry to outdo each other, they were apt to arrest people for little more than spitting on the sidewalk, especially if one of the ten cells in the jail happened to be empty.

Sugar looked over at the pile, then noticed for the first time a tall woman with long, iron-gray hair in braids and a fringed shawl about her shoulders watching them from a window on the second floor of the house. "I'm just doing what the man told me to do," he said to Lester.

"What man?"

"The barkeep in there."

"Who? Pollard?"

"I don't know his name. He just told me he'd give me two dollars to clean out his jake, said to put it over the fence there."

Lester got out of the car and pounded on the back door of the Blind Owl. A minute or so later, Pollard opened it and stuck his head out. "Can I help ye?" he said in a casual tone, an innocent look on his meaty face.

"Did you hire this man to empty your shithouse?"

Pollard squinted past the policeman at the black man standing behind him, and his brow furrowed as if he were puzzled. "What the hell you talkin' about?" he said. "I've never seen this fucker before in my life."

It took Sugar a moment to realize what was happening, but when he caught on, he kicked at the bucket and yelled, "That's a lie, you sonofabitch!"

"Now settle down," Lester told Sugar. "You don't want to be talkin' to white folks like that." He turned back and regarded Pollard suspiciously. "You tellin' me this man just took it upon himself to dip out your crapper?"

Pollard shrugged. "I guess he musta. I don't know why, though. Maybe he's one of them perverts. I've heard some of them get their jollies rollin' around in it. Like I said, I've never seen him before."

"He's lying, Officer," Sugar yelled. "He promised me two dollars and a pint of whiskey for doing this!"

"What's this about a pint?" Lester said. "You didn't say nothing about that before."

"See?" Pollard said. "He's makin' it up as he goes along. Christ, you ought to know how them fuckers are when they get caught."

Screaming another obscenity, Sugar kicked the bucket again, and Lester drew his revolver. "I'm tellin' you for the last time," he warned, "settle down."

"But you surely don't believe him, do ye?" Sugar said.

Glancing over, Lester saw that Mrs. Grady was still watching from her window. She was bound to cause trouble if he didn't make an arrest, and, though he figured Pollard was lying through his teeth, he couldn't prove it. "Well, unless you got a paper or something saying that he hired you," he said, "I don't have no—" Just then, Sugar saw the barkeep wink, and he went crazy, lunging past the cop and trying to jerk the door open to get at the dirty bastard. "That's it!" Lester yelled, sticking the barrel of his gun in the black man's face. "You're goin' to jail." He clapped a set of tarnished handcuffs on Sugar's wrists and shoved him toward the car.

"You ain't gonna allow him to sit his ass on your seats like that, are ye?" Pollard said. "Covered in shit like he is?"

The lawman thought for a minute, then said to his prisoner, "You'll have to stand on the running board." They both heard Pollard start chuckling, and Sugar turned to stare at him, his eyeballs bulging with hate. He didn't know how long he'd stick around this cow town, but he vowed right then and there that the last thing he would do before he left was burn this motherfucker's bar down. When they arrived at the jail, the cop made him empty his pockets in the parking lot out back. "What's this for?" Lester asked, pointing at the razor. Sugar shrugged. "Shaving." Not in the mood to waste any more time messing around with a penniless vagrant when he could be out looking for real law-breakers, Lester didn't bother questioning him any further about it, even though the man didn't look like he'd done much grooming as of late. He was, however, concerned about the smell from Pollard's shitter causing trouble among the other jailbirds, simply because it would give them something new to whine about, so he allowed Sugar a couple of minutes to wash off in a bucket of water before leading him down the hall toward the cells. As they passed a bulletin board on which was pinned a copy of the Jewett Gang wanted poster, he said to the cop, "Those dirty dogs held me up the other day."

"Sure they did," Lester said.

"No, really, they did. Took my hat."

Lester shook his head. "Whatever you say, pal." It was common knowledge among lawmen that when it came to criminal types, the more miserable and luckless they were, the more grandiose and numer-ous their lies and fantasies. Did this fucker really think that he'd believe the most notorious band of outlaws to emerge since the James Gang would bother stealing a hat that a colored boy wore, especially one who used a goddamn vine to hold his pants up?

In the cell across from Sugar's was a country preacher by the name of Jimmy Beulah. He was dressed in a pair of baggy dress pants with a wrinkled white shirt buttoned tight around his neck. After a while, Sugar asked him, "What they got you in here for? Stealin' from the collection plate?"

"Attempted murder," Beulah replied blandly, brushing away one of the many flies that had followed the new prisoner in. "What about yourself?"

The man's answer took him a little by surprise, but Sugar figured he was probably trying to bullshit him, maybe scare him into giving up his supper or something. But even if he was, and the fucker turned out to be no more than a public nuisance or a petty thief, Sugar still wasn't about to admit that he was behind bars simply for cleaning out a sonofabitch's shithouse and being played the fool. He hemmed and hawed around a bit, mostly cursing the cop, and then, instead of answering the question, asked the preacher another: "Who'd ye try to kill?"

"According to them, it was some soldier," Beulah said. "To be honest, I don't really remember."

"Oh," Sugar said. Jesus, he thought, maybe he wasn't lying after all. "Why not?"

"I get like that when I drink," Beulah answered. "Why, I even forget the End Times is a-comin' if I get enough in me."

"End Times," Sugar repeated. "My mother used to talk about them."

"She was a God-fearin' woman, your mother?"

"All her life," Sugar said, recalling the number of times that he'd heard her in the other room of the house praying for his soul, fervently at first, but then, as he got older, not so much. He realized suddenly that he'd been the one who had worn her out, and that she'd been right to shut the door on him.

"Remind me again," Beulah said. "What is it you're in here for?"

Sugar spent a silent minute retracing the events of the last week or so in his mind. He thought again about Flora and her fucking boyfriend, and the bloody white woman on the kitchen floor, and the promise he had made to God on the roadside after he found his bowler shot to pieces, the promise he had broken the first chance he got. And he knew that as soon as he got out of here, he'd break another if he made one, and continue to do so until one disaster or another finished him off for good. He saw the preacher looking at him, waiting for a reply. But instead of giving him one, he rolled over in his bunk and went to sleep.

56

AT SIX O'CLOCK that evening, Chimney left the Warner to meet his brothers in the park. He was wearing his goggles and duster and holding the leather driving gloves in one hand. Thoughts of Matilda had preoccupied him all day, and he was in a hurry to get out to the Whore Barn to see her again. He had burned up two tanks of gasoline driving the Ford around and remembering the way her lips curled back when he slipped inside her, the way she had patiently talked him through his first clumsy attempts. To kill more time, he had gone back to O'Malley's for another shave, but the barber took one look at his face, still as smooth as when he'd left the shop yesterday, and just splashed a dime's worth of lotion on his neck. "Well, did ye get ye any woolly jaw last night?" he asked Chimney.

"Sure did."

The barber shook his head sadly, then glanced over at the father-in-law still sitting in the chair by the window. "Boy, whatever you do, don't get married. Me, I had to go home and listen to that goddamn Nancy bitch about money the whole evening. Shit, she even had ol' Jim there ready to crack, didn't she, Jim?"

"I don't remember," the old man said stiffly.

"Listen to him," the barber said, as he made the boy's change. "She could poison the both of us with that slop she calls supper, and he'd still take up for her."

Just then another customer walked in, and Chimney slipped out the door. He stopped at the McAdams and drank a couple of beers and ate a sandwich of bloody roast beef topped with a thick slab of onion, then returned to his room to take a bath. As he soaked in the hot, soapy water, he fell asleep and started to dream that he was back in the shack with his family at Tardweller's. They were trying to decide whether or not to eat a groundhog that had crawled into the yard and died under the front steps. It seemed that he and Cane were arguing against it, but Pearl and Cob were for it. Then a car horn honked outside the hotel, and he jerked awake and scrambled out of the tub. He leaned against the sink panting, his heart pounding against his rib cage. Must have been that damn onion, he thought. They never had agreed with him.

Cane was seated on the park bench reading another newspaper and smoking a cigarette, while Cob stood at the edge of the pond again, tearing off pieces of bread from a loaf and tossing them to some geese. For every piece he fed the birds, he ate one. A teenage boy and girl in a small boat kept rowing around in a circle out in the middle of the water, and every time they turned his way, Cob waved like he'd never seen them before. He had to give Cane credit, Chimney thought as he walked toward them, they looked more like a schoolteacher and his pet dunce than a couple of outlaws with a bounty on their heads.

"Anything about us in there?" Chimney said.

Cane put down the newspaper and dusted a spot of ash off the front of his suit. He glanced over at Cob, then across the pond at the storefronts and bars that lined Water Street. "They're still calling us cowboys," he said.

"Well, I guess it's a good thing we changed our looks then," said Chimney.

"And they're speculating we're in Ohio now."

"So? They can speculate all they want."

"Yeah, but the trouble is they just happen to be right. Did ye take it out today, the car?"

"I must have drove it a hundred miles or better," Chimney said.

"So you got the hang of it?"

"Not much to it, really. Shit, Cob could probably drive it if you tied a pork chop to the steering wheel."

"I'm thinkin' we might be ahead to get on out of here," Cane said. "Sooner we get to Canada, the better."

"Oh, no," Chimney said. "You promised me if I helped ye with that old man, I could have some fun. Hell, we've only been here two days. I'm just startin' to know my way around."

"Yeah, but shit, brother, you could—"

"I don't care. I'm not leaving till I get my fill out at the Whore Barn."

"Well, how long do you need for that?"

"I don't know," Chimney said. "At least another night or two."

Cane sighed, watched Cob toss the last of the loaf into the dirty water. "All right, you got until Saturday morning, but then we're leaving. I don't care if you got one of 'em dog-knotted."

"What's today?"

"Thursday."

"Fair enough," Chimney said, "but I'm goin' to need some more money."

"Jesus Christ, you've spent that five hundred already?"

Actually, he still had at least a hundred left, but Chimney liked the feeling that carrying a wad of cash in his pocket gave him. "Most of it," he said. "Remember, the car was two-fifty. And I went ahead and bought a couple gas cans and a gallon of motor oil for when we're on the road. Plus there was—"

"Okay, okay," Cane said. He reached into his coat pocket, pulled out a roll of bills, counted some off. "Here's two hundred. Even at four dollars a shot, that's fifty pieces of ass."

"Yeah, but what about—"

"No, that's it. You run through that, I expect to see you walkin' bowlegged."

"You sure you don't want to go with me tonight? Try out that fat one?"

"No," Cane said, shaking his head. "We're gonna go see that show at the theater, the one with the monkey."

"Well, suit yourself," Chimney replied. Secretly, he was relieved. He'd been thinking that he might spend the entire night with Matilda if the pimp was agreeable, and having his brother along would just complicate things up. "I guess I'll see you tomorrow, then."

"Be careful out there," Cane said. He finished reading the newspaper, and thirty minutes later he and Cob each paid the fifty-cent admission fee and entered the Majestic. The place was packed and their seats were near the back under the balcony. A shiny-faced man in a tuxedo came out and told a few jokes, including one about a farmer with a homely daughter who put the Jewett Gang up for a night, thinking they were traveling salesmen. Thankfully, Cob wasn't paying any attention, the main thing on his mind at the time being the popcorn he was eating. But as soon as he swallowed the last kernel, he started asking Cane when the monkey was going to appear until finally an old woman with an ear trumpet seated in front of them told him to keep quiet.

As usual, backstage the Lewis Family—Barney, Marcus, Rufus, Stanley, and Wendell—was having another crisis. Fame and women, coupled with jealousy and vast quantities of alcohol, had slowly dissolved the familial bond among the five brothers, and now it seemed as if every performance was preempted by another demand from this one or that one. Tonight, Barney was refusing to go on unless Marcus admitted that not only had he drugged and molested Barney's latest girlfriend, a burned-out torch singer named Dolly whom he'd picked up working in a five-and-dime in Pomeroy on the way over to Meade, but that he'd also given her a dose of crabs, which she had subsequently passed on to Barney. After much shouting and cursing and threatening, a fed-up Rufus jammed a derringer against the rapist brother's head, and the truth spilled out in a torrent, followed by an apology, one of seven or eight that Marcus had already made that week; and Stanley signaled the stage manager that they were ready to roll. They then each took a small hit from a treasured jug of moonshine that was all that remained of their granddaddy's last batch before he died, and then smacked each other in the balls, a ritual they had begun with their very first show back in Nitro, West Virginia, on April 3, 1909, and had continued right up to the present day, even though three of them now suffered terribly from hernias.

As they came out onto the stage, the orchestra burst into a bouncy piece of circus music, and the audience clapped wildly. For at least five minutes, Cane calculated, they ran around in a circle, five roly-poly fuckers with matching pencil mustaches, pinching each other on the ass and stealing each other's hats while making goofy faces. Then the music slowed down, and they stopped and stood in a row with their hands over their hearts and began singing. Their repertoire included a couple of patriotic anthems, a medley of old pastoral favorites, and a rollicking version of "The Old Brown Nag." Cob poked Cane in the arm. "That's one of Mr. Fiddler's favorite songs," he yelled over the music. Finally, a trumpeter stood up in the orchestra pit and blasted an ear-shattering note, and the monkey, the one and only Mr. Bentley, dropped from the ceiling and began chasing the bozos around in a fucking circle again. Cob stood up in his seat openmouthed to get a better look, and the people behind him started hissing and yelling, and Cane had to threaten to leave in order to get him to settle down. Then Mr. Bentley disappeared for a minute, only to come back out again wearing a butler's uniform and carrying a white towel over his arm. Grinning maniacally with his big yellow teeth, he walked along the edge of the stage bowing to the audience one minute, then bending over the next to shake his red ass at them. This went on for quite a while until some soldiers up front grew bored and started pelting the chimp with apple cores and bottle caps and pellets of popcorn. No sooner had Cob said, "They better not hurt him," than a peanut struck the beast in the eye, and Mr. Bentley screamed and leaped over the orchestra pit into the row of army boys. Before Cane could stop him, Cob jumped out of his seat and started down the aisle. By then, several members of the Lewis Family were trying to pull Mr. Bentley off a private before something bad happened, like a repeat of the incident at the fair in Indiana last fall when he bit a man's ear off. Fortunately, everything was more or less under control by the time Cob got to the front. The orchestra broke into an extended version of "Danny Boy," and everyone returned to their seats and enjoyed the rest of the performance, which to Cob's delight was just more of the same, though now, just to be on the safe side, Rufus, the stoutest of the brothers, kept Mr. Bentley restrained with a leash around his furry neck. Still, every time he passed by in front of the group who had insulted him earlier, he gave them a look of pure, unadulterated hatred, and several, not trusting the strap or the fat buffoon holding it, got up and left the building.

Later, on their way back to the hotel, while listening to Cob rail about the abuse the poor monkey had suffered, Cane saw the girl from the bookstore walk by with a dapper man in a nice suit holding her arm. He felt a little regret, thinking about how flustered he'd been in her presence, and he wondered if he could have been the one escorting her tonight if he had just spoken up. He stayed up half the night with *Richard III,* making his way slowly through Act Three and most of Four. Occasionally he paused to take a sip of whiskey and look a word up in the *Webster's.* The hotel was old and creaky with the past, and for some reason the noises kept unnerving him. Finally, he got up with his pistol and looked up and down the empty hallway. Closing the door, he turned out the lamp and went over to the window. He could hear the sound of footsteps somewhere down the street. The church bell chimed twice. He stood looking out for a long time, thinking again of how far they had come, and how far they had yet to go.

57

THAT SAME EVENING, a frustrated and demoralized Bovard
took a cab into Meade with the sole intention of getting plastered. Not only had his dream of dying with Wesley by his side been
ruined, but even worse, rumors were now floating around that the
343rd might not ship out until next spring. What if the war ended
before he got there? The prospect of sitting around uselessly in Ohio
for five or six more months while great battles were being waged just
a weeklong ocean voyage away was too depressing for words; and the
thought that he might be cheated out of his destiny was weighing
heavily on his mind when the driver dropped him off in front of the
Candlelight.

He had just started in on his sixth scotch and was bemoaning his
predicament to Forrester, the bartender, when the Lewis Family, still
sweaty from their performance and accompanied by several females,
came in and commandeered three tables at the rear of the room. All
of the tension and animosity they had felt toward one another before
the show had been forgotten, and within minutes their earsplitting
laughter and swinish behavior had shattered the quiet, sophisticated
atmosphere that had always been, at least for Bovard, the Candlelight's
main attraction in the first place. By the time the troupe ordered their
second round, all of the other patrons had hurriedly paid their tabs and
slipped out the door. Bovard turned and watched in disgust as one of
the Lewises forced his tongue down the throat of one of the women.
Now, it is a fact that a man will sometimes go to great lengths, even
risk life and limb, to defend the sanctity of his favorite drinking hole;
and so, when it finally became obvious that Forrester wasn't going to
do anything to restore order, the lieutenant decided it was up to him.
Adjusting his officer's cap, he staggered back to their corner, and, after

giving them a thorough dressing-down that ended with a long quote from Horace, threatened to beat them all into bloody pulps unless they started acting decently. Within seconds, three of them, including one of the females, were pointing derringers at his head, and the bartender had his arms pinned behind his back and was gently but firmly escorting him to the door. "Sorry, sir," Forrester said softly in his ear, "I don't like 'em any more than you do, but they'll spend more tonight than we usually take in all week."

For a while, he walked aimlessly around town, sipping from a flask and trying to imagine the monument his parents would erect in his honor in the family plot when they received word of his death at the Front. That is, goddamn it to hell, if he ever got there! Eventually, he ended up down near the paper mill. He had just started to head back uptown when he spotted a light still on in the Blind Owl. Hoping Malone might be there, blotto and reliving all his old horrors again, he cut across the street and entered.

To his disappointment, there was no sign of the sergeant; the only customers were a shabby, middle-aged couple arguing at a table by the door. He ordered a whiskey and beer, and Pollard served him without a word, as usual. Probably because he was drunk and in a foul mood, Bovard pictured the barkeep, with his wide nose, his broad sloping forehead, and his flabby, hairy body, as a direct descendant of the chimpanzee he'd seen performing with that family of simpletons the other night over at the Majestic. He had read newspaper articles about the search in certain parts of the world for a suspected missing link; well shit, folks, here it is tending bar in Meade, Ohio. Bovard giggled to himself and sloshed his drink down the front of his uniform as Pollard tromped back to the other side of the room. Recalling the chimp then led him to thoughts of Lucas. Maybe he'd stop by the theater on his way back to the camp, see what he was up to. And he'd go visit Wesley tomorrow in the infirmary; he felt a twinge of guilt about leaving him so abruptly yesterday morning, without even saying goodbye. It was certainly no way for an officer to behave, no matter how much of a mess the boy had made of things.

Lost as he was in his own thoughts, Bovard didn't hear the squabbling couple get up and leave, nor notice Pollard walk over and lock the front door. He picked up his beer mug to take a drink, and that's when he saw in the mirror the barkeep standing close behind him. He didn't even have time to blink before he was hit squarely in the temple with a fist twice the size of a normal man's. A bright blast of light filled his head as he tumbled off the bar stool, and he vaguely felt his shoulder smack the wood floor. Then nothing.

"How do you like them apples, you sonofabitch?" Pollard said in a low, taunting voice. "Let's hear ye laugh at me now." He turned out the lamps and grabbed hold of the lieutenant's boots and dragged him through the door that led to the back room. He went through his pockets and found some identification papers and a set of keys and thirty-four dollars in his wallet, along with two cigars in a leather case. Then he chained his arms and legs to the floor and stuffed a filthy rag in his mouth that he had used to wipe up some stains left by the late carpenter. Sitting down in a straight-backed chair, he lit one of the cigars and studied his latest victim. The soldier was tall, slim, and handsome. To Pollard, he looked like a ladies' man, something he had never had a chance to be. Never had he been to a sweethearts' dance, or had sexy words whispered in his ear, or slipped his finger up some panting girl's hot gash. Hell, he'd never even been kissed by anyone other than his mother. He thought about the only time in his life that he'd ever dared to ask a woman out, some stupid shopgirl in Jackson. He was eighteen years old, and so scared he thought for sure he'd piss his pants. But he told himself she'd be crazy to turn him down; after all, she wasn't any prize catch herself, with her double chin and the muddy brown birthmark on her forehead and the way her nose was squashed to one side. He had stood in the back of the shop on a Saturday evening for over an hour, sopped with nervous sweat and pretending to look at little trinkets while waiting on the place to empty out, and when it finally did, he marched to the counter on rubbery legs, feeling as if he was going to faint. Eager to seal the deal and get it over with, he blurted it all out in a rush, his invitation to go with him to a horseshoe-pitching tournament over in McArthur. Oh, how she had howled. Laughed so hard she choked on some sick, spat it in a wastebasket right in front of him. He'd run out the door and down an alley, knocked over an old bum who was picking through somebody's trash. With the girl's shrill laughter still ringing in his head, he had kicked the fucker's ribs in, and it had felt so damn good just to hurt somebody else. Like this did. Then he leaned over and ground the stogie out on the palm of Bovard's right hand.

58

CHIMNEY AWAKENED THE next morning with his arm around Matilda. It was the first time he'd ever woken up beside a woman, and he figured he'd remember this moment for the rest of his life, no matter how many more times it happened. He lay there for a minute, then got out of the bed. He put his clothes on and peeked through the flap, saw to his chagrin that the pimp and his man were sitting by the campfire drinking coffee and chuckling about something. To hell with them, he thought. Besides, he didn't need to feel embarrassed; he had paid for it. Forty dollars for all night. The last time he had left the tent, to take a leak in the latrine out back, everything was shut down. It must have been four in the morning. The pimp was wrapped in a blanket in the front seat of his car, and the bodyguard lay snoring in the bed of the wagon. The other two tents were dark, and as he walked by the one the French model slept in, he heard her mutter something about a rubber man. When he got back to Matilda's tent, he saw to his disappointment that she had put on a nightgown. He tried to think of something to say, but he didn't know anything about love talk, and so he asked her how she started whoring.

"It's a long story," she said, "and it's late."

"How about if I give you ten dollars?" Chimney said. "Would you tell me then?"

Raising up on one elbow, she looked at him. "Why would you want to know anything about me?" she asked.

He reached into his pants lying at the foot of the bed and laid a ten on the nightstand beside her. "Just tell me," he said.

Sitting up in the bed, she pushed her hair back out of her eyes. "Well, it's your money," she said. She was born in West Virginia, and her father died from the black lung when she was eight, leaving her mother with seven kids and a twenty-dollar gold piece. A week after his funeral, she packed their two bags and headed north to find work in a cathouse where nobody knew her. By the time Matilda turned twelve, all of her siblings were gone—either dead or in jail or married off—and her mother was sick with cancer. The last place she ever worked, in Fort Wayne, kicked her out when the clients began to complain about her bad smell and lack of enthusiasm, and they ended up in Louisville. When they first walked into the tiny one-room house her mother had rented down by the canning factories, Matilda remembered her saying, as she glanced around at the black mold on the walls and the ossified pile of gray dog shit lying on top of the ripped mattress, "So this is what the end of the line looks like." Within a week, she couldn't get out of bed anymore. It took all her strength to get from the bed to the chamber pot, and even then she only made it half the time. By chance, she heard about a pimp named Blackie who was doing business out of a wagon on the edge of town, and she gave a colored girl who lived across the street one of her last dollars to go fetch him.

When Blackie finally arrived the next morning, her mother had begged him, "You got to take my girl for me."

He looked down at the kid scrunched up in the corner of the filthy room. "She's too young," he said dismissively.

"Bullshit," her mother said. "I had my first chap when I wasn't much older than her. I never heard of a pimp that let something like that bother him."

"I got a thing against men who make money off little girls."

"Well, maybe she could clean up or run errands or what have ye. She's a good worker."

"Look, maybe you're jumpin' the gun here," Blackie had said. "Hell, you might snap out of it in a day or two."

"Sure, I'll be back to screwin' fifteen or twenty a night before you know it," she panted between efforts to catch her breath.

Blackie sighed and ran a hand through his shiny, perfumed hair. "Jesus, don't ye have somewhere else you could send her? What about family?"

"They're all gone," she said.

"How old are ye, girl?"

"She's ten, maybe eleven," her mother said. "I can't recall exactly."

"Can she talk?"

"I'm twelve," Matilda spoke up.

"You awful tiny for twelve," Blackie said.

"She don't eat much," her mother said.

"You sure about this? You don't even know me."

Her mother fell back onto the dirty, sweat-soaked pillow. "Don't matter," she wheezed. "Even you'd be better than stickin' her in some orphanage."

"Well, I don't know about that," Blackie said. "At least there—"

"I do," her mother cut in. "I was raised in one."

The pimp thought it over for a minute, then said, "Well, what the fuck. I reckon."

Her mother took several deep gulps of air, then said, "Thank God. If I was in better shape, I'd . . ." She began weeping, and Blackie turned and looked out the window until she was finished. Wiping her eyes, she asked, "How many girls ye got now?"

"Three," he said. "But the one's not workin' out. Can't get her to take a bath. If'n ye didn't know better, you'd think she had the rabies."

It was the last time Matilda ever saw her mother. Two days after Blackie took her back to his camp, they packed up and moved to another part of the state. She had to give him credit; he had waited until she was almost fourteen before he turned her out. Her first customer was a rich boy whose daddy wanted him to have a little practice breaking in a virgin, so he'd know how to go about it when he married. "He paid three hundred dollars for my cherry," she told Chimney. "Now I'm lucky to make five a day, once Blackie gets his share." Leaning across the bed, she blew out the candle on the nightstand, then she reached for his hand in the dark and pulled him down onto the bed.

He was putting his boots on when he saw the cab pull in. The driver was delivering Blackie a newspaper and a box of pastries from Mannheim's Bakery, as he did every morning. Chimney finished buttoning his pants and rushed out to catch a ride before he left. "Good Lord," the cabbie said, "you're still here?"

"Yep," Chimney said, climbing into the car.

"Hey," Blackie said to the driver, "hold on a minute. I got something for you." The pimp went over to the campfire and laid the deliveries down on a stump. Then he took a knife from his pocket and unwrapped what was left of a roll of honey loaf. He cut off a thick slice and handed it to the cabbie. "You ever try this?"

"What is it?" the man said, taking a cautious sniff at the greasy meat.

"That ol' bologna salesman called it honey loaf. It ain't bad."

The cabbie laid it on the seat next to him. "I better wait till my stomach settles down a little before I eat anything June Easter is selling. I appreciate it, though."

"What'd ye do, get on a toot last night?" Blackie asked.

"Aw, I drank some rotgut my cheap-ass cousin brought over to the house. I should have known better. My ulcers, they can't take it anymore."

"You need to coat 'em with grease," Blackie said. "That's what my daddy always did. Gravy, butter, lard, whale's blubber, you name it, he tried it."

"Yeah, that worked for me, too, up until a couple years ago," the cabbie said. "If I had any sense, I wouldn't drink nothin' but beer from here on out." Then he put the car in gear and started down the lane.

Chimney sat in the backseat looking out at the tree-covered hills shining here and there with silvery frost, mist lying like smoke in the low places between them. He'd never noticed before how pretty the land was around here. Riding in the open car, the morning air was cold, and he shivered, reminded himself to buy a decent coat before they got to Canada. Then he smiled. There had been a moment last night with Matilda when he thought he was happier than he had ever been in his life; and if he could have a minute like that even once a week, he reckoned he'd be satisfied. Suddenly, the thought of all those men sticking their dicks inside her this weekend—she had told him that Friday and Saturday nights, when most of the soldiers got their passes, were her busy times—made him half sick. But then he caught hold of himself as they passed over the bridge, and tried to look at things realistically. Christ Almighty, she was a whore, and that's how girls like that make their money. And was that any worse than being a killer and a thief, when it came right down to it? The question puzzled him. He was still debating it with himself when the cabbie said, "Which one did you screw? The yeller-haired one?"

"No," Chimney said. "I was with Matilda."

"Matilda?" the cabbie said. "Oh, you mean the skinny little bitch. The one they call Cock Gobbler."

"I don't know," Chimney answered, his face turning red.

"Me, I like 'em with a little more meat on their bones."

"You'd probably enjoy fucking a hog then," Chimney said.

"What'd you say?"

"I said you look like a pig-fucker."

The cabbie narrowed his red-veined eyes and slowed the car down just as they hit the business district. "You got a smart mouth on you, don't ye, bub?"

Chimney rested his hand on the little Remington .22 he had in his pocket. "Just shut up and drive."

"You don't tell me what to do in my own cab, you little shit," the man said.

The boy looked around at all the people on the sidewalks. He hated to leave the sonofabitch off the hook, but now was not a good time to be losing his temper. There was too much at stake, he reminded himself. Besides, what did it matter what this dried-up bastard thought of anything? You could tell by looking at him that he was on his last legs, him and his goddamn ulcers. "Just let me out here," he said, ignoring the cabbie's glare. He let loose of the gun and dug two dollars out of his pocket, dropped them on top of the greasy slice of meat lying on the front seat.

59

JASPER WAS ON his way to the bench hoping to meet up with Junior when he passed by the jail and saw Lester Wallingford tacking a new wanted poster to the billboard by the front door. Having once been instrumental in bringing a pickpocket to justice after he had seen the man's mug on a flyer, he now made it a habit to stop by at least once a week to check out new criminals. "Who they lookin' for now?" Jasper asked.

"Still hunting for them Jewetts," the policeman told him. "Jacked the reward up some more. They're thinking they might be in Ohio now. I'll tell you what, those bastards come through Meade, ol' Lester here will be a rich man."

Jasper didn't say anything. He was studying the drawing on the poster. Funny how that one looked like Junior. He'd have to tell him about that when he saw him. He read over the long list of crimes they had committed: included were arson, robbery, kidnapping, rape, murder, and several others that he had never heard of. What the hell was "bestiality"? Or "necrophilia"? He looked again at the drawings. My God, he had to say, the one on the end really was Junior all over again. But, shoot, it couldn't be. That boy wouldn't hurt a fly. Still, the more he looked at the poster, the more the other one favored Junior's brother, too. He had seen them standing in line in front of the Majestic last night waiting to buy tickets. But what about—

"What's wrong, Cone?" Lester said. "You look like you seen a ghost."

"Nothing. Just got a lot on my mind."

"Only thing you got on your mind is shithouses."

"You don't know me," Jasper said. "You don't know nothing about me."

"I know you like to watch women takin' a whiz. That's what I know."

Because Jasper spent so many sleepless hours walking the streets late at night, he knew more about the cop than the cop would ever know about him, including the fact that he almost always ended up at Lucas Charles's little room above the Majestic whenever he closed down the Mecca Bar. Jasper was right on the cusp of asking Lester if his father knew about his relationship with the theater manager when he realized such information might be put to a better use later. Instead, he pretended to storm away, but then stopped and waited at the corner. As soon as the cop disappeared, he hurried back to the billboard and tore the poster off, stuck it inside his jacket. Making his way to the park, he sat down on a rock near the pond to study it. The Jewett Gang? Surely there had to be a mistake. But then how could there be another person walking around who looked identical to Junior? Or Cob, or whatever his name was. And where was the third brother? Had he gotten killed or run off? He thought back for a minute, trying to recall everything Junior had told him about himself, and then he realized that he didn't know anything. Hell, he had done almost all the talking; Junior just nodded his head once in a while and ate doughnuts.

Jasper folded the poster carefully and put it in his pocket. He watched a small flock of geese glide in and land on the water with a flapping of wings. Before you knew it, the snow would be falling, and another year would have passed without him having his own indoor facilities. But then he thought about what had been on his mind when he opened his eyes this morning. Not the usual, not porcelain commodes or claw-foot bathtubs or running Sandy Saunders out of town or the mass of hair between Mrs. Arnold's legs. No, he had been thinking about meeting up with Junior, having him to talk to while he did his job. Bagshaw, the dump keeper, as nutty as he might be with his doll baby and rotten produce, was right. Jasper was looking forward to it, to seeing his friend. His friend. He said it aloud. "He's my friend." Except for Itchy, he had never had anyone he could call that, unless you counted his uncle the broom maker, and he wasn't all that sure a blood relative counted. True, a man could have a mighty fine water closet with $5,500—Christ Almighty, he could have one in every room of the house and still have money left over—but how much was a friend worth? You couldn't put a price on that, no matter how hard people tried. He got up and started out of the park, his measuring wand balanced on his shoulder. Sure, lots of people would give up a buddy for a lot less than indoor plumbing, or the chance to run a comb through Mrs. Arnold's pubic hair. Sure, they would. But Jasper wasn't one of them. No, sir, he wasn't. He stopped and took the poster out of his pocket, looked at it one more time. Then he balled it up and threw it in the pond, watched two of the geese start swimming toward it.

60

Bovard woke up to find himself lying flat on his back in a dark room with a rag stuffed in his mouth. No matter how hard he tried, all he could move was his head, and he finally realized that he was chained to a floor. He was confused. The last thing he could recall was listening to a couple of drunks bickering in the Blind Owl. The man kept telling the woman she had the face of a bulldog, and she kept comparing his cock to a green bean. Then they'd give each other a big, sloppy kiss—he could still almost hear their puckered lips smacking—before starting their vile insults all over again. But that was all he remembered.

He pushed his tongue around in his mouth under the rag, and discovered, to his shock, that some of his bottom teeth were missing. He twisted his head from side to side. Had he been in a fight? Was he in a hospital? Was this one of Lucas and Caldwell's crazy games? No, that couldn't be it. They'd never go this far, no matter how doped up they got. Nothing made any sense, but then slowly, as his eyes adjusted to the darkness, he became aware that someone else was in the room, sitting on a cot not more than a couple of feet away from him. Jesus Christ, it was that fucking barkeep, holding a jar in his lap. Then he vaguely recalled picking up a beer and seeing him in the mirror. He heard the man cough, then spit, felt a slimy gob of phlegm *splat* on his forehead. He struggled against the chains, but they were so tight he couldn't even make them rattle. He tried to force the rag out of his mouth with his tongue, but it was useless. Making an angry moaning sound in his throat, he banged the back of his head against the floor, tried to make the bastard understand he better turn him loose right now.

Pollard smiled at his efforts. It was nothing new; they all acted the same, at least at first. Some of them gave up quite easily, others hung on hoping for a way out almost until the end, dreaming of escape: the law rescuing them perhaps, or the man who was doing this to them experiencing a change of heart, and so on and so forth, a hundred different scenarios playing out in their terrified heads. He had wondered about that a lot, why would one man surrender his life so quickly and another never admit defeat, even when he had to know he was beaten? Did it have something to do with the way they'd been raised, or if they believed in God, or if they had a family depending on them? There was really no way of telling, but he had a feeling this one was a fighter, which was the type he preferred. The last one, the carpenter, he was ready to cash in his chips before the first night was over with, and it had been hard to keep things exciting with someone so weak and worthless.

"Do you know what I'm going to do to ye?" he asked the lieutenant. "No, probably not. I doubt if you've ever been in any kind of fix like this before. Well, for starters, I'm gonna pull all your teeth out. Don't worry, I won't break 'em, I promise. I've done it plenty of times before. See, I got quite the collection here." He held up the jar and shook it. "After that, I usually do something special with the tongue. And, no, no, don't ask me why I do it. Hell, I don't know myself really. I think it's just because I can. Let's see . . . Shit, I forgot where I was. Oh, yeah. Then I'll whittle on ye for a day or two, maybe take your guts out while ye watch. From what I've seen in the past, you won't be in too good a shape by then. And then the last thing I do, I mean after your heart quits beatin' and all that shit, is saw you into little pieces. Not to eat or anything like that. I tried that once, and I have to say I didn't care for the taste of it, though I have been thinkin' lately that maybe I didn't fix him right. No, just makes you easier to carry when I take ye over to the creek. Won't nobody know what happened to ye except me. I'll dump you in the water like fish bait, and you'll just disappear. But we'll save all that for later. Right now I hear some customers knockin' on the door." Then he set the jar of fangs and grinders down just a couple of inches from Bovard's head, and left him alone in the dark room, rank with the smell of dead men's body fluids soaked into the wood floor, to dwell on what he'd said.

61

WHEN THE BAKERY opened, Cob was the first customer in the door. He'd been waiting across the street for over an hour. "So it's you again," Mrs. Mannheim said in an agitated voice. Last night, within minutes of finally nodding off, she'd been startled awake by a dream in which one of the Von Kennels' sons had been arrested in a train station in Syracuse for possession of a pound of Wiener schnitzel that his mother had given him to eat on the journey. Greta Von Kennel was her closest friend, and Mrs. Mannheim hadn't slept another wink worrying about it. Now she had a ferocious headache.

"I'll take some more of those doughnuts," Cob said.

"Oh, you will, will you?"

"Yeah," he said. "Same as yesterday."

Mrs. Mannheim stared out the front window for a moment with bloodshot eyes, wondering what sort of trap was being laid for her. Her first impulse was to tell the fat oaf to get lost, but then maybe that's what they wanted her to do. Perhaps there was some law or town statute about refusing a customer service that she didn't know about. Her head felt as if it might explode. Just how low those people would go in their efforts to crush her was anybody's guess. She wouldn't put anything past them, especially that cane-twirling insurance salesman. No, she decided, just treat him fairly, and they won't have anything to work with. She went ahead and counted out a dozen, set the bag on the counter. She watched Cob pick them up and casually start out the door. The woman shook her head in amazement. "Where you think you're going?" she shrilled.

He stopped and looked back at her. "I got to meet the sanitation inspector."

Oh, she thought, so he wasn't afraid to admit it, he really was in cahoots with those city boys. Granted, Mrs. Cone's boy had always seemed harmless enough, but the crooks had probably promised him a promotion if he played along, served as the middleman. Either that, or they'd dug up some dirt on him and were using it as blackmail. She'd heard rumors that he had a cock the length of a French baguette, and it was hard to tell what sort of depravity something like that might lead to. She stared at Cob, her eyes blazing now. The audacity of this fat bastard, grinning at her just like he did when he attempted to trick her up yesterday. "What about some money for the doughnuts?" she said.

"Well, I thought they was . . . I thought they was *on de house*. Wasn't that what ye said?"

The woman began to tremble as she felt the headache erupt into a full-scale migraine. "If you leave here without paying, I swear to God I'm calling the police."

Cob hurriedly reached in his pocket for the five-dollar bill he still had and handed it to her, then started back out the door. "Hold on!" she screamed.

"What?" he said. "Ain't that enough?" The mention of police, as well as the woman's behavior, had him spooked. What did she have against him? What had he done? He should have asked Cane what "on de house" meant; maybe that was the problem.

She threw the money at him, then pounded her fist on the counter, even though the noise felt like someone was driving a nail through her head. Just then, Ludwig, hearing the commotion, came into the room from the back, where the ovens were located. "Gertrude, what are you doing?" He looked over at Cob standing by the door, a frightened look on his face. It was obvious that the young man was a bit touched. Or, at the very least, slow. She should have realized that; half of her family was mentally handicapped in one way or another; and Ludwig was growing increasingly concerned about his wife. For weeks now she had been going on about secret plots being hatched against them. Last week, she'd even burst into a tirade about the Lewis Family being agents of the Midwest Anti-Germanic Coalition. The Midwest Anti-Germanic Coalition! He'd checked with some of his cronies at the chess club, and according to them, there was no such thing. And the Lewis Family?

Men so besotted with skanks and booze that he doubted if they'd be able to find Germany on a map! Why couldn't she see just how lucky they were to be living here, thousands of miles away from the war?

"Ludwig, he's tryin' to set me up," she said. "Make it look like I cheated him."

The baker looked down at the money on the floor, and picked it up. "Is this yours?" he asked the chubby boy in the bibs.

"It's . . . it's . . . for the doughnuts," Cob stuttered.

"Here," said Ludwig, handing it back to him. "Go ahead and keep it."

"But—"

"No worries, my friend. The doughnuts are on the house today."

Cob left and headed for the bench uptown to meet Jasper. He sat down and dug his hand into the greasy sack, pulled out a doughnut. What the hell had happened back there? First they didn't want his money, and then they did, and then they didn't again. How could you make money selling doughnuts like that? Why, they'd be out of business real quick if they kept that up. Then he wondered if maybe the five-dollar bill Cane had given him was counterfeit. A banker once tried to pass off fake money to Bloody Bill, and it hadn't turned out good for him, not good at all. By the time the outlaw got through dragging him up and down the streets behind his horse, there wasn't enough skin left on his hide to make a pocketbook. That might explain why the woman didn't want it. But still, if that was the case, why did they give him the doughnuts anyway? He was thinking these thoughts when he looked up and saw Jasper coming around the corner, right on time. Maybe he would know, but first, Cob wanted to tell him about Mr. Bentley.

62

AFTER THE ALTERCATION with the cabdriver, Chimney had
a sweet roll and a glass of milk at White's Luncheonette, then went
to the hotel and asked the clerk for his key. He stumbled weak-kneed
up the stairs to his room. Locking the door, he laid his pistol on the
nightstand and stripped off his clothes. He fell onto the bed, intending to sleep the rest of the morning away, but within a few minutes, he
knew that wasn't going to happen. Every time he closed his eyes, he
saw Matilda as a little girl lying on a corncob mattress with a bunch of
dog turds. Finally, he gave up. He splashed some water on his face and
put his clothes back on, then went downstairs and out to the Ford. He
started it without a hitch and drove out into the country west of town.
He ended up in a little burg called Bourneville. He bought some cheese
and crackers and two bottles of warm beer at a general store and asked
the man behind the counter if he could leave his automobile parked
there for a while. He walked along the border of a field planted in winter wheat until he came to a creek. Taking out the Remington, he fired
off a few rounds, reloaded it. Then he sat down on the bank and ate his
lunch while watching the water roll by, thinking about what Matilda
had told him last night. He'd never met anyone before who'd had it
rougher growing up than he and his brothers, and for some reason,
maybe because she was a girl, that bothered him. What would happen
to her when she got older and the men didn't want her anymore? She
told him last night that the only reason Esther, the fat one, was still
working was because she'd do things nobody else would do. He opened
the other beer and drank it fast, then tossed the bottle into the water.
What if he asked her to come with them to Canada? Tell her he'd take
care of her, that . . . that he was offering her . . . shit . . . offering her
an opportunity, a chance to quit whoring. Be honest with her, so she'd

know what she was in for. Sure, Cane would pitch a bitch, but he knew his brother well enough to know he wouldn't hurt her, no matter how much she knew about them. He stood up and stretched, then started back up through the field. Wouldn't hurt to ask, he thought, and if she turned him down, well, at least he'd have tried to come to her rescue.

As he approached the store lot, he saw two dirty-faced boys looking at the Ford, though standing back at a respectful distance. One appeared to be around eleven, the other nine or so. They were weed-thin and barefoot, dressed in patched overalls and frayed, homespun shirts. They reminded Chimney of him and his brothers when they were that age. "You ain't thinking about stealin' my car, are ye?" he said, as he walked up behind them.

They both whirled around when they heard his voice, then the bigger one said, "No, mister. We was just lookin' at it." The other didn't say anything, just looked shyly at the ground.

"This here's what they call a Tin Lizzie," Chimney said. "What kind do you drive?"

"Shoot, we don't have no car. Do we, Theodore?" the older boy said. "Heck, we don't even have a bicycle."

The quiet one glanced up quickly at the man in the lavender shirt, then back down at his feet. He shook his head.

"What, two studs like you don't have a car? I find that mighty hard to believe," Chimney said.

"No, it's true, ain't it, Theodore?"

"Well, you ever rode in one?" Chimney said.

"No," the boy said. "We used to have a mule, but he got sick last year and Pap had to put him down."

Chimney looked up and down the short street. A few clapboard houses, the store, a post office, a granary. An old lady in a black dress and bonnet hanging out wash on a line. A three-legged dog sniffing around a stump. Christ, what a sad little place. Here the days would seem like weeks, and a stranger passing through would be talked about for months, maybe years. Even thinking about it made his eyes heavy. "I'll tell you what," he said. "If your wives don't care, I'll take ye all a ride."

The bigger boy laughed. "We don't have no wives."

"Ah, so you're still waiting on the right girl to come along."

"We don't even like 'em, do we, Theodore?"

"Well, that'll change," Chimney said. "You just wait and see."

"What about you?" the bigger boy asked.

"What about me?"

"Where's your wife?"

"Oh, well," Chimney said with a grin, "we're still courting." He stuck the crank in the engine and gave it three turns. "How about it? I'll drive ye up the road and back."

The boys looked wide-eyed at each other, then scrambled into the backseat as Chimney started the Ford. He pulled out of the store lot and drove west for several miles until they came to the outskirts of another burg called Bainbridge, then turned the car around in the middle of the dirt road. When he got back to the store, the boys climbed out reluctantly. They thanked him, and he started to pull out of the lot, but then stopped and waved them back. "Almost forgot," he said. He pulled out some money and handed them each a five-dollar bill.

"What's this for?" the older boy asked, a puzzled look on his face.

"Oh, I don't know," Chimney said. "I might need a favor someday, and this way you'll owe me."

"But we don't even know your name, mister."

Chimney started to say Hollis Stubbs, but then he hesitated. For some reason, lying to these two didn't feel right. They would be deceived enough in the next few years without him feeding them more bullshit. And after all, what would it hurt, telling them who he really was? He was leaving for Canada tomorrow, and would never see this place again. It would be something they could tell their kids about someday, about how they once took a ride with the famous outlaw Chimney Jewett. "If'n I tell ye, can you keep a secret?"

"Sho we can. Me and Theodore keep secrets all the time, don't we, Theodore?"

Chimney looked over at the other boy, saw him nod his head solemnly. Then, out of the corner of his eye, he saw the store clerk with his nose pressed up against the door glass watching them. Maybe it wasn't such a good idea after all. "It's Bill," he said. "Bill Bucket."

63

Sᴇʀɢᴇᴀɴᴛ Mᴀʟᴏɴᴇ ᴡᴀs called to Captain Fisher's office right after mid-morning drills. On his way in, he passed First Lieutenant Waller coming out with a devious smile on his smoothly shaven face. "So what's this about Lieutenant Bovard not showing up this morning?" Fisher asked, just before he spat a stream of tobacco juice into a large brass spittoon he kept beside his desk.

"I'm not sure what you mean, sir," Malone said, still standing at attention.

"Waller just told me you two are thick as thieves."

"That's not true, sir. I had a couple of drinks with him once or twice, that's all."

Fisher cast a skeptical look Malone's way, then rang the spittoon again. Due to the country's backward isolationist policies, most of his military career had been impatiently spent behind a desk, but last winter he'd finally seen some action, having been given the opportunity to serve as the chief interrogations officer with the 7th Calvary in Mexico during Pershing's search for Pancho Villa. However, though the experience had been revelatory in many ways, and he'd never felt more alive than when he was down there, he was now having problems adjusting to being back stateside. He had begun to doubt even the most casual comment, and something as innocent as "Looks like rain today" might propel him on a weeklong witch hunt. In Mexico, fearful that he'd be sent back home if he failed to get results, he had occasionally gone a bit overboard; and the handle of his service revolver had five neat notches in it to mark the number of suspected sympathizers he had executed after his rather brief questionings failed to turn up any useful information about Villa's whereabouts. To Fisher's way of thinking, even if he was lucky, a man would still only experience war two or three times in his sixty or seventy trips around the sun, and he wasn't about to waste any of the precious minutes allotted to him for combat with prolonged questioning of prisoners, especially those who babbled in a language he couldn't make heads or tails of. No, when in doubt, the quickest and most efficient way to get at the truth was with a gun, but, as he had to keep reminding himself, the shit he'd pulled down in Chihuahua wouldn't fly here. "Has he ever said anything about a man named Lucas Charles?" he asked the sergeant, as he opened a leather pouch and squeezed together a quid the size of a golf ball, tucked it in his jaw alongside the one he was already working on. "Some homo that runs one of the theaters in town?"

Malone rubbed at his face while trying to decide how to answer the question. He'd heard the rumors about the lieutenant, but what did playing grab-ass with some funny boy have to do with anything? There probably wasn't a man on the entire base who wasn't a sick fucker in some way or another. "Look, sir," he finally said, "I know he's my superior, and I probably shouldn't be saying this, but Lieutenant Waller's worse than an old woman for spreadin' gossip."

Fisher smiled a little then, baring his brown, ground-down teeth. "You mean he's a liar?"

"Well, I don't know if I'd go so far—"

"That's all right, Sergeant," Fisher said. "I had him pegged as a little deceiver from the get-go. Believe me, that backstabber wouldn't have lasted five minutes down in Mexico. Someone, and I'm not saying who, mind you, would have put a hole in his head the first time he let his guard down to eat one of those goddamn tacos the old women were always trying to bribe us with." He leaned back in his chair, stared at his boots for a moment. "But, that being said, I'm going to ask you one more time. Any idea where your buddy might be?"

"No, sir, but I don't think he's gone AWOL. I've seen a few deserters in my time, and he just don't strike me as the type."

"Why's that?"

Malone looked over at a tapestry hanging on the captain's wall, burros and adobe huts and a couple of cacti, evidently a memento from the Mexican campaign. He recalled the way the lieutenant had paid attention to him the other night in the Blind Owl when he went into one of his trances and couldn't stop talking. As if he couldn't get enough. He was the first man who didn't seem repulsed by Malone's descriptions of the carnage at the Front. Hell, from the way his face lit up, you'd have thought he was listening to someone talk about a beautiful woman instead of overripe, headless corpses and rats the size of beagle dogs. "From everything I've heard him say, he's keen as hell to get to France."

"When was the last time you saw him?"

"Yesterday around dinnertime. Mentioned something about going to the officers' club. That's really all I know."

Fisher bent down with a rag, wiped a speck of dust off the toe of one of his boots. "The general's already on my ass about this. Though there's been three other men skip out in the last two weeks, he's the first officer, and that doesn't look good. We even talked about draggin' that goddamn Franks out of that hospital where he's hiding and putting one through his other eye, just to serve as an example, but there's too many legal complications in the States. That's what I liked about Mexico. A man could buy himself out of any kind of trouble down there with a sack of flour and a blanket."

"I see, sir."

The captain stopped talking and chewed away like a cow with a cud for a minute or two, then swallowed. "I'm going to give you an assignment, Sergeant Malone."

"Yes, sir."

"I want you to take a patrol into town every night until we get this cowardly bullshit stopped. You won't answer to anybody but me. Pick out some men you think you can trust, say, ten or so. Be easy with the citizens, that is, if you can, but any soldiers you catch committing even the slightest infractions, I give you my permission to rough 'em up a little before you haul them to the brig. Understand?"

"I understand, sir."

"One more thing," Fisher said. "A little piece of advice I've learned along the way you might want to remember."

"Yes, sir."

"If you happen to kill anybody, make sure they got a gun on 'em before the asshole authorities show up. That'll save you a lot of headaches in the long run."

64

EULA WAS IN the kitchen baking an apple pie, and Ellsworth
was sitting on the porch smoking his pipe, when Sykes, the constable
from Pike County who had dragged him off to jail over the cattle scam,
drove into the yard. The farmer raised up in his rocker. Whenever the
law shows up at your door uninvited, it can't be good; and his immediate thought was that Eddie was in trouble. "Shit," he muttered to
himself, hoping Eula hadn't heard the car pull in. Ever since those boys
had left the other day, she had been unusually quiet, and whenever she
did say anything, she was either wondering again why Eddie hadn't
written them a letter yet, or recalling another one of the compliments
Junior had paid her. Ellsworth hurried toward the car before the lawman could get out. He noticed that an old man with a long beard sat in
the backseat, just like he himself had last fall.

To his surprise, Sykes told him that they'd caught the man who
took his money last year. "Tried to pull the same thing on ol' Stanley Starling over in Beaver," he said, "but he was a little sharper than
you were. Had him tied up and waiting on us when we got there. You
don't ever want to mess with Stanley. They say he could read and write
before he was even born. Well, anyway, we got the bastard, but he done
spent your money, I'm afraid. Calls himself Oren Malloy, but I'd bet a
dollar that's not his real name." Then he sniffed the air. "Is that apple
pie I smell?"

"Might be," Ellsworth said.

"Apple's always been one of my favorites," Sykes said, glancing
toward the house.

Ellsworth ignored the hint, recalling that when he was locked up in
the constable's jail, on false charges no less, he had been given nothing
to eat all that miserable day but a dab of cold okra spooned up from

a common pot that a trustee carried along the row of cells. Instead, he asked in a low voice if by any chance he'd seen his son in Waverly. "Name's Eddie. I heard a while back he might be runnin' around down there with some young girl named Spit something or other and an old man plays a harp."

"Lord Christ," Sykes said, "is that your boy? The one that was with ye when I had ye in the jail last year?"

Ellsworth nodded. "Only got the one."

"Why, he surely has changed a bunch since then," the sheriff said. "I didn't even recognize him."

"So you have seen him?"

"Oh, yeah. In fact, I took him and the old man down to the Ohio River the other day and dropped 'em off by the bridge. The girl slipped away before I could catch her, or I'd have got rid of her ass, too. That man, that's Johnny Marks you're talkin' about. A damn drunk if ever there was one. What in the world's your boy doin' hanging around with him?"

"I don't know. He just took off one day, never said a word to his poor mother or me, either one."

"Well," Sykes said, "I been in this business long enough to know that people sometimes do things that can't be explained."

"What'd he do?" Ellsworth said.

"Your boy? Oh, nothing much. Mostly, the store owners got to complaining about the racket they was making downtown. Johnny's always thought of himself as a musician, but he couldn't play a tune if his life depended on it. Far as your boy goes, he's pretty much got a tin ear, too, though he's not a bad dancer when he gets juiced up a little. Anyway, I hauled 'em off to give 'em a fresh start, so to speak. Just like I'm doing with this one here," he said, hooking a thumb at the passenger in the back. "Only I'm a-takin' this one to Meade. Just between you and me, I got to scatter 'em out a little bit, so my associates don't get wise to it. But, heck, I can't afford to feed every no-account that shows up in Pike County. That's the reason I be up this way."

"He a music man, too?" Ellsworth asked, taking another look at the man in the backseat.

"No, I caught him in Warren Gaston's lumberyard after closing. Had the gall to tell me he was just following a bird that flew through there, but I figure it was more like he was snoopin' around for something to stick in his pocket. Can't hardly blame him, though. If I was in his shape, I'd probably take up stealing, too. Hell, he don't even own a pair of shoes."

"A bird?" Ellsworth said. He stepped a little closer, saw that the old man was clothed in what appeared to be a robe. He had a far-off look in his eyes, and was picking something out of his beard.

"Yep. That's what he pointed to when I came up behind him, anyway. I called his bluff, though."

"What'd ye mean?"

"I shot that thing so full of holes there weren't enough feathers left to fill a thimble."

"What kind of bird?"

"Oh, it was just a little white one. I got to say I never saw one like it before."

"You mean like that one there?" Ellsworth said, nodding at a small ivory-colored bird that had just landed on the hood of the automobile.

Sykes sat silent for a minute, chewing his bottom lip, watching the bird preen itself. "That sure looks like it, but . . . but there's no way in hell that's the same one. Can't be." He mumbled something else that Ellsworth couldn't hear, then pulled his service revolver from his holster and leaned out over the car door. He squinted and aimed carefully, his mouth shut tight in a determined grimace, then popped off two rounds fast. The bird burst into nothingness, leaving only a tiny splatter of shit on the hood ornament, and a single feather floating through the air. Sykes looked back at his prisoner and grinned. "I hope that wasn't another one of your buddies," he said, but the old man just kept on calmly combing his fingers through his beard.

Right after that, the constable left, and Ellsworth walked back to the porch, sat down heavily in his rocker. Eula, who had heard the car pull up and was standing inside the parlor watching, came out and said, "What in the world was that all about?"

"He stopped to tell me they caught the man who stole our money."

"Did he give you any of it back?"

"Nope. It's gone for good."

"I figured as much. Why'd he shoot that bird?"

"I don't know," Ellsworth said, shaking his head. "Crazy, I guess. Claimed it and that ol' boy in the backseat were going around stealing stuff. Something like that anyway."

"That don't make no sense. A bird?"

"Like I said, I think he's crazy."

"So that's all he had to say?"

"That was it," Ellsworth said, and she turned and went back into the house. Jesus, he didn't know how much longer he could hide the truth about their son, or even why he still felt the need to do it. Each lie begat another, and the only purpose they served was to postpone the inevitable, because sooner or later it was all going to come out. He should have been straight with her from the beginning, told her that Eddie wasn't in the military the same day he'd found out himself. Now, however, thanks to Sykes, telling her would be twice as hard. A public nuisance dumped out along the Ohio River with some old drunk who sounded a lot like Uncle Peanut! No, he couldn't do it, not today anyway. Maybe tomorrow, he told himself, after breakfast. But then, just as Eula stepped out on the porch and handed him a piece of pie on a plate, he looked up to see a bird, the color of new snow, fly from one of the oak trees in the front yard. He watched in amazement as it headed east along the road toward Meade, the same route the constable had taken, and suddenly, for a short time anyway, all the little worries and doubts and fears that ruled his life melted away, seemed to take flight along with the bird. "Sit down," he said to Eula. "There's something I need to tell ye."

65

WHEN LESTER WALLINGFORD explained to his father why they had Sugar locked up, the police chief made a sour face and said, "How much shit we talkin' about?" His nervous system was giving him fits, as it always was immediately after returning from a trip to see his mistress in Washington Court House, a former queen of the Highland County Bell Festival who seemed determined to suck the very lifeblood out of him with her demands. Neither of his sons nor his wife knew about the affair, but he was finding it harder and harder to keep it that way.

Lester held his hand in the air. "Maybe yay high, that much around."

"He from around here?"

"No, he claims he's from Detroit, but I'd say he's just a tramp from the looks of him."

"No money then?"

"Only thing he had in his pockets was a razor and a couple of walnuts."

"Mrs. Grady's, huh?"

The son nodded. "She's already called three times this morning. Wants him and Pollard both put in prison. She's recommending five-year sentences, says she'll get her brother-in-law to fix it up." Mrs. Grady's niece was married to a judge in Pickaway County, and she had used his influence several times to get her way when the law in Ross County seemed a bit reluctant to grant her wishes. Egbert Sterling, an amateur horticulturist who had beaten her out of first place for two consecutive years in the local flower show, was the latest victim of her wrath, and was now serving a six-month sentence for assault on a Pickaway County law clerk, even though the man had several witnesses testify at the trial that he was spreading lime in his garden at the time of the alleged attack. "She also told me to let you know that, from what she hears, Washington Court House is a regular Sodom and Gomorrah these days," he said. "I think maybe she's gone a little simple."

"She said that?"

"Her exact words."

Chief Wallingford sat down at his desk and swallowed a handful of aspirins, then poured a good inch of Sir Alistair's Stomach Soother into a cup of coffee. He thought for a minute, not so much about Mrs. Grady, but about something his mistress had said that morning, about how if he didn't leave his wife, she was going to make things rough on him. After he had moved heaven and earth to cover her worthless baby brother's gambling debts! His only option was to go out to the Whore Barn tomorrow, see if he could squeeze a little bit more out of the pimp. A piece of jewelry would keep her happy for a couple more weeks anyway, maybe even longer if it was gaudy enough. Why had he ever gotten involved with the highfalutin bitch in the first place? He'd known as soon as he slipped his cock into her that he was doomed. It had always been his nature to feel a bit depressed after he got his gun off, but with Marjorie Flagstaff, he'd actually heard a death knell ring in his head the moment he'd rolled off of her. And now the old bitch Grady had found out. Goddamn it to hell. He'd be at her beck and call every minute of every day for who knew how long.

"Dad?" Lester said.

"Yeah, yeah," Wallingford said. "Take a wheelbarrow and a shovel down there and have him clean her yard up, then turn him loose."

"What about Mrs. Grady? She's gonna—"

"Jesus, Lester, I can't keep a man in jail just because she's got a bug up her ass."

"Well, where do you want me to have him put it?"

"Goddamn it, boy, I don't know. Have him dump it in the creek."

"The creek? Hell, I eat fish out of there."

"So? Won't be no worse than what the paper mill puts in it. And you keep an eye on him until he's finished, too, unless you want to do it."

"What about Pollard?"

"It's too early in the mornin' to be thinking about that lowlife."

"But it's almost three o'clock," Lester said.

"Son, just let me drink my coffee, will ye?"

Lester found a cart with wobbly wheels and a shovel buried under a pile of unclaimed stolen property in the shed behind the jail, then went in and took Sugar out of his cell. He had the prisoner push the cart back to the scene of the crime while he followed behind in the police car. "You get that yard cleaned up, and you're a free man."

"I don't see why—" Sugar started to say, but the look on the cop's blank face told him he'd be wasting his breath arguing. "Where you want me to put it?"

The policeman pointed down the alley to the creek bank. "You'll have to take it down there, dump it in the water." Then he took out his pocket watch and checked the time. "Now look, I got things to do tonight, so let's get moving. I don't want to see nothin' but elbows and assholes, understand?" Then he leaned back in the front seat of the car and pulled his hat down over his eyes.

At four o'clock, Sugar upended the last load of waste into Paint Creek. He'd kept waiting for Pollard to come around, so he could sling a shovelful in his face, but he never showed up. After waking Lester, he took the cart and the shovel back to the jail and hosed them off before he was officially released. Sugar stuck his razor in his pocket and tossed the nuts away, then headed for the colored section of town where he'd bought his bowler, thinking he might run into the whore with the wart on her lip again. If possible, he wanted to find someone to shack up with for a couple of days, so he could rebuild his strength before he proceeded on to Detroit. Walking down an alley, he happened to see the old man who had given him the drink of water just a few days ago. He was sitting on the ground at the edge of his garden with a sad look on his wizened, charcoal gray face. Of course, Sugar didn't know, and if he had, he wouldn't have given a damn, but the old man had just dug up the last of his turnips, a yearly event that always brought him much pain. It meant that cold weather was right around the corner; and within a few more weeks, he'd be shut up tight in two cramped rooms with his old woman until the spring thaw. Imagine, he'd told his daughter the last time she came down from Lima for a visit, being trapped in a coffin with your worst enemy. That's what the winters were like for them now. By the middle of February, they'd both have murder on their minds. Sugar kept on walking; and the old man got up and went around the yard looking for a rat to beat on, but he couldn't find one.

66

THE CHURCH BELLS chimed six o'clock just as Chimney headed into the park to meet up with his brothers. As he approached them seated on the bench, he saw, to his consternation, that Cob was wearing a pair of goggles just like the ones he carried in the pocket of his duster. "What the fuck?" he said to Cane. "You bought him those just to piss me off."

"No, I didn't," Cane said. "He got 'em on his own. I wasn't nowhere around." It was true. Cob was already gone when he woke up this morning, even though Cane had told him yesterday not to leave again without letting him know first. His first thought was to go on the hunt of him, but then he figured what the hell. Chances were he was with his inspector buddy, and if he wanted to spend his last day here poking around in outhouses, that was his business. Looking forward to a little time of his own, Cane had taken a hot bath, then eaten a leisurely breakfast at the Mount Logan Café. He was finishing his waffles when the well-dressed man who had been with the girl from the bookstore last night walked in and sat down at the counter. Cane watched Sandy order a cup of coffee, then complain to the waitress in an acidy tone that it was cold. As Cane walked out of the diner, an urgent need to see the girl one more time before they headed for Canada suddenly came over him. He began walking toward the bookstore. He would ask for her address, he vowed right before he got to the door, write her a letter once they were settled. But to his disappointment, she wasn't working. Instead, there was a palsied, half-blind gentleman in her place, sitting behind the counter with a woolen scarf wrapped around his thin, wrinkled neck, reading a yellowed pamphlet with a magnifying glass. Cane figured he must be the father she'd mentioned, though he seemed rather ancient to have a daughter her age. He ended up buying a copy of *The Essays of Ralph Waldo Emerson,* though he didn't know for sure what an "essay" even was, and then walked back to the McCarthy to find out. As far as the girl went, by midday he realized how stupid he had been going back there again. What the hell had he been thinking? There was no way a woman like her would ever be interested in someone like him. Even he knew that the suit he was wearing didn't fit right.

"I don't want no dirt in my eyes," Cob explained to Chimney. He had showed up at the hotel around four o'clock wearing the goggles and limping badly again from all the walking he and Jasper had done.

Chimney shook his head, but didn't say anything. He had too many other things on his mind right now to even give a damn. All afternoon, he'd been planning what he was going to say to Matilda, had probably recited the little speech twenty times by the time he left the hotel room. He was prepared to offer Blackie all the money he had on him—$316.00—for her freedom, but just in case the pimp caused any trouble, he was taking his Smith & Wesson tonight instead of the Remington. He had the duster buttoned so that Cane wouldn't notice the bulge of it in his pants.

"We all set for in the morning?" Cane said.

"Just tell me the time and the place."

"I'm thinkin' we should get an early start. Let's figure you pick us up around daylight at the entrance to the park."

"What about the horses?"

"We'll just leave 'em. Couldn't get nothing much out of them anyway."

"Shit, I still got to get my rifle," Chimney said. "I damn near forgot about it."

"Well, do that 'fore you pick us up."

Chimney nodded and started to leave, then stopped and looked back at them. He thought of the two boys he'd met earlier today in Bourneville, and it occurred to him that neither of his brothers had ridden in the Ford yet. Oh, well, by the time they got to Canada, they'd probably be sick of bouncing around in it. "What are you doing tonight?" he asked.

"We're gonna try us some lobster," Cane said, "and then go back to see that monkey again."

"Mr. Bentley," Cob said.

"Lobster? What's that?"

"It's sort of like a crawdad, only bigger," Cane explained. "Cob saw a bunch of 'em yesterday in a water tank in the window at a place uptown, and they reminded him of Willie the Whale. Remember him?"

"Who could forget anybody that goddamn stupid?"

"I bet ye I can eat four or five of 'em, no problem," Cob said.

"So I expect you're headed back out to see the girls?" Cane asked.

"Just the one," Chimney said. "Just the one." Then he turned and walked away before any more questions were asked.

Twenty minutes later, Cane and Cob passed by a group of soldiers on horseback gathered around the front of the courthouse. Wondering what they were up to, Cane stopped his brother and casually lit a cigar, listened to a man with a thick black mustache tell the others that their main objective was to find a Lieutenant Bovard. Apparently, he'd been missing since sometime yesterday. Satisfied that the patrol had nothing to do with them, the brothers walked on and entered Goldman's Restaurant, advertised in the window as THE PREMIER DINING EXPERIENCE IN SOUTHERN OHIO. A man in a slightly frayed tuxedo sat at an out-of-tune piano, sipping from a paper bag and picking out melancholy notes like might be played by a guilt-ridden ax murderer in the wee hours. After debating whether or not to even acknowledge the two's presence, a waiter in a white coat led them to a table under the chandelier in the middle of the room, then rather disdainfully placed leather-bound menus in their hands. Though Curtis Skiver had grown up the son of a penniless wheelwright in nearby Massieville, his years serving as head maître d' at Goldman's had gradually caused him to forget his roots, and he absolutely detested waiting on hicks nowadays. Besides being ignorant of the most basic table etiquette, they ordered the cheapest item on the menu and never left a tip. However, when the one in the cheap suit asked for eight lobsters, along with boiled potatoes and slaw, an entire plate of macaroons, and the most expensive bottle of champagne on the list, he perked up a bit. Perhaps Mr. Goldman was onto something after all. Curtis had thought it ridiculous when his boss had him order two dozen of the lowly crustaceans from Boston, but the old man (he was always bragging that he was an innovator, a man ahead of his time, though for what reason, Curtis had never been able to figure out) had boldly claimed that with the right marketing, lobster could be turned from a food looked upon as fit only for the lower classes into a delicacy sought after by the rich. And though the waiter insisted that the pair show him proof up front that they could pay for such an expensive spread, to his credit he subsequently took it upon himself to show them how to crack the shells and dig out the meat and dip it into the special sauce that Goldman hoped to someday peddle in groceries all over America.

Cane and Cob were still sitting at the table with white napkins tucked into their shirts when Sugar walked by the window and casually glanced inside. Perhaps because he was so weak from hunger—the only thing he had eaten in several days was a bowl of soup in the jail made from carrot scrapings and potato peelings—it took him a moment to realize that he was looking right at two of the bastards who had shot the hell out of his beloved bowler, two of the same men pictured on the wanted poster that the pack of white motherfuckers down at the river showed him right before they tossed him over the bridge like a sack of garbage, and on that other flyer he'd seen hanging inside the jail just today. They looked different—for one thing, the cowpoke shit was gone—but he was almost positive it was them. He went across the street and hunkered down in the doorway of an empty storefront and waited, wondering where the skinny one might be. Thirty minutes ticked by before they came out of the restaurant chewing on toothpicks. The fat one was limping, and Sugar remembered the rag wrapped around his leg. It was them, no doubt about it. He followed them around the corner to a theater, watched them stand in line to buy tickets and then go inside. Not sure yet how to proceed, he stood down the street half a block and waited. Fifty-five hundred dollars, that's what the poster had said. He smiled to himself. After all the torment and trouble he'd been through in the past week, things were finally starting to look up.

67

JUST AS THE still slightly baffled waiter at Goldman's was handing Cane his change from a hundred-dollar bill, Chimney walked out of a florist's shop called Charley's with a dozen red roses just shipped in from Florida by train, and laid them on the front seat of the Ford. A man who'd come to the Whore Barn last night bearing a single wilted carnation for Peaches had given him the idea. By this time, he had gone from thinking he would offhandedly offer Matilda a way out of whoring to figuring this was the most important night of his life, and he wanted to make the best impression possible. He tried not to worry, but he was growing more apprehensive by the minute. What if she refused him? How should he react? And what if the pimp wouldn't let her go? What then? He started the car, wondering as he turned the crank if he should put the top up, then decided he could do that later. Distracted by all the questions and doubts running through his head, he nearly collided with a couple of soldiers on horseback while making a U-turn in the street. Ignoring their curses, he continued south down Paint Street toward the Whore Barn, but then, just as he got to the paper mill, he decided he better have a drink to settle his nerves before going any farther. The only bar around was the Blind Owl, that dismal joint he and Cane had stopped at right after meeting Matilda for the first time, but he didn't care. It wasn't like he was going to hang out there all evening. He pulled the Ford over and shut off the engine, sat for a minute going over the speech again that he planned to dazzle her with once they were alone in the tent. The sun was beginning to set when he got out of the car and went inside. The place was empty, and only one coal-oil lamp was lit to lessen the gloom. Even it was doing little but sputtering blackish fumes. He was just sitting down on a stool when the keep came out of the back room with a sullen look on his face.

"A shot and a beer," Chimney said, pushing his derby back on his head and resting his skinny arms on top of the bar.

"Only if ye got fifty cents," Pollard said.

"Don't worry, I got the money."

"You know how many times I've heard that shit?"

Reaching in his pocket, Chimney brought out a twenty-dollar gold piece and slapped it down on the bar. Pollard stared at it for a moment, then drew a beer from a tap and poured two skinny fingers of whiskey in a glass he'd rinsed in his mop bucket a couple of hours ago. He should have locked up, he thought. After pulling off one of the lieutenant's ears with a pair of tongs—goddamn, he didn't think it would ever come loose!—he had just decided to snip the other one off with a pair of wire cutters when he heard the front door squeak open; and now he felt a bit put-upon by this sonofabitch, the same as if he'd been a normal person interrupted in the middle of making love to a woman he'd just met out catting around, but whose husband was due home by nightfall.

Chimney overlooked the bartender's surly attitude; he recalled the fucker had acted the same way the last time he was in here. Instead, he sipped the beer and studied himself in the mirror. He'd always known that he wasn't what the women called handsome—God knows, the fucking newspapers had made that clear enough—but he thought if he gained some weight and grew a mustache, maybe he'd look good enough for a whore to love. Once they got to Canada and quit all the running, maybe he'd even buy a set of those Indian clubs he'd seen in a store window uptown, start building up his muscles. He figured there wasn't anything a man couldn't do in life if he put his mind to it and didn't allow silly everyday shit to distract him.

Pollard wiped his hands on a wet rag and made the boy's change. He stared at his tan duster, the purple shirt, the striped pants, the hat cocked back at a jaunty angle. If he didn't already have one chained up in the back, he'd love to work on this little bastard stinking of shaving lotion and store soap. Another goddamn ladies' man. Images of the shopgirl laughing at him flickered in his head like a picture show, and it suddenly occurred to him that there was no reason he couldn't do two at the same time. Let this one watch while he made the other skirt-sniffer small enough to fit into a bucket. Who knew? It might be nice to have an audience.

"Looks like things is kinda slow," Chimney said.

Pollard ignored the remark and looked out the window. "That Ford out there, does that belong to you?" he asked Chimney.

"Yeah, it's mine."

"How much it cost ye?"

"I forget."

"Well, you better keep an eye on it," Pollard said. "Lot of thieves around here since they opened that goddamn army base."

"He be a sorry sonofabitch whoever tries to steal from me."

"Is that right?" the bartender said, suddenly lighting up. "You talk mighty big for someone your size."

"I ain't afraid to fight, if that's what you mean," Chimney said.

"Well, then, tell me what you'd do to them."

Glancing up from his whiskey, Chimney took note of the hateful glare in the barkeep's eyes. Tardweller had looked much the same that day he held him by the shirt collar and booted his ass in front of those women like someone would do to a little kid. As Chimney remembered the greatest embarrassment of his life, his heart started beating faster, his hands began to sweat. He was right on the verge of telling Pollard to step outside when he thought about Matilda. Within a couple of hours, if everything went as he hoped, he would have her all to himself, and there wasn't any way he was going to allow this fat bastard to fuck that up. "Ah, just give me another one," he said, pushing his whiskey glass forward.

"But you ain't answered me yet," Pollard said. "What would ye do to him, someone who stole your car? Why, for that matter, what would ye do if I was to reach over and slap that stupid hat off your head? I bet ye wouldn't do a damn thing, would ye?"

"Like I said, just give me another drink."

"Two dollars."

"It was fifty cents ten minutes ago."

"That was before I knew what you were," Pollard said.

Chimney stared straight ahead as he reached into his pocket for the money and laid it on the counter. He had been willing to let a little bit slide, but this fat cocksucker was going too far. "There," he said. "There's your damn two dollars." The lamp flared for a second, then dimmed again. He thought again of Tardweller, of how good it had felt to split his head open in the barn that night. Pushing the duster back, he rested his hand on the Smith & Wesson tucked inside his belt. "So you think you know what I am, huh?" he suddenly said, just as Pollard started to pour the whiskey.

"Sure, I do," Pollard replied, a maniacal grin spreading across his face. "I know what all ye pussies are like." The hell with it, he thought. Why worry about waiting on the right time for this puny piece of shit. He'd lay him over his knee and break his spine first, then roll him like a wagon wheel to the back room. Tossing the drink to the floor, he walked quickly around the bar to the front door, slid the lock bolt in with a loud bang. "You're fucked now, boy."

"One of us is, that's for sure," Chimney said, watching in the splotchy mirror as the barkeep started to come toward him with his fist raised and his teeth shining yellow in the lamplight. Then he pulled the hammer back on the gun and spun around on the bar stool.

"Why, you little turd, I'll stick that goddamn thing up—"

Two orange blasts exploded in the low-ceilinged room, the first bullet making a deep, puckered crevasse in Pollard's forehead, two inches or so above the bridge of his wide nose, and the second breaking his collarbone. His mouth gaped open and a shocked expression crossed over his greasy, unshaven face. He tottered back, the sound of his heavy shoes clomping on the floor; and then, as if in slow motion, the top half of his body crashed through the front window and he landed on his back on the wooden walkway outside. Before the gunshots had even stopped reverberating in his ears, Chimney had dashed around the end of the bar for the wooden cash box. He stuffed the few dollars into his pants pocket, grabbed two nearly full bottles of whiskey, a Golden Wedding and a Sunny Brook. Unbolting the door, he stepped outside and looked down at Pollard, blood dripping out of his ears, his eyes staring blankly at the darkening sky above him. "Goddamn you," Chimney said angrily, kicking him with his boot. "Why couldn't ye just leave it alone?" Then he stepped off the porch and tossed the pistol and the liquor onto the seat beside Matilda's roses.

He was still trying to get the Ford started when he heard the sharp clacking of horse's hooves on the brick cobblestones. Looking back, he saw a group of soldiers racing toward him, their service revolvers drawn and a big man with a black mustache leading the charge. In the three days he'd owned the car, the engine had failed to ignite several times, and the only thing he knew to do whenever that happened was to start the whole process over again. But that took at least a couple of minutes, and the men weren't more than half a block away. "Goddamn piece of junk," he said, throwing the crank down. He sat down in the front seat just as the clatter of the horses' hooves stopped, and all he could hear was the sound of their panting, a saddle creaking. He uncapped the fifth of Golden Wedding, and then, as the soldiers lined up behind him, he took a pull and reached over for the pistol. This probably was going to be the most important night of his life after all, he thought, just not in the way he had planned on.

He heard one of the soldiers say, "Put your hands up where we can see 'em." He looked toward the bridge, remembering a cocksure lawman using the same line on Bloody Bill when he thought he and his posse had him cornered in a corncrib. He smiled to himself. The sonofabitch had emerged from that mess without a scratch after killing every one of them. But he wasn't Bloody Bill, and this wasn't some fucking book. He went over his options in his head, either get shot now or hang later; and found both of them to be lacking in any sort of hope. He wondered what Cane would do if he were here. He'd play it smart, probably surrender, and then try to figure out a way to escape later on. Taking another quick slug from the bottle, he heard the soldier repeat the order. His skin tingled, and his hands began to tremble. He glanced down at the flowers. Well, at least he had known a woman first. But, damn, he wished . . . He wished more than anything that he could have found out what Matilda's answer might have been. It would have been nice, knowing some pretty girl wanted to be with him, was willing to travel clear to some other country by his side. "This is your last warning," the man called out.

68

THIRTY MINUTES LATER, after the Lewis Family finished
their encore and took their final bow, Cane and Cob exited the Majestic just in time to see throngs of people heading down Second Street
toward the center of town as if in a hurry. Falling in behind them, Cob
started talking about Mr. Bentley, about how he wished he could buy
him and set him free in an apple orchard somewhere. "Or maybe we
could take him to Canada with us," he said, looking over to see how his
brother reacted.

"Ah, I don't think he'd like—" Cane started to say as they got to the
corner, but then he stopped in mid-sentence. Coming down the street
was the group of soldiers they'd seen earlier, only now two of them were
pulling with their horses a car that looked exactly like the one Chimney
had bought. "Clear the way," the stout man who'd been giving orders
earlier called out as citizens jammed around the auto. "Get back, I said!
Get back!"

"Stay here and don't move," Cane told Cob. He pushed his way
through the swarm until he was within five or six feet of the car, and
that's when he saw Chimney, bound in manacles and sitting with a
stony look on his face beside a soldier manning the steering wheel. In
the backseat lay another man partly dressed in a bloody uniform, obviously badly hurt. Jesus Christ, two hours ago everything was fine. A
sick feeling swept over Cane, and his ears buzzed with all the voices
going on around him.

"What the hell happened?"

"Goddamn it, people, clear the way!"

"They say that skinny boy shot Pollard that owns the Blind Owl,
but the soldiers caught him 'fore he could get away."

"Back off!"

"Someone said he's one of them Jewetts they been hunting."

"No way."

"Hey, quit your shoving, goddamn it."

"What about the one in the uniform? Did the boy mess him up like that?"

"No, it was Pollard did it. Had him chained up in his back room cuttin' on him."

"I told my wife just the other day that damn army camp was going to lead to trouble."

"Jimmy Beulah said the same thing."

"Aw, shit, Fuller, you don't want to listen to anything that ol' coot says. He put some boy's eye out the other night at the Big Penny."

"Look there. Is his fingers cut off?"

"Just on the one hand it looks like."

"They say Triplett sold him that car."

"Well, that explains why they're pulling it then."

"Be just like Trip to sell a car to a bandit."

"Here comes Chief Wallingford. You wait and see, he'll try to take credit for the whole shebang."

"Jack Meadows said he's got a new lady friend over in Fayette County."

"Shit, she can't be much of a lady if she's hangin' around with ol' Pus Gut."

"Wonder where the other ones are?"

"Who you talkin' about?"

"The other Jewetts. There's supposed to be three of 'em, ain't they?"

Cane swallowed some bile and hurried back through the crowd to where Cob stood eating from a bag of peanuts he's picked up on the way out of the lobby. "Come on," he said in a low voice, "we got to get out of here."

"But what about Mr. Bentley? Think we could—"

"We'll talk about that later," Cane said, grabbing Cob by the sleeve. "Come on, I need you to hurry."

"Don't go too fast," Cob complained after only a few yards. "My leg's hurtin' me."

"All right," Cane said, "all right." He slowed down and glanced behind them, tried to steady himself with a deep breath. "Just do the best ye can."

"What's going on back there anyway?"

"I'll tell ye later," Cane said. "Right now we got to get back to the hotel."

69

SUGAR HAD BEEN following the two brothers the entire time, and once they entered the McCarthy, he ran the three blocks back uptown to find the police chief. Although Malone and his patrol had passed on through with Chimney and Bovard on their way to the army camp, the crowd of onlookers continued to swell. Wallingford, irate that the sergeant had acted so uppity when he asked him what had taken place, was headed back to the jail with his other son, Luther, to call the general's headquarters and make a complaint. He'd already sent Lester over to secure the Blind Owl before it was looted, and Pollard's carcass before some sicko got hold of it. When he heard footsteps running up behind him, he flinched and closed his eyes. Jesus Lord, was this the end? It was one of the downfalls of being a lawman for so many years: having a great number of enemies. You never knew when someone might get the notion to do violence to you, just for trying to maintain a little bit of order in this world of chaos. Sure, nine times out of ten the assassin might only be planning to throw a pie in your face, or call you a dirty name or two, but then again, he might gun you down in cold blood, like what had happened to his friend sheriff Buddy Thompson, over in Athens County a couple of summers ago. Blasted clear out of his chair on a Sunday while reading the funny papers, by the family of a man he'd arrested for running a white slavery ring that catered to clients looking for Appalachian females endowed with the stamina of an ox and the woodsy know-how of a Davy Crockett. It was a lot of pressure, living on edge like that day after day, and that's why, he figured, he ended up doing reckless shit like taking on mistresses he couldn't afford. "Hey, Chief," he heard someone say in a ragged pant. "Hey, Mister Police."

When Wallingford opened his eyes, he saw before him the filthy black man Lester had arrested for cleaning out Pollard's outhouse. "Jesus Christ, you again? Boy, you nearly give me a heart attack."

"I saw 'em," Sugar panted.

"Who?" Wallingford said.

"Them men on the paper hanging in your jail."

"What the hell you talkin' about?"

"The wanted poster," Sugar said, sucking in another draft of air. "With the three men on it."

"You mean the Jewetts?" Luther said.

"That's them. I seen 'em just a couple of minutes ago. Well, two of 'em anyway. Them soldiers done caught the one."

"Soldiers?" Wallingford said. "You mean the boy they nabbed at the bar for killing Pollard? He's a Jewett?"

Sugar nodded his head rapidly. "Yes, sir. Sure as hell is."

"And you know this for a fact?"

"I swear on my mother's grave," Sugar said.

"That reward's over five thousand dollars, Daddy," Luther said.

"Well, I'll be goddamned. So that's why that mustachioed bastard was so tight-lipped." Five thousand dollars, Wallingford thought. He could solve all of his problems with that kind of money. Not only could he get out from under the bitch in Washington Court House, he could retire and never have to worry again about being assassinated. He'd swear off strange pussy and renew his marriage vows, maybe even—

"We gotta hurry 'fore they get away," Sugar said urgently. "They're not gonna stick around now."

"Where did you see 'em last?" Wallingford said.

Sugar hesitated. "No, no, I can't be playin' it that way. You'd end up with the reward all to your own self."

"Well, maybe we better talk about that then. How much are ye willing to settle for?"

"All of it."

Wallingford laughed. "Bullshit. We're the ones takin' all the risk. Either cough up a figure that makes sense, or get your ass out of here."

Sugar tried to calculate in his head. He wasn't good with numbers, but he did know that half of five thousand still added up to a lot of cash. "All right then," he said. "I'll settle for half. But that's as low as I'll go."

"Half! These fuckers have murdered a shitload of people already. Hell, we'll be lucky if we don't get killed."

"Yeah, but—"

"One third," Wallingford said. "That's my final offer."

"How much is that?" Sugar said.

"I reckon that'd be around sixteen hundred, wouldn't it, Luther?" Wallingford said with a wink to his son.

"About that, yeah."

Well, Sugar thought, even with only a third he could buy an automobile and a nice suit and a new bowler and a case of whiskey and still have quite a chunk left over. "Okay," he said, sticking his hand out to shake on the deal. He could already see the look on Flora's face when he pulled up in front of her apartment and tooted the horn. It would be even more satisfying than walking into Leroy's with a new woman on his arm.

As Wallingford gripped the man's sweaty hand, he asked, "So where they at?"

"Uptown."

"Shit, that don't tell me anything. Come on, boy, time's a-wasting."

"No, I'll take ye there," Sugar said. "That's the only way I'm doin' it."

Wallingford sighed and turned to Luther. "Go back to the jail and get my shotgun and a couple rifles. Make sure they're loaded. Then meet us up at Paint and Main."

"I'll need a gun, too," Sugar said. "They already tried to kill me once."

"No way," Wallingford said. "Christ, son, I give you a gun people will think I've lost my mind. I just had you locked up this morning. Now come on, let's go."

When people saw the chief of police walking behind a black man who had shit stains on his tattered clothes, some, either out of curiosity or drunkenness or both, began to tag along. By this time, many of them had heard that the soldiers had captured one of the Jewett Gang, and since Wallingford refused to answer any of their questions, quite a few became convinced that they were hot on the trail of the other two outlaws. Some ran home to get their own guns, others slipped away to lock their doors or get another drink. By the time Luther showed up with the weapons and Sugar led the two policemen to the front of the Hotel McCarthy, there must have been fifty people behind them.

"So this is where they're staying?" Wallingford said to Sugar quietly.

"I saw 'em go in there just 'fore I came lookin' for you."

Satisfied that the informant was telling the truth, the chief turned to Luther and said, "Arrest this man and take him back to the jail."

"Who?" Sugar asked.

Luther pulled out his service revolver and pointed it at the black man. "You heard him. You're under arrest."

"For what? I showed you where they was."

Wallingford looked back at the crowd of people milling about, many of them now armed. "Disturbin' the peace."

"You dirty sonofabitch," Sugar cried. "I should've figured. God-damn white bastards are all the same."

"And verbally assaultin' an officer," Wallingford added. "Now get him the hell out of here."

For Sugar, getting gypped out of his potential share of the reward money was the last straw in the series of crushing events over the past few days that had led to this moment. He realized that he couldn't take it anymore, that he'd been beaten down too far. As Luther pulled out the handcuffs, he decided that the only thing that was going to make him feel any better about himself was to make a stand, to fight back, to cut the shit out of someone, regardless of the consequences. With all of his rage centered on the police chief, he took a step toward him, and someone yelled out, "Watch out! He's got a knife!" Fortunately, for Wallingford anyway, his son didn't hesitate to act. As is sometimes the case with those who go into law enforcement, Luther had been looking for a legitimate reason to kill a man ever since he'd taken his oath to protect people, and Sugar barely had time to snap his razor open before he was lying in the street with three bullets in his bony chest. Looking up at the crowd of white men gathering around to take a look at him, he thought one more time of many things, some of them good and some of them not: Flora's big round ass, the bowler the first time he saw it in the shopwindow, the old white woman begging him not to hurt her, the way his mother used to sing him to sleep at night, and on and on, pieces of his life flying past before he could grab hold of them; and then, just before he took his last miserable breath, he turned his head a little to the left and spat on the toe of Sandy Saunders's shoe.

70

Up in Room 8 on the second floor of the McCarthy, Cane was hurriedly packing the saddlebags when he heard the three gunshots. He looked out the window, saw a gang of citizens gathered in front of the hotel. Some cradled rifles and shotguns, others were sipping from liquor bottles. A dozen or so, along with several policemen, stood over a body lying in the street. He shoved another shirt into the bag and cinched it tight. "Cob," he said in a tense voice, "get up." He reached for his pistol on the nightstand.

"What?" Cob said. He had just learned five minutes ago that Chimney had been apprehended, and he was lying on his bed wondering how much longer it would be before they were sitting in the pokey beside him, waiting to be hanged. He wished he'd saved back some of those doughnuts.

"Get up," Cane ordered. He shoved his hand under Cob's mattress and felt for the other pistol he'd hidden there, stuck it in the saddlebag that held the money. He glanced over at the books by the chair. As bad as he wanted to find out how *Richard III* turned out, he was going to have to leave them behind. "Come on, we got to move." Sticking his head out the door, he looked up and down the carpeted hallway.

"Heck," Cob said as he rolled off the bed, "we just got back and now you—"

Grabbing Cob by the shirt, Cane shoved him out of the room. They made their way down the back stairs and out the rear service entrance, then started down the alley at a slow trot, but after a hundred yards or so, Cob stopped. "What the hell are you doing?" Cane said, turning back to him.

"I can't run on this leg," Cob said.

"Jesus," Cane said, "you're not helpin' matters."

"I'm sorry, but—"

"I know," Cane said. "Come on." They walked a few yards, then ducked into a weedy vacant lot heaped with mounds of coal cinders and trash.

"So I reckon they're lookin' for us?" Cob asked.

"You reckoned right," Cane said. "We don't find a way out of here, we're in trouble." They crouched down behind a pile of busted-up bricks, and a few moments later they heard a loud voice telling people about the Jewett the soldiers had captured, and that the other two were close by somewhere. Then someone else called out that he had dibs on the reward, and another hollered back that they'd buy the Blind Owl together.

"Take me to Jasper's," Cob said suddenly.

Cane gritted his teeth. Though his brother might be slow, he wasn't that slow. "Goddamn it, this ain't no time to be playin' around."

"I'm not. We need to get to Jasper's. He'll help us."

Just then, seven or eight men carrying guns and lanterns marched down the alley past the lot. Cane thought for a minute. They had been in some tight spots before, but never one this bad. If only they could get to their horses, they might have a chance, but the stable was on the other side of town, and they would never make it that far without getting caught, not with Cob's leg slowing them down. "So you know where he lives?" he asked.

"Yeah, he showed me yesterday. It's not that far. Come on, I can find it from here."

WHEN HE HEARD someone knocking on the back door, Jasper was lying half-asleep on his mother's couch. In all the time he'd lived here by himself, the only person who had ever visited him was Itchy, and he thought at first that he must be mistaken. But then the taps started again, and he jumped up. A sharp pain shot through his groin. He'd had another one of those evenings when his situation had gotten the best of him, and he had quelled it the best way he knew how, by thrashing his cock against the furniture until he could hardly walk. Holding a candle, he cracked open the kitchen door, and for a moment all he saw was a pistol stuck in his face. "Don't make a sound," he heard someone hiss. For a few seconds, he stood frozen, but then he made out Cob standing behind the one with the gun, and he took a step back, allowing them to enter.

Cane shut the door quietly, and motioned for Jasper to move into the next room. As they passed the stinking work gear piled in front of the cookstove—the helmet, measuring stick, truncheon, and rubber boots—he remembered that this was the same man he'd seen in the store the other day looking wistfully at bathroom fixtures. In the dim light from the candle, he glanced around the parlor at the faded embroideries hanging on the walls and the dust-covered saints on the mantel and the little wooden shrine to the Virgin Mary. He recalled something Bloody Bill had said one time, after an old Mennonite woman hid him under her hoop skirts and saved him from certain death, about how salvation is sometimes found in the strangest places.

"Howdy, Jasper," Cob finally said, smiling a little sheepishly.

"Hey, Junior."

Through the open window came more yelling, then a car horn beeping, and the echo of a gunshot. Cane wiped some sweat from his brow. It suddenly occurred to him that there was no way he and Cob could make it out of town tonight, not together anyway. There had to be another solution, another way to save them both. "Sit down," he told Jasper. Cane watched the man limp toward the couch, figured he must have a bad rupture from the looks of that bulge in his pants. "My brother keeps talkin' about you, says you're his friend. Is that right?"

"Yes," Jasper said, looking nervously at the pistol Cane still had pointed at him. "I'd like to think so anyway." He hesitated, then blurted out, "I know who you are. I saw your pictures on a poster over at the jail this morning."

"Heck, why didn't ye say nothing?" said Cob. "We was measurin' them ol' shithouses all day."

"I don't know," Jasper said, shrugging his thin shoulder blades. "I guess I didn't want to scare you off."

"Have ye told anyone about us?" Cane asked.

"No, no, I swear. I wouldn't do that."

Sensing that perhaps the man could be trusted after all, Cane sat down in a chair, laid his pistol on top of one of the saddlebags. "All that commotion you're hearin' out there, that's people huntin' us," he told Jasper.

"Yeah, they done caught Chimney," Cob added.

"I'm sorry to hear that."

"Now they'll hang him and he won't ever get a chance to sit at the heavenly table. Well, shoot, I don't reckon we will, either, for that matter. Yes, sir, I sure would've liked to seen it."

"The what?" Jasper said.

"The heavenly table. Like I told Miss Eula, it's where you—"

"Hold up," Cane interrupted. Once again, just by making some off-hand remark, Cob had given him an idea, and though it certainly wasn't perfect, it was better than nothing. "You know a place called Nipgen?" he said.

Jasper nodded. He and Itchy had rented a horse and buggy on several occasions and spent the day riding around the county talking to strangers and pretending they were looking for land to buy. "Yeah, out west of town. I been through there once." From what he could remember, they'd stopped at a little store there and bought some baloney heels and crackers from a man who wore an eyeshade.

Cane bent down and opened one of the saddlebags, started pulling money out. He counted for several minutes, then put a tall stack of bills next to one of the Bibles lying on the table in front of the sofa. "What I need is a big favor, and I'll understand if you don't want to do it, but I need to know tonight."

"A favor?" Jasper said, trying not to look at the money. "What is it?"

"There's a man and his wife got a farm three or four mile past there, and they—"

"The Fiddlers!" Cob said excitedly. "They're the—"

Cane held his hand up to signal his brother to be quiet. "They know Cob, and he knows them. Ellsworth and Eula Fiddler." He nodded at the money. "There's fifteen thousand dollars there. You get my brother to their house safe and half of it's yours. That's seventy-five hundred. What do ye think?"

Jasper's head was reeling. Why, there was more money there than he'd ever seen. He didn't know much, but he had the feeling that if he refused the offer, he'd regret it for the rest of his life. Not only that, no one, not even Itchy, had ever put this much trust in him before. But then he heard some more footsteps running down the street, saw the shadow of a lantern passing through a yard three doors down. What would happen if he got caught aiding a bank robber? And a murderer, though he still couldn't picture Cob ever hurting anyone. Would they hang him, too? No, maybe he better not get involved. Then he looked over at Cob, sitting beside him on his mother's couch, the same couch he had damn near beat his peter off on just two hours ago. But what kind of man turned his back on his friend? Let's face it, he thought, he couldn't save Meade; it didn't matter how many corrupt citizens he pretended to slay in front of his mirror. As much as he wanted to believe otherwise, it had never been a clean town. And there would never be any speeches made about him in Cone Park. Christ, who was he fooling? No matter what he did, people around here would always call him Shit Scooper. But still, maybe he could save someone, save his friend. "I'll try my best," he said.

It took him a minute, but all of the sudden, Cob sensed that something was about to happen that had never happened before. "Hold on now," he said to Cane. "You mean you ain't goin' with us?"

"No, we're gonna have to split up for a while," Cane tried to explain. "Even if we could get to the horses, with your leg like it is, it'd be—"

"But we ain't never been apart before. Never."

"I wish there was some other way, but I can't think of one. Look, all you got to do is stay at the Fiddlers and wait on me. I swear, as soon as I can, I'll come back for ye."

"Yeah, but . . . what about . . ."

"It won't be for long," Cane said. "I promise." Then he reached into the bag for Cob's pistol. "Here, take this with ye."

"No," Cob said. "I don't want no more to do with them things."

"But what if the law—"

"No," Cob repeated.

"All right then," said Cane, putting the gun back in the money bag.

Then he looked at Jasper. "There's some clothes in that bag and some stuff to dress his leg. Cob will forget, so you'll have to keep on him about it. And the way I see it, it'd be best to keep him hid here in the house a couple days before you try to move him out there. But don't try walkin' it. It's a long ways."

"Maybe I could rent a horse and wagon, cover him up with something."

Cane nodded with approval. "That should work. Just don't rush it. Wait till things have cooled down a little."

"We ought to be okay," Jasper said. "Ain't nobody ever comes around here."

Wiping some sweat from his forehead, Cane continued, "Now, when you get there, you give Cob's half to Mr. Fiddler, and go ahead and explain what happened. No sense lying to him. Tell him I'll be comin' as soon as I can. And as far as your share of the money goes, I wouldn't go spendin' it all at once. People will start wondering where it came from. You got all that?"

"I think so," Jasper said.

They all stood up then and Cane stepped over to Cob. He could see his eyes watering up. "Have Jasper buy you a big ol' ham and a bottle of whiskey for Ellsworth to take with ye. He'll like that." He grabbed hold of his brother and hugged him tightly, felt his fear, smelled the lobster on his breath. As close as they'd lived together all their lives, this was the first time he'd ever had his arms around him. Damn, he hated to do this. "Don't worry," he said, "everything's gonna work out fine." His voice came close to breaking as he remembered the promise he'd made his mother all those years ago. He'd let her down, but maybe this would help right things. And if they were lucky, maybe they'd both get out of this alive. Turning loose of Cob, he picked up his pistol and the saddlebag with the money. He shook Jasper's hand and started toward the door, then stopped and looked back at him. "Don't let me come back here and find out ye fucked us over. Understand?"

"I won't," Jasper said. "If'n something bad does happen, we'll go down together. I give you my solemn word as a sanitation inspector."

71

THEY PULLED THE Ford up to the infirmary door and one of the soldiers ran to get a stretcher. As they unloaded Bovard from the backseat and carried him in, Malone yelled at the nurse to call a doctor. Then he and two privates escorted Chimney over to the brig and took his manacles off, locked him in a cell. "Anything I can get you?" the sergeant said.

"Yeah," Chimney said, tossing his derby onto the iron bunk. "I want to see my girlfriend." Back at the Blind Owl, he'd held firm until a second or two before he sensed they were going to fill him full of holes, and then he'd held his hands up high. To look at Matilda one more time, he had decided in the end, would be worth any number of trips to the gallows.

"What?"

"My girlfriend. Her name's Matilda. She works out at the Whore Barn."

Malone shook his head. "If I was you, Mr. Jewett, I'd be worried about other things right now."

"Why should I be worried? I done told ye a dozen fuckin' times, my name's Hollis Stubbs. Shit, you should be pinnin' a medal on me instead of puttin' me in jail. I saved your buddy's ass."

"Bullshit," Malone said, "you're Chimney Jewett." He held up a wanted poster. "I'll eat my hat if this ain't you. Now where's the other two?"

Chimney sat down on the bunk and leaned his back against the brick wall. He had seen Cane out of the corner of his eye as the soldiers were pulling him and the Ford through town like trophies, and he was wondering that himself. For a brief moment, he allowed himself to fantasize that somehow his brother might save him, could almost see him slipping up behind this fucker and putting one through his brainpan. But before he let it go any further, he shook it off. There was no sense in hoping for a fucking miracle; even Bloody Bill would have had a hard time busting someone out of an army base. Still, he'd be goddamned if he was going to admit to anything. He looked over at the sergeant. "Like I said, I want to see my girlfriend."

"You fess up to who you really are, and I'll see what I can do," Malone replied. Then he walked back to the hospital and had a couple of soldiers pull the car off to the side and unhitch the horses, take them to the stables. After waiting until Bovard was wheeled into the operating room, he sent another private to fetch Captain Fisher. He was standing outside drinking a lukewarm cup of coffee when the man bounded around the corner of the building. Though it was the middle of October and the night air had a nip to it, the captain was dressed in nothing but house slippers and a pair of brown jodhpurs. A set of binoculars hung from a cord around his neck. He glanced over at the car. "So you found Bovard?"

"Yes, sir," Malone said. "He's inside gettin' patched up."

"What the hell happened?"

After the sergeant related the details of how they came upon the lieutenant mutilated in the back room of the Blind Owl, Fisher said, "A jar of teeth? Did ye bring 'em with ye?"

"No, sir, I didn't think of that."

"Shame," Fisher said. "I would have liked to have seen 'em. Was the bartender a Mex?"

"Uh, no, sir. He was a white man."

Digging a wad of tobacco out of his pouch, Fisher smiled contentedly. It had become a habit with him, ever since returning to the States, to spend time with the moon on clear nights, partly because its craters and barren plains reminded him of the Mexican landscape, but mostly because it seemed to be the most honest thing he could find to confide in anymore; and tonight he'd had a long talk with that white orb and decided that he would move to the Sierra Madre after his current commission was over with. No matter how much he cursed and ridiculed Mexico, he'd realized over the last few days that he'd never been as happy as he had been there. He'd give his wife the house in Connecticut and his pension. What did it matter? He could live on beans and frijoles and whatever he could kill. "So you think the one you hauled in is one of those Jewetts?"

"Yes, sir. Though he won't admit. Keeps sayin' he's someone else, but he's the spittin' image of one of 'em on the poster."

"Have ye tried to beat it out of him?"

"Sir?"

"The truth. I don't care how tough he thinks he is, get you a pair of brass knuckles and work him over for a while. He'll talk."

"Well, I don't think—"

"Of course, there's other ways to make a man squeal, too. If you don't like blood, take him over to that goddamn Majestic Theater and make him sit through an hour of that goddamn Lewis Family and their monkey. He'd probably rat out the whole goddamn bunch of them then."

"Sir?" Malone said. "The Majestic? I'm not sure I'm following."

"My wife's in town this week and insisted on going there last night. I'll tell you what, Sergeant, I'm still not recovered from it. The worst excuse for entertainment I ever saw in my life."

"Yes, sir."

"So you don't think this Jewett had anything to do with what happened to Bovard?"

"No, I think the barkeep tried to pull something on him like he did with the lieutenant, but the boy got the jump on him."

"And no sign of the other two?"

"No, sir."

"Well, it's late," Fisher said. "Maybe we better let someone else figure out how to proceed. From what I've read about them in the papers, he's sure to hang regardless, isn't he?"

"I expect so."

Fisher yawned and stretched. "Good work, Sergeant. Good work."

"Thank you, sir," Malone said. He waited until the captain left, then went inside the infirmary and sat down in the hallway to wait and see how things turned out with the lieutenant. The man had damn near cried when he heard they might not get to the war for another five or six months, and then this morning, contrary to the rumors that had been circulating, Malone had found out that the 343rd would be shipping out for France sometime in November. Now the poor sonofabitch would never know what war felt like. Then again, maybe he already did; the day or so he spent chained in that maniac's back room was probably as close to being horrific as anything he would have ever seen at the Front. The sergeant took another sip of the cold coffee, thought about all the men who'd voluntarily shot off their fingers and toes trying to get out of it.

An hour later, an orderly pushed Bovard out of the operating theater on a gurney and down the hall to a room. Eisner, the clap doctor, came out a minute or two later, and Malone asked him about the lieutenant's condition. "Well, he's suffered a serious shock, and there wasn't anything to be done about the hand or the ear, but from what I've heard, it could have been a lot worse. My biggest concern is the risk of infection. A tavern is one of the worst places in the world for germs. Which reminds me, have you and your men washed up since you left that filthy hole?"

"Uh, well, we haven't had—"

"I don't understand you people," Eisner said angrily. "Good hygiene is one of the most important keys to a long and happy life, and yet you refuse to embrace it." Then he turned and stomped out of the building.

Malone walked down to the room where they'd taken Bovard. He stood in the doorway and looked in. A soft light burned in the far corner. Wesley Franks was sitting in a metal chair beside the lieutenant's bed. He was talking softly to him and dabbing his forehead with a damp cloth. "Has he said anything?" Malone asked.

"No, sir," Wesley said. "They got him knocked out."

Malone stepped into the room, moved up closer to the bed. The stub of Bovard's left hand was wrapped with gauze, and another bandage covered his ear hole. A bit of bloody cotton was sticking out of the corner of his mouth. "Well, at least it wasn't his right."

"Sir?" Wesley said, squinting at the sergeant with his good eye.

"His hand. He's right-handed, from what I remember."

"Oh," Wesley said. He dipped the cloth in a pan of water, then squeezed the excess out of it. "Do you think he'll still be able to stay in the army, sir?"

Malone shook his head. "It's doubtful."

"That's a shame," Wesley said.

"Maybe," Malone said, "maybe not. What if he went over there and got himself killed? At least this way he's still walkin' around on top of the ground."

"Well . . ."

"Just like you, Franks. That Dear John letter you got may have saved your life in the long run."

Wesley shook his head. He had been thinking a lot about what his shameful return home was going to be like; and he'd spent all day wishing he could just stay here in the infirmary forever. "I don't know, sir," he said to the sergeant. "I guess that all depends on what you think it's worth."

72

CHESTER HIGGENBOTHAM HEARD the noise and sat up. It sounded as if someone was trying to jimmy the front door. The news that the stable would soon be converted into a garage still had him down, and this afternoon, as soon as Hog handed him his week's pay, he had headed for the Mecca Bar to drown his sorrows. He had passed out in the straw before sundown, and though it was now past midnight, he still felt a little drunk. He heard the noise again. "Shit," he said under his breath. In return for his six dollars a week and somewhere to sleep, he took care of the animals and cleaned out the stalls and kept an eye on the place at night. He picked up his squirrel rifle. As he stepped out the back door, he heard clamoring coming from uptown, men shouting and car engines roaring and a gunshot or two. Lord, some fools must be having a high ol' time tonight, he thought. Maybe everybody in the goddamn county's losing their job.

Slipping quietly around the side of the building, Chester saw a dark shape at the door, obviously prying on the lock. He called out, and when the man turned and started to run, he lifted his rifle and fired once without really aiming, regretting it as soon as he pulled the trigger. You dumb bastard, he berated himself. He'd been on a toot when he committed the stupid crimes that got him sent to Mansfield, and now here he was again, half drunk and shooting at somebody. Although prison was where he had learned to take care of horses, he'd vowed the day of his release that he'd kill himself before he ever went back. That's what worried him most about the stable shutting down. It was all he'd done for the past thirty years, but the job had kept him out of trouble. True, it hadn't been much of a life, but he'd seen the last time he was locked up what the young ones did to men his age, forcing them to kneel down like a supplicant beside some hoodlum's bunk and gently knead his wang and blow little kisses on the head of it while the sonof-abitch dreamed of some woman on the outside. No, he had it damn good compared to that. And, hell, you never knew, maybe Hog would change his mind about working on automobiles. So when he saw the man keep going, Chester breathed a sigh of relief and wished him luck, then went back inside the barn to finish sleeping off his debacle.

The bullet, however, didn't just fly into the air aimlessly, as the stable bum thought. Getting hold of his horse had been the only plan Cane could think of when he left Jasper's house. With the gangs of men roaming the streets, fired up on liquor and rumors and false sightings and the chance at reward money, it had taken him over an hour to sneak and dodge and crawl to the stables where he and Cob had left their rides three days ago. He was still trying to pry the hasp off the door with the barrel of Cob's pistol when he heard Chester yell; and he didn't get more than a few feet before the bullet knocked him sideways, tearing the hell out of his right kidney before lodging in his stomach wall. Stifling a cry, he kept going.

He ran on until he came to the iron railway trestle extending over the Scioto. He stumbled across it in the dark, then jogged north a mile or so along the tracks with his hand pressed against the rip in his side. By then, his new shirt and coat were soaked with blood. He stopped and pulled some paper currency out of the saddlebag and tried to staunch the wound with it. Then he walked on, panting raggedly. Three miles out of town, a freight train barreled past him; and he would have gladly given all the money he had ever stolen for one third-class ticket away from here. He managed to go a few more yards before he collapsed in a heap.

Lying in the sharp gravel, he stared wearily at some bobbing lights off in the distance for several minutes before he realized that he'd seen such a sight before, one night in Tennessee when a posse on horseback had followed them with torches. The moon came out from behind some clouds then, and he forced himself up and made his way into a grove of trees. He limped and lurched past a deserted camp of burned-out fires and tin cans and chicken bones where he figured some hobos occasionally stopped to take a respite. The wind picked up and the autumn leaves rattled in the trees. Deciding he couldn't go on anymore tonight, he got down on his knees and crawled back under a thick mass of honeysuckle bushes. By then it was two o'clock in the morning. Resting his head on the saddlebag, he cocked his pistol and set it on his chest. He thought about how Chimney always volunteered to stand watch, no matter how tired he was, as if he didn't trust him or Cob to stay awake. He wondered again what had happened exactly, how his brother had ended up in the custody of those soldiers. If he could make it to a town, maybe he could find . . .

When Cane woke up, the morning sky was overcast with gray clouds, and he was damp with drizzle and shivering with the cold. For the first time in his life, he was truly alone. He raised up on his elbows to take a look around, and as he did so, he felt more blood gush out of the bullet hole. Easing himself back down, he felt in his pockets and found his last cigar and some matches. He drew on it several times, hoping it might warm him, but then he started coughing, and stabbed it out on a wet leaf. For several minutes, he watched a cardinal hop from branch to branch, just a foot or so away from him, and then fly away.

As the drizzle became a rain, Cane drifted off again. He found himself in a house that seemed familiar, as if he had lived there for a long, long time. He was sitting in a chair by a fireplace reading a book, and from what he could tell, he was near the end of it. The smell of freshly baked bread and flowers wafted in the warm air, and through the curtained windows he could see that it was dark outside. Suddenly, a beautiful, dark-haired woman appeared in the room and started to walk by him, her dress rustling against her pale skin. Her hand reached out and lightly touched his shoulder; and he felt more at peace right then than he'd ever felt in his life. Then she paused at a stairway and looked back; and the last thing he heard as he turned another page was her wishing him good night.

Epilogue

AFTER JASPER SHOWED up at their house with Cob one night in a rented carriage, the Fiddlers hid him in Eddie's old room and then spent the entire winter trying to invent a convincing explanation as to who he was and why he was staying with them. They must have told each other a hundred different lies before they finally settled on one they thought might work. Then they went over that lie a hundred more times before Eula felt that Ellsworth was ready to tell it to someone, and in the end, they decided that that someone would be Parker. They figured with the way the storekeeper liked to spread gossip, all they had to do was get him to believe it, and within a week or two everyone in the township would.

And so one bright morning in the early spring of 1918, Ellsworth took Cob, along with a few sips of wine in a jar to give him courage, over to Nipgen to plant the seed. As they pulled the wagon into the lot, he patted the boy on the knee and reminded him again, "Just let me do the talking." When they entered the store, he saw to his relief that no one else was there. So far, so good, Ellsworth thought to himself, but when Parker suddenly raised up from behind the counter, he panicked, forgetting all about Eula's warning to just act normal, and before the storekeeper could even get a good look at who he was talking about, he'd finished the story about Junior without taking a single breath and ordered a pound of coffee, and then they were out the door.

Fortunately, though Parker did wonder a little why Ellsworth had seemed so nervous, he didn't suspect anything was amiss, at least not at first. He'd seen the farmer shook up before over stuff that most men wouldn't think twice about. Why, the Singletons could get him going with a mere smirk. And things such as what he'd described, well, they happened all the time. He sucked on a piece of hard candy while he thought it over, reworking the details a bit to give it a little more color, and by evening the storekeeper had told the story in various renditions to twenty or more customers. He was still revising it in his head when Dean Hartley came in right at closing time stinking of home brew and mumbled that he wanted a pound of salt fish.

Parker reached under the counter for a sheet of the old newspapers he saved back to wrap parcels in, and spread it on the counter. Then he took the lid off the barrel of cod and pulled four or five out. As he laid them on the scale tray, he glanced down at the paper and saw the faded drawings of the three outlaws that had caused so much commotion last fall. "Well, shit, that looks just like—" he started to say, but then stopped.

"Huh?" Hartley grunted.

"Nothing," Parker said. "Just talkin' to myself." He pushed the sheet aside and wrapped the fish in another. As soon as Hartley staggered out, the storekeeper licked the brine off his fingers and locked the door. He picked up the paper and held it under the lamplight, wishing that he'd paid more attention to the boy while Ellsworth was talking. From what he could recall, though, there wasn't a whole lot of difference between him and the chubby one in the picture other than a beard. Hell, maybe that was the reason Ells had been so jittery; maybe he was hiding something.

Pulling his visor down tight on his head, Parker tried to think it through. He might have been a meddler, but this, he realized, was a lot more serious than telling people that Lucille Adkins had gotten religion and was making her husband, Forrest, sleep in the shed because he was a sinner, or that someone saw Old Man Cottrill walking down the road without any clothes on the other day. Cutting a chunk of meat off a smoked ham hanging in the window, he chewed on it slowly. The money didn't interest him; he had enough of that saved back to last him out if he shut down the store tomorrow. So the big question was, even if the boy was one of the outlaws, what good would it do to tell the authorities? For sure, Ells and Eula would get in trouble for harboring a criminal—Lord, they'd probably even go to prison—and then everybody would look upon him as a squealer, a rat, a no-account Judas. And as far as that went, how many times last year had he heard poor men stand right in this store and talk about the gang as if they were heroes, say that they wished they had the guts to go rob a bank? Quite a few. Not only that, how many had shaken their heads sadly when they'd heard that the one had been caught in Meade? Again, quite a few. Too, what if he was wrong? Why, he'd look like the biggest fool around. The more he thought about it, the more preposterous it seemed. It was easier picturing the Singletons as sex-crazed womanizers than believing someone as tame as Ellsworth Fiddler was buddies with cold-blooded desperadoes. When he finally turned out the lamp and went to bed, it was past midnight; and in the morning, he crumpled up the newspaper without looking at it again and burned it in the stove, having decided it best to stick with the story he'd been told. And just as the Fiddlers had hoped, within a few days everyone in the township believed Junior was the son of one of Eula's cousins from up around Springfield, and that they had taken him in after both of his parents succumbed to the grippe within a few hours of each other. "Ye can tell the poor feller's slow," Parker said whenever he came to the end of the tale. "He just stood there like a statue with a grin on his face while Ells went on about his people a-dying. Reminds me of Tom Stout's boy, the one that got hit in the head by that tree."

Talk of the young man living with the Fiddlers began to die down after a couple of weeks, but then, after someone saw him and Ellsworth one Saturday at an auction in Bainbridge buying six Holsteins and a bull, it started up again for a while. Since it was common knowledge that Ells didn't have two nickels to rub together, it was speculated that maybe Junior had been left a little inheritance. But that was as far as it went. By that time, Parker had repeated the story so much that he'd convinced himself it was true, and nobody else ever really wondered about the boy's past or begrudged the farmer a few cattle for taking him in. There were, after all, new rumors every other day about the devastation being brought on by the Spanish influenza. And, too, as many pointed out whenever the subject did come up, maybe old Ells deserved some luck after losing his savings to that thief down in Pike County, and his son running off and never coming back, although everyone did agree that it was terrible the way he fell into it.

As for Cob, except when he was around Ellsworth and Eula, he kept his mouth shut. Every morning when the first cow bawled in the feedlot, he hopped out of bed and put on his clothes, headed for the barn. He liked taking care of the milking by himself. It gave him time to think about what he was going to do. It bothered him something awful, trying to decide. Every time he imagined Cane coming for him, he felt half sick, and then he'd feel guilty. But the fact of the matter was he loved it here, and he couldn't bear the thought of leaving, even with his brother. For close to two years, he agonized over it, and then one morning, as he rinsed out a bucket at the well, he realized that Cane had already made the decision for him, and was all right with letting him stay.

He'd always be finished with the milking by the time Ellsworth showed up, scratching and yawning. The old man would help him pour it through the strainer and into the metal containers they used to haul it over to Parker's, and by the time they finished, Eula would be calling them to the house for breakfast. Then they would work in the fields some; and in the afternoon, they'd take the milk over to the store in the wagon, singing "The Old Brown Nag" seven or eight times before they got there.

After he carried the containers inside, Junior would hand Parker a dime for a soda pop and a cake and go out to the porch. Owning some cattle and a little business had given Ellsworth a boost of confidence he'd never had in the past, and he would often spend an hour or more talking inside. Of course, Junior didn't mind waiting. He didn't mind anything. It didn't matter to him that the pop was warm, or the cake stale. He'd eaten a lot worse than that in his life. And who could ever find fault with sitting on his ass listening through the screen to some old men tell jokes and argue over the price of crops, or why anyone would ever want a telephone? Not him. Because he knew, with a certainty he'd never known before in his life, that no matter what was being discussed, eventually Ellsworth would come out the door and say, "Hey Junior, let's head home." And that's exactly where they would go. Home.

ACKNOWLEDGMENTS

I wish to thank the following: First and foremost, local Ross County historian Rami Yoakum, for all the talks we had about Camp Sherman and Chillicothe during 1917 (sorry I didn't stick with the facts, brother!); the Guggenheim Foundation, for helping keep food on the table; my agents and first readers, Richard Pine and Nathanial Jacks, for knowing just what to say; and my editors, Gerry Howard of Doubleday and Francis Geffard of Albin Michel, for all their advice, patience, and wisdom. Oh, and Dr. Ron Salomone, for riding my ass to finish the damn thing.